Mrs. Grant and Madame Jule

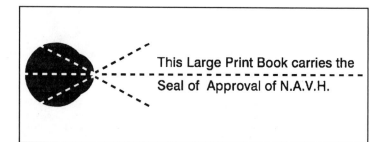

MRS. GRANT AND MADAME JULE

JENNIFER CHIAVERINI

LARGE PRINT PRESS
A part of Gale, Cengage Learning

GALE
CENGAGE Learning®

Farmington Hills, Mich • San Francisco • New York • Waterville, Maine
Meriden, Conn • Mason, Ohio • Chicago

LIBRARY OF CONGRESS CATALOGING-IN-PUBLICATION DATA

Chiaverini, Jennifer.
  Mrs. Grant and Madame Jule / by Jennifer Chiaverini. — Large print edition.
    pages cm. — (Thorndike Press large print core)
    ISBN 978-1-4104-7510-7 (hardcover) — ISBN 1-4104-7510-7 (hardcover)
    1. Grant, Julia Dent, 1826-1902—Fiction. 2. African American women—Fiction. 3. Female friendship—Fiction. 4. First ladies—Fiction. 5. Large type books. I. Title.
  PS3553.H473M765 2015b
  813'.54—dc23   2015000556

ISBN 13: 978-1-59413-811-9 (pbk.)
ISBN 10: 1-59413-811-7 (pbk.)

Published in 2016 by arrangement with Dutton, an imprint of Penguin Publishing Group, a division of Penguin Random House LLC.

Printed in the United States of America
1 2 3 4 5 6 7 20 19 18 17 16

To Marty,
my husband of twenty years,
dearest friend, and partner in all things,
with love and gratitude

PROLOGUE

June 1834

The slaves froze when they heard the old master shouting from the big house, conversations cut off in midsentence, hands grasping spoons hovering between bowls and hungry mouths. Even the little ginger-colored maid strained her ears to listen, dreading to hear her own name bellowed in anger.

For a long, tense moment she heard only the crackling of the fire from within the kitchen house and birds chirping overhead, but then Tom shook his head and resumed eating. "It ain't us," the lanky coachman said through a mouthful of oat porridge. "Something happened in the city, but it ain't nothing to do with us."

Quickly the slaves finished their breakfasts, scraping their bowls with their carved wooden spoons and licking off every last savory morsel before rising and darting to work. Only the little ginger-colored maid hung back, reluctant to return to the big house and whatever storm brewed within. She busied herself gathering up the dirty bowls and spoons and carrying them to the washbasin, but as she rolled up her sleeves, the cook shook her head. "Poppy can help me with that. You best be running off." Annie was only twenty or thereabouts, but she was the best cook in the Gravois Settlement and proud of it. "Miss Julia be looking for you. Stay out of the old master's way and you be all right."

Glumly she nodded and hurried away. She found Miss Julia seated on the front piazza, frowning anxiously at her hands in her lap, a red ribbon bobbing atop her thick, glossy, dark hair in time with the swinging of her feet. She glanced up at the sound of her maid's bare feet on the well-worn path — her expression sweet, her skin soft and rosy — but she held her head awkwardly, tilting it this way and that, trying to fix her gaze on her maid despite her cross-eye. "There you are," Julia cried, bounding out of her seat and down the stairs. She seized her maid's hand and pulled her along, her glossy curls a dark cascade down her back as they ran. The maid's spirits rose as they left the big house behind. She knew where Julia was leading her — to the stables and the family's horses.

They heard Gabriel, the stableboy, singing before they reached the corral, before they saw him emerge from the stable, a sturdy, russet-colored boy of ten years leading the missus's favorite bay mare by the reins. The boy with the voice of an angel had been given a name to suit when he had been brought into the Dent household four years before. He had been called Tom then, but the old master had renamed him for the sake of the elder Tom, the ebony-skinned coachman. The maid thought it strange that she had not been given a new name too, since she shared one with her mistress. Instead, ever since the old master had bought her when she was scarcely four years old, the family and slaves had made do by calling her Julia the maid or the little ginger girl or, more often, Black Julia.

Side by side, the two Julias stood on the lowest rail and rested their elbows on the corral fence, watching Tom and Gabriel exercise the horses, which Julia adored and rode whenever the old master allowed. When they tired of this, the mistress seized her maid's hand again and they ran off to the kitchen house, another of Miss Julia's favorite places on her family's country estate. Julia could always charm a treat from Annie and never failed to share it. "Ginger and cream," Annie often remarked when she spied the girls' clasped hands, the darker skin against the white.

Once, years before, Julia had felt a soft, quick, wetness on the back of her wrist and turned her head in surprise to discover her mistress bent over her hand, the pink tip of her tongue still protruding between her red lips. "I wanted to see if you tasted like ginger too," Julia had said, her expression embarrassed and guilty.

"Do I?"

"No." Julia had frowned in disappointment. "Just skin. And brine."

"I was helping Annie pickle cucumbers." Impulsively, she had lifted Julia's hand to her mouth, her tongue darting out for a small, swift taste. "Hmm."

"What? What is it?"

"Definitely cream." She had nodded sagely before dissolving into giggles. "The sweetest, freshest cream ever."

Julia had laughed, delighted.

Annie shooed them away soon enough, and they ran off deep into the woods encircling White Haven, to their favorite, most secret place, a beautiful, shadowy, moss-covered nook near a burbling stream that fed into the Gravois. Julia's favorite game was to pretend that this was a fairy bower and that she was queen of the fairies, ruling fairly and benignly over her kingdom, as confident and gracious in make-believe as she was shy in real life. The ginger maid portrayed her favorite lady-in-waiting, a deposed fairy princess from a far-off kingdom, bearing all the grace of royalty despite her more humble status.

When the sun shone high overhead, the maid, her stomach rumbling with hunger, reminded her mistress that Julia would be expected home for lunch. Just as they emerged from the woods, they halted at the sight of a pair of horses tied up at the front post and the old master greeting two men on the shaded piazza.

"Soldiers," said Julia, squinting enough to make out their uniforms. "See them for me."

"They're officers," her maid replied. Her mistress's poor vision was a source of endless frustration, and she often called upon her maid to describe people and scenes for her, especially at a distance. But even things close to hand, like picture books and sewing, gave her headaches if she were obliged to study them too long. When Julia was first learning to read, after squinting at the reader for a quarter of an hour, her forehead would throb so painfully that she would plaintively ask her maid to see the letters aloud for her. The missus soon put a stop to that, reminding Miss Julia that slaves weren't allowed to read and dismissing her maid with a stern rebuke.

"I see that much for myself," said Julia. "What else?"

"The tall one is younger," she continued. "He's a lieutenant. The short, stout one has gray hair, and I think he's a captain. I don't think they ever been here before."

"They must be from Jefferson Barracks," said Julia, her voice dropping to a murmur. "One of the officers did something terrible."

11

"What he do?"

"I don't know. Let's listen."

Julia took her hand once more. They darted to the house, tiptoed up the front stairs and down the piazza, and crouched silently beneath one of the parlor windows.

What they heard chilled the maid to the bone.

A few days before, Major William Harney, the paymaster at Jefferson Barracks, had become enraged with a slave, Hannah, whom he accused of hiding or losing the keys to his sister-in-law's household in St. Louis, where he was residing. He had seized a piece of rawhide and had beaten her savagely upon her head, stomach, sides, back, arms, and legs, rendering her unconscious, bruised, and bleeding. Hannah died the following day, and the coroner's jury of inquest noted that her body had been lacerated and mangled in so horrible a manner that they could not determine whether the violence had been committed with whips or hot irons. To avoid arrest — and in advance of a mob of outraged citizens intent on stringing him up — Major Harney had fled the city aboard a steamboat and proceeded to Washington City to request a transfer so he would never have to return to Missouri. The officers had come to warn the old master that anger against slaveholders throughout the county was soaring, and he ought to take care until it subsided.

Julia squeezed her hand. "Did you hear? That bad man will never come back. Papa says Washington City is about as far from St. Louis as you can go."

She nodded, her throat constricted too much to allow speech, but her heart pounded, her mind flooded with images of a slave woman screaming in anguish as the rawhide cut into her skin, falling to her knees in a pool of her own blood —

She scrambled away from the window and fled to the woods, closing her ears to Julia's beseeching cries.

She fled to the safest place she knew, the fairy bower, where she lay down on the soft moss and hugged her knees to her chest. Before long Julia arrived, breathless and anxious. "I knew you would come here," she said, sitting down beside her. "You mustn't be afraid. What happened to that poor Hannah will never happen to you. I swear I'll never beat you and I won't let anyone else either."

She felt a small measure of comfort, enough to compel her to sit up and wipe the tears from her face. But she knew Julia was just a little girl, eight years old like herself, and incapable of fighting off anyone who might want to hurt her.

"I don't like it when people call you Black Julia," the young mistress suddenly declared. "It's not a proper name, even for a servant.

But you can't be Julia, because I was Julia first."

She didn't contradict her, although she was the elder by two months and so had been called Julia longer. Her mistress was the first to be called Julia at White Haven, and she was a Dent. It was fair that she kept the name.

"I'm going to call you Jule," she said. "It's almost Julia, but different enough so no one will need to put anything else before it to tell us apart. Do you like it?"

"Yes," said Jule, after a long moment. "It's nice."

"Then Jule it is," Julia proclaimed, beaming.

Jule was proud of her new name. It wasn't quite as well earned as Gabriel's, or as fancy as Suzanne's, but it was nice, and it was hers alone.

"Miss Julia says we all supposed to call me Jule now," she told Annie that night as the weary slaves gathered at the kitchen house to eat their supper, deferred while the Dents and the livestock were seen to.

"Really." Scooping stew into bowls, Annie gave her an inscrutable sidelong look. "You proud of that odd name, ginger girl?"

"It ain't odd," said Jule, lifting her chin. "Some girls called Ruby or Opal or Pearl. Why can't I be called Jewel?"

One of the field hands guffawed into his stew; it might have been Dan, but she couldn't tell in the darkness, which on that moonless night was lifted only by the light spilling from the kitchen-house doorway and the campfire Tom and Gabriel had built.

"It's pretty," piped up Suzanne, the housekeeper's walnut-colored daughter. She would be the maid for Julia's next-eldest sister someday but as yet was too young to be much more than a playmate.

"Pretty, huh?" Still clutching her spoon, Annie planted a fist on her hip and regarded Jule from beneath raised brows. "You ain't called jewel like no pearl or sparkling ruby. You called Jule to be short for *Julia.*"

"Annie," chided Tom mildly. "She's just a girl."

"She's eight years old, old enough to know how things are. She ain't got no mamma, so it falls to me to tell her." Annie's expression turned solemn as she crouched low beside Jule and held her gaze. "Listen here. Your new name just a piece of *her* name, just like she think you no more than a little piece of her. There's us, and there's them, and you one of us."

"I know that," said Jule sullenly.

"No, I don't think you do. Listen, ginger girl. You ain't never gonna be a part of that family, no matter what Miss Julia say now, no matter how she hold your hand and tell you she love you. Soon Miss Nell gonna be old enough to be a real friend and not just a

15

pesky little sister, and as years go by you gonna be less a friend and more a slave. It always happen that way. Unless you want your heart broke, you best get ready and watch for it coming, so it don't catch you by surprise."

Miss Julia was different, Jule told herself fiercely, interlacing her fingers over her growling stomach as Annie filled bowls with stew and she waited for one to be passed her way.

Miss Julia was different, and Jule was different. They were ginger and cream. It was not their fault they were mistress and slave too.

■ ■ ■ ■

PART ONE:
LOVE

■ ■ ■ ■

CHAPTER ONE

Spring 1844

The ride through the woods from White Haven to the officers' camp was so pleasant, the soldiers so dashing in their splendid uniforms adorned with epaulettes and aiguillettes, that it was easy to forget that the men had any other duty but to parade with impressive precision, to escort pretty young belles to dances and parties, and to draw the speculative, appraising gaze of mothers of marriageable daughters.

The threat of war was, after all, the reason the gallant young men drilled and marched and prepared at the camp, ten miles south of St. Louis, five miles west of the Dent family's country home. Julia and the other admiring young ladies of the Gravois Settlement could ignore that fact no longer when negotiations resumed for the United States to annex the Republic of Texas as a slave state. The Mexicans would not countenance the annexation, and already skirmishes had broken out amid

19

the unspoken threat of worse to come. And so the Fourth Infantry was ordered south — just in case, the bold officers assured their distressed belles — first to Camp Salubrity near Natchitoches in Louisiana, and from thence no one yet knew.

On the eve of the soldiers' departure, Julia and her sister Nell decided to ride out to Jefferson Barracks to bid the men farewell. Julia dressed in her most becoming spring dress, a fawn-colored poplin with a feathery white pattern and lace trim, and sat patiently while Jule arranged her dark, glossy locks into an elegant chignon. "Perhaps I should wear a veil to conceal my horrid eye," Julia said, frowning at her reflection in the looking glass. Her short stature and rounded figure vexed her too, but her cross-eye did more to mar her beauty than the rest of her flaws combined.

"Or an eye patch, like a pirate bold," Jule remarked, smoothing a stray lock away from Julia's brow. "I could fashion you one out of white silk to match your dress."

"Jule," Julia protested, laughing. None of the other servants would dream of teasing her so, but Jule was especially dear to her and knew it. Although Papa remained Jule's legal owner, he had presented her to Julia as a gift for her fourth birthday, telling her grandly that she should think of the maid as her very own. She always had. She could not remember a time before Jule had been her steadfast companion.

"You got beautiful hair," said Jule patiently, her knowing glance reminding Julia of the many times she had enumerated her mistress's beauties to bolster her confidence. "You got such perfect hands too, so small and pretty and perfectly shaped. Your shoulders and neck look like they been carved out of marble, and your skin — What's the word the missus used last time you went stomping around moaning about your looks?"

"Luminous," Julia said, somewhat grudgingly. "But she's my mother. She has to say those sorts of things."

"Your mamma never told a lie in her life."

"No," Julia admitted, "I'm sure she never has. But I wasn't stomping about or moaning. I'm not pretty enough to be that vain. I know I'm the plainest of the Dent sisters. Everyone thinks so."

"I've never heard anyone call you plain." Jule arranged a sprig of jasmine in Julia's hair and stepped back to study the effect. "Except you, of course. You know what I hear people say?"

Julia's heart thumped. She knew people spoke too freely in front of the servants, imagining them as insensible as the furniture or the pictures on the walls. She had made that mistake herself. "I'm almost afraid to know. Perhaps you shouldn't tell me."

21

"They say you the best singer and the best dancer of you and Nell and Emma. They say you the kindest, most generous, and most amiable of the Dent girls too."

"Do they?"

"They do, and they also say you got beautiful hair." Jule tucked one last loose strand into Julia's chignon and stepped back, satisfied. "Thanks in no small part to me, if I do say so myself."

That compliment, at least, rang with truth. Rising, Julia thanked Jule and hurried downstairs to meet Nell. "We mustn't be too downcast," Nell warned as they mounted their horses. "We don't want to give the officers an unhappy memory to carry off to war."

Julia nodded and resolved to be as cheerful as Nell, or at least to seem so. At sixteen, the second eldest of the Dent sisters was a great beauty, with merry brown eyes that hinted at suppressed laughter and a mass of glossy golden ringlets that had won her the nickname "the Maid of Athens" from her many admirers. Their youngest sister, Emma, and their four elder brothers rounded out the Dent family.

Julia's heart stirred with increasing anxiety as they approached the camp, surrounded by white fences and set imposingly upon a hill, with a high ridge spiked with tall pines in the distance beyond. After the guard waved them through the gate, Julia dismounted, scanning the men's faces for the one she liked best, but her poor vision thwarted her and she dared not squint too much in case he was watching.

Nell anticipated her quandary. "I don't see him," she said, linking arms with her elder sister.

"I'm not sure who you mean," replied Julia, feigning indifference as they strolled toward the nearest group of officers. Nell merely laughed and patted her arm knowingly.

As they made the rounds of the camp and bade fond farewells to their favorite officers, now and then Julia would observe a soldier and a young lady stroll a discreet distance away from the others to exchange wistful good-byes in as much seclusion as decorum permitted. Several times she saw the promising glint of sunlight upon metal as a ring was offered and, more often than not, blushingly but charmingly refused. The scenes would have been sweet if they had not been so painfully reminiscent of her last parting with Lieutenant Grant. He had been so disappointed, though he had borne her demurral stoically. If she had known the Fourth Infantry was going to be sent away, perhaps she would have answered differently — but how could she have given him any other reply?

"There's Cousin James," Nell said, nodding toward a trio of lieutenants descending

23

the stairs of the piazza. Even Julia with her poor vision recognized their distant cousin James Longstreet, smartly attired in his dress uniform and surrounded by accoutrements of the martial life. She knew his companions too — Richard Garnett and Robert Hazlitt, frequent and welcome guests at White Haven.

James's face lit up with a smile when he spotted them. "My dear cousins," he exclaimed, hurrying to meet them and kissing each sister quickly on the cheek. "How good of you to come out to bid us one last farewell."

"Mercy," said Julia, unable to suppress a shudder. "You make it sound so final."

"What Longstreet means is, 'Good-bye, until we meet again,' " amended Lieutenant Garnett.

"Much better," said Nell, smiling so winsomely in return that a faint flush rose in the lieutenant's cheeks. "We will miss all of you very much."

"Do you know where we might find Lieutenant Grant?" Julia asked.

"I'm sorry, cousin, but he isn't here," said James. "He's still on leave visiting his family in Ohio. Didn't you know? He told me he meant to pay his respects at White Haven before he left."

"And he did," Julia quickly replied, "but that was before your new orders came. I assumed that his leave would be cut short."

Heart sinking, she looked from her cousin to his companions in turn and saw regret on each of their faces. "Won't he return before you go south?"

"If Lieutenant Grant hasn't come to see you within a week from Saturday," Lieutenant Hazlitt said, "you should assume that he's gone down the Mississippi to meet us. He won't be at Jefferson Barracks again."

"Of course," Julia murmured, flinching from his unwitting, careless cruelty. Nodding graciously to the gentlemen, the sisters strolled off — or rather, Nell supported Julia on her arm and steered her away.

"I never should have refused his ring," Julia murmured tearfully when no one else could overhear.

"You couldn't have accepted it," Nell reminded her. "You know that's so."

And Julia did, but her heart broke all the same.

In a reluctant parting from the gallant officers, the sisters rode away, waving their handkerchiefs in a lingering farewell until the forest closed around them. At White Haven, Julia curled up on the sofa with Nell's comforting arm about her shoulders and allowed her façade of serenity to fall.

How could Lieutenant Grant's absence have rendered her so unhappy, when she had known him only a scant few months, when she had never thought of him as more than a friend until that moment on the piazza less than two weeks before?

She had known of Lieutenant Grant from her brother's letters, of course, but they had offered only the barest sketch of him. Frederick, the third eldest of her four brothers, had befriended Ulysses Grant at West Point, where he had impressed his fellow cadets and instructors alike with his brilliant horsemanship. Frederick had wryly observed that in every other subject except mathematics, his friend had failed to achieve distinction, neglecting his studies but doing well enough in his recitations to get by. He had little patience for petty rules and regulations, and even less for drills, parades, and pompous ceremonies. The demerits he had accumulated were for minor infractions, but the sheer weight of their numbers dragged his class ranking below what Frederick loyally asserted was his true measure as a soldier.

As the most accomplished horseman at West Point, Lieutenant Grant had hoped to be assigned to the cavalry, but after graduating an unremarkable twenty-first in a class of thirty-nine, he was denied his first choice. Instead he had been assigned to the infantry, which would have been a complete disappointment except that he would join Frederick at Jefferson Barracks. But even that silver lining had quickly tarnished; before Lieutenant Grant arrived, Frederick's regiment had been ordered to Fort Towson in Indian Territory. "Would you make my friend welcome at White Haven?" Frederick had written home from the frontier outpost. "His family was kind to me when I visited them in Ohio. I would like to repay the favor."

Soon the lieutenant was visiting White Haven often, sometimes twice a week, or so Julia learned from her mother's and sisters' letters. After finishing her last school term, she had remained in St. Louis at the gracious mansion of her father's cousin Mrs. John O'Fallon, the wife of a Kentuckian who had earned a fortune in railroads and real estate. Mrs. O'Fallon — worldly, elegant, and greatly admired for her charitable works — had taken the shy young Julia under her wing, polishing her social graces and introducing her into the same privileged society in which her own daughter, Caroline, dwelt. There Julia had attracted the eye of a wealthy beau, but his smooth manners, extravagant compliments, and abundant gifts of flowers overwhelmed rather than charmed her.

"He's gonna ask you to marry him," Jule warned one evening as she helped Julia dress for an evening at the concert hall. "If not tonight, then soon."

Julia pressed a trembling hand to her waist. "Oh, heavens, please let it not be tonight."

"Tell him you don't want to marry him."

"I don't want to hurt his feelings." Julia sat down heavily on the edge of the bed. "I don't want to disappoint Mrs. O'Fallon. It's a fortuitous match, and Papa approves, and she's worked so hard to arrange it."

Jule regarded her skeptically, one hand resting on her hip. "You'd promise to stay with a man you don't love for the rest of your life just so you won't make other people feel bad?"

Julia knotted her fingers together in her lap. "When you say it like that, it sounds foolish."

"It sounds foolish because it *is*." Shaking her head, Jule pulled Julia to her feet so she could adjust her sash. "What a shame to watch you waste your choice on someone you don't love. Don't you know how lucky you are, to be able to choose? You can wait for love to come along."

"I can't wait forever."

Jule sighed and pulled the sash tighter. "You can choose," she repeated. "I can't believe you'd throw that away on that empty-headed peacock. *I* wouldn't, but then again, I'll never get the chance."

The rebuke stung. "Jule —"

"At least he's rich." Jule relented, loosening the sash a trifle. "You may be unhappy, but you'll be comfortable."

Jule's words lingered in Julia's thoughts as the days passed and her suitor became more urgently attentive. Finally, Julia confessed her unhappiness to Mrs. O'Fallon, who kindly sent her home to White Haven, where Julia — and Jule too, judging by her air of satisfaction — was all too happy to go.

Within a few days of her homecoming, Julia met Lieutenant Grant.

Her youngest sister, eight-year-old Emma, was proud to have met him first, and her letters had fairly gushed with admiration. "His cheeks are round and plump and rosy," she had praised, so lavishly that Julia imagined her young sister swooning upon a fainting couch. "His hair is fine and brown, very thick and wavy. His eyes are a clear blue, and always full of light. His features are regular, very pleasing and attractive, and his figure is so slender, so well formed and graceful that to me he looks like a young prince."

When Julia saw him for the first time, making his way up the zigzag path to White Haven on horseback, she was struck by the accuracy of Emma's observations. But as she welcomed him, and as she came to know him better in subsequent visits, she discovered other admirable qualities her innocent sister had missed. The blue eyes Emma had admired were contemplative and kind, and they fixed upon Julia with earnest curiosity. His quiet, composed manner was soothing and restful after the breezy boastfulness of her St. Louis suitor. His muscular hands held a horse's reins with strength and certainty, and he rode with a natural grace and power that Julia, an accomplished horsewoman herself, could not fail to admire.

"Lieutenant Grant used to be content to call on us only twice a week," Julia's mother remarked one afternoon as they tended her lavish flower garden, regarded as the most beautiful in the Gravois Creek settlement. "But since you've returned home, he visits nearly every day."

Julia had bent over a gardenia bush and busied herself with the pruning shears to disguise the color rising in her cheeks. She had not noticed an increase in Lieutenant Grant's visits, which always seemed too brief and too far apart for her liking. He did not share her fondness for music and dancing, but they both delighted in long horseback rides through the Missouri countryside, through shady groves where trailing vines and tall ferns flourished, and along the creeks, which sparkled like silver as they flowed to the Mississippi. Usually the lieutenant would return to Jefferson Barracks after supper, but sometimes he spent the night, and on those occasions he and Julia would rise early and race before breakfast, flying over rolling hills softly blanketed by morning mists. Breathless and happy, Julia enjoyed the pounding of the horses' hooves and her own heart and the sight of Lieutenant Grant leaning forward in his saddle, his often stubborn mouth breaking open in a grin, his blue eyes shining, his thick, ruddy hair tousled above a broad forehead. She basked in his unspoken admiration as he helped her alight from her mare, and he solicitously escorted her when she, an aspiring botanist, carried a magnifying glass and shears and vials off the well-worn trails into the underbrush in search of an intriguing new specimen or a particularly lovely flower. On warmer, sunnier days they might take their ease in a patch of soft grass near the creek, and while Julia examined her cuttings, Lieutenant Grant would read to her from Sir Walter Scott or Robert Burns. He was delightful company, despite his objections to slavery and his respectful disagreement with her father on almost every conceivable political issue. But Lieutenant Grant and Papa got along affably when the subject was farming, and Mamma approved of his common sense, diligent ways, and the temperate manner in which he discussed politics with her irascible, opinionated husband.

Julia had looked forward to many more swift, invigorating rides and cozy family suppers with the lieutenant, so she was sorely disappointed when, upon his arrival one afternoon in late April, he explained that he would be taking a three-week furlough to visit his family in Ohio. "I believe war with Mexico is coming," he told Julia later as they sat alone on the broad piazza after supper, as the sun

31

declined toward the horizon and the moment of his departure too swiftly approached. "I want to say good-bye to my parents and my brothers and sisters before I go."

"Of course you must," Julia said, unable to keep a tremor of apprehension from her voice.

"Oh, don't worry about me." He rested his elbows on his knees and studied her expression, which he seemed able to read all too well. "I won't get hurt. I'll be back, as whole and sound as when I left."

"Not with camp food rather than Annie's delicious cooking to sustain you, you won't," she teased. Their cook, rightly proud of her exceptional skills in the kitchen, often declared that the lieutenant was too skinny and ought to eat more, even though he rarely failed to clean his plate of whatever delicious morsels she placed before him. "I know you won't be injured or — or worse. I know you'll come back safely."

He peered at her, curious. "You sound awfully certain."

"I am." As she spoke, a familiar, uncannily powerful sensation swept over her, and she knew that she was right. Since childhood, whenever she experienced that particular, peculiar feeling, or woke from a strangely vivid dream, she knew that whatever she had glimpsed or felt would come to pass. Jule believed that Julia had the gift of prophecy, but while Julia would never make such a boastful claim, she and her family had learned to trust her intuition.

But her gift often eluded her at the most critical moments, rendering her utterly caught by surprise.

"I won't always be riding off into danger," Lieutenant Grant told her seriously, sitting back in his chair. "You know I have no real affection for military life."

"I know," said Julia, amused by the understatement. He loathed the routine of camp and the preponderance of petty regulations, and even merry military music fell like a noisy clanging of tin pans and blaring whistles upon his ear. Instead he hoped for a career as a mathematics professor, and in the evenings in the barracks, he reviewed his West Point courses to prepare himself. He had applied for a post as an assistant professor at the military academy, and the head of the mathematics department had promised him first consideration when a vacancy next appeared.

"It would be a good living," he went on, and when Julia nodded, he hesitated, turned his West Point ring about his finger, then suddenly removed it and held it out to her. "Would you not wear this?"

For a moment Julia froze, staring at the golden band on his palm. "Oh, no, I couldn't," she exclaimed, shrinking back into her chair. Once, several weeks before, when they had been walking their horses on a sunny bank of Gravois Creek, he had idly remarked that if he ever gave his school ring to a lady, he would give it as an engagement ring.

"Why not?"

"Mamma would never approve of me accepting such a gift from a gentleman."

He regarded her for a moment, clearly perplexed and disappointed. "All right, then," he said, returning the ring to his own finger. Julia was too mortified to speak, so they sat in silence, Julia with her gaze fixed on her hands clasped in her lap, the lieutenant studying the poplar and locust trees at the garden's edge.

Then he stood. "I must bid you farewell now," he said gruffly, avoiding her gaze.

"Good-bye," she replied softly. "Safe travels."

"Will you think of me while I'm away?"

"Of course," she replied, surprised that he needed to ask. "I'll think of you and pray for your safekeeping every day, as I do for my own dear brother."

To her astonishment, he winced. It was not until after he rode away that she realized he had hoped she would say that she thought of him as someone even more dear than a brother.

■ ■ ■ ■

As she went about her chores, Jule observed Nell's attempts to comfort her elder sister, noted Julia's forced laughter and poorly concealed misery, and knew that something had gone very wrong up at Jefferson Barracks. Julia wasn't wearing the lieutenant's ring, Jule was relieved to see, but she could only guess whether that was because Julia had refused it again or Lieutenant Grant had not offered it a second time.

Jule's relief was for her own sake, not her mistress's. Lieutenant Grant seemed decent enough — quieter than the other officers who visited White Haven, surprisingly courteous to the colored folk — and Jule certainly preferred him to that loud, strutting dandy who had haplessly wooed Julia in St. Louis. Jule knew Julia would marry eventually, but Jule dreaded that day, for wherever the young mistress went, the maid would be obliged to follow.

As the afternoon passed, Jule watched as Julia's composure crumbled piece by piece. At bedtime, as Jule undressed her for bed, she finally let her tears fall, pressing her lips together to muffle her sobs.

"You crying over that lieutenant?" Jule asked as she helped Julia into her cotton nightgown. "He say something unkind?"

35

"He wasn't there. He's still in Ohio, visiting his parents." Julia wiped her eyes with the back of her hand. "I miss him more than I thought I would."

Jule suspected Julia had been surprised to find herself missing him at all. "You dream about him since he been gone?"

"No — that is to say, not *that* sort of dream." As a pink flush rose in Julia's cheeks, Jule had to bite her lips together so she would not burst out laughing. What sort of dreams *had* he appeared in, if not the prophetic kind? "But — but I have a strong feeling that he won't be harmed while he's away."

"Then why carry on so?" admonished Jule, brushing out her mistress's long, thick locks. Julia winced when the tines caught on a snarl. "Shouldn't that dream put your mind at ease? Whatever quarrel you had, you can make your peace when he comes back."

"*If* he comes back." Julia inhaled deeply, shakily. "If he's already received word about the Fourth's transfer to Louisiana, he'll just meet them there or along the way. He wouldn't have any reason to come back to Missouri."

"Except to see you."

Julia laughed bleakly. "He might want to, but he wouldn't defy orders and break leave by traveling so far out of his way just to bid me good-bye."

Jule brushed Julia's hair in silence, considering. "Ain't it more likely that Lieutenant Grant didn't get the message, he being at his folks' house or traveling? Ain't it more likely that he's on his way back to Jefferson Barracks this very moment? Sure it is, and surely he'll come by White Haven before setting out for Natchitoches." Finished, Jule set the brush aside. "Seems to me you got every reason to hope to see him soon."

"You're absolutely right, Jule." Julia managed a wan smile. "I haven't lost him yet, nor have I lost hope. Nor, I pray, will I ever lose you, for how could I manage without you?"

"I don't think you need to worry about losing me," said Jule matter-of-factly, turning down the bed and plumping the pillow. "How would I get lost?"

How could she get lost, when she had nowhere to go and no way to get there? How could she leave behind every friend, every place, everything she knew?

And Gabriel. How could she think of leaving Gabriel, when Julia's marriage would likely tear her from him all too soon?

Julia faced the next morning bravely, occupying herself by playing melodic airs on the piano and weeding the garden. She passed the afternoon with a long ride on her favorite horse, Psyche, a chestnut-brown, part Arabian mare, as glossy as satin, with pretty ears and eyes that bore a faithful expression. But the day dragged by nonetheless, and the next was worse, for thunderclouds rolled in and drenched the greening land below so that it was impossible to go riding.

The weather cleared by Saturday, the sun peeping through the clouds as it rose to its zenith — but Lieutenant Grant did not appear. Restless and miserable, Julia ordered Psyche to be saddled and rode out to Jefferson Barracks, alone. The creek and all the little unnamed rivulets that fed it were swollen from the recent downpours, the road uneven and crenelated where overflow had carved channels into the mud, but Julia did not turn back. If Lieutenant Grant had returned to Jefferson Barracks, if he was on his way from there to White Haven, they would meet midway.

But although Julia slowed the mare — out of an abundance of caution as well as a desperate need to delay the inevitable — she reached the edge of the woods without encountering a single other traveler. She gazed up at the whitewashed buildings and fences atop the high hill, waiting, listening for the thunder of his bonny brown steed's hooves on the packed earth as he raced toward her, but heard only the wind in the boughs, the rustling whisper of leaves high above. Feeling foolish and unbearably sad, she turned Psyche toward home.

That night, she dreamed of him.

The next morning at breakfast, when her sisters cajoled her to explain the reason for her distraction and lack of appetite, she admitted that a dream yet haunted her. Nell and Emma, their eyes wide with excitement, begged her to describe it, and Mamma looked on with fond curiosity, but her father snorted. "Not this nonsense again," he grumbled. "Dreams and fairy tales. A leaking bucket of balderdash, all of it."

"Frederick," chided Mamma gently. Papa sighed and glowered as he stabbed a crust of bread into his egg yolk, but he did not demand they change the subject.

"Your dream, Julia," urged Emma. "Tell us your dream."

"If there is no objection," Julia began pertly, with a sidelong glance at her father. "I dreamed that it was Monday, right around noon, and who should call on us at White Haven but Lieutenant Grant."

As her sisters gasped, their father barked out a laugh. "And how, in your dream, did you know it was Monday? I understand that you could judge the hour by the position of the sun in the sky, but how did you determine the day?"

"That's the way of dreams," Emma said. "You just *know*. Isn't that so, Julia?"

"It was Monday," Julia repeated firmly. "Lieutenant Grant arrived at noon, but he was wearing civilian clothes."

"I don't know if I'd recognize him out of uniform," mused Nell.

"In my dream I did." Julia would know him anywhere, sleeping or waking. "He came in, greeted us all most cordially, and seated himself by my side. When I asked how long he would remain, he said, 'I'm going to try to stay a week.'"

"A week," Emma exclaimed, bouncing in her chair. "How wonderful!"

"That proves you couldn't've been dreaming about Grant," scoffed Papa. "Say what you will about his queer abolitionist notions, he has sense enough not to overstay his welcome."

"I know it was the lieutenant," said Julia mildly. She had seen him so vividly, heard his own true voice, inhaled deeply of his scent, slightly woodsy and spicy with a sweet whiff of horses — but of course, it had not really been him, only his dream phantom. And yet she wished she had reached out to touch his face.

"Julia, darling," said Mamma, "you know this dream won't come true. Lieutenant Grant is at this very moment sailing down the Mississippi to reunite with the Fourth. He's surely already far below the mouth of the Ohio."

Julia's soaring spirits abruptly came back down to earth. "I know, but it was a lovely dream."

Mamma smiled sympathetically and her sisters murmured agreement.

"I suppose it could still come true," Papa remarked. When they all turned to look at him in surprise, he added, "Julia didn't say what year it was in her dream. Maybe Lieutenant Grant will grace us with a visit some Monday come winter."

"Papa," scolded Nell, and Emma's mouth fell open in protest, but Julia only laughed and shook her head at her incorrigible father. He could tease all he liked, because she knew it was a Monday in her dream, and Lieutenant Grant had not been dressed for winter weather.

Sunday passed, and Monday morning found Julia in the garden, staking her water-logged bean plants in the rain-soaked soil. Jule stood nearby, shooing away the gnats and no-see-ums from her mistress's arms and face, ready to hand over the shears and the ball of twine at her request. Suddenly Julia heard hoofbeats, and when she glanced over her shoulder she spied a man on horseback coming up the zigzag path. "Jule," she exclaimed. "See him for me."

Jule studied the rider intently, shading her eyes with her hand. "He's covered in mud so I can't be sure," she said, "but I think that's your lieutenant."

Julia's heart thumped and she scrambled to her feet, brushing the soil from her hands. "It

41

is," she cried, dropping her trowel and lifting her skirts as she hurried to welcome him. The dogs barked happily; Emma burst from the house and flew down the path ahead of her, halting a few paces away as the lieutenant reined in his mare.

"What happened to you?" exclaimed Emma. "Did you fall in a lake?"

As Julia drew closer, she saw that Lieutenant Grant and his horse, too, were soaking wet. "We were submerged fording the creek," he admitted. His muddy uniform flopped about his slender frame like rags used to mop up after a deluge.

"The quiet little Gravois?" Julia said, astonished. "The one you said didn't have enough water to turn a coffee mill?"

"It's not so quiet now." Though bedraggled and shivering, the lieutenant dismounted with effortless grace. "The Gravois and all the little creeks feeding it are swollen and raging. I was almost swept away, but my horse can swim well enough and I clung to her saddle."

Julia felt a pang of fear, but it swiftly faded when she reminded herself that he was fine; he was fine and he was there. "You must come inside and dry yourself," she said, glancing over her shoulder as Gabriel came running to take the horse's reins. "My brother John surely has some clothes you could borrow. Frederick's would hang on you like a tent."

The lieutenant willingly allowed himself to be led inside, where Mamma took charge of their half-drowned visitor and shooed Julia off to attend to her own toilet. With Jule's help, she quickly washed and changed into a prettier frock and fixed her hair. When Lieutenant Grant descended, scrubbed free of the mud and clad in her eldest brother's old suit, Julia, her sisters, and her mother were waiting for him in the drawing room with tea and apple dumplings.

"How long do you expect to remain, Lieutenant Grant?" Julia asked as she served him.

"I'm going to try to stay a week," he replied, accepting the cup and plate. "Thank you."

"You've said the very words sister dreamed you would," Emma exclaimed.

The lieutenant's eyebrows rose as he swallowed a bite of apple dumpling. He turned to Julia, who felt herself shrinking with embarrassment. "Have you been dreaming of me, Miss Dent?"

For a fleeting moment, Julia considered the many ways she could later make her little sister regret her impulsive words. "Only the once," Julia said instead, not entirely honestly, and she described her dream. "And here you are, in civilian clothes, at noon on a Monday."

"And here you must stay," added Emma, with an inquiring glance to Mamma, "for a week, just as Julia dreamed."

"I see that I must. I couldn't bear to spoil any dream of Miss Dent's," said Lieutenant Grant seriously, but his eyes shone with merriment as they met Julia's.

To her delight, Lieutenant Grant's commanding officer extended his furlough, giving them ten glorious days before he would be obliged to join his comrades in Louisiana. They spent the time enjoying long rides, leisurely walks, and almost endless conversation.

One day, the Dent family was to attend a wedding, and so Julia's parents invited the lieutenant to accompany them. "I'm a bridesmaid, so I need to arrive early," Julia told him as they walked their horses after an exhilarating ride. "John will drive me out there in the morning."

"And the rest of the family?"

"They'll lumber along in the old coach afterward, and you shall accompany them on horseback."

"Your brother John admires my horse," Lieutenant Grant mused. "Maybe he'd consider trading places with me."

Delighted, Julia urged him to inquire, and John readily agreed, glad for the chance to try the lieutenant's horse. The following day, shortly after breakfast, Julia and Lieutenant Grant set out in the buggy for the neighboring farm, feeling clever and pleased with themselves for stealing some time alone.

The day was warm and bright and the sun shone splendidly, a happy omen for a wedding day. They rode cheerfully along until they reached an old bridge spanning a deep ravine, a familiar, easy crossing that had been utterly transformed by the recent heavy rains. The gentle, burbling creek had swollen until it reached the bridge, and it flowed through the gulch in a torrent of white water and rushing sound.

Lieutenant Grant slowed the horse as they approached.

"I've never seen the water so high here," said Julia, anxious. "Is this how it was when you forded downstream?"

"It might've been about this deep," he replied, studying the road ahead. "But there was no bridge."

Julia tore her gaze away from the rushing stream. "Then why on earth did you try to cross? You could have drowned."

"I have a peculiar superstition," he admitted. "When I start to go somewhere, or to do anything, I don't turn back or stop until the thing intended is accomplished. Besides, you were on the other side."

Julia felt her cheeks grow warm. "Don't think to flatter me by risking your life on my account. If you get yourself killed, you'll only upset me."

He smiled. "I'll keep that in mind." His

expression grew sober again and he nodded to the bridge. "What do you think?"

"I think it looks too dangerous to cross. Don't you?"

"The bridge looks sturdy enough, and the horse is calm."

Julia managed a shaky laugh. "Calmer than I am, certainly. I'd rather go back than take any risk."

"And miss the wedding? You love parties and dancing, and doesn't the bride need your help?"

"She'll have many other friends there eager to wait upon her, I'm sure." Nervousness made her words come in a quick torrent. "Do you really think it'll be safe?"

"Miss Dent." He turned to her, his expression calm and confident. "I'm sure that it's perfectly safe. I wouldn't suggest we cross otherwise."

Julia took a deep, tremulous breath and nodded. He chirruped to the horse, which obediently approached the bridge. Just as the horse was about to set hoof to plank, Julia blurted, "If anything happens, I'll cling to you. I won't be able to help it."

"I'm duly forewarned." Lieutenant Grant shook the reins, the buggy lurched forward, Julia shrieked and clutched his arm — and then they were on the other side, having splashed over the sturdy planks in less than a minute. The buggy quickly climbed a gentle

46

slope and the sound of rushing water faded behind them.

"We should be safe now," the lieutenant remarked, grinning.

With a gasp, Julia immediately released his arm and scooted a modest distance away.

"I didn't mean you had to go so far," he protested. "I want you always to cling to me when you're afraid. I want you to cling to me always, and I will to you, whether the creek is high or low, forsaking all others."

"Lieutenant Grant —"

"Julia, I love you." Never had her name been spoken more tenderly. "Without you, life would be unbearable. I promise I'll always care for you, and keep you safe, and make you as happy as I know how. Will you be my wife?"

"I —" Breathless, Julia pressed a hand to her chest. "I don't know what to say."

"Then say you'll marry me."

"I think it would be charming to be engaged, but to be married —" Julia shook her head helplessly, tears springing into her eyes. "Oh, no, indeed! I would much rather be engaged."

"You do know that one usually leads to the other, don't you?"

"I do, of course." She took out her handkerchief and dabbed at the corners of her eyes. "I just think that being engaged would be much nicer than being married."

He nodded and fixed his eyes on the road ahead. "Well, then," he said after a while, "bearing in mind that I hold to the time-honored custom of engagements culminating in marriages, would you consent to our engagement?"

"Yes, yes, of course," she said. "I'd be delighted to be engaged to you."

He took her hand, raised it to his lips, and held it for the rest of the drive, his fingers interlaced with hers.

The wedding was lovely, although Julia was almost too distracted to notice. She fairly burst with her secret, and when her family arrived, she was so worried they would guess the truth before she could properly prepare them that she avoided them until the attempt became comically ridiculous. Lieutenant Grant — Ulysses, she should think of him now — would not dance, as ever, but he seemed to enjoy watching her whirl about with other partners, perhaps secure in knowing that forevermore he would partner her everywhere else.

After dinner, he took her aside and quietly brought up the subject of marriage again. He wanted to fix a date, preferably soon, but Julia demurred, knowing that Papa liked Ulysses well enough as a man, but as a son-in-law — well, that was something else altogether.

After that, the rest of Ulysses's leave passed with bittersweet swiftness. On the day before his departure, he accompanied Julia out to the flower garden, where she untangled rain-battered stems and separated the blooms. With no one to overhear, they spoke quietly and heatedly about their fledgling betrothal. Ulysses wanted to marry without delay; Julia argued the merits of a long engagement. He wanted to speak to her father and set a date before he left for Louisiana; she quaked at the very thought. "Please don't speak to Papa yet," she begged. "He'll raise objections. I know he will."

Eventually, reluctantly, Ulysses conceded, but he refused to keep their engagement secret indefinitely. He would write to Colonel Dent upon his arrival at Camp Salubrity, after Julia had prepared him. "When I want something from my Papa, I can usually get it," Julia said, clasping Ulysses's hands in hers. "But it may take time. We both must practice patience."

Out of sight of everyone, they kissed to seal their agreement, and again Ulysses took his class ring from his finger and held it out to her. "Will you accept this now?"

She nodded, and when he slipped the ring upon her finger she knew she would wear it every day until he replaced it with a blessed band of gold.

CHAPTER TWO

May 1844–August 1848

Julia missed Ulysses terribly, but she occupied her lonely hours with the daunting task of preparing Papa for news of their engagement. After she confided her secret to her sisters, they gladly volunteered to help her by singing Ulys's praises whenever Papa was sure to overhear.

One Sunday morning as the family rode to church, a fallen tree reminded Nell of the time a neighbor's elderly servant had dropped his axe while cutting firewood alone in the forest. He had severed an artery in his foot and would have died if Ulys and Julia had not chanced upon him while out riding. While Julia had frozen in horror, Ulysses had swiftly dismounted and used his coat to bind the man's wound, saving his life.

"He's a steady man in a crisis," said Mamma.

But Papa shook his head. "On that occasion he performed just as you'd expect a soldier to, but he isn't a man of substance."

"How could you say such a thing?" Julia protested.

"Grant's too quiet for a man of almost twenty-two. He keeps his views too much to himself. You're never sure where he stands on the matters of the day."

"Nonsense," Julia declared. "He thinks before he speaks, a quality I admire. Would you prefer that he blurt out every idle thought?"

"No, I suppose I wouldn't." Grudgingly Papa added, "For a soldier, he might make a fine farmer someday."

Julia knew then that bringing her father around would take time and patience — but before she could warn Ulysses of her slow progress, he wrote to her father to ask for her hand.

Papa came roaring from his study into the parlor, crumpled the letter, and tossed it onto the table around which the Dent women were gathered. "Julia, you shall not marry Grant. You're too young, and he's too poor. He hasn't anything to give you."

"He has everything I want," she retorted hotly. "He's a good man, and kind, and he loves me." She turned to her mother. "You've said he shows great promise, that he'll make his mark someday."

"Yes," Mamma acknowledged, regarding Papa levelly. "I believe he will."

Papa kept his stormy gaze fixed upon Julia. "The roving military life is not for you. A soldier can't settle anywhere. Grant will drag you from one distant, desolate army post to another, likely hundreds of miles from home. You don't even like to go as far as St. Louis without your mother or your sisters." He shook his head, his thick eyebrows knitting. "No, daughter, I can't agree to let you choose such a difficult life when you don't understand what you're choosing."

Julia swiftly rose, her hands balled into fists at her sides. "I *will* marry Lieutenant Grant," she choked out, "if I have to wait ten years to receive your blessing."

When Julia called for her, Jule set her pile of mending aside and hurried upstairs. She found Julia pacing in her bedchamber, pale and trembling with unspent anger. "I'm going riding," she said, gesturing vaguely to the window, clasping a hand to her brow and fighting back tears.

Jule nodded and quickly helped her change. "Something wrong, Miss Julia?" she ventured as she accompanied her downstairs and outside.

"It's Papa." Julia strode along with such swift purpose that Jule had to leap every few steps to keep up. "He's so stubborn, so unreasonable! He insists that Ulys is unsuitable for me, but I know we're perfectly suited for each other. I know that as certainly as I know anything."

"Your papa will come around," said Jule as they approached the corral. "He always gives you your own way in the end."

"Not always." At the gate, Julia halted and clutched Jule's arm. "I won't break off my engagement. I won't. I can't."

At that moment Gabriel emerged from the stable leading Papa's stallion by the halter. His face broke into a broad grin of surprise and pleasure when his eyes met Jule's, but an expressionless mask slid in place when his gaze shifted to Julia. When she instructed him to saddle her favorite mare, he nodded and disappeared into the stable again. Soon Julia was speeding off into the forest, with no mention of when she might return.

Gabriel crossed the muddy stable yard and joined Jule on the far side, resting his hands on the corral fence between them, his skin barely touching hers but sending a frisson of warmth through her nonetheless. His shoulders were broad and strong, his hands calloused but gentle. On nights when his muscles ached badly enough to chase away sleep, Jule rubbed a liniment of her own concoction into his skin until the pain eased — although he sometimes ruefully complained that her touch relieved one kind of suffering and kindled another.

"Trouble at the big house?" he asked.

53

Jule nodded. "Same old thing. Miss Julia's pining for her soldier. Defying her papa — and she's not by nature the defying kind." The corral smelled of horses and manure and overturned soil and fresh sweat, a scent that she had come to love, for it was Gabriel's too. "I feel sorry for her. I know how she feels."

"You? No, you don't."

"Who knows better than me what she's going through?"

"The man you love is right here." He spread his hands and smiled, wistful. "Ready to marry you soon as you say."

Sharply she retorted, "Slaves can't marry."

"Not within the law, maybe." He leaned forward and rested his elbows on the fence, his foot on the lowest rail. "But before God, we could. We'd be husband and wife as true as the old master and missus."

Jule hesitated. Gabriel had made the same point many times before, and with each argument, she felt her resistance wavering. No one knew scripture better than Gabriel, not even the missus, not even the yellow-bearded white minister who came by White Haven once a month to preach to the slaves about obedience and submission and the rewards awaiting faithful servants in heaven. A Quaker lady had secretly given Gabriel the Bible he kept hidden beneath his pallet in the hayloft, and his vast store of memorized verses had helped him learn to read it. Gabriel wanted to be a minister, and he wanted to be free, and he wanted to marry Jule — but although she loved him, she could not become his wife.

"We can't get married," she told him vehemently, beseechingly, but she knew from the set of his jaw and the fondness in his eyes that she would not persuade him. "We don't know how much longer we got to be together. Soon as Miss Julia marry, she'll leave White Haven and take me with her."

"Then we ought to make the most of the time we got."

He reached across the fence and touched her shoulder, and after a moment's hesitation, she moved closer until his arm held her in a half embrace across the wooden fence. With his other hand he gently traced a line from the tiny scar at her temple nearly hidden beneath her cap — the remnant of a childhood accident, a treacherous leap between moss-covered boulders while playing with Julia along the slippery banks of the Gravois — down the curve of her cheek to her chin. She wanted him to kiss her, but she held perfectly still rather than lift her face to meet his. They never knew who might be watching, who might be upset or alarmed or offended by the sight of two slaves happy in each other.

She took a deep breath and stepped away. "If we married, it wouldn't make any difference to the old master. If I knew we wouldn't be parted —"

"Not even the old master and missus knew that on their wedding day," said Gabriel. "No man and woman do. Miss Julia and her lieutenant don't know. I say we get married and be married as long as we can. Ain't a few happy years better than none?"

All the warnings she remembered from childhood came rushing in — Annie's, that she should be vigilant so heartbreak wouldn't catch her by surprise, Dinah's that she should count her blessings and be grateful that Miss Julia liked her and would never beat or starve or sell her. "It could be so much worse," Dinah still told her from time to time, lowering her voice and glancing over her shoulder before telling her of a runaway torn to pieces by a slave catcher's dogs near Florissant, or of a girl younger than Jule who had already unwillingly borne her master two light-skinned babies the master's furious wife had immediately sold off to the far-distant South. And memories of Hannah, the poor slave woman beaten to death by an army officer, haunted her still.

"You're right," she told Gabriel, her heart cinching painfully as she turned away. "You're right, but you're wrong too."

She felt his gaze lingering upon her as she hurried back to the big house to await Julia's return.

Papa did not forbid Julia and Ulys to exchange letters, and Ulys wrote often — plainspoken, factual accounts of soldiering on the Texas border appropriate to read aloud to the family, and often a second, smaller, more tender note meant for Julia's eyes alone.

Then came autumn and a bitterly fought presidential election from which the Democratic candidate, James K. Polk, emerged victorious, much to Papa's satisfaction. On the first day of March 1845, outgoing president John Tyler signed a congressional resolution to annex Texas, and in his inaugural address three days later, President Polk spoke of expanding the United States and "extending the dominions of peace."

Texas would join the nation as a slave state, and war with Mexico was imminent.

Ulys, their cousin James Longstreet, and the rest of the Fourth Infantry expected to march into Texas at once, but when their orders were not immediately forthcoming, Ulys secured a brief leave of absence to visit White Haven. He hoped to marry Julia during his five-day respite in Missouri, but at the very least he was determined to receive her father's blessing for the marriage before he left for Mexico.

Julia told no one of Ulys's impending visit,

57

nor did she know when he might arrive. Every day she looked for him — and one morning when the family was gathered on the piazza, she saw him coming up the road on a superb dapple gray, so handsome and dashing in a splendid new uniform that the sight of him took her breath away.

After dismounting, Ulys touched Julia's hand in passing as he greeted her parents respectfully and asked for a private word with Papa. As Mamma led the two men inside, Julia and Nell quickly crouched on the piazza beneath the parlor window, where they could eavesdrop unobserved.

In the parlor, Ulys promptly got to the reason for his unexpected visit. "Mr. Dent," he began, while Julia closed her eyes and savored his voice, so dear, so long unheard, so badly missed. "I want to marry Miss Julia."

For a long, excruciating moment, there was only silence within.

"Lieutenant Grant," Papa eventually replied, "I don't believe the roving life my daughter would have to lead as a soldier's wife would suit her at all."

"If that's the only objection, I'll resign my commission," Ulys replied. "I've been preparing for a career as a professor of mathematics, and both West Point and a college in Hillsboro, Ohio, have assured me that I'll be given full consideration."

"I think it best you stick to your present occupation," Papa said. "My reluctance has nothing to do with you personally, you understand. If it were Nell you wanted, I'd make no objection, but my Julia is entirely unfit for such a life."

"I don't want Nell," said Ulys bluntly. "I want Julia. I *will* make her happy, sir, and if the military life doesn't suit her, then I'll leave it."

Julia's heart pounded as silence dragged on. Nell gave her hand an encouraging squeeze.

"If that's how you feel," Papa finally said, "I suppose it'll have to be Julia."

"Thank you, sir."

"Now, hold on. Julia's still very young. I agree that you may continue to correspond while you're apart. In a year or two, if you haven't changed your minds, *then* you'll have my blessing to marry."

Beneath the window, Julia and Nell embraced, muffling exclamations of delight.

Afterward, Ulys returned outside to the piazza, caught Julia up in his embrace, and kissed her. "I didn't expect your father to give his consent so quickly," he said, smiling down upon her, his eyes shining with love and happiness.

But Julia knew it was too soon to celebrate. "He's only granted us a cease-fire, Ulys. We haven't yet won the war."

Julia and Ulys enjoyed a few glorious days at White Haven, riding over meadows fragrant with late spring flowers, strolling along the creek, and dreaming aloud about their future as husband and wife. Never had the breezes felt more gentle and sweet, never had the locust trees and jasmine vines bloomed more beautifully — but Ulys's impending departure cast a shadow over the idyllic scenes. Ulys was leaving her again, and this time, he was heading off to war.

After his departure, the lonely days without him stretched into weeks, which Julia resolved to fill wisely. She started a quilt, hemmed linens for their marriage bed, and watched Mamma carefully to learn how she ran a household and managed the servants. Letters from Ulys came with almost every post, and she savored every line, reading aloud bits about the war and camp life to the family, but saving the words of love for herself alone. Her brother Frederick and cousin James were in Ulys's brigade now, and sometimes he sent news of them too.

The weeks stretched into months. As the nights grew longer, the winds colder, White Haven sank into a contemplative autumn stillness. With so many soldiers away at war, there were no more dances at Jefferson Barracks, and when winter blew in blustery and gray, the Dents moved to their home in St. Louis. Their city residence, a town house on the corner of Fourth and Cerre Streets near Sacred Heart Convent and the French Market, seemed narrow and cramped compared to the generous expanses of White Haven, but the city's conveniences compensated for that, and the rigors of winter were easier to bear.

The months stretched into years.

Ulys wrote that Julia would scarcely recognize him, so bronzed and hardened and aged had he become beneath the Mexican sun, though his love for her remained unaltered by time and distance. He gently chided her for not writing more often — "My Julia writes such sweet letters, when she does write" — and she tried to keep pace with him, but with her poor vision, writing for any length of time left her with terrible headaches. She wished she could have Jule see the pages for her, but of course that would never do.

One spring day Ulys wrote to Julia using a captured Mexican drum as a desk. When she read his matter-of-fact acknowledgment that a shell had nearly claimed his life a few hours before, Julia felt faint, almost too ill to read on. "There is no great sport in having bullets flying about one in every direction," Ulys told her, "but I find they have less horror when among them than in anticipation." He wrote often of his longing for peace, and Julia replied to tell him how much she wished they had married before he had left for Mexico. "I would willingly share your tent," she declared, "or your prison, should you be taken prisoner."

Then came the Battle of Molino del Rey and the terse, dreadful report that Frederick had been wounded.

Terribly afraid, the Dent family frantically sought news of his condition, but it was not until three days later that Ulys's reassuring letter arrived, written only hours after the fight. Frederick had been struck in the thigh by a musket ball as he charged an enemy gun, but Ulys had been nearby to tend his wounds, and he was expected to recover completely. Ulys was so incapable of boasting of himself that they learned not from him but from Frederick and cousin James that Ulys had almost certainly saved Frederick from bleeding to death. Afterward, Frederick and Ulys were both promoted to brevet captain — and Papa suddenly found himself unable to disparage Ulys with the same enthusiasm as before.

Ulys's letters began to speak more confidently of an end to the war, and finally, in February 1848, commissioners from both countries signed a treaty of peace. But still Ulys could not come home. "It is scarcely supportable for me to be separated from you so long my Dearest Julia," Ulys wrote.

At long last his regiment left Mexico for New Orleans, and finally Ulys was granted a leave of absence. A week later he arrived in St. Louis, swept Julia into his arms, kissed her, and declared that they must be married at once. "Will your father raise any objection?"

"No, certainly not." She had not seen her darling Ulys in more than three years, and she was breathless with joy and astonishment and something akin to shyness. The tall, strong, weathered captain who had come to marry her was both a stranger and her most beloved. And yet he was the same man, tested and tempered but still her own Ulys. "Papa left all that behind after you saved Frederick's life."

Ulys kissed her swiftly, fully on the mouth. "You can't possibly know how happy you make me," he declared. "First I have to go home to Ohio, but I can be back by the fifteenth or twentieth of August."

"You're going away again?"

"Not for long." He took her hands in his and raised them to his lips. "I want to see my parents and invite my family to the wedding. I'd like them to be with us on the day you make me the happiest man in the world."

Although Julia insisted upon a modest, simple wedding at home, she still needed the help of the women who loved her best — Mamma, her sisters, her cousins, aunts, and friends, and of course dear, indispensable Jule — to finish the final preparations. Bridesmaids and groom's attendants were swiftly alerted, invitations delivered, musicians engaged, flowers purchased, menus reviewed, marketing done. Jule's deft fingers fairly flew as she sewed the last garments and linens for her mistress's trousseau. Julia had decided, given the season and the need to economize, to wear an India mull muslin much like the one her mother had worn on her own wedding day thirty years before.

"Are you certain you wouldn't like something fancier?" asked Mamma. "Your bridesmaids will have lovely new gowns. Shouldn't you have one too?"

"My gown will be new," Julia said cheerfully. "It isn't silk, but what of that? Ulys won't know the difference."

Before her mother and sisters could protest that she ought to be married in something finer, a servant came to announce a caller. They hurried downstairs to the drawing room to greet Papa's cousin, the lovely Mrs. O'Fallon. Her footman accompanied her, carrying a large white box.

"Am I too late?" she asked, gesturing for the footman to set the box upon the table. "Have you chosen your wedding dress yet?"

"Not yet," said Julia, exchanging a glance

with Nell. "Not quite."

"I'm so glad." Mrs. O'Fallon's lovely features were rendered even more so by her joyful, affectionate smile. "I've brought you one, my dear, and I hope you'll accept it with as much pleasure as I have in bringing it to you."

Julia lifted the lid and withdrew from the box the most beautiful dress she had ever beheld, a magnificent, rich, soft, white watered silk with cascades of lace. "It's lovely," she exclaimed, holding it up so all could see, and then pressing it close to herself, imagining the fit. "I never thought to be married in such a beautiful gown. How on earth shall I ever thank you?"

"By wearing it, of course," Mrs. O'Fallon said, and they all laughed together before Mamma urged Julia upstairs to try it on. She happily obeyed, knowing that it was certain to fit, for Mrs. O'Fallon knew her measurements and employed an exceptionally skilled dressmaker.

"Jule," she called on her way to her bedchamber, wondering where her maid had gone. "Jule, come quickly."

Julia had draped the gown across her bed and was standing back to admire it when Jule appeared, breathless, smoothing her apron. "Yes, Miss Julia?"

"Dear Mrs. O'Fallon brought me the loveliest dress for my wedding," she exclaimed, reaching behind her back to unfasten her buttons. Jule promptly closed the door and hurried over to assist, swiftly undoing the buttons from neckline to waist. She helped Julia out of her dress and into the beautiful gown, which fit as perfectly as a dream, the soft silk whispering upon her skin as she turned in front of the looking glass.

"I never seen such a fine dress," Jule said, her voice strangely subdued. "You'll be the prettiest bride in St. Louis."

"Do you really think so?"

"I do." Frowning thoughtfully as she studied Julia's reflection in the mirror, Jule touched her hair, holding it back one way and then another, eventually nodding in approval. "Something fancier than your usual chignon would be best, with jasmine here and here, and some nice long curls on the sides."

"Whatever you think is best." Julia had learned to trust her maid's judgment in matters of her toilet, especially regarding her hair, her one beauty. "Oh, Jule, I don't know how I'll manage without you."

"You got by without me fine when you were at school, and your wedding trip shorter than that," Jule reminded her. "Your hostesses likely have maids to help you, and when they don't, you'll get by."

"I mean *after* the wedding trip." Julia steeled herself, knowing she had put off this conversation far too long. "Now that the war's over, the Fourth Infantry has been reassigned to the northern frontier. I'll be going with Ulys to the headquarters in Detroit, on the Great Lakes, and — well, there really isn't any place for servants there, in the North."

"I see." Jule's eyebrows drew together and a deep crease of worry appeared between them. "What about me? Where do I go?"

"You aren't going anywhere," Julia quickly assured her, whirling about to face her, to take her hand. "You'll stay with the family and look after Nell and Emma. We would never send you away."

"How long you gonna be away?"

"Oh, I don't know. A year or two, perhaps more." When Jule looked no more reassured than before, Julia added, "If Ulys is assigned to Jefferson Barracks again, or to another place where I can keep a servant, I'll send for you. I promise."

"I ain't going with you." Jule's voice was faint, her expression inscrutable. "All this time, I just figured I would be."

Julia did not know what to say. "I'm sorry if you're disappointed, but it's simply impossible."

"Oh, yes, Miss Julia. I do understand that." Jule took a deep breath and mustered a faint smile. "I think the ladies must be wondering what became of you. They're gonna think I forgot how to dress you."

"Never," declared Julia, relieved that her maid's good humor was apparently restored.

She hurried off to the parlor, where the gown met with approval all around. Mrs. O'Fallon had also brought Julia a veil of white tulle with lovely fringe, which seemed to float about her head when Mrs. O'Fallon put it on her, enveloping her in its delicate folds. For the first time in her long engagement, Julia truly felt like a bride.

She was happier than she had ever been, she thought later as Jule undressed her and put the gown carefully away. No power on earth could diminish her joy now that she and Ulys were to be united in love at last.

Ulys soon returned from Ohio, but even as Julia ran outside to greet him and took his arm to lead him into the foyer, she knew something was wrong. "Why are your parents not with you?" she asked. "Are they resting at the Planters House?"

"They're at home," said Ulys. "They aren't coming to the wedding."

"Oh, how unfortunate," said Julia. "I was looking forward to meeting them. I hope they aren't unwell."

"No, they're all in perfect health." He held her out at arm's length to admire her, but his smile seemed forced. "You'll meet them on our wedding trip instead, and when they get to know you, they'll love you as much as I do."

Something in his tone made her wary. "You

say that as if they're predisposed *not* to love me, knowing me only through your stories."

"I've said only good things about you," said Ulys. "I have only good things to say."

"What is it, then?" When Ulys shook his head, she added, "Please tell me. Does your family object to our marriage?" She had been so preoccupied with Papa's objections to the match that it had never occurred to her to wonder how Mr. and Mrs. Grant felt.

"You know I come from abolitionist people."

"You're something of an abolitionist yourself, but I don't hold that against you."

"They're deeply unhappy that I'm marrying into a slaveholding family," Ulys admitted. "They say they can't come to the wedding. Their consciences won't permit them to enjoy any fruits of slave labor, and they won't allow their presence here to give tacit approval to an institution they abhor."

"Oh." Suddenly light-headed, Julia sank into a chair. "I see."

"It isn't you they reject, Julia, but slavery. They can't abide it."

"Of course. I understand." She felt tears gathering but forced them back. "I certainly wouldn't want them to disregard their consciences."

Ulys knelt beside her chair and took her hands in his. "In time they'll grow fond of

69

you. I know they will. They won't be able to help it."

"You know them best," she said. "If you think I can win their affection, then I'll certainly try."

Candles lit the way as Julia descended the staircase on the sultry August night she married Ulysses.

She knew he waited for her in the parlor, her cousin James Longstreet standing beside him as his best man, the rest of the bridal party gathered nearby. The thunderstorms of late afternoon had rumbled and flashed furiously before moving on to the east, leaving heavy rains in their wake, the fat drops pattering on the roof like the beating of drums. The foyer smelled of the wet shawls and wraps hanging to dry in the closet beneath the stairs, and soon Julia glimpsed the friends and loved ones who had worn them — young ladies in elegant gowns, handsome officers in dress uniform, dowagers smiling and blinking away tears, beloved family who had known her all her life, all crowded into the drawing room, full of anticipation, standing witness, making Julia's happiness complete, or nearly so.

Earlier that morning Ulys had earned himself a scolding from Mamma, Nell, and Mrs. O'Fallon by calling on Julia, for it was bad luck for the groom to glimpse his bride before the ceremony. Laughing off their teasing warnings, Julia agreed to see Ulys, albeit briefly, only long enough to exchange a few heartfelt words of love and to accept his wedding gift, a chased gold locket worn by a narrow velvet strap from the wrist. Inside was a daguerreotype of the face she most loved to see, her own darling Ulysses, his thoughtful eyes and stubborn mouth. "I will wear this every day of my life," she vowed, and then she hurried off without kissing him, for she had already tempted fate enough.

The clock on the mantelpiece struck eight o'clock as Papa offered Julia his arm and escorted her into the drawing room, his face stoic as he placed her hand in Ulys's. Mr. and Mrs. Grant's refusal to attend the wedding had bolstered his own objections to the match, but the previous night, after reminding Julia that even at that late hour she could still change her mind, he sighed in resignation and announced his wedding gift — sixty acres of uncleared land about a mile north of White Haven, with the promise of one thousand dollars to stock it. "Now when that soldier tires of dragging you from post to post," Papa had told her gruffly, "you'll have land of your own not far from home to settle on."

Reverend Linn conducted the ceremony, which was mercifully brief, but Julia did not become tearful until she spoke her vows and heard Papa clear his throat, overcome with emotion. Then Ulys kissed her, and the minister pronounced them married, and all at once they were surrounded by well-wishers, caught up in embraces and basking in the joy of the smiling, happy throng.

The rain had subsided and the windows were thrown open to welcome in the cool night air, but all passed as a blur of merriment to Julia — the congratulations and good wishes from all and sundry; the parlor table laden with ices, fruits, and other delicacies; the festive supper; the merry music; the laughter that broke out when two of her bridesmaids could not resist the inspiration to dance and waltzed together around the crowded drawing room.

It was a simple, happy, poignant wedding, and after the guests departed and even family bade them good night, the newlyweds stole away, hand in hand, to Julia's bedchamber, which Nell and Emma had lovingly decorated with fragrant blossoms and twining ivy, transforming the room into a romantic nuptial bower.

"You are as lovely to me as you were that day four years ago when I first glimpsed you on the porch at White Haven," Ulys murmured after Jule had helped Julia into her nightgown and had noiselessly departed. "You'll always bloom forever young and beautiful in my eyes."

"And you are even more handsome and beloved to me tonight than you were then." Julia glowed from his words, and from his touch, and from her certainty that Ulys truly did find her beautiful in all her plainness, that he saw her with the rare vision of true love, and that in his devotion to her, he always would.

In the morning, Jule rapped softly on the door of the bridal chamber and waited for Julia's cheerful summons before entering. She was relieved to see that Captain Grant was already up and dressed, or nearly so; he sat in a chair by the window pulling on his socks and chatting with his bride, who sat in the middle of the bed in her nightgown, hugging her knees to her chest and beaming.

Their abundant happiness made Jule all the more regretful that she had too long deferred her own. Four years had passed since Julia had accepted her lieutenant's proposal, four years Jule and Gabriel could have been together if Jule had not constantly feared she would be suddenly and without warning snatched from his side. And now to learn that she would not be leaving St. Louis and White Haven for years yet, if at all —

She was determined not to waste a single precious day more.

Captain Grant stepped from the room while Jule dressed Julia for her wedding trip, and when Julia was ready, Jule watched from the top of the stairs as she went down to breakfast on her husband's arm, blushing and smiling. Jule quickly finished packing the last of Julia's bags and carried them downstairs and outside, where Gabriel waited with the carriage.

Before they could wish each other a fond good morning, the front door burst open and Julia emerged on her husband's arm, followed by a throng of family and friends seeing the newlyweds off in a cascade of tossed flowers. As Gabriel opened the carriage door and Ulys helped Julia inside, Jule waited nearby, ready to dash back inside for any essential thing Julia might suddenly decide she could not travel without.

"Jule, I do wish you could come with me," Julia lamented through the carriage window after she had settled into her seat. "I'd feel so much braver with you there, so far from home."

Jule managed a smile, though she was not feeling particularly brave herself. Except when Julia was at school — and even then she had returned to White Haven often — she and Julia had not been parted since they were tiny girls, holding hands as they scampered along the length of the piazza, ginger and cream. As soon as the carriage pulled away, everything would change. "I think Captain Grant can look after you just fine," she said.

"Yes, but —" Julia glanced over to make sure Ulys was busy speaking with the driver and wouldn't overhear. "Dare I trust him to fix my hair?"

Jule's smile deepened. "That's not for me to say, but I did put a bottle of that fragrant pomade you like so much in your satchel, brewed up fresh yesterday. It'll keep your hair as smooth and glossy as mink, so it won't matter how you arrange it."

"Oh, thank you, Jule. I'm embarrassed to admit I nearly forgot — I have a gift for you too." From her reticule Julia took a new lace handkerchief tied in a bow around something small, which she passed through the window. "A token of my gratitude for all you did to make my wedding day so wonderful."

Jule weighed the lace bundle in her palm, starting in surprise as several coins clinked together enticingly. "I'm very grateful," she said carefully, "but I wonder if I might ask another gift of you instead."

Julia's brows drew together in puzzlement. "I suppose so, but you know, those coins are gold. You could likely buy whatever it is you want."

In a sudden, unexpected surge of anger, Jule was tempted to ask what price Julia would set for her freedom, hers and Gabriel's — but of course, that would be up to the old master, and he was notoriously tightfisted.

"What I'd truly like," she said instead, "is that India mull muslin dress you meant to marry in before Mrs. O'Fallon gave you that fine lace gown."

"You want my dress?" Julia echoed, surprised. "But it's much too large for you."

"I know how to take it in."

"Well, of course you do, but what occasion would you possibly have to wear —" Julia gave herself a little shake. "Of course you may have the dress. Take the dress, and the money too. You've earned them both."

Jule stared at her, momentarily speechless. She had never heard a Dent admit that any of their servants had earned anything, except punishments — but Julia was a Dent no longer. "Thank you, Mrs. Grant."

Julia gave a little start. "Oh, my goodness. Mrs. Grant. That's who I am now."

Captain Grant gave the order for the carriage to start, and as Gabriel took the reins in hand, Jule caught his eye and mouthed the words, *Hurry back.*

She had something very important to ask him, but she already knew how he would answer.

CHAPTER THREE

August–October 1848

Julia snuggled close to Ulys as the carriage sped them to the riverfront, where they boarded a steamer that would carry them down the Mississippi to Cairo, Illinois, and then northeast up the Ohio River. She had never traveled farther from White Haven than St. Louis, and she marveled at the magnificent grace and speed of the boat as it powered through the water. Hour after hour, she enjoyed sitting alone with Ulys, watching the green countryside and thriving villages in passing. Sometimes Ulys would read to her, to "save her eyes," as he said, and she in turn would sing to him, low and sweet and melodious. He told her that her voice was the only music he cared to hear, and she glowed from the praise, just as she glowed every night in his arms.

The steamer docked at Cincinnati on a bright, sunny morning, and as they left the cabin that had been their honeymoon bower for several pleasant days and nights, Ulys almost ran into a lad of about thirteen years who stood smiling cheerfully in the corridor, his flaxen curls and blue eyes rendering him almost too pretty to be a boy. "Hello, Lyss," the boy greeted him cheerfully, then peered past him to grin at Julia. "Is this your missus?"

"Orvil," Ulys exclaimed, clapping him on the shoulder. "Yes, this is my lovely bride, your new sister-in-law. Julia, meet my youngest brother." Smiling, Julia extended her hand to the boy, who shook it and greeted her respectfully, but with an air of merry curiosity.

The same stagecoach that had brought Orvil to Cincinnati waited to carry them north. As they rumbled along out of the city, past blocks of handsome buildings that gave way to rolling hills and sweeping meadows, Orvil shared all the news from home — and Julia felt her apprehensions rising with every mile.

The stagecoach halted at a tavern not far from the Grant family home in Bethel. Word of Ulys's arrival with his new bride must have spread swiftly, for they were still organizing their luggage when a thin, sharp-featured, handsome man not much older than Ulys appeared and greeted him with a cordial handshake. "This is my brother Samuel Simpson Grant," Ulys introduced him. Julia hid her surprise as she shook his hand; in the Dent family, siblings embraced.

Simpson helped them carry their luggage across the street to the Grant residence. Julia's heart thumped as Ulys opened the door for her, and she took a quick, steadying breath before she crossed the threshold. Her gaze took in first the faces that promptly turned her way — the grave, appraising eyes, the silent, expressionless mouths — and then the subdued simplicity of the furnishings, mirrored in the occupants' attire. Julia had worn her new black-and-white-striped silk for the occasion, and she knew at once that she had overdressed and that Ulys's family would assume she was frivolous and worldly. So much could be decided upon a single first glance.

Fortunately Ulys was there, his hand upon the small of her back, his voice firm and proud as he introduced her. *This is my wife,* he announced with every glance and gesture, *and as you love me, you must love her.* Julia hoped they would take heed.

"Welcome to Bethel, Julia, and to our home," the woman who must be Hannah said, her voice low and quiet, her eyes a soft brown behind the small, round lenses of her spectacles. A delicate kerchief tied about her neck relieved the severity of her plain black gown. "I am Mrs. Grant."

I am too, Julia almost blurted, but she caught herself in time. "How do you do? It's such a pleasure to meet you at last."

Mrs. Grant nodded, her expression alert and inquiring, evidently untroubled by the nerves and expectations buzzing about Julia like so many invisible maddened hornets. She was taller than Julia — but then most people were, for Julia stood only five feet tall — with a delicate figure built upon a ramrod spine. She wore a small lace cap over her hair, which, Ulys had confided, had once been ruddy like his own but had turned chalk white during the last six months of the Mexican War, when not one of his letters from the battlefield had reached her.

"We will have supper later, here at home," Mrs. Grant said, after a lengthy silence that Julia found awkwardly long but which seemed to bother no one else. "Many of our friends wish to meet you."

"I look forward to it," Julia replied pleasantly. Then, as if Mrs. Grant's acknowledgment had given the others permission to address her, Ulys's siblings came up, one by one, to give her welcome. Ulys was the eldest, Simpson second, and following him was Clara, twenty years of age, somewhat stern and disapproving of manner. Julia knew that golden-haired, sixteen-year-old Virginia, or Jennie as she was called, was Ulysses's favorite sister, and Julia immediately took a liking to the warm, friendly girl with kind, gray-blue eyes so much like Ulys's. Orvil was the next eldest, and even though they had already met, he joined the queue to shake her hand, his merry grin lifting her spirits. The youngest of the six Grant siblings was nine-year-old Mary Frances, whose lovely features, gray eyes, and brilliant complexion promised great beauty. She spoke to Julia with grave sweetness, in elegant phrases that suggested a clever mind at work.

The Grant siblings were so cordial and welcoming after their initial reserve that Julia felt her trepidation ebbing, but she had still not met her father-in-law. He had gone out to the country to fetch back Grandmama Simpson, his wife's stepmother, who, despite her age and the discomforts of travel, had been determined to meet Ulys and his new bride. Julia found the tall and robust, warm and smiling Grandmama Simpson utterly delightful. She wore a dress of rich, chestnut-brown Irish poplin, a snowy muslin kerchief about her shoulders, and a soft white muslin cap upon her silvery gray bun, the wide ties in a bow beneath her chin. "You must call me Grandmama too," she declared, clasping Julia's hands.

As Simpson led his grandmother to a comfortable chair by the hearth, Ulys's father — for he could be no other — came forward, scrutinizing her expectantly as Ulys introduced them. Mr. Grant was much taller than his son, sturdily built but with stooped shoulders that betrayed decades of hard labor. Like Ulys he had a wide forehead, high cheekbones, and a thin, resolute mouth, but his eyes seemed small and severe behind his spectacles and his face was pockmarked from years of accidental splashing from tannic acid. As Julia well knew, Ulys had forsaken his father's trade for a West Point education.

"So," Jesse Root Grant said abruptly, "you're the western belle who captured my son's heart."

"I'm happy to lay claim to that title." Julia put on her most charming smile. "However, I was merely repaying the favor, for he stole my heart first."

Mr. Grant snorted. "That's not how Lyss tells it."

Before he could elaborate, if that was his intention, Mrs. Grant summoned the family to supper. Grace was reassuringly familiar, for like the Dents the Grants were Methodists, but conversation was restrained to murmured requests for dishes and pleases and thank-yous, until Julia began to feel oppressed and restless.

"My husband is called by so many names," she said brightly, smiling around the table. Ulys smiled indulgently, and Orvil and Mary regarded her with curious interest. "I call him Ulys, but I've overheard his army comrades call him Sam, and you all call him Lyss."

"Sometimes we call him Texas," Orvil remarked.

"Lyss or even Texas I understand," Julia replied. "But Sam?"

"Would you prefer Hiram?" Clara inclined her head toward her brother and dabbed at the corner of her mouth with her napkin. "That is his given name, after all. Didn't you know?"

Julia glanced from Clara to Ulys to his mother, instinctively following the trail of authority on the subject.

"He was baptized Hiram Ulysses Grant," Mr. Grant answered for them.

"Jesse and I chose Ulysses together," said Grandmama Simpson proudly. "We had recently finished reading Fénelon's *Telemachus,* and we agreed that it was a good, noble name."

"Grandfather preferred Hiram," said Jennie shyly, smiling across the table at Julia. "He called it a good, honest, American name."

"Mrs. Grant and I compromised." Mr. Grant's slight frown suggested that even so many years later, he wished he had not. "We named him Hiram Ulysses Grant."

"And so he remained for many years, although we always called him Lyss for short," said Simpson. "Now consider his initials."

"Hiram Ulys—" Julia gave a little laugh. "Oh, dear. HUG."

Simpson spread his palms and touched the tips of his thumbs together as if to frame the monogram. "Now you must imagine those initials pounded with brass nails into a trunk belonging to a young cadet setting off for West Point."

"I confess I find it endearing," said Julia, watching the color rise faintly in her husband's tanned cheeks, "but for a young man going off to the military academy, I suppose it wouldn't do."

"It would have been an obvious invitation to ridicule," said Ulys, "so I decided to switch the initials and call myself Ulysses H. Grant."

"But the matter had already been decided for him," Mr. Grant broke in. "Congressman Hamer, the gentleman who signed Lyss's formal application, had put him down as Ulysses S. Grant, assuming that his middle name was Simpson, for my wife's people."

"West Point knew me as Ulysses S. Grant, and since I rather liked the name, I decided to adopt it as they had it down," Ulys said. "I realized too late that cadets relish any chance to poke fun. Whenever they saw 'U. S. Grant' posted on a bulletin board, they'd call me United States Grant, or Uncle Sam Grant, and eventually, just plain Sam."

Julia laughed, delighted. "Well, I like Ulys best, but I would have loved you no matter what you called yourself."

In the days that followed, the newlyweds

made the customary round of calls to family and friends, first in Bethel and later venturing out to Georgetown, Cincinnati, and Maysville. Everyone welcomed Julia graciously, and everyone had a favorite story of Ulys to share — often of the young ladies Ulys had taken ice-skating or horseback riding, and one in particular for whom he had painted a watercolor landscape of the majestic scenery around West Point.

"I never said I didn't enjoy the company of young ladies before I met you," Ulys defended himself mildly. "I said only that I had never fallen in love."

"You never painted me a watercolor landscape," she said, unable to refute his explanation and yet still pricked by jealousy.

"I might have done, if I hadn't spent almost our entire courtship in Mexico."

Her jealousy was immediately forgotten. "I do hope you'll never go to war again."

"As do I," said Ulys soberly, taking her hands in his. "I want nothing ever to part us."

It was not unusual for the Dent sisters to bestow their worn, outgrown dresses upon their favorite servants, but the gift of a lovely, almost new India mull muslin gown had no precedent. Still, as the entire family had witnessed Julia offering it to Jule, no one objected when she retrieved it from her absent mistress's wardrobe and carried it off to the servants' quarters in the attic. There, by whatever light she could find, Jule began altering it to fit her own figure, deftly plucking out stitches and taking in seams, always out of sight of the curious Dent women.

Late one night a week after Julia's departure, Jule donned the altered gown, crept quietly down the attic stairs, slipped out the back door, and raced soundlessly to the carriage house, where Gabriel waited.

A side door opened, and faint lantern light from within briefly cast Gabriel into silhouette. "Are you ready?" he asked, quickly shutting the door behind him, his voice a warm caress in the darkness.

She nodded, breathless from apprehension and excitement.

Hand in hand, they hurried through the gate and down the sidewalk, ready to duck into an alley or a shadowed doorway at the first glimpse of anyone who might arrest them for breaking curfew. At last they came to the African Methodist Episcopal church, where their soft knock upon the door was answered by the pastor himself, a former slave twenty years free. He quickly led them into the chapel, where his wife and brother stood witness as Gabriel and Jule spoke the vows that made them husband and wife.

Jule had never been happier, but her joy was diminished by her regret that she had let fear and uncertainty restrain her from marrying Gabriel sooner — and by hot, raw anger for the old master and missus and even Julia for engendering that crippling doubt.

"Don't dwell on anger or regret another day more," Gabriel said, soothing her with kisses on her cheeks, her brow, her lips. "All that matters is that we're married now."

She spent the night in his arms, sharing his pallet in the carriage house, but she woke before dawn and stole quietly back into the house before the Dents noticed her absence. If Julia had not been away on her wedding trip, Jule never could have managed it.

In the weeks that followed, she passed the long days waiting on Nell and Emma and mixing up concoctions for the household — a hair tonic for the missus one day, a salve to soothe burns for Annie and Poppy the next.

Throughout each day, she welcomed every chance glimpse of her beloved husband, and night after night, she found comfort and tenderness in his embrace.

In mid-October, with the end of Ulys's furlough approaching, he and Julia bade farewell to his family and returned to St. Louis. The journey home should have been as delightful as their first excursion upon the rivers, but with each passing day Julia felt more sharply the pain of impending loss.

On the eve of their departure to rejoin Ulys's regiment in Detroit, Julia and Ulys sat alone in the Dent drawing room, Julia wiping her eyes after another bout with tears, Ulys trying to comfort her. "For four years I've looked forward to spending all of our days together," he said, managing a wan smile, "and yet, after only two months, you're full of regret."

"I'll never regret marrying you," Julia protested, only to fall silent as her father strode into the room.

"Grant," Papa said gruffly, "I have a solution to this quandary. You join your regiment and leave Julia here at home. You can visit her whenever you get a leave of absence."

"That would be only once or twice a year." Ulys turned a worried, appraising glance upon Julia. "But I'll do whatever's best for Julia."

Papa shook his head, frowning. "I always knew Julia wasn't suited to be an army wife, but I'm sorry to be proven right."

Ulys sat beside her and put his arm around her shoulders. "Is that what you want, Julia?" he asked gently. "Would you like to stay with your father while I go on alone?"

"No, no, no," said Julia, distressed. "If you're going — and you must — I'll go with you. I couldn't bear to be left behind."

And so she dried her tears and told Papa that her place was with her husband.

When Papa nodded and withdrew, Ulys

interlaced his fingers through Julia's and held her gaze steadily. "We're never to be parted," he said firmly. "Agreed?"

"Agreed," Julia replied. They had lived apart too much already. "Never again will we be separated. Wherever you go, I'll follow."

CHAPTER FOUR

November 1848–August 1854

In the first few weeks after the newlyweds departed, Jule felt an exhilarating rush of emotion she supposed was something like freedom. While the Dents anxiously awaited the mails and read bits of Julia's precious letters aloud to one another, news from far-off places called Sackets Harbor and Lake Ontario and Madison Barracks, Jule felt like a colt unharnessed, still confined within corral fences but able to run and buck and kick as she pleased.

"Don't let them catch you idle," Annie warned her one afternoon when she came upon Jule in the kitchen garden, picking herbs.

"Who's idle?" protested Jule, indicating her basket. "The herb lady taught me how to brew up a potion to ease sunburn." A few days before, young Miss Emma had neglected to wear her bonnet on a picnic with friends, and the skin of her apple-red cheeks had begun to slough off in thin, white flakes, sending the missus into lamentations of worry about permanent damage to her complexion. If Jule could win the missus's gratitude while soothing Miss Emma's discomfort, that would make for a good day's work.

Annie planted a fist on her hip and fixed Julia with a hard, worried stare. "A slave with nothing to do's always the first to get sold when money's tight."

Unsettled, Jule went about her work more quickly, and the next day, when she overheard Nell and her mother discussing a friend's betrothal, she suggested that they offer the bride-to-be Jule's hairdressing services for the day of her engagement party. Nell's friend was so delighted with her elegant tresses — which attracted the admiration of every other young lady at the party and won a special compliment from her fiancé — that she begged Nell to extend the favor again on her wedding day.

"This a gift to her from you like last time," Jule asked as she was packing up her little satchel of combs and ribbons and pomades, "or are you hiring me out to her?"

A thoughtful glimmer came into Nell's eye. "A gift, as before," Nell said, but a musing tone in her voice satisfied Jule that she had planted the seed of an idea.

Soon thereafter, the missus summoned Jule to the parlor and informed her that in Julia's absence, the Dent family intended to hire Jule out to ladies who required her special skills. "I realize you don't often go out amid strangers, but you needn't fear," the mistress assured her. "You'll work only for families we know well and trust, and none beyond the Gravois Settlement."

"Yes, missus. I ain't afraid of strangers." That wasn't entirely true. Jule wasn't afraid of ladies, even the short-tempered ones. Their menfolk, though — they made her wary.

"Your wages you will bring to me," the mistress continued. "Anything you earn above that, whether gifts or gratuities, you may keep."

As the months passed and Jule's fame as a skilled hairdresser spread, the old master crowed over her earnings, paid off debts, and bought his wife an exquisite pearl necklace to thank her for her ingenuity. He persuaded her to send Jule farther afield, hiring her out to acquaintances in St. Louis and then to strangers recommended by friends. Jule walked to work when the family resided in the city, but when they moved out to White Haven, Gabriel drove her to her appointments. Afterward, if they were not expected back too soon, Gabriel would direct the horses through neighborhoods where free colored folk lived.

The freeborn and manumitted colored residents of St. Louis thrived in humble alleys and grand neighborhoods, and although they could not vote or hold office, some, the self-described Colored Aristocracy, acquired great wealth and the power that accompanied it. Jule's heart quickened whenever she glimpsed the famed Madame Pelagie Rutgers, a former slave of Haitian descent who had married the mulatto son of a wealthy Dutch merchant. She had amassed a fortune in real estate, from selling tracts of land at huge profits as the city expanded and by renting her own commercial properties and tenements to white businessmen. Rumor had it that Madame Rutgers was worth almost a half million dollars, a vast, almost incomprehensible amount. To Jule, who had no surname and knew few women of color accorded so much as the respectful title of "missus," Madame Rutgers's honorific was as much a sign of her status and success as her furs and jewels and fine residence. Jule hoped someday Madame Rutgers would find herself in need of a hairdresser, and that a satisfied customer would recommend her.

"I'm saving every cent I earn," Jule told Gabriel one humid afternoon as they lingered on the bluff above the Mississippi, gazing across the churning expanse of muddy water to the Illinois shore, postponing as long as they could their return to White Haven. "I'll buy our freedom. You can be a minister in a church and I'll dress hair, and we'll keep a little house all our own."

Gabriel kept his gaze fixed on the brown ribbon of water winding ever southward. "That's a nice dream."

"Miss Julia's dreams sometimes come true. Why not mine?"

"Jule —" He sighed, shifted the reins to one hand, and rested his elbow on his knee. "It'll take years to save enough to buy freedom for even one of us, and that's if the old master agree."

"Then I'll buy my own freedom first. Once I can keep all my earnings, I'll save up faster." Jule studied him. "You know I mean it when I say I'm not bringing any babies into slavery."

"Then we better make sure you don't get any babies anytime soon."

Jule frowned and looked away. "Maybe Miss Julia will speak to the old master for me, make him set a fair price."

"Or maybe she could get him to set you free in his will." The forced agreeability in Gabriel's voice told her he was saying so only to please her. "She might do it. She likes you."

Neither of them mentioned that Julia might like her too much to let her go.

With a rueful glance at the sun in its declination, Gabriel chirruped to the horses and turned the wagon toward White Haven.

Julia liked her, Jule reminded herself resolutely, and her new husband's people were abolitionists. The longer they were married, the longer Julia lived in a free state, the more likely it was that Julia would adopt their ways.

Julia had been away so long in the North, surely she had come to see slavery for the evil it was.

Julia and Ulys spent their first winter as husband and wife at Madison Barracks in Sackets Harbor, a bleak, remote outpost on Lake Ontario in New York State. When spring came and the ice broke up, they moved on to Detroit, where Ulys assumed the post of regimental quartermaster. Julia quickly became popular among the officers of the garrison for her excellent dancing and lovely singing voice, and her generous, friendly ways made her a favorite among their wives and children. Though Ulys was not happy shifting papers, ordering supplies, and supervising commissary affairs, he was proud to serve his country.

Less than a year after their arrival in Detroit, the couple discovered that by late spring they would become a family of three.

As the months of waiting and preparation passed, they debated where their child should be born. Julia dreaded to leave Ulys, but she knew that when her labor began, she would want Mamma, her sisters, and Jule close by. And so in early spring she and Ulys parted at the train station in Detroit with a kiss and a promise that they would be reunited as soon as Julia and the baby were strong enough to travel.

The joy of her long-awaited reunion with her family eased the unhappiness of her separation from Ulys. Papa and Mamma, her siblings and friends, White Haven itself — so familiar, so beloved, changed slightly with the passing of the years but still somehow exactly as she remembered.

Jule's welcome sounded the only discordant note to her homecoming. She had greeted Julia with a warm smile and kind inquiries about her health, but there was a new aloofness to her manner, as if her mistress's needs commanded only a portion of her attention. She had blossomed into new beauty in Julia's absence too. Her skin had always been a lovely ginger color, but it had become deeper and richer and seemed to glow from within. She was much prettier than her mistress, Julia privately admitted, or she would have been if not for the firm set to her jaw, the deep crease of worry between her brows, and the guarded look in her eye.

That first night, after Jule helped Julia ease carefully into bed, she fluffed the pillows, straightened, and fixed Julia with a determined gaze. "Since you been gone, I ain't been sleeping at the foot of your bed."

"I wouldn't have expected you to," said Julia, although she had not given the matter any thought. "Mamma or my sisters wanted you closer to them, I assume."

"No, Miss Julia," said Jule. "I stay nights in the hayloft with Gabriel now."

"Oh, I see." Julia felt faintly embarrassed by all that the brief admission implied, but since Mamma had apparently not forbidden it, it was not for Julia to punish the indiscretion. "You may remain there for now, if you prefer, but after the baby comes, I'll need you back in the house."

"You going to hire a wet nurse?"

Of course. That explained Jule's reticent, almost defiant manner. She worried that she would be replaced. "No, Jule," she said, smiling reassuringly. "I intend to nurse my child myself, and you can help me with everything else."

Jule nodded, but curiously, she seemed no less ill at ease. "Can I ask you, Miss Julia," she ventured, "what Northern ladies do for help?"

"They hire servants, German and Irish immigrants, mostly," Julia replied. "I sympathize with them. I don't know how they manage."

"Them and they," echoed Jule. "You mean the servants or —"

"I mean the employers, of course," Julia interrupted. "The Irish and German girls welcome the work, and they're fortunate to have it. But their employers — let's just say they're obliged to have lower expectations for their households than we do here." She sighed and settled back against the pillow. "Nothing makes you appreciate the customs of home more than spending time away."

"I wouldn't know, Miss Julia." Jule's voice was oddly flat. "You need anything else tonight?"

Julia did not, so she reminded Jule of a few chores for the morning and dismissed her. Bemused, Julia put out the light, wondering why Jule had not seemed more pleased by the tacit compliment.

Nevertheless, Jule remained the same dear, faithful servant she had known almost all her life, and Julia was so glad to see her that she could forgive her a few small, unwitting slights.

On May 30, 1850, Julia gave birth to a strong, healthy son. As she and Ulys had agreed, she named the robust little boy Frederick Dent Grant, in honor of her father. "Someday this boy will be a general," Papa proudly declared, which Julia decided to take as a compliment to Ulys.

Little Fred was almost a year old when Ulys was assigned once more to Sackets Harbor. There Fred grew into a lively toddler and the adored mascot of the regiment — and Julia discovered that their little family would welcome a younger brother or sister for him in the summer of 1852. Happily, Julia dreamed and prepared, but in springtime, official orders from Washington threw all her plans awry. Ulys's regiment had been reassigned to Columbia Barracks, Oregon Territory.

One spring afternoon while Fred napped, Julia pulled out the trunk holding his old baby clothes. Ulys, home early from work, found her sitting on the parlor floor beside the trunk, inspecting each garment to see what could be packed for the journey to Oregon Territory for the new baby. "Julia," he scolded gently, hurrying over to help her into a chair, whether she liked it or not. "You shouldn't be sitting on the floor in your condition."

"I'm fine," she assured him, laughing. "Indian mothers-to-be sit on the bare ground when they aren't on horseback, or so you've said." Something about the set of his mouth, wariness or determination or both, chased away her amusement. "What's wrong, Ulys?"

He sat down in the chair beside her. "Julia, I've decided that it would be unwise for you to come with me in your condition."

Her heart thumped. "What do you mean? I'm perfectly healthy."

"You're with child."

"Yes, I know." A trifle angrily, she gestured to her unmistakably rounded abdomen. "I recognize the symptoms from last time."

"Julia, darling." He reached for her hand.

"The doctor agrees that you shouldn't hazard such a long and dangerous voyage."

"Many of the officers' wives are going, and some are taking their children," she protested. "Mrs. Gore. Mrs. Wallen. Most of my friends —"

"None of them are a few weeks away from being delivered of a child."

"You promised we would never be parted again. We promised each other."

"Yes, but now we have your life and Fred's and the baby's to consider." Gently he touched her cheek. "It's too great a risk."

"I know," she admitted, fighting back tears. For weeks she had worried over what would become of her and the child if her pains came upon her aboard ship or, worse yet, as they were crossing the Isthmus of Panama. "You're right. It would be best for the baby and a great comfort to me to be among family when I face my ordeal." Then she faced him squarely so he could not mistake her resolve. "After the baby is born and we're both well and strong, I want to join you, wherever you may be."

Ulys regarded her for a long moment in silence. "If you have the baby before the regiment departs for California, I'll come for you and the children, and we'll sail from New York together."

Julia knew he would offer her no more than that, and so she agreed. Within a week, she and Fred left to join Ulys's family in Bethel.

On July 5, Ulys departed Governors Island in New York with his regiment aboard the *Ohio*. Less than a fortnight later, with Hannah supervising and Ulys's sisters tending to her every need, Julia gave birth to a vigorous, red-faced little boy, Ulysses Simpson Grant Jr., who had his father's wide brow and regular features, but was more like a Dent in his expressiveness.

Julia held him in her arms and kissed him, and wept that Ulys was not there to marvel at his sweet perfection.

Julia soon learned that Ulys had been wise to discourage her from accompanying him to California. Against the regimental physician's warnings, the soldiers attempted to cross the Isthmus of Panama in the midst of a cholera epidemic, and by the time Ulys's namesake took his first breath, nearly a third of his comrades had perished and had been laid to rest in the jungle.

"You would have been so proud to see your husband rally the men through their trials, although I am grateful you were not there to suffer with us," wrote Mrs. Gore, Julia's newly widowed friend, her distress evident in the broken, staccato strokes of her pen. "He looked after the women and children most solicitously through every calamity, transporting people and goods across the treacherous

Isthmus, helping Dr. Tripler with the afflicted, attending to the burials — all manner of horrific duties fell to him, and he bore them all with a saint's patience and a soldier's courage."

"Saint Ulys," Julia murmured as she folded the letter and put it away, the stories of his valor warming a heart chilled from loneliness and worry.

After a few weeks with the Grants in Bethel, Julia had recovered enough to travel home to White Haven. Ulys had at long last arrived safely at Fort Vancouver on the Columbia River, and it was there he received the tracing she had made of the baby's tiny hand on paper. "He looks like you," she had written. "He will be as handsome and strong as you, but not, I think, even half as reticent, if his current habits remain true."

Letters arrived from Ulys in nearly every post. He was relieved to know that she had recovered from her ordeal, and that the child was a boy, and that she had named him Ulysses.

"Little Buckeye," friends and neighbors would coo as they bent to kiss the baby's soft cheek, or "Buckie," they would murmur tenderly as he wrapped his fist around their fingertips. Eventually, despite Julia's gentle protests, more people called him Buckie than used his honorable given name. Julia knew she had lost the battle the day Papa called him Buck, and her son turned and smiled brightly back at him.

The months passed and stretched into long, lonely years. Even as Ulys rose to the rank of full captain, he took no pride in it. "I think that I have been away from my family quite long enough," he wrote to Julia in February of 1854, after the day's mail had brought no response to his petitions for leave or transfer nor any letters from her. "Sometimes I feel as though I could almost go home *nolens volens.*"

Julia's worries grew when Ulys wrote with increasing vehemence of wanting to quit the army and come home. "I have the sweetest little wife in the world, a son who has likely forgotten my face, and another whom I have never met," he lamented angrily in a heart-wrenching letter that brought Julia to tears. "How can I remain in the army when it keeps me from everything I most cherish?"

There was no shame in resigning, Julia assured him through the post. The nation was no longer at war. He had served his country honorably for almost a decade. "You have always wanted to farm, and we have my sixty acres," she reminded him. "If it's my blessing you seek, know that I will be as proud to be a farmer's wife as I am now to be a soldier's."

She meant every word, and yet she was still astonished when, in late April, she received a letter he had written nearly two weeks before. "This is the third letter I write today," he said. "The first was my formal acceptance of my promotion to full captain. The second was my letter of resignation from the army."

Julia's cry of astonishment and relief brought Jule running, little Buck in her arms, Fred trotting at her heels. "Your papa is coming home," Julia cried, sweeping Fred into her embrace.

The next letter she received from Ulys at Fort Humboldt was strangely curt and cryptic. Dated May 2, it warned her not to write to him there anymore, for he would likely not receive her letters. He planned to visit her brother Louis in San Francisco while he settled his affairs and arranged transportation home. "My love to all," he concluded. "Kiss our little boys for their Pa. Love to you dear Julia. Your affectionate husbd. Ulys."

But the joy of their anticipated reunion was tainted by rumors that swirled about Jefferson Barracks and in the army circles in St. Louis. Ulys had had a confrontation with a superior officer, some whispered, and he had been given the choice to resign or face charges of insubordination. He had fallen into drunkenness and dissolution, others said more maliciously, and he had been forced to resign.

"Drunkenness?" Julia protested when a concerned friend told her the latest gossip. "Ulys has no taste for liquor. He was an officer in the Sons of Temperance in Sackets Harbor, for goodness' sake."

"But they say he takes to his bed often," her friend replied. "He closes the blinds and stuffs cotton in his ears to block out all light and sound. They say his vision is distorted, his speech slurred, his stomach upset."

"He suffers dreadfully from sick headaches," Julia said, her anger rising. "Migraines, the doctor calls them."

Her friend nodded sympathetically, but Julia knew she didn't believe her. If she could not convince a friend of Ulys's sobriety, what even worse rumors would strangers believe?

It was late summer in 1854 when Julia was called to the window by the sound of a buggy coming up the zigzag path. Although she could not see the driver, and she had been waiting for weeks for a lone rider on horseback, she knew at once that her husband had come home.

She ran outside to meet them, hurrying past Fred and Buck where they played on the grass under Jule's vigilant gaze. Bewildered, the children stared as the buggy halted before the house and a worn, bearded man stepped out. Julia froze at the sight of him, so shocked was she by the new lines of worry etched deeply into his face, the exhaustion in his eyes. But it was he, her beloved Ulys, and she flung herself into his arms, weeping with unrestrained joy and relief.

"Oh, my Julia," he murmured, kissing her all over her face, tangling his calloused fingers in her hair. "Oh, my darling Julia."

"Ulys," she choked out, hugging him with all her strength. "At last, at last, you've come."

Jule had brought the boys forward, and after one rough, lingering kiss, Ulys broke away from Julia and turned his gaze to their children, nearly staggered by the sight. "Fred," he said thickly, holding open his arms to him. "And this must be little Ulysses."

A smile slowly began to dawn on Fred's round cheeks. "You're my papa," he declared. "I remember you."

Ulys's eyes glistened. "I remember you too."

CHAPTER FIVE

August 1854–April 1860

In late September, when they could defer it no longer, Ulys and Julia left their sons in her parents' care and took the steamer to visit Hannah and Jesse Root Grant at their new residence in Covington, Kentucky, across the river from Cincinnati.

A barrage of letters had already warned them that Jesse was grievously disappointed in Ulys, that he had taken the news of his son's resignation as an almost physical blow. Ulys's sister Jennie, ever loyal, had confided that their father had written to Secretary of War Jefferson Davis in a vain attempt to rescind his son's resignation. Thus Julia was not surprised when her father-in-law spent most of their visit lamenting that Ulys had failed to meet all his proud expectations, that he could not fathom how Ulys supposed he might earn a living now that he had decided to squander his education and abandon the profession for which he had trained. Ulys listened stoically as his father complained, while inwardly Julia fumed and did her best to emulate her mother-in-law's serene calm.

On the eve of their departure, Jesse summoned Ulys and Julia into the parlor, where Hannah, too, waited. "I've decided to give you a position at the store in Galena," Jesse announced. "Your brother Simpson is doing well there, and he can teach you the business."

"Thank you, Pa."

"I do have one condition." Jesse shifted in his chair, his gaze darting to Julia before fixing squarely on Ulys. "Julia and the boys will remain here with us, or go home to Missouri and her own people."

"Why," asked Ulys, carefully measuring his words, "would you require me to leave my wife and children behind?"

"You'll learn your new occupation faster without distractions." Jesse frowned and jerked his head in Julia's direction. "And your wife will benefit from time with us. Julia's too extravagant with your money, but we'll teach her economy. From the cradle she's lived on a lavish scale at the expense of other human beings, but with us she'll learn a different way."

Quietly, Julia drew in a breath. She wanted to flee the room, and yet she could not move. Jesse and Hannah were studiously ignoring her, awaiting Ulys's reply.

"You leave me no choice, Pa," he said evenly, rising. "I must refuse your generous offer, but thank you all the same."

Hannah sighed and shook her head. As Jesse's brow knit in consternation, Ulys held out his hand to Julia. "Come on, darling," he said, helping her to her feet. "We have to finish packing."

As he led her from the room, Julia murmured, "Ulys, if you think —"

"What I think is that we must forget everything my father just said." He halted at the foot of the stairs and kissed her, firmly. "I'll forgive him for his obstinate foolishness if you'll forgive me for subjecting you to his unreasonable demands."

"I will."

"Good. Then we'll never speak of this again."

"But, Ulys —" She wanted to speak of it, if only long enough to ask him if he had been tempted, even for a moment, to accept his father's proposal. "I can't promise to forget."

"I wouldn't ask you to." He kissed her again, tenderly, and led her upstairs.

Ulys, Julia, and their sons spent the winter at White Haven, where only the discordant notes of Papa's barbed criticism for Ulys spoiled their perfect harmony. Papa's every glance declared that he had hoped for so much better for Julia than an aimless husband who, at thirty-two, had abandoned his profession and had scarcely a dollar to his name.

When spring arrived, Ulys, Julia, and their sons moved to Wish-ton-wish, her brother Louis's charming cottage three miles from Julia's sixty acres, which Ulys had begun to clear, felling trees and selling the cordwood. There, on July 4, 1855, Julia gave birth to their third child, a beautiful little girl with blue eyes, a sweet rosebud mouth, and soft, dark hair. Ulys wanted to name her Julia, but Julia insisted upon calling her Ellen, after Mamma, and the nickname "Nellie" was bestowed upon her soon thereafter. All of the servants declared that she was the prettiest baby they had ever seen, and Jule remarked that she resembled her namesake — high praise indeed, for Mamma had been a great beauty as a young woman and was still strikingly handsome at sixty-two.

When little Nellie was not quite a year old, Julia helped Ulys select the perfect place for a home of their own on her sixty acres, a sunny clearing in a grove of young oaks near Gravois Creek. The neighbors came to the house-raising, bringing delicious covered dishes to pass and putting their servants to work on constructing four ample rooms around a central hall. The walls were strong and straight and the roof as tight as a drum, but the cabin remained rustic and homely beneath Julia's quilts and curtains and wedding china.

"A frame house would have gone up twice as quickly at half the expense," Julia told Ulys one evening after they had put the children to bed and they were sitting close together in the parlor, amusing themselves by providing names for the quirks and knots and patterns they discovered in the log walls.

"Maybe we should call this place Hardscrabble," Ulys joked, and Julia laughed and agreed that they should.

When Ulys hauled wood into St. Louis, he was aware of the hard stares and curious whispers of residents who remembered that the man in the faded army coat, battered hat, and muddy boots had once worn a smart officer's uniform of blue wool and gold braid. Once Ulys ran into tall, affable Major Longstreet — Cousin James, to Julia — while delivering a load of firewood to the Planters Hotel. Major Longstreet, enjoying a furlough from his frontier post, invited Ulys to join him and his companions in a game of cards; later, when Ulys tried to give him a five-dollar gold piece to repay a longstanding debt from their Mexico days, the major shamed him by adamantly refusing it. "Sam, you're out of the service," he protested. "You need that more than I do." His words only made Ulys more determined to repay the debt, and Major Longstreet eventually took the coin to spare him further embarrassment.

On another occasion, Ulys returned from a trip to St. Louis with a curious expression on his face. Julia waited patiently for him to confide in her, and later, as they sat quietly outside the cabin watching the children play, he said, "I ran into Sherman in the city this morning."

"Captain Sherman?" Julia asked.

"Old Cump hasn't been a captain in more than three years." Ulys picked up a stick and scraped mud off the heel of his boot. "He's living with his wife's family in St. Louis until his prospects improve. He told me he's concluded that West Point and the regular army aren't good schools for farmers, bankers, merchants, or mechanics."

Julia nodded to conceal her disappointment. An old friend like William Tecumseh Sherman ought to be more encouraging. "And what did you reply?"

"I said I was inclined to believe him, but nonetheless I'm holding out hope for both of us."

Mamma knew Ulys's true worth, and Julia adored her for it. "My daughters, listen to me," she had said one summer evening a few weeks before, having joined them in the parlor after leaving the gentlemen of the family to their pipes and cigars. Her diamond ring sparkled on her finger as she pointed to each of her three daughters in turn, as if the gesture would engrave her words upon their memories. "Someday that man will rise to a higher place than we can yet imagine. His light is presently hid under a bushel, but soon his worth and wisdom will be shown and appreciated. You'll all live to see it, but I will not."

"Mamma, don't say such a thing," Julia admonished. "You'll live for ages yet."

"Do you mean my husband, Mamma?" asked Nell.

"I mean Captain Grant," she replied. "I've been sitting on the piazza for the last half hour listening to the men talk about the political divisions in our country, but Captain Grant, in a few sentences, made the subject so clear and our duty so plain that I must pronounce him a philosopher. He will be a great statesman someday."

Mamma's faith in Ulys's potential for greatness sustained Julia through many an uncertain hour, but as autumn faded into winter, cold and gray, Mamma fell terribly ill. Julia and her sisters desperately tried to nurse her back to health, unable to contemplate how they would manage without her — bereft of her practical wisdom, her gentle diplomacy, her kindness, her inexhaustible love.

But despite their tireless efforts, before the return of spring, Mamma passed away.

Weakened by grief and exhaustion, Julia suffered a lingering affliction of the chest, and Papa a deep despondency. Ulys tended the farms at both Hardscrabble and White Haven, and the crops thrived throughout the summer. Their hopes for a profitable harvest rose until a panic swept through the nation, bankrupting businesses and sending food prices plummeting. By the onset of winter, with Julia expecting another child, the situation had become so desperate that Ulys asked his father for a loan. When he was rebuffed, he pawned his gold hunting watch and chain for twenty-two dollars to buy Christmas presents for the children.

In February Julia gave birth to a son, whom she and Ulys named Jesse Root Grant after his grandfather. Soon thereafter Papa and Emma moved into the Dent family's St. Louis residence, and Ulys leased out Hardscrabble so he could devote himself to White Haven, planting potatoes, corn, oats, and wheat, as well as clover and Hungarian grass to feed the livestock.

"I believe this harvest will turn everything in our favor at last," Ulys told Julia, but in midsummer an epidemic of typhoid fever swept through the Gravois Creek settlement. Fred became deathly ill, and Nell, and her two-year-old son, Alex. Slave cabins throughout the county were rife with sickness, and even as Julia and Jule nursed the afflicted back to health, Ulys fell ill with malaria.

"I'll write to my father again," said Ulys.

"I'll explain that illness obliges me to give up farming, and I'll ask for a place in his business." He took pen in hand, trembling with fever and ague beneath the quilt she had made for him when they were betrothed, when all she wanted in the world was for the war to end so he could come home and marry her. In her innocence she had believed that she would always be perfectly content if only those wishes were granted, but marriage and motherhood had brought with them a host of new concerns, new sources of perpetual worry — for her family's health, their comfort, and their future prosperity.

When Ulys's father again rebuffed him, on the first day of 1859, Ulys entered into a partnership with Julia's cousin Henry Boggs, who ran a small real estate, loan, and rent-collection firm on Pine Street. Julia, the children, and Jule remained at White Haven while Ulys established himself, but when spring came, Ulys rented a small frame house for them at Seventh and Lynch Streets down by the river, far from the fashionable neighborhoods Julia had known as a young belle.

Soon after the family was reunited, Julia discovered that Ulys was not thriving in his new profession. The business was faltering and discord flourishing between Ulys and Henry, their estrangement worsened by rising tensions in the office that mirrored the mood of the country. Cousin Henry and

115

several other employees emphatically sympathized with the South, while Ulys and William Hillyer, an energetic young lawyer from Kentucky, supported the Republican cause. Most of their debates were friendly, but as disagreement over slavery threatened to divide the nation, their arguments became more contentious.

Julia had always known that Ulys found slavery distasteful, but she did not realize how strongly opposed to it he had become until, without giving her any warning of his intentions, he freed his only slave, earning himself fresh recriminations from his father-in-law. "I would free your slaves too, were they mine," Ulys told Julia.

"Fortunately, you can't," she retorted indignantly. Although as her husband Ulys controlled her property, Papa retained legal title to her slaves, so Ulys could not force her to give them up.

"Most of the farmers around White Haven employ paid labor," Ulys reminded her. "Your father's insistence upon keeping slaves has made him unpopular."

"Papa is good to his slaves," Julia protested. "As am I, and I'm certain Jule and the others would not thank me for casting them out and forcing them to fend for themselves."

"Why don't you ask them and see?"

Holding her breath, scarcely daring to move

116

lest they hear her, Jule froze in the hallway outside the couple's door, awaiting Julia's answer. Gabriel placed his faith for deliverance from slavery in themselves and in the Lord, but Jule had placed hers in Julia and her abolitionist husband. Would Julia call his bluff? Would she seek out her slaves, one by one, and ask them if they would prefer freedom to servitude?

Jule already knew how she would reply if asked. "You've been as kind to me as any mistress could," she would say gently, but with unmistakable certitude. "Given the choice, though, I'd like to make my own way in the world."

She and Gabriel could be free at last. He could minister to colored folk from a pulpit instead of preaching around a campfire. She could dress the hair and beautify the skin of the ladies of St. Louis, white and colored alike, and maybe someday count herself among the Colored Aristocracy like Madame Pelagie Rutgers. All Julia had to do was accept Ulys's challenge, step out into the hallway, and ask.

But instead Jule heard her mistress say, "I refuse to discuss this anymore."

Heartsick, Jule silently retraced her steps and stole away, down the hallway and outside, where she gulped air and fought back sobs of grief and frustration. Julia, the curious, questioning girl she had known in the days of ginger and cream, had grown into a woman who accepted things the way they were for no better reason than that they had always been that way.

"We could run," Jule told Gabriel the next time the Grants visited White Haven. She lay in his arms in the hayloft, having slipped away after putting the children down for their naps. "I have money saved up, not enough to buy us free but enough to get us north."

Gabriel was silent, thoughtful. "If we got caught," he eventually said, "after they brought us back, they'd be likely to sell one of us, or both. They wouldn't keep us together and risk us trying again."

"So we won't get caught." She rolled onto her stomach and propped herself up on her elbows to study his expression, her heart thudding with fear and hope. "I'm tired of living like Dinah, jumping at shadows and being grateful things ain't worse. Let's take a chance on a better life."

"Let's think about it," he said, pulling her down beside him again.

Frustrated, she bit back her protests and let him hold her. Their moments together were too few to waste in argument.

Upon the Grants' return to their rented home in St. Louis, Jule missed Gabriel terribly, though she supposed she should have grown accustomed to his absence long ago, so often had they been forced to live apart.

In their reduced circumstances, Julia paid few calls and attended even fewer parties, so Jule spent more time caring for the children than tending to her mistress's hair and dress. Almost every night after Jule put her young charges to bed, she overheard Julia and her husband discussing their prospects in hushed voices, their words often inaudible, but their tension and worry evident. The partnership of Boggs and Grant had dissolved, and stray glances at papers left on desktops told Jule that Mr. Grant was writing letters to apparently almost every gentleman of his acquaintance, hoping someone would recommend him for a position.

One morning, Julia was quiet and pensive as Jule dressed her for another worrisome day. "I had the strangest dream last night," she said, her voice subdued. "Mr. Grant was working in his father's tannery, cleaning rawhides by scraping off the flesh with a long, curved, double-handed knife. He was smiling, talking with his father, and making jokes with his brothers, thoroughly content."

"I thought you said he hated his father's trade," said Jule. "He swore he'd never work in the tannery."

"He did. That's what makes the dream so bewildering." Julia sat motionless as Jule brushed out her long, dark hair, as smooth and glossy as mink thanks to Jule's concoctions. "He was not only satisfied with the work, but proud and happy."

Jule wound Julia's hair into a smooth chignon. Jule had her own opinion about the significance of the dream, but she asked, "What do you think it means?"

"That he should go to Kentucky and see his father."

"What does Mr. Grant think?"

A flush of embarrassment crept into Julia's fair cheeks. "I haven't told him about the dream yet. His father's offers of help always come with conditions, and some of them — some of them I couldn't bear."

Jule fastened the chignon in place with a mother-of-pearl comb. "I don't think any good would come of ignoring a prophecy dream."

"No, neither do I." Julia sighed, resigned. "I suppose I must tell him."

She did so, as Jule knew she would. Later that afternoon, Julia instructed Jule to pack Mr. Grant's satchel for a week's journey. He would set out for Covington on the first steamer of the morning.

Mr. Grant's first letter home arrived within a week, and a second, more earnest dispatch quickly followed. "Ulys's father has offered him a position in the family business," Julia said softly, as if thinking aloud.

"Tanning hides?" asked Jule, astonished.

"No, not that." Julia turned her head this way and that, trying to focus on the page, which trembled in her hand. "It's a job at their retail store in Galena, in northern Illinois." She fell silent, reading. "This time there are no conditions, no demands that he leave me and the children behind."

Jule understood the great significance of the offer: Mr. Grant would have work and the family could stay together, as long as Julia agreed to leave her beloved Southern home and follow her husband again into the North.

That was what the opportunity meant for the Grants. Jule dreaded to learn what it meant for her.

■ ■ ■ ■

PART TWO:
HONOR

■ ■ ■ ■

CHAPTER SIX

May 1860–April 1861

"You couldn't possibly send our faithful servants to live with strangers," Julia protested when Papa told her about the advertisement he had placed in the St. Louis papers.

"You can't take them with you," said Papa, annoyed. "Not into northern Illinois. They'll run away."

"My servants would never leave me. They've always been loyal, and where would they go?"

"No servants are so loyal that they won't walk off if they get the chance. Grant agrees with me that they should stay behind."

"But for entirely different reasons," said Ulys, who would probably be perfectly content to sit back with his pipe and wave farewell to their servants should they all decide to pack up and leave one fine morning. "The citizens of Galena are likely to regard slave-owning neighbors with contempt and distrust. I don't think that's the impression we want to make."

"Let me take Jule along, at least," Julia implored, looking from her husband to her father and back. Her heart sank with dismay when she realized they were adamant. The best she could do was to make Papa promise that he would place Jule and the others with respectable people who would treat them kindly.

None of the servants would welcome the news, but Julia dreaded telling Jule most of all. "I don't know what to do," she confessed to Ulys that evening after Jule dressed her for bed. "Should I tell her tomorrow, to give her time to get used to the idea and say good-bye to her friends, or should I wait until the day of her departure, so she has less time to worry?"

"An interesting question." Ulys sat down beside her on the edge of the bed, took her hand, and regarded her curiously. "How would you feel in her place?"

For a moment Julia could only stare back at him, bewildered. "How would *I* feel in *her* place?"

"Yes, Julia. How would you feel?"

"I don't know." She found she could not meet his gaze. "It's — it's simply incomprehensible that I would ever be in her place."

"Try to imagine it all the same."

To humor him, Julia tried — but almost immediately shook her head. "I don't know. I suppose I'd want to know ahead of time so I could prepare. Otherwise it might come as quite a shock."

Ulys patted her hand, rose, and resumed undressing for bed. "Very good, Julia. Very good."

She was not sure if he meant her decision or how she had come to it.

She told Jule first, apart from the others, and she felt sick at heart as Jule gazed back at her, first uncomprehendingly, and then with bleak despair. "Please don't do this, Miss Julia," she murmured, giving her head the barest shake. "Please."

"It's not my choice," said Julia. "I would take you with me, but Papa insists that you stay, and Ulys is determined not to take any servants with us."

"But you need me. How you gonna to manage four children in a new house in a strange town all on your own?"

Julia could hardly bear the pain and confusion in Jule's face. "I know I'll need you — believe me, I do — but they've made up their minds."

"If I can't go with you, then can't you just hire me out by the day, as the missus used to?" Jule reached out as if to place her hand beseechingly on Julia's forearm, but at the last moment she held back. "That way I can still look after the old master evenings and mornings, and I won't have to live with

127

strangers."

"I'm sorry. I truly am. I'll make it up to you."

Jule put her head to one side and fixed her with a gaze so penetrating that Julia flinched. "Will you, Miss Julia?" she asked, her voice hardening, though it grew no louder. "Do you promise?"

"Yes," Julia quickly replied, unsure exactly what sort of pact she was making, and how she would keep it. "Yes, I will. I promise."

On the day Jule was sent off to her interim employers — her few belongings tied up in a calico bundle, her back ramrod straight, her expression brittle yet stoic — Julia's regret and shame infiltrated her dreams. She and Jule were children again, ginger and cream, playing in Papa's library. Squealing and laughing, they chased each other around his great oak desk, upon which a map of the United States and its territories was spread. Pausing to catch her breath, Julia planted her dimpled hands upon the smooth, polished surface of the desktop, inadvertently touching the map. Mischief in her eyes, Jule halted on the other side and mirrored Julia's gesture, shifting her weight from one foot to the next so that Julia would not know which way she intended to run. Suddenly Jule laughed and bolted to her right, and with a shriek Julia darted away — but their hands, sticky from sweets, clung to the fragile parchment, tearing it lengthwise. As Julia gasped in alarm, from the opposite side of the desk Jule fixed her with a solemn, steady, unflinching stare. *This is your fault,* her expression said as clearly as if she had spoken. *You and your people did this.*

The same dream haunted Julia again their first night on the river, but her apprehension faded over the four days it took the *Itasca* to reach Galena. Regarding the hilly city from the deck of the steamer, Julia was reminded of sketches she had seen of Alpine villages, the quaint houses and shops clinging to the slopes on terraces, with crooked streets and steep steps binding them together.

The steamer docked at the landing and the Grants disembarked in a stream of passengers. "Lyss," came a familiar shout from within the crowd on the shore, followed by a fit of coughing. Julia and Ulys spotted Simpson waving as he made his way toward them, tall and lean, his face flushed, his cheeks cavernous. Shocked, Julia stole a glance at Ulys and saw that he, too, struggled to hide his dismay.

"It's wonderful to see you," Simpson declared, smiling as he shook hands with Ulys, kissed Julia on the cheek, and greeted his niece and nephews with pats on the head and tickles under the chin.

"How have you been, Simp?" Ulys asked as the porter loaded the luggage onto a rented carriage and Julia helped the children inside.

"Oh, better, much better —" Simpson covered his mouth with a handkerchief as his words were cut off by another fit of coughing. "Don't let this cough fool you. The air here is very healthful, much better than in Covington. I've gained five pounds since moving here."

Sick at heart, Julia wondered how much weight he had lost before the move North if five new pounds of flesh hung so invisibly upon his narrow frame.

Orvil and his pretty young wife, Mary, would see them that evening at supper, Simpson explained as they drove along the river and up a hill to his home, where the newcomers would stay until Ulys found them a suitable residence. Within a few days, Ulys secured, at a fairly reasonable rent of one hundred twenty-five dollars a year, a two-story, seven-room brick cottage on Hill Street, high on a bluff in a fine neighborhood on the west side of town. One day Ulys stayed home from the leather goods shop to help Julia unpack trunks and place furniture, but upon opening a box of cherished treasures, she was terribly upset to discover that an old mirror that had belonged to Papa for more than fifty years had broken to pieces.

Ulys came hurrying down to the parlor at the sound of her cries and heaved a sigh of relief when he saw that she had not cut herself on the shards of glass. "Julia, calm yourself," he said, drawing her into his arms. "It's just a mirror. It's broken, and tears won't mend it."

Julia pulled away from him to dab at her eyes with her handkerchief. "It's a sign that someone in the house will die before the year is over."

"You don't really believe that breaking a mirror will cause misfortune, do you?"

"Of course it doesn't *cause* misfortune. It merely *foretells* it."

"Julia, darling, listen." Ulys placed his hands on her shoulders and met her gaze with reassuring certainty. "No one in this house is going to die anytime soon. This broken mirror isn't a sign of anything except that we didn't pack carefully enough."

Later that afternoon, when Julia was tired and perspiring and wondering what she would put on the table for supper, she was startled from her weary reverie by a series of thuds followed by an ominous silence.

"Mamma," Nellie suddenly shrieked. "Jesse's hurt!"

With a gasp, Julia darted into the foyer, her heart constricting at the sight of Nellie sitting on the floor beside Jesse's crumpled, motionless figure, one of Ulys's boots on his little leg, the other lying at the foot of the staircase. As Julia flew to gather him in her arms, she realized at once what had happened — Jesse had woken from his nap, stolen quietly from bed, put on his father's boots, and tried to descend the stairs.

"Jesse, darling," she said, kissing his cheek and forehead, rocking him back and forth. "Jesse, darling, wake up."

His long eyelashes fluttered and he let out a sob. Suddenly Ulys was there, swiftly examining Jesse for broken bones while Julia stroked his soft curls and murmured that he was fine, he was a great, strong boy, and he was going to be all right. Ulys soon determined that he had not broken his neck, thank God, but when Jesse opened his mouth to howl out his misery and fright, they saw that his four front teeth had been broken squarely off.

"Look at that," exclaimed Fred, crowding closer. "His teeth are just little stubs!"

"Never mind," said Julia briskly. "Those are baby teeth. New ones will grow in by the time he's a big boy."

She watched Jesse vigilantly throughout the day, and by bedtime he seemed restored to his usual happy self. "You're remarkable," Ulys told her as they, too, retired for the night. "You sobbed like one bereaved over a broken mirror, but you kept perfectly calm when Jesse had a terrible accident."

"I may have *seemed* perfectly calm," Julia said as she snuggled up beside him, "but I felt quite otherwise."

Ulys came home from the Grant leather goods store for lunch every day at noon, and in the evenings, the older children would meet him at the top of the two hundred stairs from Main Street and escort him home. Usually Jesse challenged Ulys to a wrestling match the moment he crossed the threshold, and as he removed his hat and boots, Ulys would warn him with mock solemnity, "I'm a man of peace, Jesse, but I can't stand being hectored like this by a man of your size." In reply, Jesse would gleefully strike him on the knees with his dimpled little fists, whereupon Ulys would roll on the floor with Jesse in his arms, pretend to struggle for a bit, then roll onto his back with a groan, set Jesse astride his chest, and protest, "It's not fair to strike a man when he's down." He would endure a dozen or so more punches, and then declare, "I give up! You have my unconditional surrender."

As summer waned and the autumn elections approached, presidential politics drowned out every other topic of discussion. Two sons of Illinois were among the contenders for the highest office in the land, and Galena had divided into two camps — those who supported Democratic senator Stephen A. Douglas, the "Little Giant" who had promoted the Compromise of 1850 and the Kansas-Nebraska Act, and those who preferred Mr. Abraham Lincoln, a Republican lawyer and former one-term congressman from Springfield.

Julia, who considered herself a staunch Democrat, like Papa, supported Mr. Douglas, but Ulys, who had not lived in Illinois long enough to be permitted to vote anyway, preferred Mr. Lincoln. In his letters from White Haven, Papa sang the praises of a third candidate, Vice President John C. Breckinridge, a former congressman from Kentucky who emphatically opposed any restrictions upon slavery but also rejected secession as a solution to the nation's crises. "Mr. Breckinridge is the man to put things right," Papa wrote to Julia a week before the election. "Mr. Lincoln's election would be an utter calamity, and Mr. Douglas's a catastrophe of only slightly lesser proportions."

In early November, Papa's worst fears were realized when Abraham Lincoln was elected president of the United States. On the night after the election, Mr. Lincoln's supporters organized a triumphant torchlight parade through Galena, and although Julia mourned Mr. Douglas's defeat, at twilight she took the children high up on a bluff overlooking the town to view the spectacle. The children were enchanted by the sight, but to Julia the long stream of blazing torches filling the winding streets below resembled a great, fiery serpent strangling Galena in its coils, just as Mr. Lincoln and his followers intended to crush the party of Jefferson, Jackson, Douglas, and her beloved papa.

In the aftermath of Mr. Lincoln's election, warnings of secession appeared with increasing frequency in the Southern press — and yet the citizens of Galena were shocked when, on December 20 at a state convention at St. Andrew's Hall in Charleston, the delegates of South Carolina voted unanimously to secede from the Union.

On the night of December 26, Union major Robert Anderson moved his troops from their vulnerable position at Fort Moultrie on the mainland to the more defensible Fort Sumter in Charleston Harbor. The next day, South Carolina militia seized Fort Moultrie and Castle Pinckney and demanded Major Anderson's surrender. In response, Major Anderson ordered his men to reinforce their position.

Whenever the people of Galena discovered that Ulys had been a captain in the regular army and had served in the Mexican War, men would engage him in earnest discussions about Fort Sumter and what new calamities might await the fragmenting nation. In the first week of January, *The Galena Daily Courier* reported that a steamship called the *Star of the West* had set out from New York en route for Charleston with supplies and troops to relieve Major Anderson's men. The *Galena Daily Advertiser* soon confirmed the story, noting where and when the merchant vessel had been spotted as it journeyed south along the coast. "The insurgents in Charleston can get news from the eastern papers as easily as we can," Ulys said. "They'll be ready and waiting when the *Star of the West* arrives. If any blood is shed on board that ship, those reporters will be to blame."

A few days later, the newspapers reported that on January 9, the *Star of the West* sailed into Charleston Harbor and was fired upon by militia and young military cadets. Struck in the mast but not seriously damaged, the steamer nonetheless was forced back into the channel and out to the open sea. On that same day, far to the south, delegates in Mississippi voted in favor of secession. The next day, Florida seceded from the Union, and the next, Alabama, followed by Georgia, Louisiana, and Texas by the first day of February.

Every night Julia listened intently as Ulys read aloud from the papers the speeches for and against secession, appeasement, and war. Every night she became increasingly upset and conflicted. "I believe the states have the right to leave the Union if they wish to," she told Ulys one evening after she had finally sorted out her feelings. "And yet I think the national government has an obligation to prevent the dismemberment of the Union, even if coercion should be necessary."

"You're a little inconsistent on the subject of states' rights," Ulys replied, amused, "but you're sound on the duties of the federal government."

"The duties of the people to the federal government are more clear to me every day."

On March 4, Abraham Lincoln took the oath of office and became the sixteenth president of the United States. The local press glowed with pride when they reported how the two favorite sons of Illinois had shown restraint and solidarity in a remarkable display of reconciliation at the inauguration. When the time had come to address the crowd, Mr. Lincoln had risen from his chair on the platform on the east portico of the Capitol in Washington City, serene and calm as he put on his spectacles. He had removed his hat, but then he had suddenly halted, looking about for someplace to put it while he took his oath. Senator Douglas had promptly come forward to take the hat, which he had held on his lap while Mr. Lincoln addressed an enthusiastic audience of thousands.

Julia found it a hopeful, heartening omen that two former rivals could make peace after their great contest, but events had begun that could not be restrained. On the morning of April 12, the insurgents in South Carolina attacked Fort Sumter, and after exchanging fire with Confederate guns for thirty-four hours, Major Robert Anderson was forced to surrender.

Outraged, the people of Galena closed their shops and took to the streets, where Wide Awakes marched in their black cloaks and brass bands played stirring martial tunes. Red, white, and blue bunting hung from windows and balconies; the Stars and Stripes flew from nearly every mast and flagpole. Vanished entirely were thoughts of appeasement, of coaxing or bribing the rebellious Southern states to return to the Union.

"They've proclaimed themselves aliens," Ulys said of the Confederates. "By attacking the United States, they've relinquished all right they had to claim protection under the Constitution. They should expect no better treatment than any foreign power that would wage war upon an independent nation."

CHAPTER SEVEN

April–July 1861

On April 15, President Lincoln issued a call for seventy-five thousand troops to suppress the insurrection, with a certain quota required from each state. Ulys agreed with the president that these troops, enlisted to serve for ninety days, would be sufficient to put down the rebellion.

Galena fairly burst with patriotism. Town fathers scheduled public meetings and called for volunteers. Fred, Buck, and their friends played at war, marching with popguns, donning military caps, guarding crossroads and bridges, and inventing signs and countersigns. Julia stayed home with the children when Ulys, Orvil, and their neighbor John Aaron Rawlins went to the first citizens' meeting at the court house, and after putting the youngsters to bed she stayed up to greet Ulys upon his return.

"I thought I was done with soldiering," Ulys told her, sitting beside her and absently taking her hand, "but as someone who's been educated at the government's expense for exactly this sort of emergency, I don't see how I can stand idle if my services are needed."

The moment Mr. Lincoln had summoned troops, Julia had known her husband would answer the call. If the government had any sense, they would put him on horseback and make him a leader of men.

The following evening, a second meeting was held to organize a recruitment drive. Illinois had been assigned a quota of six regiments, and Galena was expected to provide one company. On the basis of his wartime experience, Ulys was appointed chairman of the meeting. Local politicians and prominent citizens made speeches, fiery and spirited, and Ulys, too, was called upon to speak, something Julia knew he hated. Later, Orvil told her how Ulys had risen from his pine bench when the crowd called him forward, his hat slouched above his wide brow, his face flushed with embarrassment. He had spoken quietly, without any bluster or embellishment, as he told his listeners how to form a company. "I am in for the war and shall stay until this wicked rebellion is crushed at the cannon's mouth," he had said, but even that came in measured tones, as if he were simply stating the facts.

Ulys, ever dutiful, wrote to his father to seek

his advice and approval. "We are now in the midst of trying times when every one must be for or against his country, and show his colors too, by his every act," he wrote. "Whatever may have been my political opinions before, I have but one sentiment now. That is, we have a Government, and laws and a flag, and they must all be sustained. There are but two parties now, traitors and patriots, and I want hereafter to be ranked with the latter, and I trust, the stronger party."

Julia thought Ulys's father would respond well to his letter, but she was alarmed to discover that Ulys had not modulated his tone for Papa. "The times are indeed startling," he had written while informing her father of his plans, "but now is the time, particularly in the border slave states, for men to prove their love of country. I know it is hard for men to work with the Republican party but now all party distinctions should be lost sight of, and every true patriot be for maintaining the integrity of the glorious old Stars and Stripes, the Constitution and the Union. The North is responding to the President's call in such a manner that the Confederates may truly quake."

" 'In all this I can but see the doom of Slavery'?" Julia protested, reading his letter over before he sent it. "Did you have to end on that note?"

"That's my informed opinion," Ulys replied, taking the letter from her gingerly as if concerned she would tear it up in a fit of anger.

"Well, I hope you're wrong," she retorted. "But even if that *is* how you feel, must you taunt Papa with it?"

"It's no taunt. It's a cautionary observation your father would do well to consider."

"He'll see it as a taunt, but even if he doesn't, he'll never give you his blessing to wage war upon the South."

"But do I have your blessing?"

"Yes, of course." Julia was for the Union, but more important, she was for Ulys, always. "Without question."

"Even if this war leads to the destruction of slavery?"

"I don't see that one must necessarily follow the other."

He studied her a long moment in silence, his expression both sad and sympathetic. "It will, and when it does, I hope you won't reproach me or regret giving me your blessing today."

Before his father and father-in-law had time to reply to his letters, Ulys had assembled enough volunteers to form a company — and was promptly offered a commission as its captain. Ulys declined, for he had reasonable hopes of being offered command of a regiment, but he did agree to help the troops prepare before they reported to the state capital for assignment. He divided the men into squads, taught them to march, drilled them, and, drawing upon his experience as a quartermaster as well as a veteran of war, advised them as they assembled their gear.

Here Julia's expertise as a longtime military wife proved invaluable. The ladies of Galena, determined to sew uniforms for the brave soldiers representing their city, consulted her about how an army uniform should be fashioned. Julia, who was accomplished with her needle despite the headaches sewing inflicted upon her, knew well the precise details of an army uniform, and she found herself leading the project as the ladies bought material, found tailors to take measurements and cut the pieces, and distributed the sewing among their circle.

When the handsomely attired Galena company was about to depart for Springfield, Ulys was asked to accompany them in order to continue their training until they could be assigned to a regiment. Soon thereafter, he wrote to Julia to explain that he would be delayed in returning home, for Governor Yates had asked him to stay on to assist in the adjutant general's office. The state legislature had authorized the governor to accept ten additional regiments, and Ulys was charged with mustering them into state service.

Yet although lesser men were named colonels and placed in command of Illinois regiments nearly every day, no appointment came to Ulys. The state's negligence only fueled Papa's irate condemnation of Ulys's choices. "Grant could easily win a high command if only he would join the Confederate Army," he argued in letters to Julia. "James Longstreet has been made a brigadier general. Your husband could surely do just as well."

Julia was dismayed to learn that her cousin had joined the rebels, as far too many other friends and family had done, but she was not surprised. Papa, brother John, and sister Emma were staunchly for the South, as were several of Julia's former beaux from her time as a belle in St. Louis, and the husbands of many of her schoolmates. Even the Grant family suffered divisions; Ulys's aunt Rachel Thompkins, with whom he had exchanged many a cordial letter through the years, wrote from her expansive plantation in Virginia to declare, "If you are with the accursed Lincolnites, our ties of consanguinity shall be forever severed."

The venom in the letter chilled Julia. Would Papa ever go so far as to disown her for her loyalties? Mamma would never have allowed it, but Mamma was gone, mercifully spared bearing witness to the rising turmoil within her beloved family.

■ ■ ■ ■

The family of Edmund Slate, Esquire, kept three slaves to do the work of more than twice that number. Lisette, fifty years of age, was cook, housekeeper, maid, and laundress. Jacques, the only one of Lisette's five living children not sold off long ago, was groom, footman, and gardener. Jule, the only servant the Slates did not own outright, was ladies' maid, seamstress, and Lisette's assistant in everything the debt-ridden Virginia natives desired.

Jule marked the passing of the hours by the gnawing in her stomach and the fogginess of her thoughts. The servants could go without food more readily than the Slate ladies could endure wearing last season's gowns, so Jule, Lisette, and Jacques were ordered to exist on a diet of cornmeal porridge for breakfast, cornmeal porridge with a thin slice of bread for lunch, and cornmeal porridge with a gray chunk of salted pork for supper. At the end of the month, when the total of bills due regularly exceeded what Mr. Slate earned at his law practice, the bread and pork tended to disappear from their tin plates. Mrs. Slate had a sharp eye and a tight fist, and she kept a ledger of every penny and every ounce of goods that crossed her threshold. Scraps from the family table were bestowed upon the hogs and chickens, and once the missus had whipped Jule across the shoulders for salvaging an apple core from the slop bucket as she carried it to the sty, devouring all but the stem on her walk back to the house.

Jule had always been small, but after a few weeks in the Slate household, her dress began to shift loosely about her waist and shoulders, gaping at the sleeves and neckline as she went about her work. Her skirts concealed her protruding hipbones, but when she slept on her side, she woke with the insides of her knees red and bruised from the pressure of bone against skin. If she lay on her back, her breasts seemed to melt into her rib cage until they were as flat as the soft, swelling bosom of a girl barely out of childhood. In autumn her menses ceased, and for one fleeting, terrifying, hopeful moment she thought she was with child, until she remembered that she could not possibly be, for she had not lain with Gabriel since the previous spring. Blinking back tears, she secretly gathered herbs from the Slates' garden and brewed the tea that would make her bleed again, wondering why she bothered, whether instead she ought to let her body save its diminishing strength for keeping her heart beating and her lungs drawing breath.

She had seen Gabriel only once since she had left the Dents' city house with her dovegray shawl around her shoulders and her belongings tied up in a calico bundle she carried beneath one arm. It was early winter, and Jule was walking down the sidewalk, market basket in the crook of her arm, eyes downcast, giving way to white pedestrians rather than risk a blow to the head or arrest, when she heard her own name called out by a familiar voice. She turned in the direction of the sound only to discover the Dents' carriage passing her in the street, her own beloved husband at the reins.

"Gabriel," she breathed. He held her gaze, his expression shocked and exultant, until the carriage, carrying Miss Emma and a young lady Jule did not recognize, pulled too far ahead. He could glance quickly over his shoulder back at her and slow the carriage, but he could not stop for her.

Mustering her depleted strength, Jule hurried in pursuit, following the carriage through Mrs. O'Fallon's neighborhood and into another, where it came to a halt before an unfamiliar house. Miss Emma and her companion were apparently inside visiting, while Gabriel paced beside the carriage, looking frantically down the street, searching for her.

When his eyes met hers, she halted, fighting for breath. He ran to her and caught her up in her arms just as her knees gave way. "My beautiful girl," he said, his breath warm upon her cheek, tears in his voice. "My Lord, what have they done to you?"

She was newly aware of her scrawniness, of her worn dress and chapped skin. "I'm glad you knew me."

He held her tightly, rocking her slowly back and forth as if he were soothing a terrified child. "Oh, Jule, Jule, my sweet love." Then he held her out at arm's length and looked her up and down, eyes narrowing with anger. "How are you? How they treating you? You get anything to eat there?"

"Not much." There was no point in denying the obvious to spare him worry. "The missus has a temper and a free hand with the rawhide, but it could be worse."

He frowned, his mouth tight with anger. "You sound like Dinah."

"Dinah was right."

"Come here." One strong arm around her waist, he guided her to the carriage, where he settled her inside it despite her feeble protests that they would both be severely punished. He left her alone for a moment to climb up to the driver's seat, but soon returned with a bundle wrapped in cheesecloth. "Here," he said, placing it on her lap. "Eat."

When her trembling hands were slow to untie it, Gabriel gently reached around to open the bundle — and her mouth watered at the smell of sausage, cheese, bread, dried apples, and a perfectly ripe, sweet, fresh plum. "I can't take your lunch," she said, although she wanted nothing more.

"Eat it. I can get more from Annie later. Dear God in heaven, Jule, it's so good to see you."

She swallowed a mouthful of bread and cheese, forcing herself to eat slowly lest it all come back up again. "But I guess you hoped to see me looking better."

"I'd hoped the old master kept his promise to Miss Julia, to hire you out to people who'd treat you kindly."

"Maybe he don't know."

"More likely he don't care, as long as the money still comes in." He shook his head as Jule picked the last crumbs from the cheesecloth and licked them from her fingertips. "There's gonna be a reckoning someday, Jule. They're gonna answer for what they've done."

Jule's heart stirred with a tired flicker of the righteous light his fireside sermons had once kindled within her. She lacked the strength for anything more.

She lingered as long as she dared, but all too soon, they parted with fervent kisses and vows that they would find a way to be together. Jule raced off to finish the marketing and hurry home, but she had been gone too long, and dinner was delayed, and she endured a beating to remind her not to tarry next time. Nevertheless, her heart was full, her lips still warm from her husband's kisses, her stomach comfortably full for the first time in months — and although she did not know

149

it then, for the last time in many more.

In the days immediately following their brief reunion, Jule knew Gabriel must have told the old master about how he had found her, for Mrs. Slate inexplicably added butter and potatoes to her servants' meals, and she ordered Lisette to do the marketing in Jule's place. But the hollows in Jule's cheeks had scarcely begun to fill out when the butter and potatoes were taken away without warning.

In the Slate household, the winter passed in worry and speculation about the rising conflict. The government of Missouri had voted to remain in the Union but not to supply men or weapons to either side, a decision that had not prevented Unionists and secessionists alike from forming militia units and jostling for control over federal armories within its borders. Although reports warned of scattered bands of secessionists skirmishing in the Missouri countryside, Mr. Slate assured his anxious wife and daughters that they were safe in the city.

Five months had passed since Jule had last seen Gabriel, and she felt herself as insubstantial as the breezes that carried the fragrances of spring blossoms and horses past the door of the kitchen house where she slept on a pallet on the hard earth floor, longing for the comforts of Gabriel's hayloft. Mrs. Slate had restored Jule to her marketing duties, and on one sunny May morning, her head aching from hunger, Jule took a precious coin from the dwindling stash tied up in Julia's handkerchief. She had stolen a crumpled sheet of paper and a discarded stub of a pencil from Mr. Slate's wastebasket, and after she bought something to eat, she would have enough pennies left over to post a letter to Galena, Illinois. She could no longer wait for Julia to return to St. Louis and reclaim her, and she had abandoned hope that a prophetic dream would alert Julia to her misery. Writing to plead for help would reveal Jule's crime of literacy, but Julia was complicit in that too, and Jule knew she had no other choice.

She was so intent on her mission, clutching her market basket in both hands and feeling the condemning letter like a heavy weight in her pocket, that she only gradually became aware of a stir of apprehension in the air, the worried expressions of passersby. Then she heard it — the sounds of hundreds of men marching in the streets. Heart thudding, she drew back until she stumbled against the brick façade of a dry goods store. There she watched, stunned, as hundreds of secessionist militiamen — angry, resigned, defiant, scowling — marched past under guard by Union troops clad in the uniforms of the regular army and newer garb that marked the German Missouri Volunteers.

"They're the secesh General Lyon captured at Camp Jackson," Jule overheard a young

151

gentleman tell a companion. "Since they refused to take an oath of allegiance to the United States, he's marching them through the city to the arsenal, and once there he'll parole them and order them to disperse."

"He could've paroled them at Camp Jackson," the other man replied. "This display is humiliating."

The first man grinned wolfishly. "It's meant to be. They should've taken the oath when they had the chance."

As the men strode off, arguing, Jule realized that all around her, disgruntled murmurs were turning into angry shouts — directed not at the rebels, but at the soldiers guarding them. "Damn the Dutch!" a voice rang out, and others quickly took up the refrain. More harsh insults followed, and soon men and boys began hurling rocks and bottles upon the Union troops from the sidewalks and second-story windows. As Jule watched, horrified, a drunken, disheveled man stumbled into the path of the marching troops, shouted a hoarse stream of oaths, and fired a pistol into their midst. Women screamed as a captain in the Third Missouri clutched his abdomen and collapsed. Immediately other soldiers halted and opened fire, first above the heads of the civilians and then into the crowd.

Instinctively Jule threw herself to the ground and covered her head as screams and cries and gunfire erupted all around. A store window shattered above her, showering her in fragments of glass. She gasped in pain as a man stepped on her leg as he fled, and as more shots rang out, she scrambled on hands and knees into a doorway. Terrified, she closed her eyes, steeled herself with a few deep breaths, bolted to her feet, and ran — ran as fast and as far away from the escalating riot as she could.

When the screams and gunfire faded behind her, she slowed to a walk, gasping for breath, shaking, a painful cramp stabbing her beneath her rib cage with every step. Men and boys, wild-eyed and eager, streamed past her heading in the direction of the violence and madness. Unsteadily Jule made her way back to the Slate residence, realizing only when she stumbled into the kitchen house that she had somehow held on to her basket, but the letter to Julia was no longer in her pocket.

As the terrified Slate ladies queried her about what she had seen, Jule's thoughts were with the missing letter. She could only hope that someone would post it unread or that it would be destroyed in the chaos. If someone recognized Julia's name and gave it to the old master instead — not even Julia could protect Jule from the consequences.

When Jule served breakfast the next morning, she listened, heart in her throat, as Mr. Slate read aloud bits from the paper to his frightened family. Twenty-eight people had been killed in the furor, including women and children, and some fifty more had been injured. In a shaking voice Mr. Slate ordered the family and servants to remain indoors as several days of rioting followed, with most of the secessionist hatred and violence directed toward German immigrants and Union soldiers. Civilians shot at soldiers from the windows of their businesses and homes, and troops once again fired upon throngs of angry rioters in the streets. Martial law was imposed, but the uproar was subdued only after troops from the regular army arrived to replace the German volunteers.

Jule waited in dread for news of her letter, but nothing good or ill ever came of it. She dared not write another.

"I've decided to offer myself for national service," Ulys said to Julia, shifting restlessly in his chair during a long-awaited leave of absence from the state capital. "Stuck in the adjutant general's office, I feel as if I'm neglecting a duty that's paramount to any other duty that I ever owed."

"Then I wholeheartedly agree that you should," Julia said, managing a tremulous smile, "though I'll be very sorry indeed to be parted from you again."

"We'll be together as much as we can," he

said. "You, me, and the children. We'll find a way."

Julia nodded, though she knew it would not be easy — but what was, in those unprecedented times?

In late May, Ulys wrote to Adjutant General Lorenzo Thomas detailing his past military experience and offering his services. "I feel myself competent to command a regiment if the President in his judgment should see fit to entrust one to me," he said, with the characteristic humility Julia usually found endearing but worried was not, perhaps, quite the tone to strike in such circumstances. But she would never ask him to be a lesser man than he was, a braggart and boastful, so she said it was a fine letter and the adjutant general would be foolish not to respond with a commission. Ulys returned to his post in Springfield, and the weeks passed, and other, less-qualified men were named colonel while he was overlooked. The adjutant general not only did not reply as Ulys wanted, but he failed to respond at all.

In early June, Ulys wrote to Julia that he no longer expected a reply from Washington, but undaunted, he had decided to pursue another course. General George B. McClellan, whom Ulys had known at West Point, in the Mexican War, and at Fort Vancouver, had established his headquarters in Cincinnati. Ulys had secured another week's furlough to visit his family in Covington, and while there he intended to call on the general and offer him his services. "While I am gone," he asked in closing, "please open my letters, and if any are important, forward them to me."

Julia waited anxiously for word from Covington, praying that Ulys's interview with General McClellan would meet with success. She dreamed of Ulys every night, sometimes as the young lieutenant she had known at Jefferson Barracks, often as the sun-browned captain who had returned to her from the war, but forebodingly, never as a colonel leading Illinois troops into battle. What she did dream, curiously enough, three distinct times in a single night, was that she had received an unusual package in the mail. When she opened it, a small item wrapped in tissue paper tumbled out. Removing the wrappings, she discovered a familiar, cherished ring that had belonged to Mamma, and as she admired it, the diamond refracted a circle of bright stars of light upon the paper.

The dream brought Julia great satisfaction, for as the eldest daughter she had always believed she would inherit Mamma's favorite ring upon her death. Nell had claimed it, and at the time, Julia had been too overcome with grief to object. The dream gave her the reassuring sense that what she had long desired would soon be hers. "I will surely receive the ring before the week is over," she wrote to sister Emma. "Nell will remember it was supposed to be mine and send it to me."

For several days thereafter, Julia awaited the mail, her faith in her dream unshaken by the failure of the peculiar package to appear. Then, only days after she wrote to Emma, an envelope arrived, addressed, "Colonel U. S. Grant. Official Business."

Her heart leaping at the unexpected title, Julia opened the envelope and withdrew a sheet of vellum covered with tissue paper. As she drew the tissue paper aside, her gaze fell upon on the great seal of the State of Illinois in the masthead — encircled by stars, just like the lights cast by the ring in her dream, the ring Mamma had worn that long-ago summer evening when she declared Ulys a great statesman and predicted that his worth would someday be known to all.

Julia's hands shook and the paper and vellum fell to the floor, but she quickly snatched them up again. She scanned the page and discovered that she held the commission of U. S. Grant as a colonel and commander of the Illinois Seventh Congressional District Regiment.

Thrilled, she shared the letter first with the children and next with their bustling housemaid, and then she hurried across the street to tell her friend Emily Rawlins, who congratulated her with genuine warmth, lamenting that she was too ill to rise from her bed and celebrate properly. Returning home, Julia took pen in hand and made a copy of the commission to send to Jesse and Hannah Grant and all the family in Covington, and then, prompted by a perverse streak of mischief, she made one for Papa too.

She assumed that Ulys had already learned of his appointment through other channels, and his next letter home confirmed this. General McClellan deserved no credit for the commission, he wrote, for although Ulys had called at the general's headquarters twice, he had not been granted an audience. Instead, while traveling back to Springfield, he had received a telegram from Governor Yates offering him the command. Shortly after accepting the post, Ulys learned that when the regiment had first formed, the soldiers had elected as their commander an amiable and popular but very young and inexperienced fellow from their hometown. Later, when confronted by the reality of following an untested officer into battle, the soldiers had urgently demanded that someone more qualified be appointed in his stead. Ulys was that replacement.

Julia didn't care what unusual circumstances had brought about Ulys's appointment, only that it had come at last. She needed but a moment to count back the days and confirm her suspicions: Ulys had learned of his commission on the same day she dreamed of Mamma's ring, the long-awaited treasure, the circle of stars.

In the last week of June, Ulys managed a quick visit home to see Julia and the children and to collect supplies — namely, a horse and a uniform. When Ulys had formally taken command of his regiment three days before, he had found the men in a demoralized condition, wholly undisciplined, lacking tents, uniforms, and in many cases, weapons. "They weren't terribly impressed at the sight of me in my civilian clothes," Ulys said, "but they came around quickly enough once I began drilling them."

Julia glanced up from sewing the badges of his rank on his new uniform. "They'll need your firm hand."

"They'll get it." Ulys shook his head as he leaned forward in his chair, resting his elbows on his knees. "My predecessor did his best to develop their recklessness. He even went so far as to occasionally take the guard from their posts and go with them into the nearby village, where they'd all make a night of it."

"Goodness! It's little wonder the men didn't want him to lead them into battle."

"Most of them realize they badly need discipline." Ulys grinned as Jesse ran into the room, whooping with delight, and launched himself at his father, who snatched him up and flung him over his shoulder. "I'm sure that with the application of a little regular army punishment, I'll get as much discipline from them as I could possibly want."

During his all too brief furlough, Ulys spent every possible moment with Julia and the children, as if their company and laughter were water he must store in vessels for a long desert crossing. Eleven-year-old Fred was always by his side, engaging him in serious discussion about the soldiers' weapons and the enemy's positions, poring over maps he had drawn himself, proudly demonstrating how well he marched. "You should let me come with you," he often remarked, feigning nonchalance, as if his wild suggestion were so undeniably reasonable that he need not beg. "I'm old enough, and I could be a big help to you."

On the last night, after putting the children to bed, Ulys mused, "I'm of a mind to grant Fred's wish."

They were sitting on the front steps, savoring the cool night breezes. Seated two steps below Ulys, Julia had closed her tired, strained eyes and was resting her head on his knee, but at that her eyes popped open and she sat upright. "Take a boy into battle?"

"Not into battle, only so far as Springfield. Seeing the encampment might satisfy his appetite for the army life —"

"Or whet it."

Ulys nodded, acknowledging the possibility. "The excursion would teach him responsibility and discipline, and I would surely welcome his company."

"That would make Fred immeasurably happy, I know — but Ulys, think of the danger."

"If we're ordered to march on the Confederates, I'll send him home."

The regiment was unlikely to run into real danger in Illinois, Julia silently conceded, and everyone believed the whole conflict would be settled within a few months. "I suppose that would be fine," she said. "As long as you keep him out of danger, it should be a very pleasant summer outing for you both."

Ulys smiled and drew her close for a kiss. She recalled, as she often had throughout that frenzied spring, the overwhelming, almost debilitating homesickness that had overcome him when he was stationed in Oregon Territory. If Fred's company would spare Ulys that melancholy, how could she let her motherly fears keep her son at home?

Little Buck, naturally, was terribly jealous when Fred proudly departed with their father the next morning, his knapsack on his back, his attire as much like a soldier's as Julia had managed to put together on such short notice. "I want to do my part," Buck said after they left, and when Nellie chimed in that she did too, Julia told them they could help best by remembering their father, their brother, and all the other brave Union soldiers in their prayers every night.

Julia shared her children's patriotic desire to contribute to the cause, and, somewhat shyly, she decided to attend a meeting of one of the many ladies' organizations founded to support the Union cause. "May I assist you?" she timidly asked one of the busy leaders at a strawberry festival, a fund-raiser to purchase tents and rifles. Wordlessly the woman gave her a quart bowl of strawberries to hull, and when she finished, another, chattier woman asked her to help drape black crepe above a portrait of the late Stephen A. Douglas, who had died only three months after Mr. Lincoln's inauguration.

Another day, Julia offered her services at a sewing bee, but she arrived after all the piecework had been distributed. "Can you knit?" the lady in charge queried, peering at her over the tops of her spectacles.

Julia considered the muffler she had knit for Papa as a schoolgirl. "Yes, a little."

The woman took from her basket two long, slender knitting needles and a skein of yarn. "This is enough to make a pair of socks," she said, placing them in Julia's hands. "Try to get them done by next week's meeting."

Julia felt the heat rise to her face. "I'm terribly sorry. I confess I don't even know how to begin, and I fear the war will be over before I could possibly finish them."

She held out the needles and yarn, and after studying her a moment, lips pursed, the woman snatched the yarn away and gave her a different skein, one attached to the sleeve of a sweater that some other, more competent lady had begun. Julia accepted the new assignment with a nod and quietly stole away, taking the sleeve home to work on it in the safety of solitude. She eventually finished it, returned everything she had borrowed to the lady in charge, and silently vowed never to attend another meeting. The sight of the other women knitting away, piles of finished socks accumulating in their baskets, shamed her. At White Haven, a lady was considered accomplished if she could mend and embroider prettily and if she could capably manage servants who knit and sewed well. In the Yankee North, a lady was expected to be able to mend, embroider, quilt, knit, and sew expertly, even if she hired a girl to do the household chores.

All the while, Ulys and Fred had been at Springfield, where Ulys's troops had been mustered into the national service for three years as the Twenty-first Illinois Volunteer Infantry Regiment. They were in a good state of discipline, he informed Julia in a letter, as disciplined and up on the company drill as any in the army. Ulys wrote home often, and Fred wrote occasionally, but mail delivery was inconsistent, so sometimes she would receive their letters out of order, or a few days would pass with nothing in the post, followed by a delivery of a bounty of a week's worth of news.

It was from the newspaper, though, that Julia learned that the Twenty-First Illinois had been ordered to Quincy, Illinois, a town on the Mississippi River more than one hundred miles west of Springfield, about two hundred and fifty miles south of Galena. Soon thereafter, Julia received a letter from Ulys confirming that the regiment was on the march. "Fred has little Rondy to ride and he enjoys it hugely," Ulys reported, and Julia smiled, imagining the scene. "The Soldiers and Officers call him Colonel and he seems to be quite a favorite."

A few days later, Ulys sent another, longer letter noting that the regiment was already preparing to leave Quincy, having been ordered to Missouri. Although Missouri had remained within the Union, small bands of Southern sympathizers had formed regiments and threatened to make trouble, which the Union army was determined to swiftly quell. "Fred started home yesterday," Ulys had written, "and I did not telegraph you because I thought you would be in a perfect stew until he arrived."

With a gasp, Julia checked the date of the letter — July 13, 1861. "Oh, no, Ulys," she murmured. "What were you thinking?"

Quickly she read on in hopes of finding the answer. "He did not want to go at all and I felt loath at sending him but now that we are in the enemy's country I thought you would be alarmed if he was with me. Fred is a good boy and behaved very manly. Last night we had an alarm which kept me out all night with one of those terrible headaches which you know I am subject to."

Julia felt a headache of her own coming on. Quickly she sat down to pen and paper and ink and wrote a hasty reply that Ulys must not send Fred home alone, that even though he would remain within Union borders, Fred was safer with his father in Missouri than traveling alone among strangers in Illinois. "If you do not want me to be in a perfect stew as you say, do not send Fred home," she urged. "Alexander the Great was no older when he accompanied his father Phillip of Macedon. Do keep him with you."

She sent off the letter suspecting she was already too late, and with steadily increasing apprehension, she studied riverboat and railroad schedules, trying to determine when Fred might arrive if he had taken the steamer from Quincy to Dubuque and the train from Dubuque to Galena. But Fred did not appear the morning she expected him, nor did he come on the afternoon train, and as dusk fell she became frantic with worry. She had just decided to telegraph the railroad office in Dubuque and ask them to begin a search when the front door banged open and in trooped Fred, disheveled, exhausted, and thoroughly disgruntled.

"Where have you been?" Julia cried, flying to embrace him as he let his knapsack slump to the floor with a heavy thud. "What happened to you?"

"I missed the train in Dubuque," he said with a mutinous scowl, "so I walked the rest of the way."

"That's seventeen miles!"

"That's why I'm late." Suddenly the soldier disappeared and a forlorn little boy stood before her. "And I didn't get any dinner, Mamma."

She hurried to fix him a hearty meal, and when he had eaten his fill, she sent him off to wash up and change. Then, with her anger still at full boil like a covered pot on a hot stove, steam shooting out from beneath the clattering lid, she wrote Ulys a furious, indignant letter. By morning it was evident that Fred had suffered no more than a few blisters on his long hike, so Julia wrote again to Ulys, slightly less stridently than before. She knew full well that if Ulys was on the march, he might not have received her accounts of Fred's shame and suffering, much less found an occasion to respond to them.

At last, he did. "I have received two letters from you since our arrival," he wrote to her from Mexico, Missouri, on the third day of August, "one in which you gave me fits for sending Fred home by himself and one of later date. Fred will make a good general someday and I think you had better pack his valise and start him on now."

Ulys's gentle rebuke and easy jest made her regret her hasty words, but in early August, an astonishing, wonderful announcement chased away her lingering chagrin. A Grant would indeed become a general, but Ulys was not the prophet Julia was, for he had the details wrong. Ulys and Julia both learned the good news the same way, though hundreds of miles separated them: not by a prophetic dream, nor by a thick letter from army headquarters, but from the press, which seemed to take a reckless pleasure in wantonly divulging military secrets unknown even to the men involved.

Ulys had been promoted to brigadier general.

CHAPTER EIGHT

August–December 1861

Jesse Root Grant reveled in his son's achievements, and soon his loud, public boasts ensured that everyone in Covington knew it. He read Ulys's private letters aloud to any audience he could muster, and he sharply criticized other Union generals as if they were his son's rivals. Whenever unflattering reports of Ulys appeared in the Cincinnati press, Jesse fired back sharply worded refutations, stirring up controversy that created trouble for Ulys at army headquarters.

Equally vexing to Ulys was his father's determination to profit from his son's high rank. Jesse encouraged acquaintances to write to Ulys and request certain staff appointments, and he tried to obtain a government saddlery contract for the Grant leather company using his son's position as leverage.

As Ulys traveled about Missouri chasing Confederates, he bluntly rejected all such requests for patronage, especially as he assembled his personal staff. He thought it proper to select a man from the regiment as one of his aides, but the other two appointees were men he had known before the war: William Hillyer, the young Republican lawyer from Kentucky with whom Ulys had worked at cousin Henry Boggs's real estate firm in St. Louis; and John Aaron Rawlins, their neighbor across the street in Galena, recently bereaved of his dear wife, Emily, who in August had lost her long struggle with consumption.

In early September, Ulys occupied Paducah, Kentucky, without bloodshed, giving the Union a strong foothold in the West, but his family's proud elation was cut short by tragedy. On September 13, Simpson, who had been traveling in Minnesota on company business, died of consumption at St. Paul. Ulys's elder brother had endured his terrible affliction for so long that his death surprised no one, and when his father and sisters traveled to Galena for the funeral, in the midst of their mourning they took comfort in knowing that he would suffer no more.

As soon as Ulys left Paducah and returned to his headquarters in Cairo, he urged Julia to visit him. He assured her that she would be perfectly safe — so safe, in fact, that he wanted her to bring the children along.

Her friend Katharine Felt offered to help

her prepare for the journey, but on the afternoon of her departure, Julia had worked herself into such a state of nerves that she was obliged to excuse herself and go upstairs to lie down for a few moments while Katharine continued packing.

As Julia reclined upon the bed, resting her eyes, she felt a strange, prickling chill and sat up to draw the quilt over herself — and gasped to discover that she was not alone. "Ulys?" she cried, quickly recognizing his head and shoulders, sharply distinct a few rods in front of her, about as high above the ground as if he were on horseback. He regarded her so earnestly, so reproachfully, that her heart plummeted and she scrambled backward on the bed until her shoulders struck the headboard. "Ulys!"

She heard footsteps on the stairs, and suddenly the bedroom door swung open. "Julia?" Katharine asked. "Did you call?"

Julia had turned at the sound of the door opening, but she quickly tore her gaze away from Katharine and returned it to Ulys — but he was gone. "I saw — Ulysses was here. In this room, moments ago."

"Little Buck? But I just saw him outside in the yard playing with Fred."

"Not my son. My husband."

"The general isn't here." Katharine sat down on the edge of the bed. "You must have been dreaming."

Julia pressed a hand to her chest and willed her heart to stop racing. "It was no dream. He was several rods away, but I saw him as clearly and distinctly as I see you now."

"Well, that's proof it was a dream," said Katharine soothingly, patting her hand. "You can't see anything clearly at that distance, nor is this room large enough to contain anything several rods away."

Confronted with irrefutable logic, Julia felt foolish. "I would have sworn it was Ulys, truly him, truly here."

"You're thinking of him constantly and you're nervous about your travels. It's only natural that you'd have a troubling dream."

Julia conceded that Katharine was probably right, and after taking another moment to allow her shock to subside, she resumed packing the children's clothing, filling two sturdy trunks for them and a third for herself.

Katharine and her husband escorted Julia and the children to the evening train bound for Cairo. Thankfully, the children were cheerful and well behaved, and Julia managed to get some sleep despite the incessant rattling of the car. In the morning she overheard two gentlemen discussing a battle that had occurred in Missouri somewhere south of Cairo, and all of her anxieties returned in an instant, for Ulys had surely been at the center of any engagement.

At last the train reached Cairo, and as it

pulled into the station, Fred, peering eagerly through the window, suddenly shouted, "There he is, on the platform! There's Pa!"

The other children crowded the window to see for themselves, and before the train had stopped entirely, Ulys climbed aboard, strode down the aisle, and took Julia in his arms. "My darling," he murmured, kissing her in front of the children and the other passengers without a hint of embarrassment. "At last you've come. The children are well?"

"See for yourself," she teased, as if he could do otherwise as they promptly fell upon him, flinging their arms about his waist and demanding kisses. With some effort and lots of laughter, Julia and Ulys managed to scoot them off the train before it steamed away to its next destination. As the porter stowed their luggage on a carriage Ulys had hired, Julia managed to take him aside. "I heard you were in a great battle," she said quietly. "I had a vision of you that same day, though perhaps it was only a dream."

He urged her to tell him what she had seen, and at what hour, and when she finished, he shook his head slowly. "That is singular," he said, his gaze fixed on her face, curious and appraising. "Just about that time I was on horseback and in great peril, and I thought of you and the children, and what would become of you if I were lost. I was thinking of you, my dear Julia, and very earnestly too."

"I thought the look was reproachful," she admitted. "I thought you were displeased with me for not coming sooner."

"I ought to have been, but I knew you had a good reason for not coming," he assured her. "You're here now, and we'll make up for lost time, the six of us."

As they drove off, Ulys told her he had written her a long letter the day after the battle, and it was probably waiting for her back in Galena. On November 6, he had stealthily moved his troops by riverboat from Cairo to the Confederate stronghold at Columbus, Kentucky. The next morning, he discovered that enemy troops had crossed the Mississippi and had camped at Belmont, Missouri, so he transported his forces to the Missouri shore, marched on Belmont, and surprised the rebels in their encampment, scattering the men and destroying their supplies. The Confederates quickly reorganized, and, strengthened by reinforcements from Columbus and heavy artillery across the river, they counterattacked, forcing Ulys to retreat to the riverboats.

"We were very soon out of range and went peacefully on our way to Cairo," he said, patting her hand reassuringly, reading the worry in her eyes. "Every man felt that Belmont was a great victory and that he had contributed his share to it."

"As they should," said Julia shakily. Belmont had been his first major battle as a general, and she was too busy thanking God that he had come through it unharmed to care about the details of the victory, what territory had been gained or ceded, what artillery captured or lost to the enemy.

"Keep in mind that until then, my men were green," Ulys said. "Untested, most of them, and yet in our withdrawal there was no hasty retreating or running away. Their discipline under fire gives me confidence in them, and I'm sure it gives them confidence in themselves. I've no doubt I'll be able to lead them in any future engagement without fear of the result."

Julia clasped his hand in hers and managed a smile, but she said little more as they drove along.

Before the war, Cairo had been a charming, bustling town, or so it had always seemed to Julia as she viewed the peninsula at the confluence of the Mississippi and Ohio Rivers from the deck of a passing steamboat, but on that day it struck her as desolate, the streets almost empty save for a few citizens who hurried along on foot, their expressions haunted and anxious. The river surged high and angry in the banks around the city, and Julia shuddered as she wondered how near the rebels were, if even at that moment, snipers had their rifles trained upon the carriage.

Ulys had established his headquarters in a

gracious, three-story stone residence on a main street in a fashionable neighborhood, keeping his offices on the first floor and residing on the second. Julia settled the children in a pair of adjacent rooms, and she was pleased to discover that Colonel Hillyer and his family would be sharing the house — his wife, Anna, whom Julia had known and admired in St. Louis, and their three young children, Willie, Jimmie, and Mamie. Their landlord had hired a colored man to do the cooking and serving at table, and the services of a pair of housemaids were soon acquired.

Ulys was often in the field or sequestered at headquarters with his aides and officers, but Julia delighted in his company whenever he could spare the time. Often she, Anna, and the children rode out in an ambulance to observe Ulys reviewing the troops, an exercise that Julia soon noted usually preceded a significant movement of the army. She watched proudly as Ulys — her General Grant — rode down the columns inspecting the soldiers, the stirring music of the army band and the sweeping white mane and tail of his beautiful light sorrel, Jack, adding to the pageantry of the scene. Afterward, many of the gallant heroes would crowd around the ambulance to pay their respects to Julia and Anna, bowing and smiling. When asked if she was pleased with the review, Julia always responded that nothing could be more interesting, more thrilling, than watching the columns of brave and gallant men. "There is poetry in every movement," she enthused, and was rewarded by the proud, admiring smiles from all who overheard.

At the end of November, Ulys and Julia decided that she should take the children to St. Louis to visit their grandfather, for it was impossible to say when she might have another opportunity. When Ulys saw them off at the landing, she clung to him fiercely. "We'll see each other again soon, I promise," he said. "Don't fear for my safety, Julia darling. I won't be harmed."

"Yes, I know." And somehow she did. Whatever dangers he faced on the battlefield, she knew he would always return safely to her.

When they arrived in St. Louis, Papa sent his carriage and a servant to meet them at the landing, and soon the children were scrambling through the front door of the much-beloved house on Fourth and Cerre Streets, at the very moment the bells of Sacred Heart Convent rang out the noon hour as if to welcome them home.

Julia had feared that she would find Papa much aged from the strain of the national conflict, but if anything, his outrage and righteous indignation seemed to have rejuvenated him. She discovered a new, defiant light in his eye when he rose from his favorite chair to bid her welcome, and as he tousled the boys' hair and queried them about their prowess in their boyhood pursuits. "Nellie, my beauty," he greeted his granddaughter, smiling so tenderly upon her that Julia felt a pang of wistful love and vowed to forgive him every unfair demand, every slight against her beloved Ulys.

With all the fuss and excitement surrounding their homecoming, it was not until the family had exchanged warm embraces and shared all the news that Julia noticed a curious absence. "Where's Jule?"

"I hired her out to the lawyer Mr. Edmund Slate," Papa replied.

"Yes, Papa, I know you did, but why is she still there?" She turned to Nell, perplexed. "Didn't you receive my last letter? I'm sure I remembered to say that I wanted her help during my visit. I was counting on it, and I daresay looking forward to it."

"One maid is like any other," said Papa, waving a weathered hand dismissively. "They all can do hair. They all get you girls in and out of your frocks the same way. Emma's maid can look after you both. You won't be here long enough to warrant disrupting our agreement with Mr. Slate."

Julia was deeply disappointed, but she managed to keep her vow of forgiveness and tolerance for a few days — not coincidentally, the precise length of time Papa refrained from denouncing the Union and Ulys and all who served its so-called oppression of the South. "You realize that you condemn your own son," she chided him one evening after supper. "Captain Frederick Tracy Dent, Ninth United States Infantry?"

"Frederick is stationed in San Francisco. He'll have nothing to do with this unconscionable Yankee aggression."

"You say that as if he chose to be in California. If his regiment is transferred to the field of war, you'll find that his loyalties align with my husband's."

"Not so, daughter. If ordered to take up arms against his native South, Frederick would resign his commission."

Julia's correspondence with her brother and sister-in-law suggested otherwise, but again and again Papa provoked her, expounding at length on the constitutionality of secession whenever they entertained dinner guests, all of whom shared his sympathies. Julia felt quite alone on such occasions, a sole defender of the Union in St. Louis as she had been the lone champion of the South in Galena.

Once, while watching from the back porch as the children played in the garden, dressed in their warmest wraps as they chased a few icy snowflakes drifting lazily down from a bright blue-and-white sky, she endeavored to be a dutifully uncomplaining audience for

178

Papa's latest diatribe against Mr. Lincoln. After Papa had consumed nearly a half hour lambasting the president as an Illinois ape who either hadn't the brains to comprehend the Constitution or flagrantly ignored it, he had so exhausted her patience that she finally exclaimed, "Why don't they make a new constitution if this one is such an enigma?"

"Whatever do you mean?"

"A new constitution, you know, one to suit the times."

Papa looked aghast. "One does not simply write a new constitution."

"Why not? Our times are vastly different now. We have steamers, railroads, telegraphs, etcetera. The gentlemen who wrote the Constitution could not possibly have imagined what we contend with today."

"Good heavens." Papa clapped a wrinkled hand to his brow. "The problem isn't the Constitution but Lincoln's refusal to abide by it. Grant put this nonsense in your head, I've no doubt."

"That's not so. I came up with it entirely on my own."

"That's even worse," he retorted, shaking his head as he hauled himself out of his chair and made to return inside. "This never would have happened had Old Jackson been in the White House. Jackson would have hanged a score or two of them, and the country would have been at peace. I knew we would have

179

trouble when I voted for a man north of Mason and Dixon's line."

Astonished, Julia called after him, "Do you mean to say you voted for Mr. Douglas after all?" But the back door crashed shut after him, and she doubted he had even heard the question. The sudden quiet made her wary, and she turned to see the four children watching her solemnly.

"It's all right, my darlings," she said. "You know how Grandpa gets about politics."

Fred nodded seriously, but Jesse looked dreadfully worried.

Later that night, after Julia tucked the children into bed, Nellie's little hand slipped from beneath the covers and took hold of hers. "I love Grandpa very, very much," she confessed, "but when he says mean things about Pa, it hurts me in my tummy and in my heart."

"I understand completely, darling," she said gently, brushing Nellie's soft, dark locks from her eyes. "I hurt exactly the same. But I'll always love Grandpa, even when he says things that I know are wrong about people I love, and you must always love and respect him too."

Nellie nodded and promised that she always would. Julia smiled, kissed her smooth brow, and put out the light. When she stole quietly from the room, she discovered Papa standing in the hall, frowning. "Those who eavesdrop rarely hear any good of themselves," she whispered sharply, brushing past him on her way to her own room.

The next day, Papa displayed remarkable restraint and what was, for him, contrition. Not a word against Ulys escaped his lips, and he waited until the children left the room to mutter invective against the Union. Later that afternoon, he even managed an apology of sorts.

The children had been full of nonsense all day, and Julia had just pulled Jesse off Buck and had sent both naughty boys to separate corners when she heard a carriage come to a halt outside their door. Papa's butler answered, and a moment later Papa himself poked his head into the parlor. "Daughter," he said, a hopeful smile tugging at the corners of his mouth. "You have a caller."

Julia instinctively touched her hair to be sure no unruly locks had come free of her coiled braids. "Please show her in. Or him," she added, just in case.

"I think you should meet her in the foyer instead."

Curious, Julia nodded. "Buck and Jesse," she warned, "you are not to budge from those corners. Fred will tell me if you do." She ignored their plaintive sighs as she followed Papa into the hall — but she stopped short at the sight of a tiny colored woman standing just inside the front door, a bundle tied up in calico under her arm. "Jule," she exclaimed, hurrying forward to welcome her, halting an arm's length away. Her maid was so much thinner than Julia remembered, and her gaze carried years of misery. "How good it is to see you!"

"Thank you, Miss Julia." Jule had not removed her wrap, the familiar lovely, warm, dove-gray shawl she had knit from yarn salvaged from an old sweater of Papa's. "If you won't be needing me, I'd like to go see Gabriel, please."

Before Julia could dismiss her, the sound of Jule's voice brought the children running, and they happily embraced her, each professing to have missed her more than the other three. Jule smiled and tried to hug them all at once, and the calico bundle fell to her feet. Without thinking Julia stooped to pick it up, and then held it awkwardly while the children and their nurse enjoyed their reunion.

Julia remained in St. Louis long enough to assist at the birth of Emma's first child, a robust little fellow the proud parents named Frederick Dent Casey after Papa. Ulys was eager to see his family again, so within a fortnight of the baby's arrival, Julia was packing their trunks for the trip back to Cairo. In his letters Ulys had hinted that he was planning a major offensive, and he urgently wanted her and the children to fit in another visit before he was obliged to send them away for their own safety.

Julia already felt the pangs of homesickness, and the thought of the long steamboat ride alone with the children filled her with misgivings. She recalled how easily Anna Hillyer managed her three youngsters with the assistance of their Irish nurse, and she wished she did not have to do without help.

Upon further reflection, she wondered — why should she?

With a new lightness to her step, Julia fairly flew down the stairs to consult Papa, and when he gave his approval — with the usual cautions — she quickly found Jule in the children's room, where she was folding Nellie's pretty dresses and placing them carefully in her trunk. She had filled out somewhat since returning to the Dent household, and the strain around her eyes had eased. Her ginger skin was as warm and luminous as ever, her hair ebony without a single strand of silver. Julia was suddenly conscious of how her own waist had thickened, how she had begun plucking the occasional gray hair from her crown.

"Jule," Julia said, clasping her hands together with delight, "I have wonderful news."

Jule eyed her warily. "And what might that be, Miss Julia?"

"You'll need to pack your bundle, because you're coming with us to Cairo."

CHAPTER NINE

December 1861–April 1862

Jule must have been even more surprised than Julia had anticipated, for her first reaction was to stare at her, expressionless, before she resumed folding Nellie's dresses, more quickly and crisply than before.

"Well?" Julia eventually prompted her. "Won't it be exciting to travel?"

"Maybe too exciting." Jule placed the last little gown in the trunk, frowning. "You want me to go with you into a war?"

"You won't be anywhere near a battlefield. General Grant would never summon me and the children to him if he thought we would be in any danger."

"Even a general can't always know where the danger's gonna be."

Jule made a fair point, but Julia could not afford to cede any ground. "General Grant's headquarters are at Cairo, Illinois — well, I know you don't know where that is, but it's perfectly safe. You'll have a nice bed in the servants' quarters in the attic."

"But I've only just gotten home." Jule peered into the trunk as if wondering what she had forgotten. "I'd rather stay here — with Gabriel."

"Jule, I know you fancy him —"

Jule planted one hand on her hip. "He's my husband."

For a moment, Julia could only stare at her, speechless. "Your husband?"

"That's right. We were married a few weeks after you and General Grant, in a church, with a minister."

Dismayed, Julia sat down heavily on the edge of the bed. "You know that's against the law."

"You gonna turn me in? You gonna tell your papa?"

"Of course not, but you can't let him know." Julia inhaled deeply, imagining Papa's reaction. "Why didn't you tell me?"

"Because it's against the law," said Jule pointedly, echoing Julia's own words.

"Of course." Julia clasped her hands together in her lap, thoughts churning. When she considered how unhappily she had endured Ulys's numerous and lengthy absences, it pained her to think she had inflicted that keen sense of loss and separation upon someone else.

Jule fixed her with a level, determined gaze. "When you went off to Galena and hired me out, you said you would make it up to me. Now's the time — please. Let me stay here with Gabriel and hire me out to dress hair like you used to. Let me stay with my husband and earn some of my own money again."

"Jule, listen," Julia said. "My father has the final word. It's not a choice between accompanying me to Illinois or staying here with Gabriel, but coming with me or returning to Mr. Slate. They still have your contract."

Jule pressed her lips together, but her chin trembled and angry tears gathered in her eyes. "That's no choice at all."

"I know. I'm sorry."

Jule looked away. She pressed a hand to her cheek, to her brow, her expression shifting from grief through resignation to resolve. "Illinois, you say?"

"Yes, in Cairo. It's a charming little town on a peninsula between the Mississippi and the Ohio. You like the river, don't you?"

"I do, yes." Jule closed the lid to the trunk but remained bent over it, bracing herself with her arms. "The old master don't mind? He wouldn't let me go to Galena."

"He understands that I need help with the children and that I'm not likely to find anyone more suitable to hire there."

"All right, Miss Julia." Jule straightened and tucked her hands into her apron pockets, a new, inscrutable glimmer in her eye. "It might be good to travel. When I finish packing Buck's trousers, I'll get my bundle together."

When their steamer arrived at Cairo, Ulys met them at the landing, his joy abundant as he embraced Julia and the children — and when he glimpsed Jule standing at a respectful distance with the luggage, his consternation was equally evident. "Hello, Jule," he greeted her. "I didn't expect to see you here."

"I didn't expect to be here, General, sir."

Ulys laughed, and Julia, who had been holding her breath, exhaled with relief. He could have ordered Jule back aboard the next steamer for St. Louis, but it appeared that she could stay. Impulsively Julia kissed Ulys on the cheek, beaming, and he gave her a wry look and took her hand. He was an indulgent husband and father, and she knew she was fortunate that he so often let her have her own way.

She was delighted to see Anna Hillyer again, to find the stouthearted soldiers in excellent spirits, but she soon realized that something was afoot at headquarters. Someone — Julia suspected a disgruntled transportation officer named William Kountz, who had made trouble after he was blamed for irregularities in the quartermaster's department — had complained to Washington of intemperance in the camp. Ulys had enough to do without playing the schoolmarm to his officers, so it was true that he took a lenient approach to how they spent their time off duty, as long as the encampment was never disorderly or rife with drunkenness. Nevertheless, the rumors of dissipation in camp persisted, and before long, certain gossipy, malicious folk dragged out the old accusations against Ulys.

"How can anyone who knows you believe you're a drunkard?" Julia protested in an undertone one night as they prepared for bed. She trusted the Hillyers never to repeat what they might overhear, but others could be walking by or toiling away in the offices below, taking note of every word that passed through the thin walls and floorboards. "General Rawlins is a zealot about temperance. I've heard him say he would rather have a friend take a glass of poison than a glass of whiskey. If you were a drunkard, he would know, and he would report you himself. How do these rumormongers believe your alleged drunkenness has escaped his notice?"

"I don't know." Ulys sighed heavily. "Julia, I haven't been a perfect man —"

"But you're no drunkard."

"No," he said. "No, I would not call myself that."

"No one should."

He put out the light, and she pulled the quilt over them, shutting out the world.

■ ■ ■ ■

Julia found Christmas melancholy rather than merry that year, far from home in a temporary residence that resembled an army barracks, with war lurking just beyond the light of her hearth, but she resolved to hide her feelings for the sake of Ulys and the children, so they would know only the joy of the season and none of the loneliness and regret. She was ever mindful, too, that she lived among thousands of brave men who also had not expected to be so far from home in that holy season, men who had not seen their families for many long months. Julia had Ulys and the children, as well as Jule, for comfort and company. How could she bemoan her state when she was surrounded by people far less fortunate? Casting aside her self-pity, she gathered the other officers' wives and walked along the rows of white tents distributing Christmas delicacies to the soldiers while the children sang carols in their sweet treble voices. She spied a tear in the eye of many a stalwart soldier, but they seemed pleased to be remembered, and Julia hoped their homesickness had eased at least a little.

Throughout the holidays and into the New Year, Ulys was preoccupied with planning assaults on Fort Henry and Fort Donelson in Tennessee, two Confederate strongholds protecting the Tennessee and Cumberland Rivers. If Ulys could wrest those forts from the enemy's grasp, he would open two routes for a Union invasion deep into Tennessee and beyond.

It seemed a good idea to Julia, but Ulys's superiors needed to be persuaded, and even as he made his case via letters and telegrams, he suffered distractions and interruptions from Captain Kountz. Julia disliked the officer intensely, certain he was responsible for the slanderous accusations against her husband. Her enmity seemed justified after the riverboat captains under his command formally complained about him to Ulys, declaring that he was obnoxious and that they would not obey his commands. "Captain Kountz has been appointed by the president and must be obeyed," Ulys reminded them. "There's no time to discuss whether that's agreeable or not, and I hope, gentlemen, that you'll do your duty."

The riverboat captains acquiesced, but Kountz continued to make a nuisance of himself around headquarters. One morning while Ulys was off inspecting the troops, Julia was drawn from her sitting room by the sound of a fierce argument downstairs. From the top of the staircase, she glimpsed Rawlins and Kountz squared off in the foyer, glaring at each other with almost tangible enmity.

"Your constant interruptions have driven

the general from his office," Rawlins said, his voice growing louder with each word until he was almost shouting.

"I'm doing my duty," snapped Kountz, "which is, I'm sure, a concept so unfamiliar to you that it's no wonder you don't recognize it."

Rawlins cursed and rushed him, and as they grappled, two other soldiers came running. "Restrain him," Rawlins ordered, tearing himself free as the soldiers seized Kountz's arms. "Escort him back to his barracks at once."

"You're drunk," Kountz hollered, struggling to break free. "You're all drunk — you, General Grant, the entire staff. Drunkards, every one of you!"

That evening at dinner, Colonel Hillyer told Ulys what had occurred in his absence. "I ordered the scoundrel gagged," the colonel said, disgusted. "He should be ousted from the army. He's nothing but trouble."

"Gagged?" Ulys winced and shook his head. "He must be released at once."

"But General —"

"We must bear with this man," Ulys said. "He's overzealous in doing his duty; that's all."

Colonel Hillyer rose to carry out the order, but his expression made it clear that he was loath to obey. "We can't trust him, sir. *You* can't trust him. He's a menace."

■ ■ ■ ■

Although Ulys confided nothing of his strategies to Julia, as January passed, she could not fail to observe that he was preparing to send his troops into battle. Something — a new intensity in his manner, the escalating fervor of his closest advisors — told her that he had finished planning the assault and had chosen the day to send the army to meet the enemy.

One afternoon he found her in her sitting room mending Jesse's torn trousers, and he lingered quietly in the doorway watching her so long that she was finally compelled to ask him what he wanted.

"I intend to move the army tomorrow," he said. "While I'm gone, I think you and the children should go to Kentucky and stay with my family."

Julia's spirits dipped. "Couldn't I wait here until you return?"

He shook his head. "I don't know how long I'll be away, and Covington is safer."

"I feel perfectly safe here," she replied, trying her best to sound confident rather than forlorn. "Please don't send us away. The children will be heartbroken."

"Fred, Buck, and Nellie really ought to be in school," Ulys reminded her. "Covington is as good a place to enroll them as anywhere, and it's close enough that if I want you to visit, you can leave the children with my family and come to me without fear for their safety."

Julia set her sewing aside, closed her eyes, and pinched the bridge of her nose to ward off a headache. "What about Jule? I can't imagine that your parents would permit me to bring her along."

"They couldn't abide it," he said shortly, and a flush of mortification rose in her cheeks when she understood that his displeasure was directed toward her for keeping a slave, not to his parents for objecting. "A messenger will be carrying my dispatches to St. Louis early tomorrow morning. I've arranged for him to escort Jule to your father's house."

So he had already decided; she was being informed, not consulted. "If I can't talk you out of this," she said, "and I see from your scowl that I dare not attempt it, please send word to my father that he mustn't hire out Jule to Mr. and Mrs. Slate. I absolutely must insist. She won't tell me all that she suffered there, but you saw for yourself that she returned to us half-starved and aged beyond her years. I won't put her through that again."

Ulys ran the fingers of his right hand through his beard, considering. "I'll give the messenger a letter for your father explaining that she isn't to be hired out to anyone because you expect to need her yourself again soon. I'll even send along money for her

193

keeping, so he has less reason to ignore the request. Will that do?"

"I'd much rather have her remain here with me and the children while we await your return."

"That's not possible."

"Then, yes, it will do." Julia managed a smile. "And thank you, Ulys."

To her astonishment, he next handed her a thick roll of bills — six to eight hundred dollars from the weight of it. "Ulys, this is a small fortune," she exclaimed. "What on earth would you have me do with it?"

"Take care of it," he said. "You'll need it. It may be some time before I can give you any more, as I expect to be on active duty from now on."

Unsettled, she promised to do so. As soon as he left her, she put the roll of bills away for safekeeping and then set off to break the news to Jule and to begin packing.

Jule accepted General Grant's decision with practiced outward stoicism, but inside, unseen, hope warred with trepidation. Her heart soared to think that she might embrace her beloved Gabriel soon, but the general's letter seemed a flimsy weapon against the old master's stubbornness. She did not trust him to abide by Julia's wishes.

The next morning, Ulys's messenger arrived early to collect Jule. Lieutenant Aaron

Friedman was a tall, lanky officer with olive skin and dark curly hair, who curiously offered to carry her calico bundle — which she adamantly refused to relinquish — and extended his hand to assist her into the ambulance. Belying those kindnesses, as they rode to the dock, he said, "I'm only taking you to your master because General Grant expressly commanded it."

Jule said nothing, but only inclined her head in acknowledgment.

As they boarded the ship, a member of the crew directed the lieutenant to take Jule to the hold. "Absolutely not," he barked in reply, his height and uniform giving the illusion of greater authority than his rank commanded. "This is Mrs. General Grant's handmaid, and the general himself has ordered that she be given all due consideration."

Jule kept her features smooth but could not refrain from studying the lieutenant from the corner of her eye. Nothing of what he said was true, except that she was Mrs. Grant's maid, and he knew it.

The crewman hesitated before sending them to other quarters — still belowdecks, still small and windowless, but much better than the hold.

"Have you eaten?" the lieutenant asked after she looked the place over. He smiled boyishly and seemed extraordinarily pleased with himself. She was too bemused to do more than shake her head.

He produced a bundle of paper-wrapped sandwiches, the sort she recognized from the officers' mess, and he persuaded her to come above decks to dine in the fresh air. She hid her incredulity as he cheerfully engaged her in a mostly one-sided conversation, ignoring, or perhaps oblivious to, the curious or hostile glances of other passengers.

"You'd like my hometown, Columbus," he assured her, which struck her as rather odd, since he had known her only a few hours and had no idea what she might like or dislike. "Friendly, kind people everywhere. Helpful people. The best way to get there, if you're traveling on the river, is to disembark at Cincinnati. Do you know the city?"

When Jule wordlessly nodded, he went on to describe a church she ought to visit, the Zion Baptist Church on Third Street between Race and Elm. Finally curiosity compelled Jule to speak. "Why would a white man like you worship in a colored church?"

The lieutenant had just taken a bite of apple, and a laugh turned into a cough so suddenly that Jule thought he might be choking. He cleared his throat, shook his head, and grinned at her. "Oh, I've never worshipped there. I'm a Jew. But you, Miss Jule, you would find the sermons illuminating, I think."

Miss Jule. Astonished, she stared at him as

he rambled on about how one could travel from Cincinnati to Columbus and to parts farther north — and suddenly the light of understanding broke through her bewilderment. He regretted taking her back to her master because he was an abolitionist, not because he craved more warlike duty. He could not help her escape because of his sworn loyalty to General Grant, but if she should happen to have another chance, he hoped she would make the most of it.

She hung on his every word all the way to St. Louis, breaking in to murmur questions from time to time, committing every detail to memory.

Two days after Jule left Cairo, Julia, Anna, and the children reviewed the troops as they set out for battle. Julia's heart seemed to beat in time with the music of fife and drum as she watched the men form ranks and march to the landing. As the young officers hurried along, she overheard them cheerfully boasting to one another that they would win their spurs or a strawberry leaf, an eagle or a star — the insignia of the higher ranks to which they aspired.

"We'll all come to you to set them in place, Mrs. Grant," a lieutenant called to her in passing.

"And I shall be happy to do it," she declared, waving. "I'll have my needle and thread ready."

As the lieutenant's companions laughed and clapped him on the back, another young fellow shouted, "We're sure we all have your kind wishes, Mrs. Grant."

"Of course you do, as well as my prayers."

The men filed aboard the steamships, which looked grand and proud as they pulled away from the shore, their decks filled with eager soldiers, every railing adorned with bright flags waving in the wind.

"Is that Pa, Mamma?" asked Nellie, tugging on Julia's coat and pointing.

Julia shaded her eyes with a gloved hand and searched for Ulys, but to her disappointment, she did not find him. "I don't know, darling. I don't see him." They had exchanged private farewells at headquarters earlier that morning, but it would have been lovely to catch one last glimpse of him before he departed. She wished Jule were there to see for her.

"Is he going to be all right?"

Swiftly Julia bent to hug her daughter. "Yes, of course he is." She had told him in parting that she was sure he would return victorious. It was not a prophecy, just an ardent wish, but he had seemed glad to hear it all the same.

A few days after the troops set out, three of the steamers that had carried them up the Ohio River returned, bringing with them the wounded, the deceased, and the glorious news of Ulys's victory. Breathless from relief, Julia sank to her knees on the landing, her heart overflowing with gratitude to Almighty God. Kneeling, clasping her hands, she prayed for his continuous favor for her nation and her beloved husband.

She was terribly disappointed when she discovered that Ulys had not returned aboard one of the steamers, but he had sent her a letter telling her of his intention to attack Fort Donelson without delay. "Fred may accompany one of the staff officers to Fort Henry for a brief visit, if that would not make you too anxious," Ulys wrote.

The very thought of it filled Julia with apprehension, but Fred pleaded so earnestly that she eventually acquiesced. After subjecting him to a lengthy lecture about safety and responsibility, she let him depart the next morning with an officer she knew well and trusted, and by evening he returned bearing war trophies he had collected from the field of battle — a handful of grapeshot, two empty cigar boxes, and several pipes, which he generously divided among the other children, who regarded him as a hero.

Fred saved the best treasure, a small cannonball, for four-year-old Jesse, whose eyes widened with wonder as he accepted the gift. Jesse amused himself by rolling the cannonball back and forth on the windowsill, the rumble of iron upon wood strangely reminiscent of distant thunder — until suddenly it tumbled off the sill and landed on his foot. He cried out in pain, but Fred quickly exclaimed, "A soldier never cries, Jess." At that Jesse gulped back his sobs, clutched his injured foot in both hands, and sank trembling and pale to the floor. Julia immediately summoned the doctor, and to her relief, when he examined Jesse's foot he found no broken bones, only some vivid, painful bruising that would fade with time.

Julia had made up her mind to remain in Cairo as long as she could, but all too soon Ulys wrote to tell her that she must go to Covington at once and remain there until he sent word. Aboard the steamer to Cincinnati, by day Julia was preoccupied with the children, but at night she was overcome with loneliness. One evening, sitting alone on the deck, she felt so desolate that she buried her face in her hands and broke down in sobs, releasing into the night the unhappiness she struggled to conceal from the children throughout the long days.

"Are you quite all right, madam?"

With a start, Julia looked up to discover an elderly woman looking kindly down upon her. "Yes, yes," she stammered, suddenly ashamed. Other women had lost husbands, brothers, fathers, and sons in the previous week's fighting, and she was blubbering away over a little homesickness. She would have made a terrible soldier.

"Shall I call someone for you?"

"No, I'm quite fine, thank you." Forcing a smile, Julia rose and hurried away.

In Covington, she found Jesse Root Grant in excellent spirits, as well informed about Ulys's maneuvers in the field as many of his officers. He recited facts and statistics and compared his son's strategies with those of military geniuses of bygone eras, always to Ulys's advantage. For her part, Hannah confided that she did not worry as much about Ulys as she had in the Mexican War, when his inadvertent silence had caused her hair to go white. "I believe that Ulys has been raised up for the particular purpose of fighting this evil rebellion," she said with quiet certainty. "The same power that raised him up will protect him."

One afternoon in mid-February, Mary darted into the parlor where Julia and Jennie were sewing. "Have you not heard the great news?" she exclaimed, breathless and pink cheeked. "Richmond has fallen!"

"That is not and cannot be true," Julia declared, as Jennie gasped with delight and clapped her hands. "Richmond will fall only before Ulys and his army."

"Oh, Julia," Mary said, fondly exasperated. "We're all proud of Lyss, but does it matter which general takes Richmond as long as it falls?"

"I wish it were true, but Richmond hasn't fallen," insisted Julia.

Soon enough, news reports proved her right: It was Fort Donelson that had fallen, and to her beloved Ulys, in a joint effort with the navy. After enduring the Union assault for several days and failing to break through Ulys's lines, the Confederate commanders had realized that their position was hopeless. Confederate Brigadier General Simon B. Buckner, left in charge after his two superior officers relinquished their commands and fled, sent a message to Ulys proposing an armistice and the appointment of commissioners to settle the terms of his capitulation. Ulys's response was reprinted in all the Cincinnati papers. "No terms except an unconditional and immediate surrender can be accepted," Ulys had written with his usual brevity and directness. "I propose to move immediately upon your works."

General Buckner was said to have sent back a bitter, petulant reply, stating that Ulys's overwhelming forces compelled him, despite the "brilliant success of the Confederate arms yesterday, to accept the ungenerous and unchivalrous terms you propose."

"How can this rebel suggest that Ulys is anything less than a gentleman?" Julia protested, but her indignation was but a drop compared to the wave of exultation that swept through Covington, Cincinnati, and the entire Union. Here is a general who fights, the people declared in the streets and the parlors and in the press. Ulys's victories thoroughly rejuvenated the depressed morale of the people of the North, and soon his letter to General Buckner inspired a new nickname: Unconditional Surrender Grant.

The day after Fort Donelson fell, Ulys was promoted to major general — so Julia was astonished when, after making a quick trip to Nashville to consult with General Don Carlos Buell, he was accused of leaving his command without permission. Other bewildering accusations quickly sprang up — Ulys failed to maintain order in camp, he failed to communicate his plans to Commander of the Department of the Missouri Major General Henry W. Halleck, and he refused to answer Halleck's daily messages. Scarcely a month after his triumphs, Ulys was suspended from his command, and the expedition into Tennessee he had so diligently planned was assigned to another general.

To Julia's dismay, the controversy stirred up the old malicious lies about Ulys's sobriety, prompting army headquarters to order an investigation. No evidence of drunkenness could be found, and other officers rushed to defend him on the other charges, testifying with adamant certainty that Ulys had always sent General Halleck frequent reports, sometimes two or three a day.

Eventually the truth came out: After a Southern sympathizer employed in the telegraph office deserted, it was discovered that he had intercepted numerous messages that were supposed to have been sent between Ulys and General Halleck. Thus exonerated, Ulys was reinstated to his command in the middle of March, and he immediately joined his army in Savannah, Tennessee.

The uproar following the capture of Fort Donelson had barely subsided when Ulys and his brave army defeated the rebel forces at Shiloh in Tennessee. "Again another terrible battle has occurred in which our arms have been victorious," he wrote to Julia. "I got through all safe having but one shot which struck my sword but did not touch me."

Julia's heart thumped so hard it pained her. A strike upon his sword was still much too close.

A week later he wrote that General Halleck had arrived and had taken command, although Ulys and General Buell remained in charge of their separate armies. "I am looking for a speedy move, one more fight and then easy sailing to the close of the war," Ulys wrote. "I really will feel glad when this thing is over. The battle at this place was the most desperate that has ever taken place on the Continent and I don't look for another like it. I suppose you have read a great deal about the battle in the papers and some quite contradictory? I will come in again for heaps of abuse from persons who were not here."

As trainloads of wounded men were carried from the battlefield to hospitals, tales spread that the Confederate attack had caught Ulys entirely by surprise, that he had not established adequate defenses, that he had ineptly directed his forces, that green troops had turned cowardly and had refused to charge until their own guns were turned threateningly upon them. Ulys was blamed for the more than thirteen thousand killed, wounded, or missing on the Union side and nearly eleven thousand for the South; was called bloodthirsty, a butcher — charges that brought angry tears to Julia's eyes.

"If the papers only knew how little ambition I have outside of putting down this rebellion and getting back once more to live quietly and unobtrusively with my family, I think they would say less and have fewer falsehoods to their account," Ulys wrote to Julia two days before his fortieth birthday. "I do not look much at the papers now, and consequently save myself much uncomfortable feeling."

"Someone has to set the record straight about my boy," Jesse declared. His anger filled Julia with foreboding, but no prophetic dream warned her of his intentions. She learned along with everyone else in Cincinnati that he had forwarded a private letter from Ulys and another from Colonel Hillyer defending Ulys's actions at Shiloh to *The Cincinnati Commercial,* which immediately printed them. Rather than silencing Ulys's critics, the letters provoked more criticism as other newspapers picked up the story.

One day, Julia was alone in the Grants' parlor reading yet another scathing editorial in the *Cincinnati Daily Gazette* when Hannah appeared in the doorway. "You have a visitor," she said, showing in a tall, slender woman clad in black crepe. Despite her pale face and melancholy expression, she was stunningly beautiful.

Julia invited the woman to sit beside her on the sofa, where she introduced herself as the widow of Lieutenant Colonel Herman Canfield, one of the many brave Union officers who had perished at Shiloh.

"Oh, Mrs. Canfield," said Julia, stricken. "I'm so sorry for your loss. Is there anything I can do to help you?"

"No, there is not, and that is not why I wished to see you." The beautiful widow pressed her lips together, fighting back tears. "I've come because I must tell you of your husband's kindness to me."

Puzzled, Julia folded her hands in her lap and nodded for her to continue.

"A few days before the battle commenced,

I was seized by a strange, uncanny feeling that my husband desperately needed me, and I resolved to go to him." Mrs. Canfield hesitated. "You will think me a superstitious fool —"

"I think nothing of the sort," Julia assured her. "I've been known to have such feelings myself."

"I arrived in Shiloh on the evening of the first day of that dreadful fight, and I was told — and I had felt it in my heart all along as I traveled — that my husband was among the wounded and was at that moment lying in a hospital a few miles down the river. I despaired when I learned that I was forbidden to go to him, that it was against orders and absolutely impossible."

"How dreadful, after you had come so far!"

"As I stood there, utterly despondent, a cavalcade rode up, and I at once recognized General Grant and his staff. I saw, too, that the general was unable to dismount, but was helped off his horse and all but carried aboard his dispatch boat."

"What?" Julia exclaimed. "Was he wounded?"

Mrs. Canfield clasped her hand reassuringly. "I tried to see him, but the guard told me that I could not, that the general was injured. I hesitated, but my intense anxiety to go to my husband overcame all else, and I boldly passed by the guard and boarded the boat. As I approached the general, I saw the doctors cutting the boot off the general's foot."

"Oh, my goodness."

"I learned that the previous evening, his horse had stepped on a rolling stone and had fallen, landing upon his ankle. It hadn't troubled him all day, but when he dismounted, he was astonished to find his leg quite swollen and numb."

Julia felt faint. Had Ulys lost the leg? Was that what the grieving widow had come to tell her?

"I explained that my husband had been wounded and needed me and that I had been told I could not go to him. I begged the general to allow me to proceed." Mrs. Canfield took a quick, quavering breath. "Your gallant husband said, 'I will write my report at once, and you may go on the dispatch boat that will deliver it.' Paper and ink were brought, and as soon as the general had written and sealed his report, he wrote an order to pass me on the dispatch boat, and to grant me permission to visit my husband in the hospital. Then he bade me good-bye with his sincere hopes that my husband and I would soon be reunited."

"That is the General Grant I know," said Julia. "Did you reach your husband in time?"

Two large tears trickled down Mrs. Canfield's face. "I was too late, too late," she choked out. "I was conducted down an aisle between the cots in the hospital, and my escort paused and pointed to a figure on a cot, the blanket drawn up to cover the face. I knelt beside the cot and drew the blanket down and lay my hand upon my husband's bosom. He was still warm, but his great heart had ceased beating. The blood was clotted on his beard and breast." Her chin trembled, she took another deep breath — and then she could restrain her weeping no longer. "I think he might have lived if I had been near."

Julia embraced her, murmuring words of comfort even as her own tears began to fall. The poor, good woman — nothing Julia could say or do, no prayers or patriotic words about the lieutenant colonel's sacrifice, could ease her suffering.

When Mrs. Canfield's tears were spent, she composed herself and continued her tale. "I'm determined to devote my time to the wounded soldiers for the duration of the war," she said. "My husband might have lived if he had only had the services of a kind nurse. I hope to spare other wives and mothers this cruel, terrible grief."

"How noble you are!"

"No, not at all, not I. It's something I'm compelled to do."

"And I'm determined to help you." Excusing herself, Julia hurried upstairs to her bedchamber and retrieved the roll of bills Ulys had given her in Cairo. After briefly considering how much Ulys would insist she save for herself and the children, she divided the bills in half, made two rolls, put one away, and hurried back to the parlor with the second. "I hope this will help you purchase supplies and make your travel easier," Julia said, closing Mrs. Canfield's hands around the roll of bills.

"Mrs. Grant," she protested, astonished. "I didn't come seeking donations. My only intention was to tell you of your husband's great kindness. One sees such horrid things in the papers of this good man, and he has been greatly wronged, for in my hour of need he was so kind, so gentle, so full of sympathy."

"Yes, he is," said Julia, "and he would be the first to agree that you must take this offering for your work."

Eventually Mrs. Canfield agreed, and when she was quite restored to herself, and braced with tea and Hannah's wholesome bread and apple butter, they parted with embraces and promises to write. Julia knew that Mrs. Canfield would offer faithful service to the Union, and for a wistful moment, she wished she could join her.

Afterward, whenever the press vilified Ulys, Julia reminded herself of Mrs. Canfield's kind words and took heart. Although the Battle of Shiloh provoked many people to call for Ulys to be removed from his command, President Lincoln would not bow to their demands. "I can't spare this man," he was reported as saying. "He fights."

Chapter Ten

May–December 1862

At the end of April, Ulys's army advanced on Corinth, Mississippi, settling into a long, slow siege that rendered Ulys impatient and restless. He wrote of beautiful apple and cherry orchards blooming all around the encampment, but also of the tedium of routine duties and of hundreds of men dying of dysentery. He spent his evenings around the campfire with the other officers, smoking, sharing tales of the Mexican War, and playing whist and twenty-one. The attacks in the press continued, and it vexed Ulys that the men subject to his command could not help hearing of the ludicrous charges against him.

At his new headquarters in Memphis, Ulys met his family at the wharf, all smiles for the children and tender kisses for Julia. His beard, chestnut brown with tawny threads, was neatly trimmed, and the injury to his ankle had apparently fully healed, leaving not even a trace of a limp. "My dear little wife," he said as he embraced her, his voice a sigh of relief, and when he held her she could feel his strength and good health, but also his frustration and loneliness. Weather-beaten, he looked every bit of his forty years, and a troubled, wary look seemed permanently etched upon his features, but his eyes were as startlingly blue as ever, and they regarded her with the same love and admiration she had discovered there when she was a belle rather than a matron of thirty-six.

They had barely settled in Memphis when Ulys moved his headquarters to Corinth. When Julia and the children arrived a few days later, he sent an ambulance to meet them at the depot. Ulys rode on horseback alongside, reaching through the window for Julia's hand. "Did you miss me as much as I missed you?" he asked.

"I missed you more," she said warmly, smiling up at her beloved general.

Dusk was falling as they approached the Corinth encampment, the campfires alight, the rows of white tents illuminated like thousands of lanterns. "What are they singing?" Buck asked, crawling over Julia in his eagerness to listen.

"John Brown," said Fred, and soon Julia, too, could make out the familiar melody, the verses carried by perhaps a hundred voices, with what must have been almost the entire army joining in the choruses, so powerfully did the glorious anthem ring out.

Julia did not approve of John Brown, the white abolitionist who had been hanged for attempting to lead a slave uprising in Virginia a few years before, but it was a stirring tune, and as she listened, she realized that the lyrics were quite different from those she had heard before.

In the beauty of the lilies Christ was born
    across the sea,
With a glory in His bosom that transfigures
    you and me.
As He died to make men holy, let us die to
    make men free,
While God is marching on.
Glory, glory, hallelujah!
Glory, glory, hallelujah!
Glory, glory, hallelujah!
While God is marching on.

They were in the midst of the most anxious weeks of the war thus far, Ulys confided to Julia later that evening. The Army of the Tennessee had been ordered to guard all the territory acquired by the fall of Memphis and Corinth, dangerously extending Ulys's lines. He lacked sufficient reinforcements to form an attack, and guerrillas lurked in copses and hollows in every direction. Julia knew that his restless nature was better suited for waging an offensive campaign than for remaining constantly on guard throughout a tedious siege, but she hoped that having his family near would help him better endure the interminable waiting.

In July, Major General Halleck was promoted to general in chief of all the Union armies, and when he was called to Washington at the end of the month, Ulys was placed in command of the rebellious territory between the Mississippi and Tennessee Rivers from the Ohio River to northern Mississippi. He was charged with protecting miles of river, railroad, and telegraph lines, even though his forces were steadily diminished by orders to send troops to the East.

Julia was proud of her husband, certain that his new responsibilities reflected his superiors' increasing recognition of his worth. Yet her heart sank when Ulys found her in her sitting room one afternoon, invited her to sit beside him on the sofa, and gently told her that he suspected that the change in orders presaged a significant movement of the troops.

She knew before he spoke another word that he intended to send her away again.

White Haven buzzed with excitement when Julia's letter arrived announcing that she was bringing the children home for a brief visit. In recent months, Jule had been as close to content as she could have reasonably expected. She and Gabriel were together. The old master regularly hired her out, but only by the day and never to the Slates, so she was earning a little money of her own again. But Julia's visits home always disrupted the reassuring pattern of Jule's days, and upon her departure the pieces never quite settled back into their original places.

Her apprehension eased somewhat when Julia greeted her warmly upon her arrival and the children threw their arms around her and declared that they had missed her terribly. "I missed you too," she told them sincerely, hugging them in turn. She wondered how much longer they would love her; Dinah had warned her that white children outgrew their affection for their colored nurses over time, yet another heartbreak on her horizon.

In mid-September, word came of a fierce, bloody battle along a creek called Antietam in the far-off state of Maryland. The Union had declared victory, but most of Julia's neighbors claimed the battle had ended in stalemate, since Union general McClellan had allowed General Robert E. Lee's army to withdraw to Virginia without pursuit. Less than a week later, the St. Louis newspapers published a proclamation in which President Lincoln declared that "on the first day of January in the year of our Lord, one thousand eight hundred and sixty-three, all persons held as slaves within any State, or designated part of a State, the people whereof shall then be in rebellion against the United States shall be then, thenceforward, and forever free."

It was lawyer's language, the same sort of phrases Jule had heard Mr. Slate intone as he paced in his study preparing for a trial, but she understood enough of it to tuck the discarded newspaper under her skirt and smuggle it out to Gabriel. "What does it mean, exactly?" she asked later, sitting close beside him in the hayloft as he read.

His eyes shone and a slow smile spread across his face. "It means come the New Year, slaves in rebel territory will be free."

"Missouri too?"

"There were rebel militia in Missouri at the start of the war, and may still be." He set the paper aside and seized her hands. "Whether freedom comes in January for us or later, it will come. It has to. That's what General Grant's fighting for. He'll win, and when the war's done, slavery will have to end too, or the fighting never will."

"It can't come too soon," said Jule, more sharply than she intended. She was tired of waiting for Julia, for the old master, for the president, for whole hosts of other people to decide to set her free.

Gabriel raised her hand to his lips. "Keep listening, keep reading," he urged. "Learn all you can about what this means for us."

Jule did, and in the days that followed the

announcement, she realized that the new law would not affect the status of slaves in loyal Missouri. Even so, the old master and his eldest son, John, were furious that any slaves anywhere would be declared free.

"This is such an unfortunate development, isn't it?" Julia lamented one morning as Jule arranged her hair.

"How so, Miss Julia?"

"Well, the younger slaves have already been so demoralized since this dreadful rebellion began. What will it do to them to hear that soon, all the old comforts of slavery will pass away forever?"

Jule paused, but after a moment she resumed arranging Julia's chignon. "The old comforts of slavery," she said, a flat echo of her mistress. "You must mean the comforts the master's family enjoys."

"Those exist, certainly, but the comforts I refer to are those bestowed upon your people." Julia held her gaze in the mirror, her expression all earnest sympathy. "All your life you've had someone to look after you, to take care of you. You never need worry where your next meal is coming from, or whether there will be a roof over your head, or how you should spend your days. You need only to do as you're told, to obey your master or mistress, and all is well in your world."

"Unless I'm beaten." Jule set down the hairbrush, her expression hardening in the mirror above Julia's. "Unless my children are sold away from me. Unless the master decides to increase his property by getting a baby on me —"

"Jule," Julia exclaimed. "What's gotten into you? I'll have none of this vulgar talk."

The truth was vulgar, and cruel and painful to hear. That didn't make it any less true. "All I mean is —"

"How can you say such things? You have no children, and you've never been beaten, at least not in this house, and to suggest that Papa would —" Julia pressed her lips together and shook her head, too distressed to continue.

Jule was careful to keep her voice low and calm. "I was speaking of others and their hardships, Miss Julia, not myself."

"I can't help what goes on in other households. What would you have me do? Tell my neighbors how they should treat their servants?"

Jule put her head to one side as if she needed to give her mistress's words serious consideration, and then she nodded sagely. "That would be a good start."

"You don't understand, nor would I expect you to. That sort of thing simply isn't done."

"Shouldn't it be, though?" Jule countered. "And shouldn't you be the one to do it? Since your husband's the general fighting the war to end slavery?"

219

Julia clenched her hands together in her lap, a flush rising in her fair cheeks. "General Grant is fighting to preserve the Union. His mission is not to end slavery but to end the rebellion."

"Is that what you think or just what you say because it's expected?" Jule knew she ought to close her mouth and gaze meekly at the floor, but she had held back the questions and accusations too long, and once the floodgate was opened, she could not close it again. "What happened? Remember our ginger-and-cream days? You used to be the girl who asked questions, who spoke up when you saw wrongdoing."

"Jule —"

"When your papa said you can't ride this or that horse, you didn't say, 'Yes, sir.' You asked, 'Why?' When the missus told you to punish me for learning my letters, you said, 'I won't.' When your papa said you couldn't marry your lieutenant, you vowed you would someday. What happened to make you close your mind?"

"Stop it!" Julia bolted to her feet. "I am quite out of patience with you. No more of this, no more. Go call the children inside and be sure they wash before breakfast. As for myself, I have completely lost my appetite."

She waved Jule out of the room and shut the door behind her.

For a moment Jule stood with her hand on

the knob, her forehead resting against the door, heart pounding, wondering if she had gone too far, if she should hurry back into the room and beg forgiveness. Then something hardened within her. She had spoken too frankly, but she had said nothing untrue.

Julia was in the wrong. It was she who ought to beg forgiveness from Jule.

But instead of an apology, which would have astonished Jule, or a punishment, which she would have expected, Julia acted as if the incident had never happened. Only a new chill in her manner, a distance in her voice when she issued instructions, revealed her displeasure. And yet there was an element of uncertainty too, as if she did not understand the nature of their argument and wished desperately that it had never happened.

Julia was not so displeased with Jule that she wished to leave her behind when she and the children left White Haven. In late October, after General Grant led his armies to victories at Iuka and Corinth, he established his headquarters at Jackson and sent word for Julia to join him there. "You will accompany me," Julia told Jule evenly, not quite meeting her eye. "I will leave Fred, Buck, and Nellie in Covington with General Grant's parents. You will continue on with me to Jackson so you can look after Jesse."

"Yes, Miss Julia," Jule said quietly, for she knew it was pointless to protest.

On the night before her departure, Jule lay in Gabriel's arms in the loft, the hay crackling around them beneath the pallet they shared, the chirping of cicadas a forlorn accompaniment to the soft sighing of the autumn winds. Her heart ached with pain and uncertainty, not knowing when she would feel the warmth of his embrace again.

"Jule?"

"Yes, Gabriel?"

"You remember everything that lieutenant told you when he brought you here, everything about Cincinnati and how to find your way north?"

"Every word."

"After you leave here with Miss Julia and the children . . . if you get the chance, run."

"Not without you I won't."

"Jule, listen." He shifted in the darkness, rolling onto his side to gaze into her eyes firmly but lovingly as he traced the lines of her face with his hand. "I'm not likely to ever find myself aboard a steamer to Cincinnati."

"When we run, we run together," she replied. "If we can't, then I'll wait until the president frees slaves everywhere. I'm not going without you, so don't ask me again."

In Jackson, Ulys had chosen as his headquarters a sprawling old country residence, part frame house and part log cabin, with a long, low piazza on the southern exposure. Julia immediately set about making the unfamiliar place feel more like home, sorting out bedchambers for herself and Ulys, Jesse, and Jule; inspecting the kitchen; and introducing herself to the household staff, a single maid who assured Julia she could cook if need be.

The domestic flourishes were, perhaps, more for herself and Jesse than for Ulys. He was never one to fuss about his attire, dressing not as a general on parade but as a soldier in the field, a man who could expect exertion and mud and rough weather. His endurance had become legendary among his troops; he could outride every officer on his staff, he could go without food or sleep longer than his youngest and strongest men, and he seemed unaffected by the cold, heat, fatigue, and exposure to the elements that brought other soldiers staggering into shelter. Julia too was impressed by her husband's extraordinary fortitude, but when she was in camp, she wanted a proper home, even if it was only a tent.

Julia had not been long in residence when General Rawlins called to pay his respects. After the usual pleasantries, Rawlins said, "I wonder if you would have a word with the general on my behalf."

Julia had to laugh. "General, if he won't take your advice regarding a military matter, he's hardly likely to accept the same suggestions from me. In fact, that's more likely to prove to him that his original judgment was sound."

"This is too important not to make the attempt." Rawlins fairly crackled with agitation. "General Rosecrans ought to be relieved of duty."

He went on to describe the general's offenses, including an address he had recently published that had upset his officers, but as Julia listened, nodding, her heart filled with dismay. She liked General William Starke Rosecrans because he was handsome and brave, and because she knew Ulys liked him. To appease Rawlins, however, and in fond remembrance of his late wife, Emily, she agreed to bring his concerns to her husband.

Ulys hated to linger at the table, so as soon as he sat down to his noon lunch, she quickly passed along his assistant adjutant general's concerns. "Rosecrans is a brave and loyal soldier with the best of military training, the kind of man we can't spare," Ulys replied. "He's a fine fellow — a bit excited at present, but he'll soon come around all right."

Later, after Julia returned from visiting the soldiers on the sick list, five other officers called on her, echoing Rawlins's entreaties about General Rosecrans.

"I'm reluctant to part with him," Ulys admitted after Julia shared his officers' confidences. "I know what it's like to face this sort of criticism."

"Not quite this sort," Julia countered. "*You* never merited a word of the criticism spoken against you."

Ulys thanked her for the compliment, kissed her cheek, and returned to his office, his brow furrowed.

Not twenty minutes later, he returned to her sitting room, smiling broadly. "This is good news, very good news," he said, holding up a telegram. "Rosecrans is promoted and ordered to take command of the Army of the Cumberland. Now we can part on cordial terms."

Ulys's officers were pleased that all had been resolved to their satisfaction — and despite Julia's protests that she had played no part in it, they thanked her profusely for advocating their cause so persuasively. In the days that followed, she realized that she had unwittingly become the favorite intercessor for anyone with a difficult case to plead before the general.

From Jackson, Julia, Jesse, and Jule accompanied Ulys and his army to La Grange, Tennessee, following the line of the Mississippi Central Railroad. A week later, Ulys's cavalry captured Holly Springs, Mississippi, where, to minimize the risk of long munition and supply lines in enemy territory, he decided to establish a depot.

Ulys had gone ahead with his army, and Julia's escort was delayed several days, so by the time her little household arrived in Holly Springs, Ulys had already moved on. He wrote to tell her that he greatly regretted not meeting her, and he promised she could join him in Oxford as soon as the railroad was repaired.

Holly Springs bustled with activity despite the cold, which had frozen the muddy roads into hard, furrowed avenues where wagon wheels had passed during an icy rainstorm the night before. "Will you see it for me?" Julia asked Jule as they rode along. Jule dutifully described the signs of Ulys's preparations for the anticipated thrust toward Vicksburg — a long train of boxcars loaded with clothing and rations ready to be shipped to the field, bales of cotton piled in the court house and the public square, warehouses full almost to overflowing with essential supplies. "It seems a charming sort of place despite all this frenzy," Jule concluded, with a reassuring smile that told Julia that the ice between them had thawed. "Safe and hospitable, or so it looks to me."

Ulys's staff had arranged very nice lodgings in the fine house of Harvey W. Walter, a lawyer who had left Holly Springs to become a Confederate officer. He had placed his residence, a large, new, Greek Revival mansion with Gothic towers, in the care of a Mrs. Govan, whose husband, son, and brother-in-law had joined the Confederate army. Despite their political differences over secession, Julia found her landlady a fine, noble woman. She and the other ladies of the household — her two daughters and her daughter-in-law, all displaced from their own home after it had been commandeered as a hospital — had waited up late to receive Julia and Jesse upon their arrival, and served them a much welcome supper before showing them to their apartment.

"Breakfast will be about nine o'clock," Mrs. Govan said in parting. "I will have it announced to you."

Julia slept comfortably and woke refreshed, and in the morning after Jule had tended to their toilets, Julia and Jesse joined the family for breakfast. Jesse was funny and charming, the Govan ladies were excellent conversationalists, and Julia felt herself utterly at home, except for Ulys's absence. After the servants cleared the dishes away and Jule came for Jesse, Julia rose from the table with the family and, without thinking, turned toward the drawing room where she had been received the night before. Suddenly Mrs. Govan stepped between Julia and the door. "Excuse me, Mrs. Grant," she said gently, placing a smooth, white hand on the doorknob. "I have set aside another drawing room for your use."

For a moment Julia had forgotten that she was not a welcome guest but the wife of the occupying general. She was the enemy. "Thank you," she managed to say, and waited for Mrs. Govan to indicate the proper sitting room for chagrined Yankee ladies.

She never again entered the private family apartments except by special invitation. The ladies of the household did not neglect her entirely, however; from time to time they visited her in her drawing room, and on one occasion, when they learned that Julia had never heard of any of their favorite songs, they gathered a few friends together and invited her into the family drawing room for a concert. Julia had never heard ladies' voices ring out so grandly except in church, nor with such feeling, power, pathos, and enthusiasm. But oh, the lyrics! They sang "Dixie," of course, which was harmless enough, but also "God Save the South," with its appeal to heaven to "Lay Thou their legions low, roll back the ruthless foe, Let the proud spoiler know God's on our side." One lady was so moved that she began to weep during the chorus of "The Battle Cry of Freedom" — "Our Dixie forever! She's never at a loss! Down with the eagle and up with the cross!" — and she practically shouted the last verse:

While our boys have responded
And to the fields have gone,
Shout, shout the battle cry of Freedom!
Our noble women also

228

Have aided them at home,
Shout, shout the battle cry of Freedom!

"My," Julia said, breathless, when the ladies had finished and stood watching her expectantly, awaiting her verdict. "You certainly do shout out your own battle cry quite . . . melodiously."

"You must come again and listen to us," said a friend of Mrs. Govan's.

"No, never again," Julia exclaimed, rising. "It was bad enough that I listened to your rebel songs once. I would be a traitor indeed if I listened a second time."

She fled the room, the sound of amused laughter following her down the hall.

Mrs. Govan was too gracious to bear a grudge, and that same afternoon, she invited Jesse to play with her own young son, and the boys became good friends. Encouraged by her reluctant landlady's kindness, when she needed alterations made to a favorite gown, Julia asked her to recommend a dressmaker.

"I know just the one," Mrs. Govan replied. "Would you like me to take you to her tomorrow?"

"Oh, yes, please," said Julia. "I would very much enjoy the company."

The following morning shortly after breakfast, Mrs. Govan escorted Julia to the dressmaker's shop. As soon as she crossed the threshold, Julia discovered that word of her visit must have preceded her, for she found nearly a dozen ladies already present, a few who apparently had business of their own with the seamstress, but others who apparently had come only to satisfy their curiosity regarding the Yankee general's wife.

Julia soon had them engaged in friendly conversation, scrupulously avoiding the subject of their favorite music. The dressmaker was deftly attending to Julia's alterations when one of the ladies asked, "You are Southern, are you not?"

"No," Julia replied. "I am from the West. Missouri is my native state."

"Yes, we know," said a gray-haired woman in small round spectacles, smiling with disdain, "but Missouri is a Southern state. Surely you are Southern in feeling and principle."

"No, indeed," Julia said, lifting her chin. "I'm the most loyal of the loyal."

"But you own a slave," exclaimed a younger, dark-haired woman in a yellow dress. "You can't be for the Union and for slavery both."

"The Yankee aggression against the South is unconstitutional," the bespectacled woman declared, and a chorus of approving murmurs went up from the Southern ladies.

"I cannot speak to that," said Julia testily. "I don't know a thing about this dreadful

Constitution."

The other ladies stared, astonished. "Why, surely you've studied it," said Mrs. Govan.

"No, I have not," said Julia. "I wouldn't know where to look for it even if I wished to read it, but I do know that the people of the North believe it's unconstitutional for any of the states to secede. How useful a document can it be, if it's subject to such vastly different interpretations?"

As the ladies exchanged glances, Julia, much embarrassed, resolved to become as knowledgeable about her government as were the ladies who had rebelled against it.

Northern ideals descended anew in the person of Jesse Grant, who unexpectedly arrived in Holly Springs to escort Julia and his grandson to Ulys in Oxford.

Full of misgivings, Julia instructed Jule to pack sufficiently for a few days away. She considered leaving Jule behind, but she was afraid that some unscrupulous person might decide that she had been abandoned and put her to work, or worse yet, assume that she was a runaway and sell her off deep into rebel territory. So Julia steeled herself for Jesse's sanction and summoned the carriage to take them to the depot, informing Mrs. Govan that they would soon return.

At the depot, the elder Jesse greeted his namesake with great delight and Julia with a perfunctory kiss on the cheek, sparing a grimly sympathetic nod for Jule as she left them to sit in the rear with a few other colored travelers.

Julia soon discovered that Jesse had not traveled alone, but in the company of three gentlemen, whom he introduced as the brothers Harman, Henry, and Simon Mack, prominent clothing manufacturers from Cincinnati. Julia's polite, circumspect questions availed her little, except the knowledge that they were of the Hebrew faith, and that they were intelligent, courteous, and generously tolerant of little Jesse's exuberant antics. She also discerned that Ulys was unaware of his father's traveling companions.

Ulys had sent an ambulance to meet them at the depot, and he was waiting outside headquarters when they arrived. "Jess, you little rascal, are you glad to see me?" he asked, snatching up his son and tossing him into the air. He kissed Julia and shook his father's hand, and although he seemed surprised to discover his father's entourage, he welcomed the men cordially as each was introduced. "As my father's friends," he added, "you're welcome to join us for dinner."

"We'd be delighted," said Simon Mack, and his brothers readily agreed.

Later, over beef, canned vegetables, rice, bread, coffee, and condensed milk at a private table in the officers' mess, the Mack brothers

232

praised Ulys for his handling of the war, but since Ulys was ever reluctant to speak of himself or to discuss military strategy, Jesse soon turned the conversation to the news from Cincinnati, which prompted the subject of the brothers' clothing business.

"Our company has suffered since the rebellion began," Henry Mack admitted. "Our mills need cotton to weave the cloth from which we make our clothing, but embargoes and blockades have made cotton a rare commodity in the North."

"So I've heard," said Ulys, but Julia suspected no one but she recognized the irony. The authority to grant cotton-trading permits so that Northern manufacturers could purchase cotton from loyal Unionists in the South resided with Secretary of the Treasury Salmon P. Chase, but the enforcement of it fell to military officers in the field.

"We have associates in the South, loyal Union men we've known since before the war, with cotton to sell and nowhere to sell it," said Simon Mack.

"If you would provide my friends here with a cotton-trading permit," Jesse said, shifting eagerly in his chair, "I could help them arrange to transport it to New York, and from there to the mills."

Julia stole a glance at her husband, whose features had not changed expression, though his cheeks had become florid. "At a tidy profit, I don't doubt," Ulys replied in a level voice.

As Jesse shrugged, embarrassed to be caught out, Harman Mack quickly said, "Mr. Grant has agreed to become our partner in this venture, so it is only right for him to earn a commission."

"How much?" Ulys asked.

"Twenty-five percent of the profits."

Abruptly Ulys stood, his back stiff, his eyes bright with anger. "It is unfortunate that you will all be disappointed." In two strides he was at Julia's side, and she quickly rose and took the arm he offered her. "If you'll excuse us, gentlemen."

Ulys waited until they were safely alone in their quarters before unleashing his anger. "My father is determined to make his fortune from my position," he stormed. "I can't allow that. I can't bring the taint of scandal upon my command."

"Of course not."

"Julia —" Suddenly he strode to the door. "Julia, I'm sorry, but I must resolve this immediately. I might not be back until late."

Julia promised to wait up, but he did not return until long after she had put young Jesse to bed and had dismissed Jule for the night. "I've arranged for my father and his friends to depart on the first train North, and I've written an order that will solve this problem once and for all," he informed her as he undressed and settled into bed.

In the morning, Julia devised for her son a tour of the encampment so that Ulys would not be disturbed. Bundling Jesse in his warmest clothes, Julia took him by one hand, Jule by the other, and together they went exploring. Each camp was new and enthralling to Jesse, though they all looked much the same to Julia, but she and Jule both enjoyed his delight, and hours later, when they headed back to meet Ulys for lunch, they were all red cheeked, breathless, and happy from exertion.

Just as they reached headquarters, a man called out, "Mrs. Grant, may I have a word?"

She turned to discover a man in a long black coat, black hat, and white minister's collar hurrying toward her. "Reverend Briggs," she greeted him. "How delightful to see you again. How are the sheep in your vast flock?"

Reverend Briggs was one of the tallest men in camp, in his early sixties, with a slight stoop to his shoulders that suggested many a long night bent over his Bible with a pen in hand, composing a sermon. "Some of them are quite distressed today, Mrs. Grant, and not for the usual reasons."

"I'm sorry to hear that. Is there anything I can do?"

The minister rubbed his hands together; she saw that they were red and chapped and made a mental note to procure him some warm gloves and one of Jule's miraculous salves. "I certainly hope so. The men know of your kindness, and of your religious devotion, and they trust that you empathize with people of many different faiths."

"We are all God's children," Julia said, regarding Reverend Briggs curiously while keeping an eye on Jesse, who was not one to remain sedately at his mother's side while she conversed with another adult. Fortunately, Jule, ever watchful, followed after as he began to wander. "Whether we are Methodist or Lutheran or even Papists."

"Or Hebrew?"

"Yes, of course."

Reverend Briggs looked relieved. "Then, in the spirit of religious tolerance, I hope that you might speak to General Grant on behalf of our hundreds of soldiers of the Jewish faith. They are to a man loyal, dutiful soldiers."

The minister's vehemence caught Julia by surprise. "I'm sure they are. What can I do to help them?"

"As you may well imagine, the general's order has upset them greatly." His voice was clipped and hurried with unmistakable anger. "Nevertheless, they're determined to do their duty, once they understand it. Are General Grant's Jewish officers and men to hold to their original commitment to the United

States Army, or should they obey the general's new order? They cannot, as the general must surely realize, do both."

"Reverend," said Julia, startled, "I'm sorry, but I don't understand. I've been out since breakfast and I know nothing of any new order."

"My apologies. I assumed you knew. It's the talk of the camp." The minister gestured toward the far end of the headquarters piazza, where notices were posted. A crisp new page had been tacked up to a column, the lower corners rustling in the wind.

"Jule, will you take Jesse inside?" asked Julia, gathering her skirts and climbing the stairs. "Please change him out of his muddy clothes and give him his lunch in the kitchen."

"But I want to eat with Papa," Jesse protested.

"You'll see him at suppertime." Jule gave him a winning smile and extended a hand. "Have lunch with me, and I'll finish that story I started last night."

Jesse beamed and took her hand, and as she led him inside, she and Julia exchanged a worried, wary glance before Julia strode down the piazza to read Ulys's order.

Headquarters 13th Army Corps,
Department of the Tennessee,
Oxford, Miss. Dec. 17 1862.
GENERAL ORDERS, NO. 11

The Jews, as a class violating every regulation of trade established by the Treasury Department, and also Department orders, are hereby expelled from the Department within twenty-four hours of the receipt of this order.

Post Commanders will see that all of this class of people be furnished passes and required to leave, and any one returning after such notification will be arrested and held in confinement until an opportunity occurs of sending them out as prisoners, unless furnished with permit from headquarters.

No passes will be given these people to visit headquarters for the purpose of making personal application for trade permits.

By Order of Maj. Gen. U. S. Grant:
Jno. A. Rawlins
Ass't Adj't Genl.

"Oh, no, Ulys, what were you thinking?" Julia murmured. Quickly she turned back to the minister. "I assure you, I'll speak to the general, and I'll advocate for the Hebrews among your flock. I'll try to convince him to rescind the order altogether."

"Thank you very much, Mrs. Grant," the minister said. "The men have the utmost faith in you, and I know now that it was well placed."

"That remains to be seen." She bade him good afternoon and hurried inside.

Ulys was late coming to the table. Julia had no appetite, so after they said grace, she kept her hands folded in her lap while Ulys tucked in. "I read your new order expelling the Jews," she said.

He eyed her warily while he chewed and swallowed. "From your tone I gather you wish to register an opinion."

"I do. I must." She took a deep breath. "Ulys, I would never second-guess your decisions on the battlefield, but this order — it is scarcely to be believed. It's wrong. It's obnoxious."

His eyebrows rose. "Obnoxious?"

"Yes, Ulys. Obnoxious and offensive and unjust. Reverend Briggs called to express his grave concerns. Did you forget that hundreds of Jews are serving in your own army? Did you consider how your order would affect their morale?"

Thunderstruck, Ulys set down his fork and sat back in his chair, and she had her answer. "I didn't mean all Jews," he said. "Only those involved in the cotton trade."

"Your order clearly stated, 'The Jews, as a class.' Oh, Ulys. These men have served

239

honorably, risking their own lives for the Union, and you've shamed them. If there are certain Jews who have committed offenses, then by all means punish those individuals, but you cannot condemn an entire race, the good with the bad."

"You're a fine one to speak of condemning an entire race."

Julia felt heat rise in her face, for she knew he spoke of slavery. "That's not at all the same. You know this order is really about your father and the Mack brothers."

Ulys pushed back his chair and rose from the table. "I believe you're a woman of limited understanding."

"And I believe," Julia replied shakily, "that we have both today discovered that the one we love is far less perfect than we imagined them to be."

In the days that followed, Julia took little comfort in learning through Reverend Briggs and other sympathetic officers that Ulys's generals were almost insubordinately slow to carry out his order and expel the Jewish men serving in their ranks. Even Ulys soon seemed to regret his decision. "I've heard talk that some generals aren't carrying out the order because they believe it's illegal," he told her as they lingered over breakfast. "I'm not certain that it's illegal, but I am beginning to think that it was wrong."

"Then rescind it," she urged, reaching for

his hand.

He managed a wry smile. "Make a strategic withdrawal?"

"Call it whatever you like, as long as you call it back."

Suddenly Rawlins burst into the room. "General, sir, you're needed at once," he said, telegram slips clutched in his hand. "The rebels have captured Holly Springs."

CHAPTER ELEVEN

December 1862–April 1863

Throughout the morning, grim reports of Confederate general Earl Van Dorn's whirl- wind attack on Holly Springs continued to filter in, shocking Julia with news of the capture of the entire garrison of twelve hundred Union soldiers. Munitions, food, and forage had been confiscated, warehouses destroyed. After capturing the depot, General Van Dorn's soldiers had burned and plun- dered the town for hours, turning it into a veritable inferno, cheered on by delighted Southern ladies who had emerged from their homes into the frosty dawn still clad in their dressing gowns, clapping their hands and shouting encouragement to the raiders. Confederate officers learned that Julia was boarding at the Walter residence and raced there on horseback to apprehend her, but upon discovering that she was no longer there, they settled for capturing her horses and burning her carriage.

"If General Grant had not summoned you to Oxford," said Jule, visibly shaken. "If we had still been in Holly Springs when the raiders came —"

"Let's not speak of it," Julia interrupted, feeling faint. She could imagine it all too well — herself sitting on the floor of a dark prison cell, comforting a terrified Jesse; Jule snatched away and sold off into the Deep South, never to be seen again.

Ulys quickly organized a response, sending his calvary to drive Van Dorn away, dispatching teams into the countryside to gather food and forage. But Julia knew that replenishing their supplies would only partially restore all that had been lost in the raid. Communications had been badly disrupted, and Ulys had been forced to abandon his main line of attack into Vicksburg, a city essential to the rebel defenses because it connected regions of the Confederacy separated by the Mississippi. The city occupied the first high ground near the river below Memphis as well, and it was the origin of important railway lines leading into all points of the South. If Vicksburg fell, the Confederacy would eventually follow.

Ulys soon reestablished his headquarters in Holly Springs, but not in the Walter house. William Henry Coxe, a cotton planter who represented himself as a Union man, invited Ulys to occupy his home, a lovely four-year-old Gothic villa on Salem Avenue.

As soon as Julia settled her small household into their new accommodations, she called on her former landlady, concerned for the family's well-being after the frightful raid. Mrs. Govan invited her in for coffee — the last they had, she remarked with a wistful smile. "When the raiders came for you, I said that you had already left to meet General Grant in Oxford, which was true." Mrs. Govan smiled as she stirred a scant pinch of sugar in her coffee. "They then demanded I relinquish your personal effects. I said that you had taken everything with you, which was not entirely true."

Mrs. Govan beckoned to a servant and issued instructions to load Julia and Jesse's trunks onto Mrs. Govan's carriage.

"You saved our belongings," Julia exclaimed, wishing, not for the first time, that their husbands fought on the same side. "I had given them up for lost. Thank you very much indeed."

"I would have saved your horses and carriage too, if I could have hidden them."

Soon thereafter, in consideration of the courtesy shown his wife, Ulys ordered a guard placed upon Mrs. Govan's home and issued a guarantee against search, trespass, or devastation by federal parties for the remainder of the war.

On Christmas Eve, Mrs. Govan sent Julia a fine turkey and several grouse for the Grants' holiday dinner. "I wish I could return the compliment with some delicacies from the North," Julia fretted to Jule, "but these days our mess is indifferent at best. All the nice things I brought with me from St. Louis are long gone."

"Not everything," said Jule. "You still have a few jars of quince jelly from White Haven."

"Where?"

"At the bottom of your trunk. I wrapped the jars for safekeeping in the pieces of that quilt you're never going to finish."

"I certainly shall finish it someday." Julia had begun the patchwork quilt as a bride, but what with raising the children, her persistent headaches from eyestrain, and many tasks to occupy her time, she sewed on it only infrequently. Ulys teased that she took it with her everywhere, and yet it never came any closer to completion. It had become something of a family joke, common ground between Dents and Grants.

"Don't you find it curious," Jule remarked, "that a lady who can see into the future often can't see what's right in front of her?"

Abruptly Julia stopped searching through the trunk, sat back on her heels, and frowned up at Jule, exasperated. "I'm going to give you the benefit of the doubt and assume you're still referring to the overlooked jelly."

"Of course," said Jule, feigning innocence, but the determined set to her mouth betrayed her. "What else would I be talking about except your poor vision, and how much good it does you when I see for you?"

"What else indeed." Usually Jule was better able to conceal her discontent, which had increased steadily ever since President Lincoln's Emancipation Proclamation had gone into effect. Jule thought she should be free too, and she stubbornly refused to accept the wording of the document and facts of geography: Papa was exempt from the decree since Missouri was not in rebellion. By law, Jule was still a slave, and by choice, she had become an ever less manageable one.

"However the jelly came to be spared," Julia said briskly as she unearthed the jars from their patchwork nest, "it will make a wonderful gift."

She arranged the four jars in a basket, cushioned in a bed of pretty fabric, and sent Jule off to deliver her gift to Mrs. Govan.

Van Dorn's raid had disrupted communications, but word of Ulys's dreadful Order No. 11 had spread nonetheless. As Jewish families within the Department of the Tennessee were forced from their homes, rabbis and other influential Jewish leaders throughout the North lodged official protests. Delegations from Cincinnati and Louisville had met with President Abraham Lincoln at the White House, and soon thereafter, General Halleck telegraphed Ulys, "A paper purporting to be a Genl Order No. 11 issued by you Dec 17th has been presented here. By its terms it expels all Jews from your Dept. If such an order has been issued, it will be immediately revoked."

Ulys promptly had Rawlins issue another order declaring, "By direction of the General in Chief of the Army at Washington the General Order from these Head Quarters expelling Jews from this Department is hereby revoked."

Julia privately rejoiced, and she knew from Ulys's haggard looks that he deeply regretted the entire affair and wished it could be expunged from the pages of history. "I fear that when this war is done, all I will be remembered for is my shameful behavior toward the Jews in this one moment of anger," he confided one evening as she nursed him through a particularly severe sick headache.

"That is not all you will be remembered for," Julia had consoled him, entirely certain of it, and ever mindful of her mother's prophecy that someday his true greatness would be known to all.

Julia's household remained in Holly Springs into the New Year, but after repairs to the railroad through Grand Junction were completed in early January, Ulys moved his headquarters fifty miles northwest to Memphis. Upon their arrival, Ulys took rooms for the family at the Gayoso House, a gracious hotel on Main Street, and established his offices in a bank building nearby. The Gayoso was a fine establishment, the rooms comfortable, the staff courteous if aloof, but the ladies of the city were openly hostile to the Yankee occupiers, and Julia had little hope of forming cordial acquaintances as she had in Holly Springs.

A few days after their arrival, Ulys left Memphis, having resolved to relieve General John A. McClernand of his command in Arkansas and to lead the expedition upon Vicksburg himself. A week later he returned to Memphis to make the necessary arrangements for securing the rear territory before moving on Vicksburg. On the morning of his departure, he had solemnly told Julia that the real work of the campaign to capture Vicksburg was about to begin. "I don't know how often I might be able to see you and the children until the city falls," he warned, taking her hands.

"I understand," she replied, smiling bravely. "Ulys, you know how much I long to see Fred, Buck, and Nellie again. If you're going to be away indefinitely, should I not go to them?"

He brought her hands to his lips and agreed that a visit might be possible, and a few days later he wrote from Young's Point, Louisiana,

"I shall not return to Memphis until the close of this campaign. You had better make your visit to the children at once. As soon as I am stationary I will write to you to join me." Happy tears filled Julia's eyes as she imagined embracing her three eldest children again. She would have departed at once, but various arrangements had to be made first, and the vagaries of the post complicated their planning. Ulys wanted Fred to accompany him as he had in Springfield in the early months of the war, and Fred, who seemed destined to become a military man like his father, was very eager to go. As for Buck, Nellie, and little Jesse, Ulys preferred for Julia to take them back to Memphis so they would be nearby in case an opportunity came for them to visit him. Finally everything was in place, and by the end of March, Julia and all four of her children had settled happily into larger quarters in the Gayoso House, where they awaited a summons from Ulys to visit him at his headquarters near Vicksburg.

Fred did not remain with them long. The day after the children arrived in Memphis, Colonel Hillyer escorted Fred and his own son to Ulys's encampment. "Fred is looking well and seems as happy as can be at the idea of being here," Ulys wrote, despite a terrible storm that had delayed the travelers at Lake Providence. He assured Julia that he would require Fred to read every day and study his arithmetic, and write to her at least twice a week. "Kisses for yourself and children dear Julia," he ended his letter. She hoped it would not be long until he could deliver those kisses himself rather than through the post.

At long last, Ulys wrote with instructions for Julia to bring the children on the next boat for a few days' visit.

How wonderful it was to have her whole family around her once more! Fred looked dashing in the uniform she had made for him, wearing a sword with a yellow sash at his side. He had a clever little Indian pony to ride, he shared the soldiers' mess, and he slept on a cot in his father's tent. "He never knows what it is to be afraid," Ulys confided proudly when Fred couldn't overhear.

"A little healthy fear might be prudent," Julia reminded him, and Ulys assured her yet again that he kept Fred well out of harm's way.

They toured the camp, and all the officers they met paid their kindest regards to Julia. She received them graciously, admired the encampment, and inspected a canal that the men had apparently been digging and reinforcing for many days. "They named it after me," Ulys remarked.

A dubious honor, Julia thought, considering that the river had flooded the canal and had filled it with backwater and sediment. It was a remarkable feat of engineering — but Julia could see no point to it whatsoever.

She waited until Jule had led the children off to their lunch before she unburdened herself. "Why don't you move on Vicksburg at once?" she asked as they strolled along a well-worn path between regimental banners. "Do stop digging this silly canal. You can't possibly mean to use it."

"General McClernand before me was charged to widen and deepen this canal," Ulys replied, amused. "President Lincoln navigated the Mississippi in his younger days and he understands the river. He sets much store by this endeavor."

"Well, I think it's a waste of time and effort."

Ulys laughed heartily — and the sound reminded her how long it had been since she had last heard him laugh. "It's true that I won't use the canal," he admitted. "I never expected to, but it served its purpose by giving the men something to do while I waited for the waters to subside. It also gave any observers something to watch while I made plans elsewhere."

"I suppose you had to give the reporters something to write about," Julia acknowledged. "If the papers proclaimed that absolutely nothing was going on here, the people of the North would be calling for your head."

"And I would be so bored that I might willingly let them take it. I only hope the Confederates observing us from Vicksburg won't realize it's a ruse as quickly as you did."

"Don't give them enough time to figure it out. Move upon Vicksburg now and you'll take the city."

Ulys's eyebrows rose. "I suppose you have a plan of action to propose?"

"I do. Mass your troops in a solid phalanx at a point north of the fortress, rush upon it, and the enemy will be obliged to surrender."

"I'm afraid your plan would involve great loss of life without any certainty of success. I'm sorry, Julia, but I can't adopt it." Ulys halted and took both her hands in his. "You needn't worry. I'll move upon Vicksburg, and I'll take it too."

"I know you will, but when?"

"When the time is right and not an hour before. You must never forget that each and every one of my soldiers has a mother, wife, or sweetheart whose life is as dear to them as mine is to you."

"But Adjutant General Lorenzo Thomas has been sent to relieve you for inaction. Everyone in Memphis talks of it."

"Then everyone in Memphis is wrong." He kissed her cheek and cupped her chin in his hand. "The president sent Adjutant General Thomas here to devise a plan for taking care of the contraband — the newly freed slaves."

"Are you sure?" asked Julia. "Perhaps that's

another ruse."

"I'm sure. We've already spoken about it."

"Thank goodness." Julia sighed and pressed a hand to her brow. "I can't tell you what a relief this is."

"I didn't realize you were so concerned about the plight of freedmen."

"Don't tease, Ulys. You know I mean that I'm glad you aren't going to be relieved of your command." She thought for a moment. "Although I do feel for the slaves. I can only imagine how it must feel to find oneself suddenly at liberty after a lifetime of servitude. Where does one even begin? It must be terrifying."

"But also exhilarating." Ulys studied her. "I'm glad that you *can* imagine how they might feel, Julia. Try to do more of this." Before Julia could ask him what he meant, he added, "I'm also glad you've arrived in time to witness the running of the blockade."

Julia gasped and seized his arm. "Is that what you mean to do?"

Ulys nodded. "I've ordered three transports prepared. Tonight after dark, they'll go silently down the river as far as possible, then put on all steam, fly past Vicksburg and its batteries, and end up exactly where I want to use them, south of the city."

"Are you going with them?"

"Not this time. I thought we could watch

from the river as they set out, though, if you'd like."

Julia nodded eagerly, her heart pounding with excitement — even as she realized that Ulys had let her go on and on urging him to action, and had even pretended to consider her strategy, though all the while he intended to move that very evening.

"Admiral David Porter insists on taking two or more gunboats as escort and to return the rebel fire," said Ulys. "He's a gallant fellow, and he says it would look bad if they ran past without returning the rebel broadside."

Julia felt a swift thrill of alarm. "Then the gunboats will be mostly for show?"

"Mostly," Ulys agreed, but he had hesitated a moment too long, and she understood what he did not say: This was a military exercise, and although every precaution would be taken, the potential always existed for something to go dangerously awry.

She was ashamed that she had, even for a moment, considered the running of the blockade a spectacle for her entertainment, like the foolish citizens of Washington City who had set out from the capital in carriages with picnic hampers to watch the Battle of Bull Run. She was Mrs. Grant, the general's wife, and she had seen enough of war to know better.

As evening approached, Ulys escorted Julia and the children aboard the *Henry Von Phul,* where they were met by many officers and several of their wives. The Grants dined with them on board the transport, and after nightfall, the ship moved out on the river just out of range of the rebel batteries on the bluffs high above the opposite shore.

Everyone, including the children, quietly stole out onto the deck into the clear, moonless night, crowding the rail, shawls and overcoats drawn close against the night air and the steady wind. They watched as the Union flotilla stealthily advanced from Milliken's Bend, a thick, black mass lost in shadow.

Suddenly the rebel battery between Vicksburg and Warrenton roared to life, and an enormous splash rose just ahead of Admiral Porter's flagship. Then a shower of detonations boomed all along the line, rockets burst fore and aft, and geysers of water shot into the air and rained down upon them, sparkling in the lights from the rockets and shells.

"Pa!" Jesse shouted, clutching his father's leg. The Union gunboats ran close to the bluffs and opened fire, but the rebel assault continued unabated. Again and again the flotilla was hit, yet it moved ever forward. Nellie shrieked and buried her face in Julia's skirt; gaze riveted on the transports, flinching at every explosion, Julia stroked her daughter's head and murmured comforts lost in the thunder of cannon. Fred and Buck stood together on her other side, pale, open-mouthed with awe, determined to stand their ground though they jumped at each scream of the rockets.

Suddenly a ten-inch shell pierced the boiler of the Union transport ship *Henry Clay* and it went up with an earsplitting bang. Julia watched in horror as fire spread to its barges, sending up sheets of flame. All the while, more and more light shone down upon the ships in the river, as if day were breaking in sudden increments. Sulfurous smoke filled the air. Tearing her gaze from the transports, instinctively pulling Nellie closer, Julia looked to the opposite shore and saw that the rebels had lit bonfires and set houses ablaze on the east bluff to illuminate the ships on the river below.

And yet the Union flotilla pushed on, though the rebels poured shot and shell down upon them — and suddenly she realized that for some time, the barrage had struck only water. The gunboats and transports had passed out of range. The deadly batteries fell silent. The fiery beacons on the east bluffs were extinguished. A murmur of excitement went up from the officers aboard the *Henry Von Phul,* but Julia waited, her gaze flitting from Ulys's face to the bluffs to the darkness into which the flotilla had disappeared.

The sulfurous smoke dissipated. From the riverbanks, katydids and frogs resumed their summer songs.

"Admiral Porter is to be congratulated," Ulys said quietly.

The *Henry Von Phul* retreated to a more prudent distance to await official reports from Admiral Porter. Miraculously, although there were numerous injuries, no lives had been lost on the Union side.

Ulys was moving his army south of Vicksburg, and he would soon open siege in earnest.

CHAPTER TWELVE

April–August 1863

Jule had never witnessed a sight more terrifying and exhilarating than the running of the blockade. The flotilla had carried with it not only armaments and supplies, but her most ardent hopes and wishes as well. When Vicksburg fell, the Confederacy would be divided. The rebellion would be put down, the war would end, and slavery would crumble. She and Gabriel and all their colored brethren would at last be free, not only in rebel lands but everywhere.

The running of the blockade had succeeded so spectacularly that General Grant repeated the operation on April 22, sending six more transports loaded with supplies and several additional barges past the Confederate batteries to the Union foothold south of Vicksburg. Early the next morning, the encampment bustled with activity as he prepared to move out with the advance of his army.

Young Fred would go with him, and although he had assured his mother that he could manage fine packing his gear on his own, Julia, preoccupied with the younger children and her own travel preparations, sent Jule to assist.

She found Fred waiting for his father outside headquarters, his arms folded across his chest, looking about eagerly in case any of the officers should need a hand, his gear already packed and piled neatly on the ground beside him.

"You need any help?" she called as she approached, drawing her gray shawl closer around her shoulders to ward off the morning chill.

"I've been ready to go for an hour," he replied, grinning. "Pa's going to take Vicksburg in a week or two. I just know it."

"I hope you're right." Jule was less certain victory would come so quickly. As she had dressed Julia earlier that morning, Julia had described a curious dream from the night before — General Grant seated with his legs crossed on a camp chair, his brow damp with perspiration, his collar open in the summer heat, thousands of cigar stubs littering the ground all around him. Julia worried, and Jule agreed, that the dream meant Ulys would still be laying siege to Vicksburg well into summer.

"Vicksburg will fall," Fred replied confidently, his gaze traveling around the encampment, taking in the quick, steady preparations to move out. "Pa will capture it." Then his gaze lit upon Jule and turned curious. "Jule, have you seen the contraband?"

"They'd be hard to miss." Hundreds, perhaps thousands of newly freed or runaway slaves trailed after General Grant's army, establishing camps of their own on the outskirts of the neat rows of Union tents, finding work as cooks or laundresses or laborers, eking out a living as best they could, impoverished and hungry but free of the chain and the lash. From what Jule overheard around headquarters, the authorities in Washington City were unsure what to do with them, but they were determined not to send them back to the plantations and workshops they had fled, where their labor would sustain the rebel cause. Their camps were haphazardly constructed, their clothes bedraggled, their rations scant, yet Jule envied the contraband, for although they were poor, they were free.

"My mother says the contraband would be happier if they'd stayed with their masters."

"Better fed, maybe, in some cases, but happier?" Jule shook her head. "No."

"Grandfather Dent says colored people are most content when they're serving good masters."

Jule managed to stifle a derisive snort. "I doubt your grandfather ever asked the opinion of a colored person on that subject."

"Do you want to be a contraband?"

She regarded him levelly. "I want to be a free woman. Can you understand that?"

"I guess so." Suddenly his face fell, his grin vanished. "You don't like living with us?"

"Oh, Fred." She rested a hand on his shoulder and realized that he had grown so tall that she had to look up to meet his eyes. "I've cared for you since you were a babe in arms. I love you and your brothers and sister very much. But I'm not happy as a slave, though that's not your fault."

"I'm never going to own a slave."

"I'm very glad to hear that, but can I trust you with a confidence?"

"Of course."

"I don't think it's enough not to own slaves yourself. If you turn your back on other people's misery and say it's got nothing to do with you, that's just as bad."

Suddenly he looked very young. "Has it really been so terrible with us?"

She sighed and looked away, more to give him a chance to blink away embarrassing tears than to allow herself time to reflect. "Well, Fred, think about it. You've been on the battlefield. You've seen something of war."

He nodded.

"I know your pa's kept you away from the worst of it, but you've seen the dead and injured. You've seen the sick and wounded in

261

the hospital tents."

He nodded again.

"And yet as terrible as war is, young men keep signing up to be soldiers." She held his gaze steadily. "No one's ever signed up to be a slave. No one. That's how terrible slavery is. Do you understand, Fred?"

He swallowed hard and nodded.

"You take care, now," she said, hugging him as she had when he was a much smaller child, woken in the night by bad dreams. "Stay out of range of those rebel guns."

Shortly after they parted company, Fred, General Grant, and the Union army moved upon Vicksburg, and an hour later, Julia, the three younger Grant children, and Jule set out for St. Louis aboard the *Henry Von Phul,* the same ship from which they had observed the running of the blockade. Julia and the children would spend the summer with the old master, alternating as the whim struck them between their city residence, White Haven, and Wish-ton-wish, the pretty villa where the Grants had lived before moving to Hardscrabble, which the general had recently purchased from Julia's brother Louis.

When the steamer landed at St. Louis, it was all Jule could do to stay with Julia and the children rather than racing ahead to search for the carriage the old master had promised to send for them. Her excitement grew as they sorted their luggage, took the children in hand, and disembarked, but when they finally reached the Dent carriage, Jule was disappointed to see Tom at the reins.

After Jule assisted Julia and the children into their seats, she lingered, catching Tom's eye as he helped the porter stow the luggage. "Where's Gabriel?" she asked, smiling. "It's not that I didn't miss you, but I missed him more."

"Jule —" Tom hesitated, his expression so grim, so sympathetic, that for a moment she forgot how to breathe. "I'm sorry. Gabriel's gone."

"What do you mean, gone?" she said, her voice rising with each word. "Do you mean — is he dead?" It couldn't be. She would have known. She would have felt it if his soul had been torn from the world.

"No, not that." Tom climbed down from the wagon seat to place his hands on her shoulders, and she was dimly aware of Julia breaking off her conversation with Nellie to watch them through the window. "Sold. About three weeks ago."

"Oh, dear Lord, no." Jule pressed her hands to her mouth, heart thudding, vision graying over.

"Jule, what's wrong?" called Julia, alarmed. "You look ill. Come sit down."

Somehow, with Tom's help, Jule found herself seated in the carriage between Julia and little Nellie, who took her hand and peered up at her worriedly. As the carriage lurched and pulled away from the station, Julia fanned her with her handkerchief. "My goodness, what's wrong? What did Tom say to you?"

"Gabriel's been sold."

Julia's hands fell to her lap. "What?"

"Gabriel's been sold." Jule enunciated each word with perfect clarity. "Your father sold my husband. He's gone."

"That can't be. Papa would never do that."

"But he did." Jule's head ached. Suddenly nauseous, she buried her face in her hands and bent forward, resting her elbows on her knees. "Tom says he has."

"There must be some mistake," said Julia, her voice shaking. "We'll get this sorted out, I promise."

When they reached White Haven and Julia hurried into the house to speak to her father, Jule made her way to the stable, dazed and heartsick, and climbed into the loft. Gabriel was not there. His few possessions were missing. The pallet they had shared was gone, with fresh straw covering the depression their bodies had made.

Annie and Dinah found her there, her arms wrapped around her waist as she sat rocking back and forth, too shocked and grief-stricken for tears. The old master had sold Gabriel to pay a debt, they told her gently when she begged them to explain.

"We'll buy him back," Julia promised as Jule undressed her for the night. Jule nodded woodenly, and a small light of hope flickered to life, but in the weeks that followed, Julia's flurry of letters brought only dismaying replies. The old master's creditor had taken Gabriel into Arkansas, where he had sold him to a slaver, who had in turn sold him to a Georgian migrating to Texas. There the trail ended.

"I'm sorry, Jule," Julia told her repeatedly, her eyes shining with tears. "I'm terribly sorry."

There were no words adequate to her grief, and Jule could manage only the barest of nods in reply. Gabriel — her love, her dearest friend, the source of her only happiness on earth — was lost to her forever.

Julia continued to make inquiries long after she had exhausted any hope of locating Gabriel. "It was wrong of you to send him away," she chided Papa. "He was a faithful servant and a good worker. He deserved better."

"I don't need two grooms anymore, and it was an extravagance; I couldn't afford to keep them both," Papa retorted, glowering. "Would you have had me pay the debt with Tom instead? That wouldn't have been fair. He's been with the family longer." With slightly less bluster, he added, "Gabriel was younger and stronger. He fetched a better price."

By early May, even Jule — outwardly, at least — seemed to have resigned herself to his loss. One morning she struck out alone into the forest and returned with a basketful of twigs, bark, and roots, which she brewed up into an odoriferous concoction in a kettle on an open fire behind the kitchen house. She seemed so intent on her work, stiff backed and straight mouthed and curiously blank of expression, that Julia left her to it. When Jule next appeared at the house later that afternoon, she was wearing an old dress of Annie's, and the next day, Julia discovered that Jule had dyed all her own clothes black, even her lovely dove-gray shawl.

"She drifts through the house like a grim specter," said Emma with a shudder after Jule wordlessly served them lemonade on the piazza and returned into the house, as silent as smoke. "Aren't there enough poor war widows clad in mourning without her going around all in black? She makes a mockery of their suffering. You should speak to her."

"She's suffering too," Julia said, but Emma only sighed and gazed heavenward.

Amid the glorious beauty of White Haven — the lofty trees, the cheerful birdsong, the rushing creeks, the flowering meadows — Jule's quiet, relentless grief dimmed the brightness of what should have been a happy visit home. But other sources of consternation provoked Julia's discontent — in particular, acquaintances who strongly sympathized with the Confederacy and could not believe that Julia did not also.

"It's not right for you to say you're for the Union, Julia," an old friend of her dear mother's scolded her when they struck up a conversation after church one balmy Sunday.

"We know better, my child," an elderly dowager chimed in, wagging a finger. "It is not in your nature to be anything but Southern."

They refused to entertain her suggestion that as a westerner, one could be Southern in birth and custom but Union in loyalty, and they were not alone. On another occasion, Julia invited several childhood friends to White Haven for dinner. Afterward, as they relaxed in the cooling shade of the piazza, her friends discussed the many ingenious methods they employed to exchange letters and packages full of contraband goods with friends throughout the Confederate South.

"You should not speak of such things in front of me," Julia remonstrated. "I might feel it my duty to repeat it to the authorities."

"We know you won't," retorted the wife of a Confederate colonel, laughing.

"We know how you have been brought up," teased another longtime friend, clad in half mourning, her husband having fallen at Shiloh. "An oath would not be more binding than the sanctity of your roof."

And Julia was confounded, for they were right.

Whenever they visited their city residence, Julia could scarcely walk the length of the block without encountering old acquaintances, some of whom she scarcely remembered, others who had once been good friends but who had turned chilly toward her as Ulys rose within the Union army.

"When are you going to join your husband the general?" inquired one lady with cloyingly false concern.

"I shall go as soon as Vicksburg is ours," Julia replied.

"Not until then?" the first lady's companion asked, arching her eyebrows. "Don't you know that Vicksburg is as strong as the Rock of Gibraltar? How can it ever fall?"

"I don't know how it will be taken," said Julia, "but I do know that General Grant will never lift his siege until the city has surrendered. As soon as Vicksburg is ours, the same messenger who brings the news of victory will escort me back to the general. That is how you will know your Gibraltar has fallen."

As the weeks passed, letters came from Ulys regularly and less frequently from Fred. In late May, Julia was alarmed to read that her son had been nicked in the thigh by a musket ball at Big Black River Bridge. Ulys assured her that Fred bore his slight wound proudly and was already up and about, practicing his marching and riding his pony, but Julia felt sick and light-headed whenever she envisioned a garish scar marring her son's perfect young skin, and she became nearly petrified with horror when she considered what might have been, if the rifle had been aimed a little higher.

She read of furious battles at Port Gibson, Raymond, and Champion Hill. Within a month of running the blockade, Ulys had marched his men more than two hundred miles and had defeated two rebel armies in five battles. By the time he reached Grand Gulf, he wrote, he had been without luggage for a week, had not changed his clothes or slept within a tent in all that time, and had nothing to eat except what he could forage by the wayside. Julia wished he and Fred were more comfortable, but Ulys's stamina and endurance were legendary, and she was not surprised to hear that Fred had inherited his father's hardiness.

One afternoon in early July, Julia was sitting in an upper room chatting with her sister Nell, who had brought her children for a visit, when they were startled by a sudden salvo of artillery somewhere not too distant. Julia bolted from her chair, flew to the window, and thrust her head and shoulders outside, but she saw nothing, not even a telltale puff of smoke.

"Papa," she called down, spotting him on the piazza below. "What do you suppose the matter is? Do you think Vicksburg has surrendered?"

Without looking up from his newspaper, Papa turned the page and shrugged, frowning. "Yes, I should not wonder if both Vicksburg and Richmond have fallen from the infernal noise they're making."

"Perhaps it's in honor of Independence Day," Nell suggested.

Julia supposed that could be the reason, but later they learned that the canon salute was in celebration of a Union victory, for even as Ulys was ferociously bombarding Vicksburg, the Army of the Potomac had halted General Robert E. Lee's invasion of the North in a tremendously bloody battle at a small Pennsylvania town called Gettysburg.

On a morning shortly thereafter, Julia, Nell, and Emma sat on the piazza, watching the children play in the shade of the locust trees, and talking somberly of friends who had gone to the war and friends who would never return from the battlefields. Jule sat in attendance nearby, clad in fading black. Julia's thoughts were with Ulys and young Fred, and she wished so fervently to be with them, if only for a day, just so she could embrace them and be certain that they were safe, that she almost imagined she heard the pounding of hooves and glimpsed Ulys riding urgently up the zigzag road to come to her.

At the same moment she realized the hoofbeats were real, she glimpsed a rider clad in Union blue. "Jule, will you see him for me?"

Jule rose and approached the railing, shading her eyes with her hands. "His uniform's dusty from the road, but I see a major's insignia." Her hands fell to her sides. "It's Major Dunn."

"Major Dunn," Julia echoed, rising slowly from her chair as every nerve in her body screamed warning. Why would a member of Ulys's staff have come to White Haven so unexpectedly? Why was he approaching at such a rush if not to tell her —

A few yards from the house, Major William Dunn brought his horse to a halt and swiftly descended. "Mrs. Grant," he said, removing his hat as he strode toward them. "Ladies. I bring news from Vicksburg."

Julia took a deep, shaky breath and held fast to Nell's arm. "What news?" she demanded, and by some miracle, her voice was steady and clear.

"General Grant sent me from Vicksburg to Cairo to telegraph to the secretary of war that he has taken the city," Major Dunn declared proudly. "I was then ordered to come immediately here, to escort Mrs. Grant and her children to Vicksburg to visit the general."

Nell let out a cry of joy, Emma sighed in relief, and Julia sank back into her chair, murmuring fervent prayers of thanksgiving.

Julia and Jule swiftly packed for the journey, a task that had become so familiar it was completed in less than an hour. The family accompanied them to St. Louis, where they would spend the night before departing on the first steamer of the morning, and since Annie had remained at White Haven, they dined at the Planters House. Gentlemen, some with ladies on their arms, offered their congratulations, and as Julia graciously thanked them, she observed Papa sitting taller in his chair, holding his chest out a trifle more, with something suspiciously resembling a proud smile playing in the corners of his mouth. In the distance, a salvo of artillery proclaimed the good news over the river. Singing and music came through the windows and down the halls.

Julia's gaze was turned toward the window when a gentleman she knew approached the table. "Mrs. Grant, please pardon the interruption."

"Why, if it isn't General William Strong," she said, smiling as she offered him her hand. "You'll never guess what has happened at Vicksburg."

"I've heard a rumor or two," he replied, "but *you* may not guess what is happening outside the hotel at this very moment."

"A parade!" Jesse exclaimed.

"Yes, Master Jesse, that's so." The general smiled indulgently and offered him a little bow. "But do you hear that singing? People have come to serenade your mother."

"What?" exclaimed Julia. "Why on earth would they serenade me?"

Nell raised her glass to her sister, her eyes full of merriment. "Because you are Mrs. Grant."

"They're asking for you to come to the window and address them," said General Strong. "I would be honored to escort you, if you care to go."

"I couldn't possibly," Julia protested, mindful of the other guests watching and smiling and making no polite pretense to the contrary.

"Of course you must," said Emma. "Someone must answer. If you won't, I'll go and pretend to be you."

"Julia isn't obliged to appear," Papa said, "but I could say a few words —"

"No, thank you, Papa," said Julia quickly, rising and taking the arm General Strong offered her. "They're asking for me, so I must answer. I should at least bow to show how deeply I appreciate their affection for my husband."

General Strong gallantly escorted her to a window on the second floor, and as she approached it, she gasped to behold a vast crowd gathered below. "I had no idea there were so many loyal Union folk in St. Louis."

"Would you like me to say anything on your behalf?"

Julia nodded and shared a few scattered thoughts. Then she stepped forward to the window, the general a reassuring presence at her side. The crowd roared with approval when they spotted her, and she felt her legs trembling beneath her flowered poplin skirts. Goodness, she should have worn something finer, one of her silks perhaps — but she never could have anticipated this.

The general raised his free arm for silence. "Mrs. Grant thanks you for your kind regards," he began, his voice ringing out above the crowd. "She departs tomorrow to visit General Grant in Vicksburg." A great, triumphant cheer broke out; someone pounded a drum, while another sounded a blast on a trumpet. "General Grant has not taken one day's absence since the war commenced, nor has he troubled himself about the political opinions of his soldiers or what papers they read. He has allowed no censorship of that sort, his rule being simply that his men should be true to the flag and fight like heroes when required."

Applause rang out. "Hear, hear," someone shouted. "Grant for president!"

"Oh, dear me, no," Julia murmured.

"If I might add an observation of my own,"

General Strong continued, "General Grant has extraordinary common sense and has proven himself a great commander. He and his men have won immortal honors."

"Three cheers for Grant and the Union," called a man in the front of the crowd, waving his hat in the air, and the crowd enthusiastically complied.

When the shouts subsided, General Strong said, "Mrs. Grant now bids you good night, and she begs you to accept her thanks."

Julia offered the crowd one last gracious nod and withdrew from the window, but even as the general escorted her back to her family, the cheers and applause went on and on.

The crowd had dispersed by the time they departed the Planters House, and as they walked home, Emma linked her arm through Julia's. "You'll never guess what Papa said while you were addressing your admirers."

"Ulys's admirers," Julia corrected her. "What did Papa say? Something outrageous, I suppose?"

"You might think so." Emma smiled and lowered her voice. "He said that if Vicksburg had to fall, he was glad it had surrendered to your husband."

When their steamer docked in Vicksburg, Ulys met them with his ambulance, and all was a great commotion of hugs and kisses and congratulations. "Hail, my glorious

275

victor," Julia teased softly, brushing her cheek against his, enjoying the tickle of his beard on her skin.

"Welcome, my lovely bride," he murmured back, his eyes shining with warmth and affection.

Fred greeted her proudly, addressing her formally as Mother before flinging his arms around her with unrestrained cheerfulness as in the old days. At thirteen he stood several inches taller than she, his eyes clear and blue, his ruddy hair tousled, and his skin tanned and glowing with good health.

"I'm pleased to see that your wound hasn't left you with a limp," Julia told him.

"But it has left me with a scar," he boasted casually as his younger siblings listened, awestruck. "I'll carry it always as a memory of that battle."

"Don't be alarmed," Ulys murmured for Julia's ears alone. "The scar's barely visible."

Julia nodded, much relieved.

As the ambulance carried them through Vicksburg to Ulys's headquarters, Julia's happiness ebbed as she took in the sights of the battered city encircled with barricades and rifle pits. Once gracious homes and charming cottages were pockmarked with shell holes, while others had been reduced to dusty rubble or charred ruins. Cannonballs were stacked into pyramids on piazzas and street corners, and unexploded thirteen-inch shells topped gateposts and tree stumps.

At last they reached the city heights, where Ulys had supplanted Confederate General John C. Pemberton in the Lum residence, a gracious white colonial that reminded Julia of sketches she had seen of the Executive Mansion in Washington. Shade trees surrounded the house, which commanded lovely views of the Mississippi from its double piazzas, and pastures for the horses lay nearby. In the gardens, hedge roses bloomed in abundance and figs ripened on the trees.

Less than a week after her arrival, Ulys found Julia enjoying the breezes on the shaded upper piazza. "I've just received a letter from the president," he said, handing her a piece of paper.

Julia glanced at it, squinting, enough to make out the familiar signature. "Does this confirm your promotion?" Shortly after Ulys took Vicksburg, he had been appointed a major general in the regular army.

Ulys shook his head. "It's a letter of thanks."

"How lovely," said Julia, handing it back to him. "Do read it to me and save my eyes."

Executive Mansion,
Washington, July 13, 1863

My dear General:
    I do not remember that you and I ever met personally. I write this now as a grate-

ful acknowledgment for the almost inestimable service you have done the country. I wish to say a word further. When you first reached the vicinity of Vicksburg, I thought you should do, what you finally did — march the troops across the neck, run the batteries with the transports, and thus go below; and I never had any faith, except a general hope that you knew better than I, that the Yazoo Pass expedition, and the like, could succeed. When you got below, and took Port Gibson, Grand Gulf, and vicinity, I thought you should go down the river and join Gen. Banks; and when you turned Northward East of the Big Black, I feared it was a mistake. I now wish to make the personal acknowledgment that you were right, and I was wrong. Yours very truly

A. Lincoln

"How remarkable for a president to make such an admission," said Julia.

"By all accounts, he's a man of great humility," Ulys replied, folding the letter. "He's also an excellent commander in chief."

"You didn't vote for him," Julia teased.

"I couldn't vote for him," Ulys corrected her. "I hadn't lived in Illinois long enough. But I'm very grateful that so many other men did vote for him, for he's the man we need in the presidential chair right now."

Julia nodded. President Lincoln's letter was so gracious, and Ulys so obviously appreciative, that she hadn't the heart to point out that if Abraham Lincoln had not been elected, the South might not have seceded, and there might never have been a war.

The hungry citizens of the beleaguered city readily accepted rations from the Union army, but some officers warned Julia not to mistake that for tolerance of the occupiers or their wives. "No one who sees and hears the women of this city can but feel the intensity of their hate," General Sherman told her one afternoon when she and Ulys rode out to see him at his army's camp at Big Black. "With one breath they beg for the soldiers' rations, and with the next they pray that the Almighty or Joe Johnston will come and kill us, the despoilers of their homes and all that is sacred."

As the weeks went by, while the children played or rode out on their ponies to inspect the troops with their father, Julia forged acquaintances with the ladies of the neighborhood, and the dreadful stories of all that they endured evoked her greatest sympathies. With their homes under the constant threat of bombardment, many families had retreated to caves dug into the clay hillsides, with multiple entrances to allow for air circulation and to lessen the danger of entrapment.

"It's not as dreadful as it sounds," one lady told her. "We carved niches for flower pots, and closets for food, and bookshelves. We brought in our carpets and a dining room table too, although all cooking took place outside, of course." Her gaze turned distant. "We could not change our clothes for weeks. Once during a bombardment, a chunk of earth broke free from the ceiling and nearly crushed my niece." She gave a little start and forced a wan smile as if she suddenly remembered she was speaking to the general's wife and ought not give offense.

When one young matron asked if Julia felt any guilt or responsibility for how they had suffered, Julia confessed, "No, I do not."

"Have you no compassion?"

"I have compassion and sympathy in abundance," Julia assured her, "but I feel neither guilt nor shame nor responsibility for what has befallen you. Nor should my husband, though he commands the army that held you under siege for so long. The people of Mississippi brought calamity upon themselves by rebelling against the United States. The citizens of Vicksburg have only themselves and their leaders to blame."

"I didn't vote for any of them," the young woman said hotly as she turned and strode away.

In mid-August, Ulys and Julia agreed that

they should enroll the three eldest children in boarding school in St. Louis for the upcoming term. As they expected, Fred strongly objected to any plan that would take him from the field, but Ulys convinced him that he must continue his education if he hoped to enroll at West Point someday.

Ulys accompanied Julia and the children as far as Cairo, where Julia embraced him and made him promise that he would summon her back soon, after he attended to important matters in Memphis and New Orleans. Then Julia and the children stood at the rail and watched him disembark, flanked by two aides. When he turned on the landing and waved, Julia felt a sudden, sharp stab of worry. Always before she had held fast to a quiet certainty that he would return safely to her, but on that day her faith eluded her.

Julia and Ulys had agreed that the children deserved a holiday with the family before reporting to school, so they spent a week at White Haven, riding through the forest, fishing in the creek, running happily wild with their cousins. Julia and Nell went riding too, not as swiftly or daringly as they once had, but with the same exhilaration she remembered from girlhood.

One afternoon, she and Nell invited several ladies from their church to White Haven for a sewing bee to make pinafores and trousers for children orphaned by the war. Everyone was eager for news from the battlefield, and they peppered Julia with so many questions about Ulys and his armies that she chatted much more than she sewed, which was perhaps just as well, for it spared her eyes the strain.

The matrons of White Haven were curious about the nation's leader, and one friend of Julia's was disappointed to learn that neither Ulys nor Julia had ever met President Lincoln. "But Mr. Lincoln and General Grant do exchange letters on occasion," Julia said, and was pleased when her friend brightened. "Recently they've exchanged a few letters discussing the arming of the Negroes, a policy which they both believe will strengthen the Union army a great deal."

Although only a few of her guests owned slaves, Julia did not confess the rest of it: that Ulys had spoken as eagerly of emancipation as he had of forming colored regiments. "I have given the subject of arming the Negro my hearty support," he had written to Mr. Lincoln on the day she and Ulys had parted in Cairo. "This, with the emancipation of the Negro, is the heaviest blow yet given the Confederacy."

Suddenly their conversation was interrupted by the sound of a horse's hooves pounding up the zigzag road. Even before she turned to look, Julia knew it was an officer bearing terrible news.

She took a deep, steadying breath and rose to meet him. She watched, squinting and shading her eyes, as the officer dismounted and strode toward them. He was Captain George Maheu of Iowa, she recalled. He had a pretty sweetheart in Dubuque. He had shown her a daguerreotype.

"Good afternoon, Mrs. Grant," he said, removing his hat as he halted at the foot of the steps. "General Grant has ordered me to escort you and young Master Jesse to Vicksburg."

A sigh of relief went up from her companions, but something in the captain's expression told Julia this was not the usual summons to rejoin her husband. "Is the general well?"

Captain Maheu hesitated, took a deep breath, and shook his head grimly. Nell gasped. Someone took Julia's hand and held it tightly, lending her strength.

"General Grant was injured after a review at New Orleans," the captain said. "His horse reared, but he kept his saddle, and the horse fell back upon him."

One of the ladies cried out. Another whispered a fervent prayer.

CHAPTER THIRTEEN

August 1863–January 1864

"General Grant can't be too badly injured," Jule reassured her as the carriage raced to take them to the dock to board the next steamer south. "They wouldn't have taken him from New Orleans back to Vicksburg if he was hurt too bad to travel."

"Perhaps that's why no prophetic dream warned me of his accident," Julia said, feigning confidence. "Though hundreds of miles separate us, I surely would have sensed it if my husband's life were truly in danger."

Jule regarded her wanly before turning her gaze out the window. "I don't have your prophetic gifts, but I like to think I would too."

And Julia felt wretched anew, knowing that no steadfast messenger would ever bring word of Gabriel to Jule, no swift train or steamer carry her to his side.

Aboard the steamer, Julia pressed Captain Maheu for every detail of her husband's accident. On the fourth of September, Ulys had attended a military review in Carrollton, Louisiana, where Major General Nathaniel P. Banks had presented him with a fiery, blooded warhorse from Virginia. Astride the magnificent stallion, Ulys had galloped swiftly beneath towering oaks, a superb rider in a well-worn brown duster coat and slouch hat surrounded by officers brilliantly attired in their dress uniforms, all polished brash and glittering emblems.

But as they rode back to the city, a blast from a train whistle startled the spirited charger, and it dashed headlong into a freight wagon. A lesser rider would have been thrown, but Ulys remained in the saddle, and when the horse fell, it rolled on top of him, knocking him unconscious. Some time later, he woke at the Carrollton Hotel to find himself in bed, his body swollen to the armpit and several doctors bent over him, conferring in hushed voices.

"He spoke of pain almost beyond endurance," Captain Maheu told Julia, as gently as he could. "That he survived the crushing weight of the horse at all is a testament to his extraordinary hardiness."

When Julia arrived at Ulys's Vicksburg headquarters, she found him working from bed, still in great pain, badly bruised from feet to shoulders, more concerned about General Rosecrans's stunning defeat at

Chickamauga than his own injuries. With Jule's help she nursed him tenderly, and within days of her arrival, Ulys was up and moving about on crutches. Dr. Henry Hewit examined him daily, marveling at his progress and urging him to rest, knowing military necessity would trump his advice every time.

On the third day of October, General Halleck sent Ulys a dispatch summoning him to Cairo at "the wish of the Secretary of War."

As soon as he could make the necessary preparations, Ulys placed Major General James B. McPherson in command of Vicksburg and embarked via steamer for Cairo, accompanied by two aides and Julia, Jesse, and Jule. Though he was still quite lame from his injuries, he endured the travel without complaint, reaching Memphis on October 14; Columbus, Kentucky, the following day; and Cairo the day after that.

The next morning, Ulys received a telegram directing him to proceed by train to the Galt House in Louisville.

"This is all very cryptic," said Julia, wondering at the vague instructions, the circuitous route. Ulys murmured agreement, but if he suspected the reason for all the secrecy, he did not confide in her.

Hours after they set out from Cairo, the train stopped at Indianapolis, but just as it lurched forward to continue on to Louisville,

Julia glanced out the window and spied a young man in a dark blue coat and hat running toward the engine, waving his arms frantically and shouting. Somehow he must have caught the engineer's attention, for the train shrieked to a halt.

Once aboard, the man came directly to Ulys's car. "The secretary of war is here," he announced, panting. "He would like to see you."

Astonished, Julia tried to catch Ulys's eye, but he had risen painfully from his seat, his gaze fixed on the doorway, where another man had appeared. Short, stout, and jowly, with a long beard and dark hair patched with gray, he peered at Ulys unsmilingly through round wire spectacles.

Introductions were made, and as the staff filtered out, Julia handed Jesse off to Jule, then settled quietly in the far corner. Secretary Edwin M. Stanton glanced her way as he seated himself, but he turned his attention to Ulys without asking her to depart.

The train whistle blew, the wheels began to move, and Secretary Stanton gave Ulys two sheets of paper. "These are the orders for two different commands," he said. "President Lincoln would like to offer you your choice between them."

Ulys carefully studied each order, then handed one back to the secretary and set the other on his desk. "I will accept this one."

For the first time, Secretary Stanton smiled. "The president will be pleased."

"The honor is all mine," Ulys told him sincerely. "I will give him no reason to repent placing his trust in me."

The men conferred quietly, somberly, as the train made its way to Louisville. Eventually it reached its destination, and through a downpour of frigid rain and sleet, the delegation made their way to the Galt House, where Ulys and his companions bade the secretary's party good evening and settled into their own rooms.

"Come, tell me," Julia said after changing into her nightgown, sitting beside Ulys on the bed and rubbing his hair dry with a towel. "What mysterious orders did Mr. Stanton give you?"

"The two orders were identical, except for one particular," he said. "Both create the Military Division of Mississippi, including the departments of the Ohio, the Cumberland, and the Tennessee, and all the territory from the Alleghenies to the Mississippi River north of Banks's command in the Southwest."

"My goodness, Ulys," Julia gasped. "Such a vast area, and so many men to command!"

"And so many enemies to confront," he added soberly. "But here is where the two orders differ. One leaves the department commanders as they are, while the other relieves General Rosecrans and assigns General George Henry Thomas to his place."

Julia sat back against the headboard, the damp towel on her lap. "And which did you choose?"

"I accepted the latter."

She nodded, not at all surprised. "General Rosecrans won't bear that easily."

"He'll bear it like a soldier," said Ulys firmly. "He'll be little use to anyone if he doesn't."

But the next morning, a messenger knocked on their door with an urgent summons for Ulys to report to Secretary Stanton's suite, and more than an hour elapsed before he returned. "I found Secretary Stanton still in his dressing gown, pacing the floor," Ulys told her, scooping up Jesse and settling him on his lap on the sofa. "He received reports that Rosencrans might retreat from Chattanooga."

"What did you do, Pa?" asked Jesse.

"I telegraphed Rosecrans to tell him I was assuming command." Ulys lifted Jesse off his lap and set the boy on his feet on the floor. "You're getting to be more than a lapful, you know." As Jesse grinned and darted off to his toys, Ulys told Julia, "I next telegraphed General Thomas that he must hold Chattanooga at all hazards, and that I would be at the front as soon as possible."

Julia's heart sank, for she knew she could not accompany him. "How soon will you depart?"

"The day after tomorrow, sooner if I can manage it." He gave Julia a fond, encouraging smile and took her hand. "Don't be distressed, my dear little wife."

That was far easier said than done, but Julia took a deep breath and lifted her chin. "I, too, can be brave, when I have to be."

On the twentieth of October, General Grant and his staff set out for Chattanooga, while Julia, Jesse, and Jule remained in Louisville at the home of Julia's aunt Emily Wrenshall Page, the old missus's younger sister. Mrs. Page's housekeeper, a stout, coal-black woman in her mid-fifties, showed Jule to the slaves' quarters in the attic, where Jule would have her own bed, three pegs to hang her clothes, and her own washstand.

"It used to be crowded up here," the housekeeper remarked. "Two to a bed, shared quilts, no washstands. Now we have half the slaves and twice the space."

"And twice the work for those left behind, I bet," said Jule. "The others get sold off?"

"They run off," said the housekeeper, lowering her voice to a conspiratorial whisper. "The young men first, some of the women later. They got brave when they saw how the men never got caught."

"But not you?"

The housekeeper shrugged, but her look

spoke volumes. Too old, too stout, too comfortable, too afraid — even after Mr. Lincoln's proclamation, running away remained a dangerous gamble. Jule's own willingness to risk everything for freedom had dwindled in her mourning. She could hardly run away to Texas, a vast territory controlled by the Confederates, and fleeing to the North would only put more miles between her and Gabriel.

But whenever she came close to abandoning all hope, she seemed to hear a faint echo of Gabriel's exhortation: "If you get the chance, run."

Later that autumn came word of General Grant's two great victories at Lookout Mountain and Missionary Ridge, and in mid-December, he summoned Julia to join him at his new headquarters in Nashville.

Their train to Nashville chugged past hills and fields clad in the drab green, gray, and brown of early winter. General Grant's ambulance met them at the station, and as it carried them through the city to their lodgings, Julia was unusually still and silent. "Jule," she asked, her gaze turned to the window, "will you see it for me?"

Jule complied, but even as she described the passing scenes, she knew her words failed to capture its air of desolation and ruin. Gracious mansions and modest townhomes alike had been reduced to rubble. Fences and bridges were down; factories lay in ruins. Offices and hotels had been commandeered as hospitals, and harried orderlies and somber nurses bustled in and out, while soldiers with bandaged limbs sat outside resting or limped along the sidewalks on crutches. A few black-shrouded women glanced up at the ambulance as it went by, their eyes fathomless with sorrow, but most ignored it, and all held their worn shawls closed at the neck to ward off the cold, empty market baskets dangling from thin arms.

"The Nashville of my memory is sunny and warm and adorned by flowers," said Julia, her words a quiet lament. "Now families go hungry and cold and clothed in tatters. This dreadful war has wreaked havoc on us all."

"Some folks were suffering worse than this long before war broke out," said Jule.

She pretended not to notice the sharp, wary look Julia gave her in reply.

Julia was happy and relieved to be with Ulys again, though from the moment of her arrival, he was so preoccupied with telegrams and dispatches that she rarely saw him except at meals and bedtime. On Christmas Eve, he spent all day conferring with his staff and telegraphing his commanders in the field. That night, after putting Jesse to bed, she waited up late for him, hoping that they might enjoy a few moments alone. He finally

292

came upstairs shortly after midnight. "Longstreet's making trouble around Knoxville," he explained wearily, undressing and draping his clothes over the back of a chair.

"Cousin James?" It was impossible to think of him only as Confederate General Longstreet, without the entanglement of family relations. "I thought he abandoned the siege."

"He did, but he didn't lay down his arms." Ulys climbed into bed and reached for her, and she snuggled up beside him. "I'll have to start for Knoxville at early dawn. I'm sorry to leave you and the little rascal alone at Christmas."

"If you must go," she said, resting her head upon his shoulder, "you must."

After Julia and Jesse saw Ulys off the next morning, she resolved to spend the day being useful rather than dwelling upon her own loneliness with her family scattered on Christmas Day. Few Union officers' wives resided in Nashville, but Julia quickly summoned them together and proposed that they provide a bit of holiday cheer for the soldiers. She opened her own purse and sent out ladies in search of delicacies from local shops and farms, and she divided the wives and their children into two groups, one to visit the soldiers encamped outside the city, and the other to go to the hospitals. Then off they went to distribute tasty treats and small gifts and to sing carols.

At dusk, as Julia escorted her little band from the last hospital, a nurse thanked her for coming. "You've brought the men some comfort on this holy day," she said. "Come back again. Their great need will remain long after Christmas has passed."

Julia promised that she would return, and in the weeks that followed, she often entrusted Jesse to Jule while she visited the hospitals, distributing books to soldiers convalescing from illness or surgery, writing letters home for the men who could not do so themselves, offering cheerful conversation to the lonely, and granting requests to sing favorite songs that raised the men's spirits and reminded them fondly of homes far away.

Then, in January, she received alarming news from her own far-off home in the form of a telegram from Louisa Boggs, the wife of her cousin Henry in St. Louis. Fred had been afflicted with a stomach ailment ever since Vicksburg, but his illness had taken a serious turn, and Louisa strongly urged Julia to come at once. "Typhoid fever and dysentery," Julia read aloud to Ulys, her voice breaking. "That's what claimed the life of young Willie Sherman last October."

Ulys took the telegram from her. "Fred will not die," he said firmly. "He's always had a strong constitution and he's receiving the best of care. He'll recover. I'm sure of it."

Nevertheless, Julia would go to him immediately. She and Jule quickly packed while Ulys arranged for Major Dunn to escort them to St. Louis. As the major loaded their baggage onto the ambulance and Jule helped Jesse into his seat, Julia embraced Ulys in the doorway, trying to absorb his reassuring strength into herself.

"Telegraph me every day," Ulys said. "Even if there's no change, tell me so."

"Pray for him," Julia said, her throat constricting. She climbed into the ambulance where Jesse and Jule waited, and they raced off to the train station.

Julia kept up a cheerful façade for Jesse's sake as the train sped them northward, but behind it all was turmoil and worry. Louisa had mentioned Fred's illness in previous letters, but even after she and Cousin Henry had taken him out of boarding school so that she could nurse him properly, Julia had not feared for his life. All had changed in a moment, in the reading of a telegram. She prayed for the Lord to shine his healing grace upon her son, but she also willed the train to move faster, faster, so that she might be with him in his final moments if her prayers failed.

They were obliged to switch trains in Louisville, and as Julia took Jesse in hand and followed Major Dunn across the platform, she lost sight of Jule in the press of the crowd. "She hurried off that way," Major Dunn said, nodding to the baggage car. "I think she went ahead to collect your luggage."

Julia tightened her grip around Jesse's hand and followed the major along the platform to the rear. A porter was attending to their bags, but Jule was nowhere to be found.

Julia felt as if a cold fist had seized her, squeezing the breath from her lungs. She looked wildly about — and then, in the midst of the throng, she glimpsed a familiar head-scarf and a black shawl that had once been dove gray, but they were immediately swallowed up in the bustle of passengers and porters.

"Jesse, stay with Major Dunn," she ordered, quickly making her way through the crowd. Inside the station, she glanced this way and that, increasingly frantic — and then she spotted Jule passing through the doors to the street. "Jule," Julia cried, waving, but Jule neither stopped nor turned. Gathering up her skirts, Julia ran after her, but by the time she reached the sidewalk, Jule was already halfway down the block.

Julia cupped her hands around her mouth. "Jule," she cried. "Come quickly! We'll miss the train!"

Jule's quick strides slowed. After a moment, she turned deliberately around, but the distance between them was too great for Julia to read her expression.

"We aren't staying over," Julia called, hurrying after her. "We're going straight on to

St. Louis."

"You are," said Jule flatly. Only a few yards separated them, but something in her voice brought Julia to a halt. "I'm going my own way. I won't go back to Missouri."

"But, Jule —" Then the full meaning of her words sank in. "You don't mean you're running away?"

"I shouldn't have to." Jule's face was stone. "Mr. Lincoln signed that Emancipation Proclamation. I should be free."

"But Missouri isn't —"

"Don't give me more of that 'exemption' talk." Jule shifted her calico bundle to one arm and planted her other fist on her hip. "Don't talk to me about the law. Talk about what's right. You say you're for the Union and Mr. Lincoln — well, prove it. Grant me my freedom. Go on. Do it."

"You know I can't." Julia raised her hands and took a few tentative steps forward, expecting any moment to hear the train whistle shrill its warning. "Papa owns you, for all that we say you're mine. It would be meaningless for me to declare that you're free. You know that."

"I'm not free because you don't want me free," Jule countered. "Did you ever ask your papa to free me? Did you and the general ever ask to buy me from him, so you could free me yourself?"

297

Julia hesitated. "No, but that doesn't mean —"

"Did you ever pay me wages for my work, like you would've if I was a free woman, to show you think I ought to be free?"

"Jule." Julia felt close to tears, frantic. "I was kind to you, I —"

"You kept me a slave. How is that kind?"

"You had a roof over your head, plenty to eat —" With every word, Jule's frown became more scornful. Desperate, Julia said, "Jule, please. After all our years together, how could you leave me now, in my hour of greatest need?"

For the barest of moments, uncertainty and defiance warred in Jule's expression before resolve won out over both. "I pray Fred gets better, but you'll have to tend him without my help." She took two steps backward. "I don't hate you, Miss Julia, but I don't forgive you either."

She turned and darted off, her footsteps drowned out by the blast of the train whistle. Julia watched her go, stunned and despairing and angry. She was tempted to shout for a constable, but then she remembered the departing train, and Fred languishing in his sickbed, and she turned and ran back to the station.

Major Dunn was pacing anxiously on the platform, and when he saw her coming, he shouted to the conductor to wait one moment longer. His request was either unheard or ignored, and the train was already moving as Major Dunn seized her arm, heaved her on board, and quickly jumped on after her.

Jesse was fidgeting in his seat, peering anxiously out the window. "Did Jule get lost?" he asked when he saw them coming down the aisle without her.

"Yes," said Julia shortly, fighting back tears. "Jule is lost."

CHAPTER FOURTEEN

January–February 1864

It was after midnight when Julia, Jesse, and Major Dunn finally arrived at the Boggs residence in St. Louis, half-frozen and exhausted from arduous travel and worry. Louisa met them at the door, red-eyed and fatigued from sitting up with Fred day after worrisome day. Julia quickly shrugged out of her wraps and hastened upstairs to her son, who tossed fitfully in bed, burning with fever and shaken violently by hoarse, hacking coughs.

"He declines by the hour," Louisa told her softly, putting an arm around Julia's shoulders as if to bear her up. "But Dr. Pope says we have every reason to believe he will rally."

All through the night Julia tended her ailing son, and all the next day. On the second morning, Papa brought Buck and Nellie to see her; she embraced them tearfully in the parlor but forbade them to enter the sickroom.

"Is Fred going to be all right?" asked Nellie, ever gentle and tenderhearted.

"Of course he will," Julia said, forcing confidence into her voice, "but you must pray with all your might. Can you do that?"

Nellie and Buck both nodded vigorously, their little faces drawn and worried. Then Papa placed his hands on their shoulders, told them to kiss their mother good-bye, and took them away again as quickly as they had come.

Dr. Pope attended Fred every day, but his medicines seemed to have little effect. In the last week of January, he somberly told Julia that she must prepare herself for the worst and that Ulys should be summoned at once, to say his good-byes before it was too late.

Later that day, she received Ulys's terse telegram announcing that he was on his way.

As the hours passed, she tried, as the doctor had urged, to prepare herself for the worst, but she could not do it, she could not — and somehow, knowing that Ulys would soon be there infused her with new hope.

She was sitting in a chair at Fred's bedside, clasping his hand in one of hers, resting her aching head on her arm on the bed, when she heard a faint whisper. "Mamma?"

She bolted upright. "Yes, Fred, my darling." Her heart clenched as she brushed his sweaty locks off his forehead. "I'm here." And then she froze, her hand on his brow, hardly daring to believe it, wondering if it was only the workings of a mother's anguished imagination or if he truly did feel cooler.

"I'm thirsty."

She filled a cup from the pitcher and helped him sit up to drink. Then, with a sigh, he settled back against his pillow and drifted off to sleep again, his breaths deep and even. She pressed a hand to her mouth to hold back sobs of joy and disbelief before hurrying off to share the good news with Louisa.

Later that day Ulys arrived. Julia heard his boots pounding as he raced up the stairs two at a time and burst into the sickroom. "Does my boy yet live?"

Julia held out her hand to him, smiling, tears in her eyes. "His fever has broken," she said quietly, beckoning him to the bed. "He's going to be fine."

Heaving a sigh of relief, Ulys took her hand and looked down upon his sleeping son. "Thank God," he said, his voice trembling. "Thank God."

Fred stirred at the sound of his father's voice, blinked sleepily, and smiled in recognition before sinking back into sleep.

Ulys had brought with him an expert telegrapher so that he could retain direct command of all his forces and maintain communications with Washington. As Fred steadily improved, Ulys turned the Boggs's parlor into his headquarters, reading telegrams, sending off dispatches, and studying maps.

"I never thought the Yankee war would be fought from my own house," Cousin Henry remarked without rancor.

An entire day passed before Ulys noticed a conspicuous absence from the household. "Where's Jule?" he asked Julia.

"She abandoned me in Louisville," said Julia, distressed anew by the memory. "Oh, Ulys, she said such unkind things."

"Is that so?"

"Yes, but I'll forgive her if she'll only come back. She couldn't have gone far. I'm sure she made her way to Cincinnati — she knows the city well and they're known to be tolerant of runaways." She rested her hand on his forearm. "Ulys, you know so many people in Ohio. If you send word for the authorities to search for her —"

"Absolutely not," he interrupted. "I forbid any attempt to bring her back. In fact, I'd be only too glad if we could be rid of your other slaves in the same manner."

"Ulys," she protested.

"I only wish I had known she was planning to run. I would have given her a fat purse for the journey."

Inexplicably, Julia suddenly realized that she wished she had thought of that. What would become of Jule — a colored woman, penniless, alone, and on the run? But even as she wondered and worried, a faint hope stirred that perhaps after a day or two, Jule would decide to return home, chastened and wiser — though Julia did not confess those feelings to Ulys.

When Jule quit Julia outside the train station, she had hastened away as quickly as she dared, balancing speed and discretion. An icy prickling went up her spine as if hundreds of pairs of accusing eyes were upon her, but she dared not turn around. She expected any moment to hear Julia cry out for the constable, to feel strong hands seize her roughly, but nothing followed after her, not even the sound of pursuit.

Blood pounding in her ears, she ducked down a narrow alley and pressed herself so hard against the wall she felt the bricks through her wool dress and shawl. The train whistle had blown, signaling its departure, but was Julia aboard? Had she and Major Dunn remained behind to search for her?

She waited, shivering from cold, thoughts churning. No. Julia would never linger to pursue a runaway slave while her son lay on his deathbed.

Her spirits dipped as she remembered young Fred, but she steeled herself and made her way down to the riverside, her stride purposeful, her gaze lowered deferentially. At the docks, a surreptitious glance told her which steamer was bound for Cincinnati, but to cross the gangplank, she would have to pass between two crew members.

She had no ticket, no papers, no pass, and no other way to board that ship.

As the passengers began to file aboard, she observed a family on the landing, an elderly couple, a young widow swathed in black crepe and heavy veil, and four children who looked to be under eight years of age. The second smallest child dawdled behind the others, a rag doll dangling from her hand. Jule quietly fell into step behind them, and when the little girl approached too closely to the edge of the pier, Jule quickly placed a hand on her shoulder and drew her back. "Careful, Miss Sarah," she said, mindful of the crewmen's watchful gaze. "You don't want to lose your dollbaby in that deep water."

The little girl gaped up at her, too surprised to wrench herself free or protest that her name was not Sarah. Jule released her and smiled, and as the child scampered ahead to catch up with her family, Jule hurried along behind her, shaking her head and sighing as she had many a time over the antics of the Grant children, for all the world as if she were the four children's overworked, long-suffering nurse.

The crewmen gave her only the barest of glances as she boarded the steamer. As soon as she was sure they were not watching, she turned and strode briskly away in the opposite direction from the unwitting family.

She had traveled on the river so often with Julia that she knew the best places to avoid other passengers and crew, and when she did cross paths with anyone, she carried herself as if she were on an important errand for her mistress. No one challenged her.

As the hours passed she grew hungry, but although her handkerchief of coins was hidden in a secret pocket in her skirt, she dared not draw attention to herself by purchasing anything to eat. Her stomach was rumbling by the time she disembarked in Cincinnati, so she quickly seized up the flow of passersby and followed other colored folk to a neighborhood northeast of the landing, where she bought a cup of hot cider and a loaf of bread at a market. Cradling the cup in her hands to warm them, she made a quick meal of the bread before asking the vendor to point her in the direction of the Zion Baptist Church.

A prayer service was under way when she arrived, so Jule slipped into the back pew and bowed her head, closing her eyes against tears. The preacher's voice, while raspier than Gabriel's, resonated with faith and feeling as his had, flooding her with memories and a renewed sense of loss and absence almost too painful to bear.

Worship ended with a rousing hymn of love

and redemption, and Jule opened her eyes to discover that she was the only one not standing, clapping, singing in the spirit. She quickly rose but could not find her voice, and as the service ended and the worshipers fell to embracing one another and laughing and chatting like longtime friends, she felt heat rise in her face, shaken by the sudden fear that she was too conspicuous even here, even among people of her own race.

As the worshipers filed from the church, some gave her kindly, knowing glances, and suddenly she found the minister at her side. He was tall and solidly built, with two straight creases across his brow and a wreath of black-and-silver hair encircling a bald pate. "Are you in need, sister?" he asked in an undertone.

She nodded and gripped her shawl more tightly around her shoulders.

He glanced warily to the tall double doors that flanked the entrance, but then turned his gaze back to her, searching her face, warm and sympathetic. "Come with me," he said, offering her his arm.

She hesitated only a moment before taking it.

Word that General Grant was in St. Louis spread quickly, and soon the Boggs residence was besieged by callers and invitations. One morning Julia glanced out the sickroom window and saw a woman, her face hidden beneath a black bonnet, draw her cloak close about her and walk dejectedly away from the house. Curious, she descended from the sickroom and came upon Major Dunn in the foyer. "Who was that caller?" she asked.

"She gave her name as Mrs. Mary Simmons," he replied. "She wants a pass through the lines, but the general can't meet with her now."

"Why, she's an old acquaintance of mine. Did she ask to speak with me?"

"No, Mrs. Grant."

"If she calls again, I'd like to see her."

The major bowed assent.

Fred improved dramatically hour by hour, so much so that Ulys arranged for a nurse to sit with him so that he and Julia could take Henry and Louisa out for a night at the theater. They rode the streetcar downtown to see *Richelieu* at the St. Louis Theatre, but although they were escorted to a private box and Ulys seated himself near the back, he was soon recognized. As the curtain came down on the first act, rapturous cries of "Grant! Grant! Speech!" rang out from the audience.

His cheeks flushing, Ulys reluctantly rose, bowed to a crash of applause, and abruptly sat down. As the applause continued, Julia's gaze traveled from one beautiful young lady to another, their lovely faces turned to Ulys like spring daisies to the sun. Keeping her smile in place, she leaned closer to him and rested her hand upon his arm, reassured when he took her hand and smiled briefly at her, as he had not to the others.

The next day, when Dr. Pope came to the Boggs residence to examine Fred and declare him entirely cured, Julia escorted him to the foyer, where she sent the servant away with a discreet nod. "Doctor," she said quietly as she helped him into his coat, "I wondered if I might speak to you on a most delicate subject."

"Certainly," he said. "Is anything the matter?"

Julia shook her head, then nodded, then took a deep breath and handed him his scarf. "Many years ago, you spoke to me and my parents about a simple operation you could perform upon my eyes to improve their appearance."

"Yes, I recall."

"I was too frightened to consent at the time, but now — well, at the risk of seeming terribly vain —" She broke off and glanced quickly over her shoulder before continuing. "I don't wish to put myself forward in public, but my husband has become so famous that people recognize and watch me too, and I think it behooves me to look as well as possible. So I think I should like to go through with the surgery as soon as it can be arranged, please."

"My dear Mrs. Grant," said Dr. Pope. "It grieves me to tell you this, but it's too late, much too late. The operation I described could have succeeded only if it had been performed when you were still a child, with the marvelous resilience and recuperative powers of youth. There's nothing to be done for it now."

"I see." Bitterly disappointed, Julia nonetheless managed a smile. "Thank you just the same."

Promising to call on Fred again the next day, Dr. Pope bade her good-bye, and when he left, he took with him Julia's last wistful, fleeting hope to reclaim some of her faded beauty.

Later that afternoon, she was taking a slow stroll in the Boggs's winter-bare garden with Fred on her arm, as thin as a rail but in good spirits, when a servant hurried out to inform her that Mrs. Mary Simmons had returned. After seeing her son back upstairs and comfortably settled in bed, she hastened to the sitting room to receive her visitor. "Welcome, Mrs. Simmons," she said, offering her a seat in the chair adjacent to her own. "Is there anything I can do for you?"

"The general alone can grant my petition." Mrs. Simmons hesitated before plunging ahead. "I lost my husband at Vicksburg."

"Oh, dear. I'm so sorry."

A bit of fire appeared in the widow's clear blue eyes, illuminating the shadows beneath. "He fought for the Confederacy, against your husband. Does that make a difference?"

Julia reached out and clasped her hand. "Your sorrow is no different, and neither is my sympathy."

"You're very kind." Mrs. Simmons bowed her head in a vain attempt to conceal her tears. "I would like to join my late husband's family in Georgia, but I can't cross through the lines without a pass."

"General Grant can't see you because his every minute is occupied with the war." Julia rose and gave her an encouraging smile. "He *will* see me."

Julia excused herself and went to Ulys's office, where she found him at his desk, handing a dispatch to the telegrapher. "Come in, Mrs. Grant," he greeted her, rising, and the two officers seated in front of his desk quickly stood as well. Julia presented her petition more humbly than she would have were they alone, and as she soon had the pass in hand, she thanked Ulys and hurried upstairs to retrieve a thick roll of Confederate bills a young officer had captured at Vicksburg and had given her as a souvenir. The denominations amounted to about four thousand Confederate dollars, but what that represented in real, United States currency, Julia was unsure.

She found Mrs. Simmons gazing out the sitting room window, wringing her hands. "My dear Mrs. Simmons," she said, handing her the pass, "you may join your husband's people in Georgia as soon as you wish. And this" — she placed the roll of Confederate notes in the widow's hands — "I hope this may be of some use to you."

Mrs. Simmons's eyes widened. "I couldn't possibly accept so much."

"I insist. They're of no use to me. Think of the scandal if I tried to spend them!"

It was not until later, when she considered how furtively Mrs. Simmons had tucked the precious pass and the roll of notes into her reticule, that Julia's conscience troubled her. The Confederate bills were nothing to her but scraps of paper, but had she done something terribly wrong in giving them to Mrs. Simmons to carry into the South?

The minister and his wife sheltered Jule in their home adjoining the church for several days, until the immediate danger of pursuit subsided. Restless in confinement, Jule assisted her benefactors as much as they allowed, cleaning and helping in the kitchen. She wanted not to take her ease after a lifetime of forced labor but to be useful, to distract herself with activity, to occupy her hands while her mind churned ceaselessly over what to do next.

"We'll search for advertisements in the papers and keep watch for handbills," the minister told her. "When we're sure your owners haven't sent slave catchers after you, I can find you work and a place to live in the city."

"I thank you," said Jule, "but I can't stay in Cincinnati. My mistress's husband grew up not far from here and his people live across the river. I might cross paths with them someday, or if not them, someone else who'll recognize me."

The minister turned to his wife, and after a long, wordless look that Jule knew conveyed the substance of a much longer conversation, the minister's wife nodded.

"In that case, we'll have to find some means to carry you from the city," the minister said, turning back to Jule. "Have you trained for any occupation?"

"I've worked as a ladies' maid nearly all my life," she replied. "I dress hair, and I make my own salves and ointments."

"You're a nurse, then?" the minister's wife prompted hopefully. "There's a great deal of work for nurses these days."

"No, ma'am. I don't make medicines, not really. Just treatments for rashes and chapped skin and sore muscles and the like. And pomades for hair." The minister's wife looked so disappointed that Jule felt compelled to explain, "I've cared for sick folks, of course,

313

and tended babies and children. I'm just no proper nurse. Just like I can cook, but I'm not *a* cook."

"I'm sure you've done the work of an entire household of servants," the minister's wife said.

"I can read," Jule hastily added, "and write some."

They brightened considerably. "Excellent, excellent," the minister said, clasping his hands together and exchanging a smile with his wife.

Later that evening, the minister's wife came to her bedchamber to report that they had made inquiries among their friends and fellow longtime abolitionists, and they were optimistic that they would soon find a way to deliver her to a safe haven in the North. "In the meantime," she said, dropping her gaze abashedly and peeling off her gloves, "I wonder if you can help me."

She extended her hands to Jule, who took them in her own, carefully keeping her expression impassive. The backs of the woman's slender, copper-hued hands were covered in patches of dull, leathery skin interspersed with blisters, some oozing fluid, others crusted over.

"I'm afraid even a minister's wife is not immune to the sin of vanity," Mrs. Shaw said, managing a faint, apologetic laugh. "I should be content to wear the gloves and endure the blemishes."

"It's not vanity to want to ease your pain," said Jule, studying the woman's skin. "I bet this hurts close to unbearable. Itches, too."

The minister's wife pressed her lips together and nodded.

"How long they been this way?" Jule asked.

"For months, ever since the weather turned colder. The condition returns every autumn and fades with the spring."

Nodding thoughtfully, Jule released the woman's hands. "I can mix you up a salve if you can find me what I need," she said. "Try to keep your hands out of very hot water, and stop drinking cow's milk and eating eggs for a while. You should eat fish and bone broth every day if you can."

Mrs. Shaw nodded as Jule listed the ingredients she would need — beeswax, yarrow, rosemary, comfrey leaves, and the rest. Mrs. Shaw went out to the market first thing the next morning, and by late afternoon, Jule had prepared the healing salve. Within a few days, the minister's wife happily confided that she was already feeling much relief, and a day after that, Reverend Shaw announced that he had devised a plan for Jule's escape.

"Two parties of trusted friends are traveling to the East soon, and you may have your choice between them as escorts," he said. "The first is a Quaker family traveling to Philadelphia, and you would travel in the guise as nurse to their three children. If you prefer to settle in Washington City, you could travel as ladies' maid to a longtime friend of ours, a widow and a native of this city who writes for an abolitionist paper in the capital."

From the depths of childhood memory, Jule recalled something Julia had said to reassure her that the murderer Major William Harney would never return to Missouri. "Papa says Washington City is about as far from St. Louis as you can go," she had told Jule. Time had proven Julia wrong in one respect — Harney had returned to Jefferson Barracks, and as a general — but perhaps she was right about the distance separating the two cities.

"I'll go to Washington," she told the minister, marveling at the unexpected luxury of choice.

On the eve of Ulys's return to his headquarters in Nashville, Colonel John O'Fallon hosted a grand banquet in his honor at the Lindell House. General Rosecrans, General John M. Schofield, and numerous other high-ranking officers were present, as well as Papa. Although ladies were not invited, an exception was made for Julia, Mrs. O'Fallon, and cousin Louisa, who observed the event from an adjoining parlor, nibbling on delicacies and indulging in gossip about the men. When Ulys entered the room, the band played "Hail to the Chief" and the gentlemen broke into thunderous applause.

"I seem to recall, only a few years before, a certain obscure army veteran selling firewood to make ends meet," Mrs. O'Fallon mused aloud, smiling. "If memory serves, many prominent men of this city dismissed that farmer or pitied him. How interesting that a great many of those men are here tonight, cheering him on and speaking of him as a presidential candidate."

As the banquet drew to a close, it was announced that a vast, ardent crowd had assembled on the streets outside, and they refused to disperse until they had a word from their hero. Resignedly, Ulys stepped out onto the balcony, and when the doors were opened the cries of "Grant! Grant! Speech!" sent a thrill of shock and wonder through Julia. Poor Ulys, she thought. He cannot avoid it now.

"Gentlemen," he began, barely audible in the ladies' parlor over the cheers of the crowd. "Making speeches is not my business. I never did it in my life, and never will. I thank you, however, for your attendance here."

As the people burst into deafening cheers, he bowed and withdrew from the window.

"The people will not be satisfied with that," declared Mrs. O'Fallon with a laugh. "They'll surely demand another, longer speech before the night is through."

Julia foresaw a great many speeches in Ulys's future, and needed no prophetic dreams to tell her so.

"Before we part, my dear, I have a confession to make," Ulys said the next morning as he prepared to return to military headquarters. "Some well-meaning but badly misguided gentlemen are talking about me as a candidate for president."

"Yes, I've overheard the talk."

"I've told them I'm not interested, but that hasn't discouraged them." Ulys shook his head, frowning. "I'm exactly where I need to be, and so is Mr. Lincoln. It would be a disaster to replace the commander in chief before the war is won."

"You would make a fine commander in chief yourself."

Ulys smiled fondly and caressed her cheek with the back of his fingers. "Thank you, Julia, but my only political aspiration is to be the mayor of Galena — and that's only so I might order a new sidewalk built from our home to the train station."

Julia laughed. "Oh, Ulys." Then her mirth faded. "I have a secret to confess too."

The story spilled from her — how she had been moved by Mrs. Simmons's plight, how she had given the widow nearly four thousand dollars in Confederate notes. "I meant no harm, but I'm afraid that by giving her that roll of bills, I might have aided the rebel cause and betrayed my country, and worse yet, you."

She steeled herself for his recriminations, but to her astonishment, Ulys smiled. "You needn't worry, my dear little wife. In fact, you've done the Union a service."

"I have?"

"Of course. The more of those Confederate bills in circulation, the better it will be for us." He kissed her on the cheek. "However, the next time you want to dispense funds to rebels, or to rebels' widows, ask me first."

"I will," she solemnly replied. "But, darling . . . I suppose I have a second confession to make."

His eyebrows rose. "You've kept two secrets from me?"

She wrung her hands. "I spoke to Dr. Pope about surgery to correct my dreadful cross-eye, but he says it's too late."

"What put such a thought in your head in the first place?"

"You're getting to be such a great man, and I'm such a plain little wife. The more famous you become, the more —" She broke off, embarrassed. "The more people will be watching you closely — not only you, but me too. I thought that if my eyes were as other ladies' are, my plainness might not be such an embarrassment."

"Listen to me," he said, drawing her near. "Didn't I first see you and fall in love with you with those same eyes?"

"Well . . ." She hesitated. "Yes, I suppose so."

"You know I did, and I liked them then and I like them now exactly as they are." He tapped her twice on the bridge of her nose. "You are not to interfere with them. I might not like you half so well with any other eyes."

Unburdened of their secrets, they parted with quiet laughter, promises to write, and words of enduring love.

From the day of her darling husband's departure, Julia waited for letters from Nashville, anxious most of all for the one that would summon her to his side. In the meantime, she sent regular reports that Fred grew stronger every day, until he was almost as vigorous as he had ever been, though still much thinner than she liked. Ulys wrote to tell her of General Sherman's maneuvers in Mississippi, of President Lincoln's order for a draft of half a million men to serve for three years or the duration of the war, and of new regulations he had issued for the cotton trade.

But as February passed, the most shocking news Julia received came not from her husband, but from her eldest brother, John, an ardent rebel whose loyalties had compelled him to relocate to the South.

There, while visiting friends in Louisiana, he had been arrested on suspicion of Union sympathies and had been thrown into a Confederate prison in South Carolina.

CHAPTER FIFTEEN

February–March 1864

"His captors would only have to talk with him for five minutes to know that he's Confederate to the core," Papa protested when they received John's letter from prison in Columbia, a few shaky lines scrawled on a scrap of paper, barely enough to let them know he was alive and unharmed.

"They must assume that General Grant's brother-in-law is for the Union," said Henry. "How could they not?"

Papa glowered at Julia. "Since your husband got John into this wretched mess, he can very well get him out of it."

"John got himself into this mess," countered Julia. "He chose to repudiate his country, and if the rebels doubt his sincerity, that isn't Ulys's fault. John must accept the consequences of his poor choices." But the thought of her eldest brother suffering in prison, guilty of nothing more than expressing his opinion and being disbelieved, left her sickened and afraid. "Nevertheless, I'll ask Ulys to do all he can."

But there was little Ulys could do. John was a civilian, not a soldier, so he was not eligible for the usual prisoner exchanges, nor did Ulys seem willing to take extraordinary measures to secure his release. "I sympathize with John in his sufferings, and with your family and all who love him," Ulys wrote in response to her pleas. "But Julia, do you really think it would be just to give a rebel prisoner of war in exchange for your brother, when so many brave, deserving soldiers who fought for the Union languish in rebel prisons?"

Julia knew he was right, but when she told her father that Ulys would not petition the Confederacy on John's behalf, he became incensed. They exchanged heated words — Papa furious, Julia tearful and defensive — and when they parted, Julia knew that the rift between her husband and father, so recently closed, had been torn open anew.

Even as she grieved for John and Papa and the rest of her family, her thoughts turned to Jule. For almost a year, Julia had believed she understood Jule's anguish, for she, too, had endured many lengthy separations from her husband throughout his many years of military service. Yet even amid the hazards of war, Ulys's absences never filled her with the searing pain and apprehension as John's did now, knowing that he was being held against his will far from all he loved, suffering untold deprivations, beyond reach, beyond hope.

Julia longed to tell her erstwhile servant that she finally understood, to commiserate with someone who understood her in turn. But Jule, the trusted confidante whom she had always relied upon to see clearly for her, was gone.

Jule discovered that Reverend Shaw and his wife had taken up a collection for her train fare only after they presented her with a ticket and informed her she would be leaving the following morning. "I can pay the fare myself," she said, surprised. "I have money."

"Keep it, dear," Mrs. Shaw urged. "You'll need it in Washington City."

Jule thanked them and asked them to thank their parishioners on her behalf, but although she was grateful, she was also disappointed. Depending upon charity made her feel less like a free woman than a parcel to be transported.

And yet she had no misgivings about their second gift — a heavy tapestry satchel with leather handles for the journey, and clothes to fill it. "It's not new, but it's in fine condition," Mrs. Shaw said, somewhat apologetically.

"It's better that it's not new," said Jule, admiring the bag. "Mrs. McGuigan's satchel is likely well used from all the traveling she does, and wouldn't it look suspicious if the servant had better luggage than her employer?"

She had met Adelaide McGuigan only once, for a brief interview over tea to discuss their upcoming travels, and she had taken an instant liking to her. She was a large woman, easily head and shoulders taller than Jule, sturdily built rather than softly plump. Her curly, gray-streaked red hair was gathered in a silken net of dark blue, its evident weight suggesting great thickness and length. Examining it surreptitiously, Jule hoped that in her role as Mrs. McGuigan's maid, she would be allowed to brush out her hair, trim the ends neat, and apply oil to correct the dryness.

Jule had expected Mrs. McGuigan to be clad in black like herself, albeit in finer fabrics, but Mr. McGuigan had died six years before, and the widow had put off mourning attire long ago. "He was founder, publisher, and editor in chief of an abolitionist newspaper," Mrs. McGuigan had explained. "He had championed the cause of an enslaved man suing his owner in the Cincinnati courts for kidnapping and false imprisonment. He argued that his client ought to be free because he had been born in Ohio while his owner was traveling through the state with his mother. The case was quite controversial, and when the judge seemed to favor the plaintiff, supporters of the defendant rioted. They forced their way into my husband's office, knocked him unconscious, broke up his printing press with axes, and set it on fire." She fixed her gaze steadily upon Jule. "As the blaze spread, they carried my husband up to the third story and threw him out the window."

"Oh, my Lord," breathed Jule.

Mrs. McGuigan had managed a tight, grim smile. "It could have been worse. They could have left him there to burn alive. I count my blessings where I find them."

Her husband had been martyred for the great cause of abolition, Mrs. McGuigan had said proudly, and in his memory she would continue to serve it. That was why she had taken up her pen after his death, why she traveled the country making passionate speeches on behalf of the enslaved to any audience who would listen, and why she was happy to escort Jule to a new life in freedom.

The clothes Mrs. Shaw had packed in the satchel for Jule were also secondhand, but well made and finer than any of those she carried in her calico bundle. Jule sorted through them, speechless, admiring the soft muslin undergarments, the wool dresses of dark blue and tan, calico skirts and blouses for spring, several pairs of newly knit stockings, and new leather boots, scuffed and yet finer than anything Jule had ever worn.

"I don't have the words to tell you how grateful I am," said Jule, overwhelmed. "Thank you."

"You're truly welcome." Gently Mrs. Shaw added, "The dresses aren't black, as you see. From your dyed garments, I assume that you've been in mourning. I don't mean any disrespect for your lost loved one, but perhaps you should put aside your mourning clothes before you depart."

Her lost loved one — yes, Gabriel was exactly that. Lost, but not dead, she hoped, and therefore perhaps not lost to her forever.

She had mourned him less than a year, but it was time to leave her widow's weeds behind.

Mrs. McGuigan called for her early the next morning, and soon they were boarding a train for the east. Mrs. McGuigan had paid for a private car, but when they were obliged to mingle with the other passengers, Jule fell easily into the role she knew so well, ladies' maid. On the second morning, Jule offered to dress Mrs. McGuigan's hair, and although the widow professed herself indifferent to fashion, she cheerfully accepted. "Gracious me," she exclaimed afterward, studying her reflection in the looking glass with utter astonishment. "You have rare talent."

"It's just a little oil and fragrance."

"And the skill to mix and apply them." Mrs. McGuigan regarded her appraisingly. "You may be able to make your living from this."

Jule smiled her thanks, but her heart gave a crashing thump. She had not envisioned her future beyond disembarking the train in Washington City. Reverend Shaw had written to an acquaintance there who had promised to help her find work and lodgings, but shortly thereafter, Jule would be on her own.

It was terrifying and exhilarating all at once.

At long last they reached Washington City, where Mrs. McGuigan delivered her safely to Reverend Shaw's friend, a minister at the Union Bethel Church. "I'll call on you before I return to Cincinnati," Mrs. McGuigan promised, embracing her.

By the time Jule saw Mrs. McGuigan again a few days later, she had found work at a barbershop serving prosperous colored gentlemen. She only swept floors, but it was a start, and her employer indulgently permitted her to recommend her services to their customers' wives and daughters. Perhaps soon she would have customers of her own.

Her wages were enough to pay for a comfortable room in a boardinghouse with a little left over for her savings. Her neighborhood was humbler than those where the shop's customers resided, but it was safe and quiet, almost opulent compared to the makeshift shacks and fetid camps where thousands of contraband had settled in Washington after fleeing slavery in the South. Jule was ever mindful that she was vastly more fortunate in comparison, and in her prayers she never forgot to ask for God's blessing for her brethren — and for Lieutenant Aaron Friedman, who had told her where to find the trailhead that led to her new life.

In the last week of February, Dr. Pope examined Fred and concluded that although he was steadily improving, he should not return to school until the fall term. While Julia worried that his education would suffer, Fred accepted the doctor's advice with restrained jubilation, which soared when Ulys wrote to suggest that Fred could spend a few weeks with him in Nashville instead. Julia was skeptical of the notion that Fred was too weak for school but hearty enough to travel to military headquarters, but Ulys and Fred insisted so relentlessly that she soon acquiesced.

Julia, Fred, and Jesse set out for Nashville soon thereafter, where Ulys arranged for them to board in a comfortable private home across the street from his offices. They had barely settled into their quarters when Ulys told Julia that a measure to reinstate the rank of lieutenant general had recently passed both houses of Congress and that President Lincoln had nominated Ulys for the first appointment to that rank since General Washington. While nothing was certain, General

Halleck had telegraphed to report that he believed Ulys would surely be confirmed immediately.

"Oh, Ulys, I'm so very proud of you," Julia cried, embracing him, but even with her poor vision she could perceive his considerable lack of enthusiasm. "Aren't you pleased?"

"I don't want the promotion if it will take me from the field before the war is won." Ulys grimaced. "And I have one other regret."

"Regret?" exclaimed Julia, astonished. What could there be to regret about better pay, higher rank, and greater recognition? He would outrank even General Halleck.

"Yes, regret, for if I'm named lieutenant general, I'll surely be stationed in Washington." He shook his head, resigned. "I had hoped when the war was over that I might have my choice of posts, and I'd prefer the Pacific Coast."

Two days later, General Halleck sent another telegram: "The Secty of War directs that you will report in person to the War Dept as early as practicable considering the condition of your command."

"A summons to Washington," said Julia, thrilled. "Surely this means your appointment has been confirmed, or it will be soon."

"Yes," said Ulys shortly. "It surely does."

As reluctant as Ulys was to leave the field, he was mindful of the high honor the president meant to show him, and Julia never heard him complain about the summons except in the privacy of their bedchamber.

Julia's eyes were troubling her too much to travel, but she saw Ulys and Fred off with proud kisses and orders to remember for her every detail about the Executive Mansion, the president, and his wife. She loved them beyond measure — her son, almost fourteen and nearly a man, tall and still thin from illness but broadening in the shoulders, and her husband, her darling Ulys, who grew more handsome as he aged, hardier and healthier than he had ever been, his blue eyes and bearded, weathered face strikingly handsome and virile. It was little wonder the ladies admired him so, when even after fifteen years of marriage, Julia still felt her heartbeat quicken and her knees tremble whenever he held her gaze or touched her hand.

Soon thereafter, glorious accounts of Ulys's enthusiastic reception in Washington began to appear in the Nashville papers. When the ache in her eyes and head subsided enough to allow her to read, Julia found Jesse a rapt audience as she read the reports aloud, but it was not until Ulys and his companions returned to Nashville on March 14 that she learned the rest of the story. Fred and Rawlins told her everything, beginning with Ulys's inconspicuous arrival at the Willard Hotel — carrying his own bag, his faded uniform hidden beneath his old brown duster coat. When he signed the register as U. S. Grant and son of Galena, Illinois, the clerk, failing to recognize him, disdainfully assigned them to a small, inconvenient room on a high floor.

"They expect all generals to carry themselves like McClellan," Rawlins said, a little scathingly, and Julia had to smile. She knew that the fashionable, impeccably attired General McClellan suffered in comparison to Ulys in the eyes of the public and, apparently, the president. Whereas General McClellan had drilled and dithered and complained that he was perpetually, hopelessly outnumbered, Ulys planned shrewdly and advanced persistently and unrelentingly. McClellan had invited mockery when the Washington press reported that he had needed six wagons, each pulled by a team of four horses, to carry his attire and personal belongings to the front, while reporters marveled that Ulys often took the field carrying only a spare shirt, a hairbrush, and a toothbrush. McClellan enjoyed lavish champagne and oyster banquets at his gracious mansion on H Street in Washington City; Ulys preferred pork and beans cooked over a campfire. McClellan had graduated second in his class at West Point — but that was the only measure by which he exceeded her Ulys.

The clerk at the Willard soon learned his mistake. Ulys and Fred had gone upstairs to change for supper, and soon after they were seated in the dining room, another guest recognized Ulys, pointed at him in astonishment, and exclaimed, "There sits General Grant!" A shout of welcome rang out and swelled into a chorus of cheers, and the crowd cried out his name and pounded the tables with their fists until Ulys rose and bowed.

Ulys and Fred had been immediately reassigned to a room befitting a general, and after seeing Fred upstairs, Ulys had made his way on foot to the Executive Mansion to meet the president. Mr. and Mrs. Lincoln had begun receiving guests for their weekly reception in the Blue Room at eight o'clock, and when Ulys and a few of his aides arrived ninety minutes later, their entrance caused great commotion.

"What did Mr. Lincoln say when he met you?" asked Julia.

Ulys's cheeks took on a slight flush. "His face lit up in a broad smile when saw me coming toward him, and rather than wait for me to reach him, he came to me. He said, 'Why, here is General Grant! Well, this is a great pleasure.' He shook my hand with brotherly warmth and we talked a little, and then he introduced me to Secretary of State William Seward, who tried to help me navigate the crowd."

"That was not easily done," Rawlins broke

in. "The cheering throng was calling the general's name and descending upon him in a mad, rapid, frantic crush of torn laces, mashed crinolines, and trod-upon boots."

Julia felt a sting of jealousy as she looked from Rawlins to Ulys and back. "You make it sound as if the reception was comprised solely of admiring ladies."

Rawlins shook his head. "No, he was swarmed by ladies and gentlemen alike. The crush was so intense that Mr. Seward steered him into the East Room and made him stand on the sofa so everyone could see his face better."

"I imagine his face was as red then as it is now," mused Julia, imagining a crowd of beautiful, adoring ladies in fine silk gowns pressing themselves toward her husband, their pretty gloved hands patting out applause.

With the hearty, indefatigable Secretary Seward at his side, Ulys had received the frenzied crowd for an hour before he was escorted to a drawing room where he, President Lincoln, and Secretary of War Stanton discussed the next day's ceremony. The president, aware of Ulys's well-known disinclination to speechify, kindly provided him with a copy of his own remarks so that Ulys could prepare a response.

"When Pa came back to the Willard, he wrote a few lines on a half sheet of paper,"

Fred added. "I was standing right beside Pa the next afternoon at the White House when President Lincoln gave him his commission. Mr. Lincoln gave his speech, and then Pa read his, and I think Pa was every bit as good as the president."

"That's high praise indeed, considering that Mr. Lincoln is such a renowned orator." Smiling, Julia reached out to squeeze her son's hand. "I wish I could have been there."

"Lots of people were," said Fred. "The whole cabinet, and important men from the government, and some ladies."

"Was Mrs. Lincoln present?" asked Julia. "What was she wearing?"

Fred shrugged. "She was there all right. She wore a fancy dress."

"Is that the best you can do, when I asked you to remember every detail?" Turning to her husband, Julia prompted, "Ulys?"

"It was a fancy *white* dress," he added helpfully. "And she wore a lace shawl around her shoulders and flowers on her head."

"That's a little better, I suppose," said Julia, too fascinated to be truly exasperated with them.

The next day, while Ulys was consulting with General George Gordon Meade at the headquarters of the Army of the Potomac at Brandy Station, President Lincoln telegraphed to invite the two generals to a military dinner Mrs. Lincoln had arranged in their honor. On Thursday morning Ulys called at the White House, where the president interrupted a cabinet meeting to see him. "I asked to be excused because I felt most urgently that I should return to the field," said Ulys. "The president smiled in a frank and friendly way and said, 'I don't see how we can excuse you. It would be like *Hamlet* with the prince left out!' "

"I must say I agree with him. What was your reply?"

"I told him that I fully appreciated the honor Mrs. Lincoln meant to show me, but time was very precious just then, and I'd had enough of the show business."

"You said that to the president?" Julia exclaimed, mortified. "You turned down an invitation from Mrs. Lincoln because your time was too precious?"

"She'll despise you for that," Rawlins remarked.

"She despises me already." Ulys drew deeply from his cigar and studied the burning end as he exhaled. "I've heard she calls me a butcher and tells the president that I have no regard for life. She was perfectly pleasant to me at her reception, though, so maybe that's just idle gossip."

"If she *has* made such ridiculous disparagements," said Julia, "the president evidently doesn't agree."

"Apparently." Ulys brushed ashes from his

336

trousers and sighed. "After that, I left immediately for the West, so I missed the dinner with the dozen or so other generals — and I missed what followed after."

When Ulys paused, Rawlins straightened in his chair, which told Julia he knew what Ulys was going to say. "And what was that?"

"When President Lincoln and I spoke alone, he confided to me that he had never professed to be a military man or to know how campaigns should be conducted. He never wanted to interfere in military matters, but the procrastination of his commanders and pressure from the Congress and the people of the North forced him to issue certain orders throughout the war." Ulys puffed on his cigar, brooding over the memory. "All he'd ever wanted, he told me, was a general who would take responsibility and act, calling on him for assistance as needed. I assured him I would do the best I could with the means at hand, and I'd avoid annoying him and the War Department as much as possible."

"Then —" Julia paused, weighing the men's words. "He expects you to be that general."

"Yes, Julia." Ulys set the stub of his cigar in the ashtray and leaned forward to take both of her hands in his. "The day after I left Washington, President Lincoln appointed me general in chief of all the armies."

As Julia sat quietly absorbing the revelation, Ulys dismissed Rawlins and sent Fred off to tend to his pony. "I would have you and Jesse come with me to Washington," he told her when they were alone. "For a few weeks at least, or maybe a few months, for as long as my headquarters is close enough for me to visit you, and safe enough for you to visit me."

"Of course," said Julia, her heart thumping with trepidation curiously mixed with delight. "As you wish, Ulys."

She was going to Washington City. She shook her head in disbelief at the very thought. A greater distance than could be measured in miles stretched between Hardscrabble and the nation's capital, and she had never thought to cross it.

Fred protested when Julia informed him that he must return to St. Louis and, if Dr. Pope thought him healthy enough, back to school. "A soldier must follow orders, son," Ulys reminded him, and so Fred swallowed his complaints and packed his satchel, emulating as best he could his father's stoicism.

Ulys's promotion obliged him to make changes to the command structure, which he revealed to General Sherman, his successor as commander of the Army of Tennessee, aboard a train to Cincinnati. As she listened to their conference, Julia admired her husband's tact and fairness. "I want to restore to duty some officers who have been relieved from important commands," she overheard him tell Sherman. "They're all good, loyal soldiers, and we must not let them go under if we can avoid it. I'd like you to look out for those who have been removed from the West."

"Send them out and I'll see they're provided for," Sherman replied.

"Don't make any assignments until after I've spoken to Stanton."

Sherman nodded and made a foreboding remark in an undertone, something about whether certain generals would be willing to serve under commanders they had once outranked. Julia hoped he underestimated the officers' dedication.

Before they parted company in Cincinnati, Julia, anxious and uncertain about the proper etiquette in Washington City, found a moment for a private word with General Sherman. "I've never sought the public eye, but I fear it will fall on me regardless now that my husband has risen to such heights," she said. "I want always to conduct myself so that people will think well of us both. You've been to the capital often. What do you think I should do while I'm there?"

"What should you do in Washington?" Sherman looked a trifle annoyed, as if it were a ridiculous question or she had interrupted his contemplation of some serious war matter. "Return all your calls, every one of them, and promptly too."

Chastened, Julia thanked him with a bow and wished him safe travels and great success in his new command.

Aboard the train that would carry them to the East, Ulys offered no such advice on public life. "If all goes well," he said, digging into the pockets of his duster for a cigar, "I'll defeat Lee in Virginia, Sherman will capture Atlanta, and Lincoln will be reelected in November. I don't envy the president. I saw enough of the burdens of his position while I was in Washington to know that I'd be a fool to covet them."

CHAPTER SIXTEEN

March–April 1864

Julia's first glimpses of the capital through the carriage window revealed a startling juxtaposition of elegance and squalor. The tall marble dome of the Capitol, still under construction, rose proudly above snow-dusted streets where cows, pigs, and geese freely roamed. Pennsylvania Avenue and a few adjacent blocks of Seventh Street were paved, but the carriage rattled painfully over broken, uneven cobblestones. The opulent marble edifices housing various federal departments inspired awe, but the one-hundred-fifty-six-foot stub of the Washington Monument stood forlornly in the midst of an open field where cattle grazed.

"It was begun with such good intentions," Rawlins remarked, peering past her, "but construction was halted thanks to political squabbling, economic uncertainty, and vandalism."

"Do you suppose they'll ever finish it?" Julia asked.

"Perhaps," said Rawlins, frowning skeptically. "After the war is won."

"After the war is won, the South will need to be rebuilt," said Ulys. "I think President Washington would agree that houses and towns should come before monuments."

As they rode on, the white tents of the soldiers' camps provided a reassuringly familiar scene, but the overcrowded hospitals served as a painful reminder of what became of the wounded soldiers carried from Ulys's battlefields. Though it was late March, the city clung to the vestiges of winter, and Julia shrank back from the window and pressed her handkerchief to her nose when a gust of wind carried to her the fetid miasma of innumerable outhouses and refuse dumps. Eyes watering, she fervently hoped that come springtime, flowers budding on the trees lining the broad swath of grass south of the Executive Mansion would release their lovely fragrances throughout the city, masking the stench.

Their carriage soon arrived at the Willard Hotel, an elegant, five-story structure on the corner of Fourteenth Street and Pennsylvania Avenue. The Willard, Rawlins informed Julia, was not only the city's finest and largest hotel but also a nexus of Washington society and politics. Some observers considered the Willard more the center of Washington and the Union than the Capitol, the White House, or the State Department.

The hotel had endured the hardships of war, the front desk clerk told them, but not without great effort and ingenious diplomacy. When tempers first flared over secession, the Willard brothers had tried to maintain peace between contentious factions by assigning Southern guests rooms on a single floor and urging them to use the ladies' Fourteenth Street entrance, while Northerners were encouraged to use the main doors on the Pennsylvania Avenue side.

"Which entrance should I use?" Julia inquired as the clerk passed Ulys their heavy iron room keys. "I am a western woman for the Union."

"You are the wife of our great general Grant," the clerk said graciously. "You may use whatever entrance you like."

It was a relief to enter their lovely suite on the second floor and shut the door against the noise and bustle. Their rooms were comfortably furnished and appointed with all the modern conveniences — gaslights, polished mirrors, running water, and toilets. Best of all, the windows offered enticing views of the White House, rising tall, proud, and breathtakingly elegant on the other side of Lafayette Square.

Julia scarcely had time to rest and unpack before the bellman began bringing up cards from callers. While Julia went down to receive them in the ladies' parlor, Ulys went out to sit for a photograph at the offices of Matthew Brady. Julia wished she could have accompanied him instead, not that she wanted her heavy features and cross-eye preserved in all their imperfection. She was gratified that the ladies of the city's political and social elite wished to make her acquaintance, but hours of smiling and clasping hands and conversing with dozens of friendly callers wearied her, so after supper, when Ulys left to spend the evening at the White House with Mr. Lincoln, she and Jesse retired early.

She woke when Ulys climbed quietly into bed beside her sometime after midnight, smelling of tobacco and coffee. "How was your evening?" she murmured sleepily, rolling onto her side to snuggle up to him.

"I would've enjoyed it more had my lovely wife been on my arm." He kissed her on the forehead. "Tomorrow I'm leaving for the field. General Meade will meet me at Brandy Station, and he'll accompany me to Culpeper Court House. I think I'll make my headquarters there, but I want to take another look at the place before I decide."

"Shall Jesse and I accompany you?"

"Not this time, my dear little wife." He drew her closer. "But I'll be obliged to return to Washington now and then to consult with President Lincoln and Secretary Stanton, so you'll see me often."

"Not as often as I'd like."

"Nor I."

Ulys and most of his staff departed for Brandy Station at ten o'clock the next morning, but in his absence, Lieutenant Colonel Adam Badeau, Ulys's military secretary, dutifully escorted her whenever she needed to venture from the Willard. He was of Huguenot descent, a short, stoop-shouldered, red-haired, thinly bearded, blue-eyed fellow who would have had a scholarly air even without his wire spectacles. Before joining Ulys's staff, he had served as a clerk in the War Department, as a reporter for the *New York Evening Express,* and as a brigadier general's aide in Mississippi and Louisiana. Nearly a year before, Badeau had been severely wounded in the Siege of Port Hudson, and he had been sent to his home in New York City to convalesce. There, he confided to Julia as they strolled through the muddy streets as she returned her calls, he had been tended and entertained back to health by two friends — the famous actor Edwin Booth and his somewhat less celebrated brother, John Wilkes Booth.

"I imagine they made rather diverting nurses," Julia remarked.

"Quite so," said Badeau, still limping from his injuries, as he probably would for the rest of his life. "I never knew whether my bandages would be changed by one of my friends or by Hamlet, Bottom, or King Lear."

As Jule lifted her skirts clear of the mud and studied the street for the least treacherous crossing, the trill of a familiar laugh riveted her in place. Flooded with apprehension, she held her breath and turned her head slowly, scanning the faces of the passersby — and discovered Julia on the opposite sidewalk, laughing merrily on the arm of a short, red-haired, bespectacled officer.

Quickly Jule turned back to face front. Julia and her escort were walking west on Pennsylvania Avenue, as was she. If Jule retraced her steps and fled home, she would surely draw Julia's attention, but if she continued on, Julia's gaze might alight on her all the same.

Before she could decide what to do, an impatient gentleman brushed against her in passing, propelling her forward. Walking sedately, she silently berated herself for wearing her favorite knitted shawl, once dove gray but now fading black. She should have left it in Cincinnati with the rest of her old clothes, but it was warm and soft and boasted some of her finest, most intricate knitting. Gabriel had thought her especially beautiful in it, and she had kept it out of vanity, out of a foolish hope that he might admire her in it again one day.

Although the afternoon was chilly, Jule

casually slipped out of the shawl, folded it, and draped it over her arm, forcing herself to breathe steadily, to keep to a walk. Julia was not likely to recognize her. Unless she had trained that officer to see for her as Jule had done for so many years, from that distance her former slave would be only one more blurred figure in a plain dress going about her errands.

What was Julia Grant doing in Washington City? Had she somehow discovered that Jule was there?

Her heart in her throat, Jule ducked inside the nearest shop and watched through the front window until Julia and her escort passed. She knew she ought to hurry home, but she was determined to keep her appointment. In recent weeks she had been hired to dress the hair of well-to-do colored ladies in their homes, and thanks to the recommendations of Mrs. Elizabeth Keckley, a popular, very successful dressmaker she had met at Union Bethel Church, she had added several white ladies of Washington's most elite social circles to her clientele. After a fellow resident of her boardinghouse employed as a bellboy at the Willard mentioned her services to the concierge, she had begun receiving occasional requests from hotel guests who needed their hair dressed for whatever important occasion had brought them to the capital. Jule was steadily accumulating clients and experience, but she was too new to her profession to risk damaging her reputation by failing to show up for an appointment.

Steeling herself, Jule emerged from the shop and followed behind Julia and the officer, keeping her distance, silently willing them to enter a building or turn down another block. But they kept to the same route Jule intended, and before long they confirmed her fears by entering the Willard through the Pennsylvania Avenue entrance. Without breaking stride, Jule continued around the corner and slipped quietly into the hotel through the rear door reserved for employees and servants.

When she emerged into the lobby, she hung back and surreptitiously scanned the room until she was certain Julia was not among the busy throng. The hotel's public rooms were illuminated by gaslight and opulently furnished in rosewood, damask, lace, and velvet, and they smelled of cigar smoke and spilled whiskey. Everywhere gentlemen hurried back and forth, their arms full of documents, their lapels adorned with bright pins declaring their various allegiances. Julia was not among them.

Jule discreetly inquired with the concierge and was sent upstairs to the suite of Mrs. Bramlette, the wife of the governor of Kentucky, who had come to Washington to confer with President Lincoln on the contentious issue of Negro enlistment. "What do you think, Jule?" Mrs. Bramlette queried after describing at length and with great enthusiasm how her husband's position conflicted with the president's.

"I know General Grant's in favor of it," Jule said, frowning in concentration as she wound locks of Mrs. Bramlette's long, wheat-brown hair around a hot iron, framing her face in glossy ringlets. "He's sure colored soldiers will strengthen the Union army so much that the Confederacy will reel from the blow."

Heedless of the hot iron, Mrs. Bramlette turned to peer up at her in surprise. "How would you know so much about General Grant's opinion?"

Quickly Jule assumed a knowing expression. "Oh, I hear things — but I never say where or who. You understand."

"Of course." Mrs. Bramlette made a little pout as she turned back to the looking glass. "In your occupation, discretion is everything. I'm glad to know that my secrets — and my husband's — will be as safe with you too."

If the governor's wife was disappointed that Jule refused to gossip, she was thoroughly delighted with her hair, and she promised to recommend Jule to all her friends whenever they visited the capital. With her wages — as well as a generous gratuity — tucked safely into her reticule, Jule bade Mrs. Bramlette good afternoon and left the Willard as inconspicuously as she had come.

From her first day as a fugitive, Jule had followed the Grants in the papers, not only to see if Julia would advertise a reward for the capture and return of her fugitive maid, but also to gather news of young Fred's recovery from his illness. She had read about the general's promotion and had known that he had come to the capital to see the president, but she had seen no mention of Julia's arrival in the city.

The next morning, still shaken from her narrow escape, Jule went to Union Bethel Church to seek her pastor's advice. Astonishment pushed him back in his chair when she revealed the identity of her former mistress, but he listened intently as she described her plight, without warning her that she had made an enemy of the wife of one of the most powerful men in the country. That, Jule already knew.

"I've just gotten settled," she lamented when her tale was done. "I'd hate to start over somewhere else, but don't see how I can stay in Washington if Mrs. Grant means to live here too."

"She's taken rooms at the Willard," the minister said. "If she meant to stay longer, wouldn't General Grant rent a house for her?"

"I suppose so." A faint hope stirred. "She'd likely have all the children with her too, and one of the bellboys told me he's seen only the youngest."

"You're probably safe for now. Mrs. Grant may be entirely unaware that you're in the capital. Avoid the Willard, watch for news of her travels in the press, and if you discover that she means to settle here — well, let's not worry about that unless it happens."

Much relieved, Jule thanked him, but as she made her way back to her boardinghouse, she felt as if she were already bidding a sad, reluctant farewell to the street corners and shops and friends she had only recently come to know.

"A messenger brought this while you were sleeping," Ulys said after kissing Julia good morning. Newly returned from the front to confer with President Lincoln, General Halleck, and Secretary Stanton, he kept to military hours and had been awake to receive the cream-colored envelope on a silver tray.

"It's addressed to both of us," Julia said, squinting at the elegant script.

"I thought you'd enjoy opening it."

Julia broke the seal and peered carefully at the paper, bringing it closer to her eyes, moving it farther away, tilting her head. Then she gasped and thrust the page toward Ulys. "Darling, tell me if my silly eyes deceive me or if we've been invited to a reception at the White House this evening."

"It appears that we have been," said Ulys, barely glancing at the paper, enjoying her excitement.

"Oh, we must accept right away! I wonder what I shall wear — one of the gowns I bought in Philadelphia, perhaps. Do you think them elegant enough?"

"You'll be lovely in anything you wear," Ulys assured her, but then he hesitated. "I'll find someone to escort you."

"Can't you delay your return to the field one day more?" she cajoled. "You can't decline an invitation from the president."

"I have before and survived to tell the tale," said Ulys. "You can give the Lincolns my regrets — and yours, if you refuse to go without me."

Julia had no intention of declining, and so later that evening, hours after Ulys had departed for headquarters, she donned her most becoming new gown, a deep-green watered silk trimmed in eyelet lace, and engaged a maid to brush her long, thick locks and arrange them into a stylish coil. Jule would have done better, Julia thought with a pang as she studied her reflection in the mirror, but it would suffice.

The night air was brisk, but Julia found the exercise invigorating as she walked the few blocks to the White House accompanied by her two dashing escorts, Lieutenant Colonel Badeau and Admiral David Farragut, whose recent successes at sea had earned him great acclaim throughout the North.

Carriages filled the circular drive in front of the White House nearly all the way to Lafayette Square, but Julia and her companions easily made their way past the bronze statue of Thomas Jefferson in the center of the driveway and proceeded beneath the tall white columns of the front portico. The burly, white-haired doorman greeted them in an Irish brogue and admitted them into the vestibule, and from there they strolled down the brightly illuminated corridor to the Red Room. The public parlor was richly furnished in crimson satin and gold damask, with heavy gilded cornices framing the windows and a profusion of ormolu work gleaming in the gaslight. Elegant vases, some of them appearing quite ancient, adorned polished tables along the walls, and in a corner sat a grand piano, unattended at the moment, but hinting at the pleasing possibility of music later. An impressive full-length portrait of George Washington commanded attention from the wall to her left, and although Julia was much too far away to read the artist's signature, she was certain she beheld the work by Gilbert Stuart that Dolley Madison had famously saved from being consumed in flames when the British destroyed the first Executive Mansion. A lovely new red carpet softened the footfalls of the dozens of guests mingling and chatting or standing in the line to pay their respects to the president and his wife.

Admiral Farragut drew admiring glances and respectful murmurs as they joined the queue, and Julia observed a few curious looks for herself, as if everyone wondered who the plain, sturdy woman on the arm of their valiant hero could be. Julia smiled and nodded pleasantly, knowing that her anonymity would be short-lived, for the ladies in the crowd who had called upon her at the Willard would quickly enlighten the others.

Before long she and her escorts reached the top of the queue. President Lincoln — clad in a handsome black suit, tall and gaunt and melancholy of expression — immediately recognized Admiral Farragut and welcomed him heartily. The admiral presented Julia, but his words were drowned out in the din. "I beg your pardon?" the president said, bending his lanky frame toward them and smiling kindly.

"This is Mrs. General Grant, Mr. President," said Badeau, loud enough for all nearby to hear. Heads turned, eyebrows rose, interested gazes took in Julia up and down and politely flitted away.

"Mrs. General Grant," the president echoed. He beamed warmly as he took both her hands in his. "Mrs. Grant, it is truly my great pleasure to meet you at last. But where is the general?"

"I begged the general to remain and accompany me," Julia explained, "but he said he must go to the front, and that he was sure the President and Mrs. Lincoln would excuse him."

Mr. Lincoln seemed delighted with her reply, and he assured her that General Grant's absence was entirely forgivable. He presented her to his wife, who smiled so cordially and took her hand so readily that Julia could hardly believe she despised Ulys or had ever called him a butcher. Mrs. Lincoln's expression was intelligent and inquisitive, her complexion white and smooth except for faint shadows beneath her clear blue eyes, her neck and arms elegantly molded, but otherwise, like Julia herself she was plain and tended toward stoutness, which her short stature and her husband's great height unfortunately exaggerated. Her elegant gown of deep lavender silk was masterfully fashioned, if a trifle too elaborately embellished for Julia's simple tastes, but it unquestionably outshone any Julia had seen in the fine shops of Philadelphia. She knew it was the handiwork of the gifted, generous woman she had met at Union Bethel Church, Elizabeth Keckley.

"My dear Mrs. Grant," Mrs. Lincoln said warmly. "Mr. Lincoln admires General Grant very much. He is convinced that the general will bring about a Union victory at last."

"The general has dedicated himself to that great endeavor," Julia replied. "I speak as a partial judge, but I'm certain the president will have no cause to regret entrusting General Grant with his high command."

Mrs. Lincoln smiled knowingly. "I'm not one to dismiss the judgment of a great man's wife, partial or not."

They chatted pleasantly for a few moments, and upon discovering a mutual fondness for flowers, Mrs. Lincoln invited Julia to tour the White House conservatories. "But first, would you care to join me in receiving our guests?" she inquired, gesturing to a place at her side. "I'm sure they would all welcome the opportunity to meet the wife of our new general in chief."

"Oh, thank you, Mrs. Lincoln, but I couldn't," Julia replied, a trifle bashfully. "You are Mrs. President, and I am merely a guest. This place is rightfully yours alone."

Julia had spoken with her usual sincerity, but Mrs. Lincoln drew herself up and beamed proudly, obviously flattered.

The queue moved along and Julia and her escorts with it, but when they withdrew to the Blue Room, the press of the crowd was so great that Admiral Farragut proposed that they pass on to the Green Room. Lowering his voice, he added, "The commonality gather there. Do you dare venture it?"

Smiling up at him, Julia replied, "I think I

may venture anywhere on the arm of Admiral Farragut."

He smiled, bowed, and led her off, while Badeau remained behind, cornered by a distinguished-looking gentleman in civilian attire who probably hoped to petition Ulys for a favor or an appointment. Ulys's aides had become quite popular of late with opportunists who sought a quick and easy way to reach the great man.

No sooner had they found a good place to stand and observe the beautiful ladies and brave men in attendance than the guests from the Blue Room followed after and, without any instructions whatsoever, formed another queue to pay their respects. To Julia's astonishment, cabinet ministers, senators, foreign dignitaries, Supreme Court justices, distinguished officers of the army and navy, and a hundred or more of the beaux and belles of Washington passed before her and Admiral Farragut, smiling, welcoming her to the capital, and cordially shaking her hand.

More than an hour elapsed before the entire receiving line passed before them, and everyone Julia met showed her the utmost courtesy for her husband's sake. Afterward, Julia reminded Admiral Farragut of Mrs. Lincoln's gracious suggestion that she tour the conservatory. "I believe Badeau claimed the honor of escorting you there," the admiral said, offering her his arm and leading her back to the Green Room.

They found Badeau standing a little apart from the throng, engaged in a quiet, heated conversation with the loveliest woman in attendance, quite possibly the most beautiful young woman Julia had ever seen. The auburn-haired beauty looked to be in her early twenties, with intelligent green eyes flecked with hazel. Graceful and vivacious, she was becomingly attired in a gown of pale green silk, her hair arranged in an elegant Grecian twist adorned with pearls and diamonds.

As Julia and the admiral approached, the young woman and Badeau broke off their muted argument. "Mrs. Grant," Badeau said, "May I present Mrs. Senator William Sprague. Mrs. Sprague, please allow me to introduce you to Mrs. General Ulysses S. Grant."

"Mrs. Grant," said the young woman warmly, clasping her hand. "It is such pleasure to meet you. My father and I — and my husband — trust that he will bring about a Union victory soon."

"Thank you, Mrs. Sprague," Julia replied.

"Mrs. Sprague's father is Mr. Salmon Chase," said Admiral Farragut.

"Yes, of course." Julia had never met Mr. Chase, but she certainly knew of him. As secretary of the treasury, he was responsible for issuing cotton permits and making trading policies that Ulys had been obliged to spend far too much of his time enforcing. He was also a teetotaler — quieter on the subject than the fiery Rawlins, perhaps, but just as adamant in his views and suspicious of drinkers, even those who indulged in only a rare tipple. According to trusted friends, it was Secretary Chase who had passed along to the president scurrilous rumors that during the siege of Vicksburg, Ulys had been drinking excessively out of sheer boredom. Ulys was, reporter Murat Halstead was said to have written to Mr. Chase, "Most of the time more than half drunk, and much of the time idiotically drunk." After Secretary Stanton ordered an investigation, he had concluded that Ulys's drunkenness — of which no proof had been discovered — clearly did not interfere with his ability to win battles. No action been taken against Ulys, and rumor told that Mr. Lincoln had joked that if he knew which brand of whiskey Ulys favored, he would immediately distribute bottles of it to his other generals.

Julia had been outraged when she learned about the investigation, but Ulys had reminded her that petty, cowardly folk had been raising the same accusations against him for most of his military career, and no one had ever found a scrap of evidence against him. "It could be worse," he had said as Julia fumed. "Sherman was accused of being insane — not reckless or foolhardy, but entirely insane — and it wasn't easy to defend himself against that."

But Julia decided there was nothing to be gained by introducing this long, fraught history into a conversation with Mr. Chase's lovely daughter, who was being quite friendly and perhaps did not know what her father had done. "You're a native of Cincinnati, are you not?" Julia asked instead. "I've had the great pleasure of visiting the city often, as General Grant's family live across the river in Covington."

"Yes, I am, and I'm proud that General Grant represents our home state with such distinction." Mrs. Sprague had an enchanting voice, rich and musical. "I do hope I'll have the honor of meeting him soon."

"I hope so too, because that will mean he's returned to Washington, and I do miss him when duty calls him away."

Mrs. Sprague smiled sympathetically and rested a graceful hand on Julia's forearm. "I completely understand. Business often calls my husband home to Rhode Island, but I find consolation in the company of my father and sister — and in meeting pleasant ladies such as yourself."

Charmed, Julia smiled and thanked her. With a gracious bow, Mrs. Sprague bade her good evening and moved on in a whisper of silk, gracefully gliding across the floor until she was detained by several handsome officers.

"Take care with her," Badeau warned, offering Julia his arm as they watched the younger woman smile up at her admirers, engaging them in what seemed to be lively banter. "She's someone to be reckoned with."

"Oh, come, now. She seems lovely." Julia took Badeau's arm and strolled alongside him to the East Room and down the corridor to the conservatory. "Although I could not help noticing that my arrival interrupted a heated exchange between the two of you."

"She is her father's official hostess and a dominant figure in the Republican Party in her own right," said Badeau, glowering. "It's her life's ambition to see her father president and herself as First Lady. Mrs. Lincoln believes her husband to be the best man for the job, so naturally the two ladies have become bitter enemies."

"That's not natural at all," Julia protested. "Gentlemen can disagree fiercely over politics or business and their ladies remain good friends. Our friendships are a constant that helps restore civility when our gentlemen's disagreements are resolved. I'm sure I could never hate my dear friend Mrs. Longstreet, and I would probably like Mrs. General Lee too, although their husbands are fighting for the rebels."

"That's probably because good ladies such

as you remain above politics. Mrs. Sprague, the Belle of Washington as they call her, strides right into the midst of it. She won't rest until her father is made president, and after that, she'll probably want her husband to succeed him. They say a tremendous amount of her father's success is due to her political maneuvering and his greatest missteps befall him when he fails to consult her."

"Really," said Julia, intrigued. She liked to think that her support and affection helped Ulys to succeed, but she could not plan military strategy. It astonished her to think that a woman half her age could have such influence.

"Indeed," said Badeau shortly, "but her charms and demands will not move me. Whenever I encounter her — and she seems to descend upon me wherever I go —"

Julia gave him a sidelong look. "I daresay that prospect would please most gentlemen."

"Not I." Badeau stopped short in the corridor and clasped a hand to his brow, shaking his head in weary exasperation, inspiring other guests to glance curiously their way in passing. "I wish she would relent. Her persistent demands that General Grant call on her father are driving me to distraction."

Julia laughed, astonished. "General Grant and Secretary Chase have had some disagreements through the post and the telegraph, but if the Chases invite the general to call, why shouldn't he accept?"

"You don't understand."

"No, evidently not."

"When General Grant comes to Washington, he calls on the president and the secretary of war. Every other gentleman calls on *him.*"

"I see," said Julia, hiding her amusement as Badeau resumed walking toward the conservatory, his pace brisker than before, spurred by indignation or an unconscious desire to escape Mrs. Sprague. "It's a question of rank. Whoever calls first shows deference to the other."

"Yes, and I will not allow Mrs. Sprague to contrive to have General Grant defer to Secretary Chase. The general is the better man."

"I can hardly disagree with that," said Julia, "but all this fuss seems very silly to me, and I don't think the general would countenance such machinations."

Badeau made no reply, but his expression, somehow both sheepish and resolute, told Julia he had no intention of surrendering the point to the lovely Kate Chase Sprague.

And yet he lost the battle nonetheless. Soon after the reception, Julia sent an amusing account of the conflict to Ulys, and in his reply, he wrote that he had no time to waste on such trivial matters as who called on whom. One April afternoon, while out riding during one of his brief visits to Washington, he abruptly put an end to the contrived conflict by calling on Secretary Chase at his home, a gracious three-story Greek Revival brick mansion at the corner of Sixth and E Streets. He was warmly welcomed by Mr. Chase, Mrs. Sprague, and her husband, the junior senator from Rhode Island. "You pay too much attention to such trifles," Ulys scolded Badeau afterward. Julia felt sorry for the chastened aide, who had not meant any harm and had acted only out of loyalty and respect for his general.

The call was immediately returned, and an invitation for the Grants to dine at the Chase residence soon followed. Other invitations came in flurries whenever the newspapers reported that Ulys was expected in the capital. Julia delighted in the attention and praise showered upon her husband during his visits, but Ulys was, as usual, uncomfortable with the fuss and eager to return to the field. But as general in chief, he was obliged to make the rounds of Washington society, where he was cheered and serenaded and toasted with such fervor that Julia was not surprised to hear him once again whispered about as a potential presidential candidate. On one occasion, Julia was astonished to discover Ulys stiffly maneuvering about a ballroom with none other than the Belle of Washington in his arms.

"She makes him look much less awkward than he usually does in such circumstances," Rawlins observed, but Julia was not amused.

"Your dislike of dancing and music is well-known," Julia pointed out as Ulys escorted her back to the Willard afterward. "You never dance. You won't even dance with me. Mrs. Sprague must have enchanted you."

"She's a very persuasive young woman," Ulys admitted, a faint, faraway smile appearing on his lips. Frowning, Julia abandoned the unpleasant line of questioning before he inadvertently admitted something hurtful to her.

She was, to her misgivings, less wary elsewhere. The next morning, as Ulys's staff prepared for his return to headquarters, she overheard Rawlins and Badeau discussing her Washington debut.

"I think the ladies of Washington are inclined to patronize Mrs. Grant," said Badeau indignantly. "They're wrong to do so. It's my opinion that she managed her first visit to the White House with tact and grace, and ever since she has asserted herself with great delicacy and skill."

Julia crept quietly closer, warming to the praise.

"But of course," Rawlins replied. "She'll find herself liked by all, for she's too plain to induce envy, too devoted to her family to provoke gossip, and insufficiently sharp-tongued to incite controversy. I think we can safely trust that unlike Mrs. Lincoln, she'll do nothing to embarrass her husband — at least, not intentionally."

Badeau barked a laugh, surprised. "Do you mean she might do so unintentionally?"

"She *is* her father's daughter, and she shares his views on slavery."

"You don't mean to accuse Mrs. Grant of supporting the Confederacy!"

"Certainly not. She's as true a Unionist as you or I — and yet she is tragically, irredeemably ignorant on the subject of slavery. Did you know she forced her slave to accompany her whenever she came to headquarters?"

"Yes," Badeau admitted. "I've seen her. A tiny, pretty little maid, as I recall."

"What a spectacle she made, the wife of the Union general in chief striding about the encampments with her poor little slave in tow, blithely unaware of how others regarded her. Everyone is fond of Mrs. Grant, but they cannot understand her unwitting, appalling cruelty in this single regard. My wife has often been obliged to defend her to the other officers' wives."

"I think we can trust Mrs. Grant not to make any speeches advocating slavery," Badeau said. "And her little maid has run away, so we need not fear a reprise of those pathetic scenes."

Julia had heard enough — more than

enough. Cheeks burning, heart heavy, she silently withdrew.

She said nothing of what she had overheard to Ulys. Not long thereafter, on a bright, balmy day in the middle of April, Ulys escorted her and Jesse down the James River to Fortress Monroe, where they observed the gallant troops in review, toured the ruins of Hampton, and made a quick excursion out to Norfolk. Julia watched with dubious interest as a colored regiment marched and drilled, and when Ulys queried her, she was obliged to admit that they performed as well as any white troops she had seen.

A few days later, Ulys returned to Washington to meet with President Lincoln, and afterward, when he joined Julia and Jesse at the Willard, he seemed distracted. She knew many cares weighed upon him, but by evening, worry compelled her to ask if something else was amiss.

"No," he said, "but I think you and Jesse should return to St. Louis."

Julia's heart thumped. "Why? Why now?"

He puffed his cigar silently for a long moment. "Spring has come," he finally said. "The roads are passable again. Lee will be on the move, and I intend to confront him."

CHAPTER SEVENTEEN

April–June 1864

Colonel Hillyer kindly agreed to accompany Julia and Jesse to his home in New York so that Julia could visit his wife, Anna, while he arranged a suitable escort to St. Louis. Though Julia was sorry to leave Ulys, she was happy to be reunited with her friend, and she found New York City at least as exciting as Washington.

Soon after her arrival, Colonel Hillyer escorted Julia and Anna to the great Sanitary Fair at Palace Garden, a glorious exhibition of art and curiosities with a marketplace of delicacies and fine goods. The proceeds from admissions and sales would be presented to the United States Sanitary Commission, an organization that served soldiers and veterans. Ladies throughout the North had formed local chapters of the commission, and their tireless fund-raising efforts had already provided millions of dollars' worth of money and goods to support the Union cause.

Someone must have alerted the authorities to their presence, for they had not been long at the fair when a thin, mustachioed man in a dark civilian suit descended upon them, fluttering with nervousness as he bowed and introduced himself as Mr. David Elder, chief clerk of the executive committee. "We are truly honored by your visit, Mrs. Grant," he said with great dignity.

"That's very kind of you," said Julia. "I know General Grant would have accompanied me if he could have. He would want to thank you personally for all the Sanitary Commission has done for his army."

Drawing himself up proudly, Mr. Elder invited Julia and her companions to accompany him to the Curiosity Shop, where all manner of interesting artifacts from foreign lands and the American frontier were displayed. Julia recognized the lady in charge of the room as the wife of General Irvin McDowell, but before Julia could greet her, Mr. Elder introduced them with great formality.

"I know Mrs. Grant well," said Mrs. McDowell, holding out her hands to Julia. "We're old friends from our Ohio days. My goodness, how long has it been?"

"Far too long," Julia declared, taking her hands and smiling. "You've been keeping yourself very busy in the meantime, I see."

"I try to do my part," Mrs. McDowell

replied. By then a small crowd had gathered around, murmuring to one another and staring at Julia and her companions. As their numbers grew, Julia felt increasingly uncomfortable beneath their scrutiny, and she was relieved when Mr. Elder suggested they visit the parlor set aside for the ladies' executive committee. There, in relative quiet and privacy, she was introduced to two other generals' wives, Mrs. General George McClellan, a reserved, sad-faced woman, and the cordial and vivacious Mrs. General John Frémont.

After a respite, Julia approached Mr. Elder. "I'd like to see more of the fair, but I wish to remain incognito as much as possible," she explained in an undertone, well aware of the reporters taking notes just outside the doorway. "Would you be so kind as to arrange for an escort, some person well acquainted with the exhibits who could point out to me all the objects of interest?"

"I gladly volunteer," said Mr. Elder, squaring his shoulders and lifting his chin. "I hope you'll grant me the privilege of showing you the fair."

Julia and Anna exchanged a look, hiding smiles, for it seemed unlikely that Mr. Elder would be refused. "Thank you, indeed," said Julia. "I'm sure we'll enjoy the sights much better with your guidance."

Mr. Elder offered Julia his arm and led

them downstairs to the hall of arms and trophies. "This interesting department is supervised by a number of highly accomplished ladies," he said proudly, "for the most part, wives of major and brigadier generals." Two of these ladies were present at the moment — Miss Anderson, the daughter of the hero of Fort Sumter, and Mrs. General Egbert Viele.

After observing many dazzling artifacts, Julia and her companions came to a magnificent sword with a jeweled hilt and a shining silver blade engraved with Moorish designs. When Julia asked about the lists and collection boxes arrayed around it, Mr. Elder explained that as a fund-raiser, the sword would be presented to the people's favorite general as determined by popular vote. "Would you like to cast a ballot, Mrs. Grant?" he asked.

"I certainly would." Julia stepped forward, paid her fee of one dollar, took pencil in hand, and put down her name for General McClellan, who already commanded an impressive lead of more than fourteen hundred votes. Gasps and murmurs and even a smattering of applause went up from the crowd, who kept a respectful distance as Julia smiled pleasantly, bowed, and continued on her way.

Anna linked her arm with Julia's and whispered, "Well done!"

Before Julia could reply, Colonel Hillyer

exclaimed, "What? Voting for McClellan? How can this be? Don't you want General Grant to win the sword?"

"Of course I do, Colonel," said Julia, as Anna discreetly gestured for her husband to lower his voice, "but it wouldn't be very good form for me to vote for my husband, would it?"

"Why not, if you believe him to be the most deserving? I know he's your favorite general, so why shouldn't you vote accordingly?"

"I've never voted except at school when we chose our May Queen," Julia explained. "The etiquette on such occasions was always that rival queens should vote for each other. Any other course would have been regarded as selfish and dishonorable. I simply voted upon that precedent."

"And a gracious act it was," said Anna stoutly, patting her arm.

Colonel Hillyer shook his head. "Choosing according to sentiment, not reason — this is evidence enough why women must not be permitted to vote."

"I voted my conscience," Julia protested. "Is that not right? And is it not wrong to use a single woman's ballot to conclude whether all other women should be permitted to vote?"

"You must admit, your method isn't very scientific," Anna told her husband. "Are you certain *you're* not relying too much on sentiment rather than reason?"

Julia and Anna exchanged merry glances as Colonel Hillyer frowned in consternation and urged them on to the next display.

The next morning after breakfast, while Julia and Anna sat on the rear terrace watching their children play in the Hillyers' garden, the Irish servant girl hurried over from within the house clutching a small bundle of newspapers. "I think you'll be wanting to read these, Mrs. Grant," she said, handing her the papers.

Julia squinted at the paper on top of the pile, *The New York Herald.* The sunshine was bright enough, and the typeface large and bold enough, for her to make out the headlines of the first story on the front page. " 'The Fair,' " she read aloud. " 'Mrs. General Grant Pays a Visit and Votes for McClellan.' Oh, dear."

"Read on," Anna urged.

Julia took a deep breath. " 'Great Excitement About the Sword. Little Mac 1,620 Ahead Last Night.' Evidently he gained some ground after we left. 'Arrangements for Counting the Votes To-day.' "

After the headlines, the print became so small that Julia had to pass the papers to Anna, who read aloud *The Herald*'s startlingly detailed account of their visit to the Sanitary Fair — with most of the column devoted to Julia's vote for General McClellan. " 'The incident created quite a sensation,' " Anna read, " 'and was talked of the rest of the day by the visitors.' "

"Oh, dear," Julia said again, with even greater dismay. Ulys would not like her to create a sensation, and she did not like to be talked about.

The other papers offered similar reports, all of them full of praise for Julia's vote. "Her action was a graceful evidence of queenly magnanimity," declared *The New York World.* "It has never been our fortune to record a more graceful and magnanimous act. It marks the lady as the possessor of the loveliest attributes of her sex — the highest qualities of heart and soul. It was more than queenly — it was womanly."

Julia sat back in her chair. "I don't know whether to be pleased or mortified."

Anna laughed. "Then be pleased."

"What if Ulys disapproves?"

"Why should he?"

"I didn't vote for him."

"And in so doing, you earned the admiration of the press and the public. How could your husband be anything but proud of you?"

Julia suspected that Ulys would not like that she had voted at all, even for a good cause.

The voting closed at eight o'clock that evening, at which time the votes were tallied by the special committee in public view. To Julia's relief and no small delight, a messenger came to the Hillyer residence shortly after ten o'clock to announce that Ulys had overcome McClellan's substantial lead to win the magnificent sword.

But three days later — Ulys's forty-second birthday — she received a letter he had written on the evening the votes were counted. "I see by the papers you are having a good time in New York," he began. "Hope you are enjoying it. A telegraph dispatch announces that a sword has been voted to me. I am rather sorry for it, or rather regret that my name has been mixed up in such a contest. I could not help it however and therefore have nothing to blame myself for in the matter."

The letter continued for two more paragraphs, reports about the weather at headquarters and requests that she give his regards to their children and the Hillyers. He had written not a single word more about the sword — not one line of praise for her deft handling of the affair, not a single remark to say how pleased he was that she had charmed the public. Instead he wanted nothing to do with the one event that had brought her warm accolades from a particularly difficult audience to impress — the press and people of New York City.

Bitterly sorry, Julia folded the page and hid it away in her luggage, for a peculiar superstition prevented her from discarding his letters. She wished he had never sent it. She thought she had managed a fraught situation with grace and that he would reward her with praise, so his unexpected annoyance and disapproval were difficult to bear. The acclaim of the press, the praise of the entire world, meant nothing if Ulys was disappointed in her — but inseparable from her regret was indignation, for her every instinct told her that his oblique reprimand was unwarranted and unfair.

Jule felt a wave of immeasurable relief when she learned that Julia had left Washington for New York, and yet she read with great satisfaction of Julia's triumph at the Sanitary Fair. "That's Julia through and through," she remarked, smiling over a newspaper report about the magnificent sword and Julia's vote for General McClellan — but then she caught herself. How, she wondered, could she feel any lingering fondness for the woman who had kept her unjustly enslaved for most of her life?

Then she recalled the fleeting, innocent sweetness of their ginger-and-cream years and wondered how she could not.

Even so, knowing that she need not fear a chance encounter on the bustling streets of Washington brought Jule an expansive sense of release, of air enough to breathe. Despite the tensions and deprivations of war, Washington City seemed abundant with possibilities, vibrant with hope despite the squalor of the contraband camps and the horrors of the military hospitals.

There was too an air of expectation, of a long season of waiting coming to an end, for the spring sunshine had dried the muddy roads of Virginia enough to make them passable. Armies north and south would soon be on the move — and for the first time, General Grant would confront General Lee.

Jule had seen innumerable military reviews during her time with Julia in the field, but she turned out just the same on April 26 to join the crowds lining Fourteenth Street to watch General Ambrose Burnside's thirty thousand troops march out to reinforce the Army of the Potomac. In the early months of the war, her landlady told her, every parade of soldiers through the capital had drawn cheering crowds, but in recent years the sight of passing regiments had become so commonplace that they attracted little notice. But even Jule, a newcomer to the city, understood that this would be no ordinary procession, for the column would include seven regiments of United States Colored Troops.

It seemed that every person of color in Washington had come to watch the soldiers set out to confront General Lee. A thrill of joy and anticipation flooded Jule as she waited on the sidewalk among the crowd, listening for the familiar strains of fife and drums that heralded the column's approach. She joined in the applause as down New York Avenue they came, brave and dignified, turning south onto Fourteenth Street past the cheering throng.

"There they are," a joyful voice rang out. Jule glanced over her shoulder and spied a colored woman gesturing to the passing column, a toddler in her arms and two older girls by her side. "Do you see how well they march?" she asked her children, beaming. "Do you see? Those are our soldiers, our brave colored soldiers."

As the awestruck girls assured their mother that they did indeed see, Jule gazed at the dark, proud, eager faces of the colored soldiers and felt her throat constricting with emotion. Their splendid uniforms, the rousing music, the bold and steady marching, the cheering crowd — in that glorious moment it seemed to Jule that there was no limit to what the people of her race could accomplish in the years to come, unhindered by slavery, when peace once again reigned over a reunited nation. She had never witnessed a more glorious sight, and she prayed that the men would acquit themselves bravely. Everyone would be watching them, she knew, following their movements in the press, scrutinizing and debating their performance on the battlefield. Many white folks north and south alike would viciously pray for them to fail, but Jule would pray even more fervently for them to triumph. The United States Colored Troops carried the hopes and faith of every colored person with them, for in victory they would surely disprove every false, slanderous word ever spoken about the cowardice and weakness of their menfolk.

The marching regiments approached the Willard Hotel, where President Lincoln and General Burnside stood on the eastern portico to review the parade. When the colored troops passed the president, they waved their hats in the air and cheered for the Great Emancipator, the man who had set their people free. Mr. Lincoln stood with his hat off, bowing and nodding, and Jule's heart swelled with gratitude and pride to see that he showed them the same respect and courtesy he had shown every white soldier.

The column needed more than four hours to cross Pennsylvania Avenue. After the soldiers came scores of ambulances, followed by thousands of cattle to feed the troops, all heading across the river to Virginia. A sense of purpose and determination filled the city, from the marching soldiers to the people lining the streets showering them with blessings and good wishes. And then they were gone, leaving hope and fear and anticipation and apprehension in their wake.

The crowds dispersed, and Jule, too, turned toward home. Now, she knew, the citizens of

Washington City would again prepare for the inevitable deluge of casualties.

In New York, Julia anxiously awaited Secretary Stanton's telegrams bringing her news from the front.

Ulys's army and Lee's clashed in the Wilderness, and the dead and wounded poured into Washington from field hospitals, just as they had after the battles at Bull Run, the Peninsula, Antietam, and Gettysburg. Julia felt faint when she imagined the noxious odor of bodies in the summer heat hanging sickly sweet over every street and alley, no corner of it spared the miasma of death. She was stung, too, by a guilty grief when she learned that General Longstreet had been seriously wounded in the neck and shoulder in the battle, accidentally shot by Confederate troops who had mistaken him and his companions for federal cavalry. Julia did not know where her cousin had been taken or whether he was expected to live or die. When she closed her eyes to pray for him, she saw him as he had been on her wedding day, standing beside Ulys, handsome and happy and gallant in the uniform of the nation he would eventually repudiate. She knew that the best she could hope for was that Cousin James would recover from his wounds but would be unable to return to the field.

From the Wilderness the fighting moved on

to Spotsylvania Court House, and from there to the North Anna River. Casualties were massive on both sides, disproportionately so for the Union, but the outcomes of the battles were tactically inconclusive. As stunned as the people of the North were by the staggering tolls of the dead and wounded, they were also heartened by what Ulys did each time he failed to destroy General Lee's army: In circumstances where his predecessors had retreated, he regrouped and moved his valiant army forward, again and again, keeping General Lee on the defensive and inching ever closer to Richmond. Everyone then realized what Julia, well aware of his superstition about retracing his steps, had known for decades — General Grant possessed a very different military mind than the people of the Union had yet observed in that terrible war.

In the second week of May, an escort was secured at last and Julia and Jesse left New York for St. Louis, so she missed the long-awaited letter Ulys had sent her from Spotsylvania Court House. Colonel Hillyer telegraphed her the essential details, but it was not until she arrived in St. Louis several days later that she held the precious letter and read it entire.

Near Spotsylvania C. H. Va.
May 13 1864

Dear Julia,

The ninth day of battle is just closing with victory so far on our side. But the enemy are fighting with great desperation entrenching themselves in every position they take up. We have lost many thousand men killed and wounded and the enemy have no doubt lost more. We have taken about eight thousand prisoners and lost likely three thousand. Among our wounded the great majority are but slightly hurt but most of them will be unfit for service in this battle. I have reinforcements now coming up which will greatly encourage our men and discourage the enemy correspondingly.

I am very well and full of hope. I see from the papers the country is also very hopeful.

Remember me to your father and family. Kisses for yourself and the children. The world has never seen so bloody or protracted a battle as the one being fought and I hope never will again. The enemy were really whipped yesterday but their situation is desperate beyond anything heretofore known. To lose this battle they lose their cause. As bad as it is, they have fought for it with a gallantry worthy of a better.

Ulys.

As she read, Julia envisioned the scenes of carnage so vividly that she wept — for Ulys, for his courageous men, for the fallen men and widowed women on both sides.

By the first day of June, Ulys had driven the Army of the Potomac closer to the Confederate capital of Richmond than it had been in two years. At nine o'clock that night he had written to tell Julia that a very severe battle had taken place that day, and that despite the late hour he still heard firing along some parts of the battlefront. "The rebels are making a desperate fight," he had written, "and I presume will continue to do so as long as they can get a respectable number of men to stand."

Ulys wrote with such unadorned composure that if not for the press and Secretary Stanton's occasional telegrams, Julia almost could have imagined that he was back in Washington, miles away from the horrors at Cold Harbor, where six thousand brave Union soldiers died within a single hour on the way to a costly defeat.

Ulys — her valiant general, her victor — was indomitably resilient despite setbacks that would have staggered a lesser man. On June 15, he directed his engineers to construct a pontoon bridge twenty-one hundred feet across the James and stealthily moved his troops over the river, catching General Lee entirely by surprise. "Since Sunday we have been engaged in one of the most perilous movements ever executed by a large army," Ulys wrote to her later that same day, although nearly a week passed before she received the letter, "that of withdrawing from the front of an enemy and moving past his flank, crossing two rivers over which the enemy has bridges and railroads whilst we have to improvise. So far it has been eminently successful and I hope will prove so to the end. About one half of my troops are now on the South side of the James River."

Julia needed Fred to show her on his maps to be sure, but her hopes were justified — Ulys's army now threatened Petersburg, the most important supply base and railway depot for the entire region, including the Confederate capital of Richmond. When Ulys captured Petersburg, Richmond would inevitably fall — and so too would the Confederacy.

While Ulys conducted offensive maneuvers north and south of the James River to extend his siege lines and attempt to cut off Confederate supplies, Julia made what contributions she could to the Union cause. She joined sewing bees to make uniforms and necessities, often bringing Nellie along to help with the easier tasks. She visited wounded soldiers at Jefferson Barracks, which had been converted to a military hospital in 1862 and held more than three thousand beds, which were nearly always full. She patronized sanitary fairs and performed whatever kindnesses she could for Union widows and orphans, who were increasing in number day by day.

At Wish-ton-wish, where Papa resided most of the year, she could lose herself in simple pleasures — putting the pretty cottage in order with new India matting and muslin curtains, reading aloud with the children on the rose-covered piazza, strolling in the cooling shade of the forest. On rainy mornings when she could not go riding, she lingered over breakfast with Papa to discuss politics — or rather, to listen while he opined and then to tease him with questions that toppled his arguments, or at least rattled them a little. The last of the Dents' colored servants had left them long ago, but Papa had hired German and French immigrants to replace them, and he grudgingly acknowledged that they performed their duties just as capably. Why shouldn't they, Julia thought after observing them for a few days, with ambition and the lure of prosperity to motivate them rather than the fear of the lash?

She wondered what had become of Jule. She resigned herself to never knowing.

Throughout Julia's visit, the family had

many visitors, for although most of Julia's old friends with Confederate sympathies shunned her, neighbors and acquaintances loyal to the Union sought her out. Julia had never realized how much work it was to entertain guests until she had to do it without the old family servants who had been with them for years, sometimes their entire lifetimes, and knew the house and the family's needs better than they did themselves. Slavery was a selfish necessity, she had told herself in the early years of her marriage whenever Ulys's steadfast opposition made her doubt the traditions of her people. After Jule fled, so dignified in her anger, Julia had begun to question whether slavery was necessary at all, or merely selfish. Watching the colored soldiers in Union blue march and drill and suffer in military hospitals, observing that the end of slavery in Washington City and elsewhere had not brought about the economic ruin advocates of the "peculiar institution" had ominously predicted, Julia realized that the answer was obvious. She had simply been too concerned with her own comforts to see it.

CHAPTER EIGHTEEN

June 1864–January 1865

In the middle of June, Ulys established his headquarters at City Point, Virginia, fixed his sights on Petersburg, and settled in for the siege.

As the summer passed, Julia decided that she ought to establish new headquarters too: a residence in a city in the East within an easy day's journey of City Point, someplace with excellent schools for the children. Ulys agreed, and so at the end of August, Julia packed up the children, bade farewell to Papa and her sisters, and headed to Philadelphia.

Her brother Frederick, newly appointed to Ulys's staff, met them at the station. His fair hair was thinner than she remembered, and his angular face boasted a new thick mustache and chin beard, but his familiar military bearing was as upright and precise as ever. The children showered their uncle in hugs and kisses, which he heartily returned, adding a warm embrace for Julia. "Ulys regrets that he couldn't be here to welcome you," Frederick added, smiling sympathetically. "But you know as well as anyone that while the war lasts, no one can fill his position but he."

"Of course I understand." Julia embraced her brother again, overjoyed to see him after their long separation. "I'm honored that he sent his very best officer to meet us."

Fred had arranged for a carriage to take them to the Continental Hotel, and while they awaited Ulys's summons, they caught up on all the family news and made inquiries about a more permanent residence for the family. Two days after their arrival, Ulys telegraphed that Frederick should immediately escort Julia and the children to visit him at City Point.

The next morning, after Julia scrubbed the children thoroughly and dressed them smartly, they departed by train for Baltimore, where they boarded a steamer that carried them down the Chesapeake, past Fortress Monroe, and up the James River to City Point. When their steamer docked beside Ulys's headquarters boat, it was all Julia could do to restrain the children from disembarking before the crew set the gangplank in place. Then they ran ashore and raced aboard their father's boat.

Escorted by her brother and greeting officers she knew in passing, Julia followed her children's shouts and shrieks of laughter to

Ulys's stateroom. When she at last found her darling husband, she burst out laughing, for he had a child dangling from each arm, a leg, and his shoulders, his coat was askew, and his cigar, though clamped firmly between his teeth, seemed seconds away from tumbling to the floor.

"I think they're happy to see me," he remarked by way of greeting when he saw her standing in the doorway. His eyes shone with affection.

"Oh, Ulys," she murmured, hurrying to embrace him. He freed an arm long enough to pull her close and kiss her, but moments later his sons wrestled him to the floor, while Nellie danced around them, clapping her little hands and cheering, "Get up, Papa! Get up! No surrender!"

Suddenly a shadow darkened the doorway, and all the Grants as well as Frederick glanced up to discover one of Ulys's aides-de-camp, dispatches in hand, staring in mute astonishment at his general in chief, whom he had discovered on the floor, interrupted in the middle of a rough-and-tumble wrestling match.

Red in the face and chuckling, Ulys got up at once and brushed off his knees. "Well, Horace," he greeted the lieutenant colonel apologetically, "you know my weaknesses — my children and my horses."

City Point proved to be a much busier place

than Julia had imagined. Gunboats, monitors, and transports crowded the river, and vessels of every description lined the quartermaster's docks, where men unloaded stores and munitions for the army. Storehouses all around the wharf were being filled at a steady pace, and a near constant stream of wagons traveled to and from the front. It was a splendid summer day, sunny and breezy and not too hot, and the children were enchanted by the sights and sounds of the military camp — the boats moving briskly up and down the James on military missions, bright flags whipping in the breeze, bugles calling from the heights down to the river. When the children begged for a tour, Ulys obligingly led them from the headquarters mess, past the rows of white tents where his brave soldiers slept, to his own larger tent — which they thoroughly explored and insisted had room enough to accommodate them all quite comfortably if he would let them stay.

Julia held fast to Ulys's arm nearly every moment of their visit, so happy was she to see her beloved husband again, so reluctant to part from him at the end of the day, as she knew she must. They had little time alone, so it was not until the afternoon waned that she found a moment to inquire about the war. With Ulys apparently unable to advance upon Richmond except in the smallest of increments and General Sherman stalled near

Atlanta, the Union advance seemed to have ground to a dispiriting halt.

"The siege of Petersburg will succeed," Ulys told her with unmistakable certainty. "Richmond, too, is suffering the effects of the blockade, and it'll crumble from the inside out if my troops don't capture it first." He touched a finger to her lips. "Now, my dear little wife, this is for your ears alone. You mustn't repeat anything that I tell you, not even to someone you assume is utterly loyal."

"You have my solemn vow that I won't breathe a word to anyone."

Late in the afternoon, Frederick escorted Julia and the children back to Philadelphia, from whence they launched their search for a suitable residence for the duration of the war. After considering Philadelphia and other cities in the region, on the advice of friends they chose nearby Burlington, New Jersey. Frederick went ahead to scout for a house, and when he found a cottage pleasantly situated in a good neighborhood, he immediately secured it for them.

Ulys was in the Shenandoah Valley conferring with General Philip Sheridan when Julia and Frederick moved their little household about twenty miles up the Delaware River to their new home. "What an excellent brother you are," Julia exclaimed when she saw the pretty two-story cottage her brother had discovered. Verdant ivy covered the spacious porch, tall fir trees flanked the front gate, and French windows upstairs and down let in sunny views of the garden.

It was a lovely but lonely home in which to pass the long days until she could see Ulys again.

After a dismal summer full of stalemate, discouragement, and defeat, General Sherman's capture of Atlanta in early September elevated Mr. Lincoln from a beleaguered administrator into a triumphant commander in chief. As hope for a victorious conclusion to the war soared throughout the Union, Radical Democracy Party candidate General Frémont withdrew from the presidential race, and as Election Day approached, Democrat General McClellan, the popular but perpetually hesitant military commander who did not support his own party's peace platform, seemed a dangerously imprudent choice.

On the first Tuesday of November, Julia sat up late, too anxious to sleep, until a messenger brought word that Mr. Lincoln had been reelected — and decisively so, receiving fifty-five percent of the popular vote and an enormous margin in the Electoral College, two hundred twelve votes to General McClellan's twenty-one. Best of all, her home state of Missouri, so long conflicted over the questions of slavery and secession, had proven its loyalty by choosing Mr. Lincoln.

Soon thereafter, Ulys was able to leave headquarters long enough to visit Julia and the children in Burlington, but although they were happy to be reunited, Ulys could not rest for the steady stream of visitors who descended upon the cottage to pay their respects. He was constantly reading telegrams and issuing dispatches, and it seemed that no sooner had he arrived than he was obliged to depart. On his way back to City Point, throngs of admirers turned out to cheer him all along his route, and to his consternation, the press printed detailed accounts of his movements, divulging his whereabouts not only to loyal citizens, but also to the enemy, who read Northern newspapers smuggled through the lines almost as soon as did the residents of the cities where they were printed.

In early December, Julia repaid his visit, traveling by train to Washington City, where she boarded a steamer and sailed down the Potomac to Fortress Monroe. There Ulys met her, and she transferred to his boat so they could continue on to City Point together.

Julia enjoyed every moment of her visit, her time alone with Ulys most of all, but also meeting his staff officers, the corps commanders, and the many distinguished gentlemen who came down from Washington City to tour the camp and confer with the general in chief. Often their ladies accompanied them, and, by popular custom, many requested buttons from Ulys's coat as souvenirs.

"I think it is very silly for ladies to be cutting off your buttons," Julia said tartly one afternoon after lunch, sitting with Ulys at headquarters, enduring eyestrain and headache to sew buttons back onto his coat while he read dispatches. "Your loyal and devoted admirers don't seem to consider how their general appears with half a dozen buttons missing from his uniform."

Ulys looked up from his papers, mulled it over, and shrugged. "Very well. From now on, if any lady wants a button, I'll refer her to you."

In the days that followed, ladies appealed to Julia for buttons in ever increasing numbers, pretty maids and charming wives and earnest dowagers alike, and despite her reluctance she felt obliged to consent. It seemed too trifling a thing to refuse, especially since so many of the ladies were parted from brave husbands, sons, and sweethearts serving in the Union army.

On another occasion, Julia was strolling alone on the deck when she encountered a young woman clad in a simple, dark-blue wool dress and shawl approaching the stateroom Julia and Ulys shared. Her head was swathed in a veil and she carried a plump, rosy-cheeked baby.

"I would like to see General Grant, please, madam," the woman asked breathlessly, her voice shaking with agitation.

"When I left the general he was resting," Julia replied. "I don't believe he can see anyone presently." In truth, Ulys was suffering from a sick headache. Julia had applied a poultice to his brow and had left him alone in their quiet, darkened stateroom, hoping she had remembered Jule's recipe correctly, wishing forlornly that Jule had been there to guide her.

"I must see him," the young woman implored. "I must see him! I will!"

"I'm very sorry, but —"

"Oh, madam, please let me see him!" She burst into tears, and the child in her arms fussed and mewed. "My husband is sentenced to be shot!"

"Oh, my goodness. When?"

"This day, at twelve o'clock, and it's all my fault." Shaking her head, the sobbing woman paced and patted her baby on the back in a futile attempt to calm him. "Our son is seven months old, and my Bob had never seen him, so I wrote and begged him to come."

"I see," Julia replied, dismayed. "You do understand that soldiers can't simply leave the army without permission, don't you?"

"I thought they'd never miss him from out of all these thousands of men." The distraught young wife drew closer to Julia, the desperate plea in her eyes visible even through her veil. "My Bob did come home as I asked, and he was on his way back to the regiment when they caught him and now they say he must be executed for desertion. Oh, please do let me see General Grant!"

"Wait here," said Julia. "I'll see what I can do."

She slipped inside the stateroom only to find Ulys awake, dressed, and preparing to light a cigar. "Ulys, a young lady wishes to see you on a most urgent matter."

Quickly Julia told him the sad tale, but even before she reached the end, Ulys was shaking his head regretfully. "I can't interfere. The lady should petition General Patrick."

"But her husband is meant to be shot today at noon, and it's nearly nine o'clock now."

"Julia, it's not appropriate for me to intercede."

Pressing her lips together and inhaling sharply, Julia strode to the door, flung it open, and announced, "You may enter and tell General Grant yourself."

Julia stepped into the corridor and waited just outside the door, listening to the woman's soft entreaties and Ulys's rumbling questions. Soon thereafter, he called Julia back inside. "Have paper and ink brought to me," he commanded, and with a nod she hurried off.

Before long the young wife emerged from the stateroom, the baby dozing on her shoulder, a folded piece of paper in her hand. "Thank you, madam," the woman said, her face transfigured by joy. "God bless you, and God bless the general."

Julia nodded in farewell, and as the woman hurried off to see to her husband's reprieve, Julia hesitated a moment before entering the stateroom. "Thank you, Ulys."

He frowned, but without rancor. "I'm sure I did wrong."

"I'm sure it would have been a far greater wrong to deprive that young woman of her husband and the child his father."

"You may think so, but I've no doubt that I've just pardoned a bounty jumper."

Silently Julia inclined her head to him. She knew the importance of discipline in the ranks, but she also understood a soldier's longing to see a child born in his absence. Ulys ought to empathize even better than she. Surely he had not grown so great that he had forgotten the loneliness and misery that had compelled him to resign from the army when Fred and Buck were very young.

On Christmas Day, Washington City rang with the thrilling news that General Sherman had reached the Atlantic, the terminus of his march across Georgia. Word quickly spread that he had sent the president a telegram declaring, "I beg to present to you, as a Christmas gift, the city of Savannah, with 150 heavy guns and plenty of ammunition, and also about 25,000 bales of cotton."

The citizens of the capital celebrated Christmas with a fervent, patriotic jubilance Jule had never before witnessed, and their renewed interest in merrymaking kept her satisfyingly busy dressing the hair and beautifying the skin of the social elite. For the first time in her life, she had plenty to eat, nice dresses to wear, a comfortable room to call her own, and a steadily increasing savings.

Jule was aided in her endeavors by a new friend, Emma Stevens, a former slave employed as an assistant seamstress to the renowned dressmaker Mrs. Elizabeth Keckley. Although Emma was more than ten years younger than Jule, she had acquired her freedom several years sooner, and she cheerfully assumed the role of Jule's confidante and guide as she navigated the capital, her new landscape of freedom.

As a very young child, Emma had been manumitted with her mother when their old mistress passed away, but the woman's heirs had contested the will. Emma and her mother had been kept in slavery for ten long years more while the lawsuit Emma's mother brought against the heirs dragged out in court. Upon miraculously winning their case, and their freedom, Emma and her mother had adopted the last name of the lawyer who had courageously represented them in a hostile courtroom.

Emma rented a small attic bedroom in the same Twelfth Street boardinghouse where her employer resided, and she often spoke admiringly of Mrs. Keckley's extraordinary skill and the dignity and grace with which she moved among the city's elite — as an employee rather than a social equal, perhaps, but respected nonetheless. "Mrs. Keckley is not only Mrs. Lincoln's modiste, but her most trusted confidante too," Emma told her proudly. "President Lincoln respects her so much that when he speaks with her — which is often, and in the most warm and friendly manner — he addresses her as Madame Keckley."

"The president does that?"

Emma nodded emphatically, beaming.

Jule shook her head in wonder. She could only imagine what it would be like to climb so high and succeed so well that the president himself would bestow such a title upon her.

Emma generously used her intimate knowledge of Mrs. Keckley's dressmaking orders to Jule's benefit, letting her know which ladies had ordered gowns for special occasions so that Jule might leave a card at their homes announcing her hairdressing services. As the winter social season progressed, particularly busy days found Jule hurrying from one gracious residence to another from morning until early evening, arranging one lady's golden tresses and another's dark curls, dispensing ointments and balms to clear the complexion or soften dry hands. She learned the city's omnibus routes by heart and established a lengthy list of satisfied, loyal customers. She had rarely been busier, and never more confident in herself and her prospects. Though she felt a jolt every time she heard that General Grant was in the capital, Julia was rarely with him, and Jule no longer feared that she would be recognized and arrested. She only occasionally woke sweating and trembling from nightmares that she had been captured and thrown back into slavery. Far more often, terrifying visions of Gabriel suffering beneath the lash somewhere in the impossibly distant Southwest haunted her.

Her dreams had never foretold the future, she reminded herself when her fears for his safety threatened to overwhelm her. Prophecy was Julia's gift, one more blessing piled upon her abundant store.

Christmas parties kept Jule too busy to brood over her empty arms and lonely bed, and the turning of the year kept her even more constantly employed. The New Year's Day reception at the White House was the highlight of the season, and Jule learned that it was by custom a three-hour affair in which Mr. Lincoln would stand in the East Room shaking hands and welcoming visitors —

foreign diplomats first, then ranking officials, and lastly the public, anyone who wished to come. Naturally every lady who attended the reception or any of the great many private parties that followed it wished to look her best, and after the whirlwind of activity, when Jule and Emma had caught their breath, they compared notes and congratulated each other on a very profitable season.

"You spend so little on your lodging and almost nothing on indulgences for yourself," Emma noted, a slightly scolding, teasing tone to her voice. "With all the money you're saving, you should open a little workshop and hire employees to mix and bottle your various potions for you. You could keep selling them to your clients yourself, of course, but you could also find pharmacies that would be willing to sell them for you. I'm sure they would, for a small percentage of the profits."

Jule had learned to trust Emma's canny business sense, and she was tempted by the vision of expanding her trade, but she had another, more urgent use for her savings. "Every penny I don't have to spend on essentials must go to buying Gabriel's freedom," she said, "but first, to finding him. I know the search will cost money too."

"Do you really think there's any hope you'll ever find him?"

Jule's breath stuck in her throat. "Of course," she managed to say. "I have to

401

believe that. Don't you see?"

Emma regarded her with stricken sympathy. "I do see," she said, laying her hand on Jule's arm. "Maybe when the war's over, Gabriel will find you before you've exhausted your fortune on the search. Wouldn't you have a merry time spending it together?"

Jule felt tears gathering, but she managed a smile. "That's not Gabriel's way. He'd want to distribute it to the less fortunate. But I don't suppose he'd mind a little celebration too."

"I look forward to meeting him," said Emma sincerely, and Jule thought they were some of the kindest words anyone had ever spoken to her.

Early in the New Year, the deed to a fully furnished residence worth fifty thousand dollars on Chestnut Street in Philadelphia was delivered to Julia at the cottage in Burlington.

The loyal citizens of that generous city had raised the funds out of respect for General Grant and a desire to express the people's gratitude in a tangible, practical manner. Overwhelmed, Julia immediately wrote back to thank them on her husband's behalf, and after sending off the letter, she promptly telegraphed the astonishing news to Ulys at City Point. "I think you had as well arrange to move into your new house at once and get

Nellie and Jess at good schools," he replied in his next letter. "Leave Fred and Buck where they are. They have been changed from one school to another often enough. As soon as I can I will run up and see you in your new house."

Julia had scarcely begun to make inquiries when Ulys sent another dispatch summoning her to City Point, and so instead of preparing to move to Philadelphia, she quickly made arrangements for an extended absence from Burlington. Her lovely sister-in-law Helen had recently moved her children to the East to be closer to Frederick, and she agreed to watch over her nephews and niece while Julia was away. When all was in order, Julia traveled the familiar route by rail and steamer to Fortress Monroe, where Ulys met her and escorted her the rest of the way.

General Rufus Ingalls, Ulys's quartermaster and longtime friend, met them at the dock with a team of carpenters, all grinning and fairly bursting with some secret. Mystified, Julia accepted General Ingalls's arm and allowed him to escort her to a bluff overlooking the James River. There, to her delight, he led her to a charming cabin standing among a little village of smaller cabins. Bare-limbed trees surrounded it, promising cool shade come springtime, and the Stars and Stripes waved proudly from a flagpole in the front garden.

"Your new quarters, madam," Ingalls said, gesturing grandly to the cabin.

"It's lovely, absolutely lovely," Julia declared. "I cannot thank you enough."

"We built this for the general especially so you could stay with him," the general replied, beaming proudly. "We miss you too much when you're away."

"You flatter me," Julia protested, laughing, and happily agreed to let him show her around. A large front room would serve as parlor, dining room, and office, and its large open fireplace would spread warmth to all corners. Doors on the far wall led to two bedrooms, offering beds enough for all whenever the children came to visit. The cabin was simply furnished, with only the necessities, but as Julia's gaze traveled around the front room, she knew she could easily transform the rustic place into a cozy home.

She soon had the cabin in good order, and it proved to be as snug and cozy as any winter quarters she and Ulys had yet shared. As the weeks passed, many notable visitors called there to confer with Ulys — General Edward Ord, General George Meade, and others — and Julia listened surreptitiously from her chair by the fireplace while vital matters of the war were discussed. Occasionally Ulys was obliged to travel to Washington to confer with the president and secretary of war, and usually Julia would accompany him, enjoying the sights and grandeur of Washington. They never stayed long, for Ulys always felt most urgently that he should return to military headquarters before the rebels discovered he was away and took advantage of his absence to launch an assault.

It seemed to Julia as they traveled from a round of military meetings in Washington City back to City Point that there were fewer naval vessels upon the waters than on her previous journeys. "You're not mistaken," Ulys told her. "The admiral has withdrawn nearly all the navy's ships from the James in order to increase his fleet for an expedition against Fort Fisher."

"Far be it for me to question the judgment of an admiral," Julia ventured, "but doesn't that leave your headquarters vulnerable to attack?"

Ulys smiled and took her hand. "Don't worry, my dear little wife. The enemy's fleet lies near Richmond, and we've sunk obstructions in the river at Trent's Reach. The Confederate gunboats won't be able to get around them."

That evening at supper, which they shared with some of Ulys's officers and staff, Ingalls seemed both disturbed and disappointed that the rebel navy had not attempted a strike against City Point. "General, what do you suppose those fellows mean by not coming down?" he asked Ulys. "I don't understand them. By all rights, they should have been down here three days ago."

"They're coming, Ingalls," Ulys replied. "You keep a sharp lookout and be prepared for them."

As the men retired to the fireside to smoke and confer and Julia began to clear away the dishes, another messenger arrived. "The naval officer sent to place the torpedoes discovered Confederate ironclads moving down the river," he reported.

The men became instantly alert, the announcement an electric jolt through their senses. "How many?" asked Ulys.

"Six vessels, sir. By half past ten o'clock, they'd passed the upper end of Dutch Gap Canal."

Ulys inhaled deeply on his cigar, and by the time he released the plume of smoke, he had a plan. He ordered two officers to take boats out to certain naval vessels, warn them of the anticipated attack, and direct them to move up the river and prevent the enemy's fleet from reaching City Point. He sent a third officer to communicate with a gunboat stationed at some distance from the boats, and issued orders to move all heavy guns within reach down to the river shore, where their fire could command the channel. As his staff rushed to obey, Ulys sat and wrote a dispatch to Captain William Albert Parker suggesting that he immediately tow coal schooners up the river and prepare to sink them in the channel if necessary.

"We reached the naval vessel by means of steam tugs," Lieutenant Colonel Horace Porter reported more than an hour later. "Most of the vessels sent up the river as obstructions are out of repair and almost unserviceable, but their officers are determined to make the best fight they can."

"Good," Ulys said curtly. As he lit another cigar and Porter busied himself with documents at Ulys's desk, Julia understood they could do nothing now but wait, try to get some sleep, and hope the defenses held.

Much later, a sharp, nervous rapping on the cabin door jolted Julia awake.

"Hello," called Ulys, already out of bed and pulling on his clothes while Julia remained beneath the covers, groggily trying to remember where she was. "Enter!"

Julia heard the front door open, and Ulys hurried from the bedroom to meet their visitor. She climbed out of bed and groped for her clothes in the darkness, her long, loose braid slipping over her shoulder, her heart pounding.

"General," she heard Major Dunn say, breathless. "The rebel gunboats have cleared the obstructions. They're coming down the river."

A frisson of alarm ran through her as she dressed, but she composed herself before joining Ulys and Major Dunn in the front room. The major bowed to her when she entered, his hands clasped behind his back, his mouth in a hard, tense line.

"Ulys," she asked. "Will the rebel gunboats shell the bluff?"

Ulys took his cigar in hand and regarded her with level calm. "If they make it within range, we can well imagine what they would do."

Julia nodded, understanding him completely. Not only were the general in chief and his senior staff present and vulnerable, but Ingalls had accumulated an enormous amount of supplies at City Point, and their destruction would be a serious blow to the Union army.

Julia had just finished pouring coffee for Ulys, Dunn, and herself when Porter arrived with more harrowing news. "Due to the high water, the enemy's boats were able to clear the obstructions," he said, his voice brittle with anger and disgust. "Upon the approach of the enemy's vessels, the *Onondaga* retreated down the river."

"Retreated, not was driven back?" asked Ulys. "You're certain?"

Porter nodded. "The captain lost his head, and under pretense of trying to obtain a more advantageous position, he turned his vessel and moved downstream below the pontoon bridge."

Julia set the coffeepot on the table so hard the lid rattled. While Ulys issued orders for the shore batteries to respond with all possible vigor, she resumed her seat by the fire and clasped her hands in her lap. "Ulys," she asked steadily, "what am I to do?"

For a moment Ulys regarded her as if he had forgotten she was present. "You shouldn't even be here."

"You sent for me," she reminded him pointedly.

"I could drive her into the country beyond the range of their shells," Dunn offered.

"You can't be spared simply to protect one person," Julia protested. "No. I shall remain here, as safe as any of you."

The looks the men exchanged told her that they did not consider themselves safe at all.

By dawn the *Onondaga* had moved within nine hundred yards of the Confederate ironclad flagship *Virginia* and had opened fire upon her. Union batteries on the shore had trained their guns upon her and commenced a general bombardment. The Confederate flagship had been struck about one hundred thirty times, the fifteen-inch shells damaging it heavily.

That night the Confederate fleet again came down the James and mounted another attack, but before the sun rose, they were forced to retreat after meeting with disastrous fire from the *Onondaga* and Union batteries on the riverbanks.

In the morning, the crisis over, Julia woke to the sound of voices outside the cabin window. She peered outside and discovered Ulys sitting at the campfire with Lieutenant Colonel Porter, smoking and drinking coffee.

"If I may say so, sir," Porter said, "the excitement of the past few days has had everyone in a stir, and yet from the moment the attack began, Mrs. Grant was one of the most composed people in the room."

"Don't let her sweet kindness and gentle nature deceive you," Ulys warned, smiling. "Mrs. Grant witnessed the running of the blockade at Vicksburg. She narrowly escaped capture at Holly Springs. She's not one to be rattled by the threat of a few gunboats on the James."

"She seems the ideal general's wife, sir."

Ulys inclined his head to acknowledge the compliment. "She's always been the ideal wife for me regardless of my rank, and when I had no rank at all."

Tears sprang into Julia's eyes. The quiet, matter-of-fact praise from her darling husband meant more to her than had President Lincoln himself awarded her a medal for gallantry in the field.

CHAPTER NINETEEN

January–February 1865

In the middle of January, the Union navy captured Fort Fisher, closing the port of Wilmington in North Carolina and severing supply lines to the Confederacy from abroad. As Washington City rejoiced, Jule's thankfulness that the end of the war seemed imminent was tempered by worrisome rumors circulating among the worshipers at Union Bethel Church, concerns that the residents of her boardinghouse shared. After the war was won, what was to become of their enslaved brothers and sisters in states that had remained loyal to the Union?

Jule grew apprehensive anew whenever conversation turned to the Emancipation Proclamation. She had never fully trusted it, that piece of paper that had freed slaves in rebellious states where no one obeyed President Lincoln's laws anyway and kept them enslaved in places where he had the power to declare them free. How could she have any faith in the proclamation when she still stung from anger when she recalled Julia's half-hearted explanations about exemptions and geography? For months Jule had assumed that the end of the war would bring freedom to all, but increasingly, that once bright future seemed to have been built on unsteady ground.

When General Grant defeated General Lee and the rebellious states returned to the Union, would the Emancipation Proclamation be abandoned as a war measure no longer necessary in peacetime? Would Jule remain a fugitive, subject to return to Missouri and the old master? Would Annie and Dinah and Polly and Tom and the others remain the Dent family's slaves? What would be the fate of any children born to them and their enslaved brethren in the years to come?

Would Gabriel be considered legally free in a defeated, once rebellious Texas, but remain forever beyond her reach?

The previous spring, Jule recalled, Washington's colored neighborhoods had hummed with excitement as a new amendment to the Constitution eradicating slavery throughout the nation once and for all had passed the Senate — only to have their rising hopes dashed when the measure failed to pass the House. At the time, Jule had been too preoccupied with finding her own way to dwell upon the crushing defeat, but her interest was rekindled when her minister announced in his sermon one Sunday that President Lincoln had urged Congress to reconsider the amendment. Then, scarcely a week into the new year, a Congressman from Ohio reintroduced the measure in the House.

"The vote will be close, if it comes to a vote at all," warned Joshua, one of Jule's boardinghouse neighbors. He overheard scraps of many significant conversations in his job as a bellboy at the Willard, and he knew who was holding clandestine meetings with whom.

"I'm tired of waiting for other folks to do what's right," Jule fretted to Emma one afternoon as they braved a snow shower to go marketing, arms linked, heavy shawls drawn tightly around their heads, sturdy baskets dangling from their elbows.

"Give it time," Emma urged, tirelessly optimistic. "Justice moves slowly, but it moves ever forward."

Jule understood why Emma trusted the laws and the courts that had eventually freed her and her mother, but she did not share her friend's faith. Even sunny Emma admitted that time was of the essence. The Thirteenth Amendment had to pass before the war was won if it was to pass at all.

On the last day of January, Jule and Emma walked to Capitol Hill, where they hoped to observe the debate from the House gallery. Hundreds of others had preceded them, and when they tried to gain entrance they were told that every inch of space in the galleries and on the floor had been claimed. Joining the ordinary citizens who had squeezed their way inside were the justices of the Supreme Court, several members of the president's cabinet, dozens of senators, and many foreign ministers. There was not room enough for Jule and Emma and hundreds of others who crowded around the entrances, speaking in small groups in hushed, urgent voices, listening intently for sounds of cheers or derision from within, eagerly awaiting messengers who came running now and then with news of the debate's progress.

They waited, and talked, and prayed. Everyone knew the narrowest of margins separated success from defeat. The vote would fall sharply along party lines, and five Democrats would have to join the Republicans in support of the measure if it was to prevail. When a messenger announced that a few Democrats had taken the floor to justify why they intended to break with their party to support the amendment, cheers went up from one portion of the crowd, contemptuous shouts from another.

"The tally sheets are being handed around," someone shouted from a high window. Emma seized Jule's arm, and they clung to each other, hearts pounding, trembling, too anxious to speak. The crowd fell into a breathless hush as the minutes stretched on, the tense stillness broken only by occasional fragments of news passed on from within the chamber.

And then, at last, came a distant roar, the thunder of many voices shouting out in righteous triumph. Emma gasped and clutched Jule's arm tighter; Jule closed her eyes, bowed her head, and murmured a prayer.

"It's passed," a voice rang out from the top of the stairs. Trembling with joy and disbelief, Jule raised her head and glimpsed a young, fair-haired man in a stovepipe hat amid the milling throng, smiling though tears streamed down his face, reading aloud from a piece of paper held open between his two hands. "On the passage of the Joint Resolution to amend the Constitution of the United States the ayes have one hundred nineteen, the nays fifty-six. The constitutional majority of two thirds having voted in the affirmative, the Joint Resolution has passed!"

Jule and Emma cried out in jubilation and fell into each other's arms, laughing, weeping, praising the Lord. Shouts of exultation rose from the crowd; hundreds of hats flew into the air. A man began to sing "The Battle Hymn of the Republic" in a rich baritone, and just as Jule and Emma chimed in, Capitol Hill shook as a round of artillery signaled the wondrous news to all of Washington.

"It ain't over," Jule heard one sour-faced white man declare as he stalked away from the celebration. "This cursed amendment still has to be ratified, and God willing, it won't be."

Jeers followed in his wake, but Jule quickly observed that others in the crowd seemed to share his outrage. "What does that mean?" she asked, her mouth close to Emma's ear so she might be heard over the din. "What's that word, 'ratified'?"

"Now it goes to the states," Emma replied, tears of joy glistening on her cheeks. "Each will hold its own vote, and three-quarters must approve the amendment before it becomes the law of the land."

Jule stared at her, aghast. "So there's still a chance it might fail after all?"

"There's not even the whisper of a chance of it," declared Emma, her elation undiminished. "The states will approve it. They will. They must!"

Emma's certainty was so compelling that Jule felt her spirits rising again until they soared. Even so, she knew it would be many months before freedom reached her enslaved friends in Missouri — and only a victorious end to the war would deliver Gabriel.

Rumors of a peace conference had circulated for months, but Julia did not believe them until the last day of January, when delegates from the Confederate states presented themselves at the Union lines around Petersburg and were immediately conducted to City Point and placed under Ulys's authority.

The commissioners — Alexander Stephens, the vice president of the Confederacy; Judge John Archibald Campbell, assistant secretary of war; and Robert M. T. Hunter, a former United State senator from Virginia and president pro tempore of the Confederate Senate — arrived at Ulys's headquarters at dusk, so he ordered them escorted to quarters aboard the *Mary Martin,* the steamer Julia herself often used to travel to and from City Point, the one most comfortably fitted up for passengers.

After the commissioners were settled, Ulys telegraphed Washington to inform President Lincoln and Secretary Stanton of their arrival. Ulys had returned to the cabin by the time they telegraphed a reply, which a messenger immediately brought to him. "I'm instructed to detain them here," Ulys said, letting the paper fall upon his desk, "until the president's designee should come to meet these representatives of the so-called Confederate government."

"So-called?" Julia echoed.

"My words, not the president's or Stanton's," Ulys acknowledged. "I'll never admit that they represent a legitimate government. Too much blood and treasure have been needlessly wasted to concede anything of the kind."

After that stern judgment, Julia expected Ulys to detain the men as prisoners rather than guests, but instead Ulys directed the captain of the *Mary Martin* to extend every courtesy to the commissioners and make them as comfortable as possible. He set no guard over them, placed no restrictions upon their movements, and required no pledge that they would not abuse these privileges. Since the commissioners were allowed to leave the boat whenever they pleased, they did so often, strolling along the bank, observing the soldiers drill, and, as a gesture of respect, calling on Ulys at the cabin.

Ulys was out the first time they called. Julia had never met any of the commissioners and knew little about them except Mr. Stephens, who had been a good friend of Mr. Lincoln's when both had served in the House of Representatives. She had heard that Mr. Stephens was a small gentleman in his early sixties, so when the trio arrived, she was surprised to be introduced to a man of rather ample girth. He wore a coarse overcoat of thick gray wool, a heavy weave that had been adopted in the South after the blockade forced masters and servants alike to resort to homespun. When she invited the gentlemen inside and Mr. Stephens removed his coat, she was surprised anew, for all of his apparent bulk had been in his garment, and he turned out to be the slight, wizened fellow she had expected.

Julia invited the gentlemen to sit by the fire while she served coffee and fresh bread with preserves, the only suitable refreshments she had on hand. The men's great appreciation for the coffee was apparent. She wondered how long it had been since they had enjoyed real coffee, not some weak, unpalatable brew of roasted rice, peas, and chicory.

"General Grant hopes that you will be comfortable aboard the *Mary Martin*," Julia told them. "You may rest assured that he has personally guaranteed your safety while you're in camp."

The other men nodded politely, but Mr. Hunter frowned. "What is General Grant's opinion of the prospects of the peace conference?" he asked. "Does he believe peace can be achieved through negotiation? Does he know what Lincoln will demand in exchange for peace?"

"I don't suppose anyone but President Lincoln knows that for certain," said Julia, unable to resist emphasizing Mr. Lincoln's title. "President Lincoln is a good, just, and wise gentleman, and I must assume that any decisions he would make on any serious matter relating to the war would reflect that."

When Mr. Hunter's frown deepened, Julia decided to steer the conversation elsewhere. "Did you know," she said lightly, "that although you are the first three Confederate commissioners that I have met, you are not the first that I have known?"

Mr. Hunter and Judge Campbell exchanged bewildered looks, but Mr. Stephens smiled as one did when entertained with a riddle. "My dear lady, how can you know a commissioner whom you have not met?"

"Because I know him only through the post and we have never been properly introduced," said Julia. "For many months I have been corresponding with the commissioner for the exchange of prisoners at Columbia, South Carolina, where my brother John has been held for almost a year."

Judge Campbell's brows drew together in sympathetic bewilderment. "Was General Grant unable to arrange for him to be exchanged?"

"Of course not," said Julia. "My brother isn't a soldier. He is, however, as ardent a rebel as there ever has been. We had many an argument on the subject before the war."

"If he isn't a soldier," asked Mr. Stephens, prepared to take on another riddle, "how did he come to be in prison?"

"He was visiting a friend in Louisiana when he was captured," said Julia. "When it was discovered that he is the brother-in-law of General Grant, he was taken for a spy, despite his many proclamations to the contrary."

She waited, but while they expressed sympathy, not one of the gentlemen offered to intercede on her brother's behalf — and so she smiled, poured more coffee, and did not offer to intercede on their behalf to Ulys.

Mr. Lincoln had sent envoys, including Secretary of State William Seward, to meet the commissioners at Hampton Roads in Virginia. On the second day of February, he telegraphed Ulys, "Say to the gentlemen I will meet them personally at Fortress-Monroe, as soon as I can get there."

The president himself was coming to the conference. Mr. Hunter could not ask for more evidence of Mr. Lincoln's tremendous desire for peace than that.

Late in the afternoon a few days thereafter, Julia was in the cabin straining her eyes and sewing buttons on Ulys's dress uniform when a knock sounded on the door. She rose to answer and discovered President Lincoln standing before her, tall and gaunt in a dark suit and stovepipe hat. "Mr. President," she said warmly, despite her astonishment. "What an honor this is! Do come in."

"Thank you, Mrs. Grant." He removed his hat but still had to bend sharply to pass through the doorway. He glanced around their little home, and when a small, cryptic smile appeared on his weary face, Julia remembered that he, too, had once lived in a cabin. "I'd like to speak to General Grant, if he has time."

"He would always have time for you, Mr. President," she said. "He's at his office at present."

"I thought this was his office."

"He works here occasionally, but only because he is always working and is sometimes here."

Mr. Lincoln chuckled. "I understand completely. I believe I can find someone to direct me. Thank you, Mrs. Grant."

"Mr. President," Julia quickly said as he turned to go, "I assume you come directly from the conference. Have you reached any agreements in the interests of peace?"

The president hesitated. "Well, no."

"No?" Julia exclaimed, her heart plummeting. "Why, Mr. President, aren't you going to make terms with them? They are our own people, you know."

"Yes, Mrs. Grant," he said, nodding somberly. "I never forget that."

He took from his pocket a piece of paper, which he unfolded and read aloud. Julia listened intently to the terms of peace he had presented to Mr. Stephens and his companions: national authority would be restored over all the states, slavery would be abolished throughout the country, and all military forces hostile to the government of the United States would be disbanded. When Mr. Lincoln finished, he looked up, fixed his sad, rueful gaze on Julia, and returned the paper to his pocket.

"They did not accept that?" asked Julia.

"They did not."

"But those terms seem most liberal."

"The commissioners, echoing the instructions given to them by Jeff Davis, insisted that the goal was to achieve peace between two sovereign nations," the president said. "I seek peace within our one common country. I insist upon the end of slavery, while Mr. Stephens is bound to the opposite. We have no common ground to tread upon."

"I see." It was all Julia could manage to say, so profound was her disappointment.

"I thought you would, when I explained it to you." The president fit his lanky frame through the door and bowed to her before replacing his hat. "I have, for the past year or so, looked to General Grant for the end to this cruel war. The conference has failed, and so I rely upon him more than ever."

"He will not fail you, Mr. President," Julia replied. "He has his mind set upon victory, and he always was a very obstinate man."

"I know my trust could be no better placed." When the president smiled, it was like the sun breaking unexpectedly through clouds. "Mrs. Grant, did you have the opportunity to see the three commissioners?"

"I did."

"Did you meet Mr. Stephens, and did you notice his unusual coat?"

"Yes, indeed, Mr. President."

"Well, did you not think it was the biggest shuck for the littlest ear you ever did see?"

Julia laughed. "I confess I didn't think of it in quite those terms, but now I always shall."

The president rewarded her with a warm, hearty laugh of his own.

Later that day, Julia learned that Mr. Lincoln had found Ulys at his office and had conferred with him briefly before departing for Washington. "I told him I'd see him soon," said Ulys wryly.

Julia reached for his hand and gave it a sympathetic squeeze. Ulys had been summoned to appear before the House of Representatives to testify before the Joint Committee on the Conduct of the War about General Benjamin Butler's failure to take Fort Fisher. It was not a task he relished, so Julia felt a trifle guilty for looking forward to a few days in the capital.

They left City Point on February 9, arriving in Washington City the following day. Julia had grown accustomed to the fanfare and frenzy that always marked their arrivals, and she smiled and bowed graciously and exchanged pleasantries with several of the ladies in the throng as Ulys's aides swept them off to their waiting carriage. After they were settled into comfortable rooms at the Willard, Julia received callers in the ladies' parlor while Ulys met with President Lincoln and

Secretary Stanton at the War Department. That evening, after dining alone in the peaceful seclusion of their rooms, they attended the theater with Mr. and Mrs. Lincoln and General and Mrs. Burnside. The program at Ford's Theatre included the comedy *Everybody's Friend* followed by the farce *Love in Livery,* which pleased Ulys greatly, for although he detested opera, like Mr. Lincoln he loved a good play.

When the president's distinguished party arrived, the orchestra struck up "Hail to the Chief," and the audience welcomed them with such thunderous applause and powerful cheers that the performance onstage was suspended for several minutes. The president bowed to his admirers with the utmost courtesy and humility, while Ulys looked as if he wished the people would quiet down, take their seats, and allow the play to continue. For her part Mrs. Lincoln basked in the admiration, smiling proudly down upon the audience and inclining her head gracefully to one person and then another. Suddenly she threw Julia a quick, arch, sidelong smile, as if to urge to her relish the cheers, to bask in the reflected glow of her husband's glory while she could, for they would fade all too soon.

Despite Mrs. Lincoln's silent warning of the transience of fame — which might have been

Julia's imagination, too much read into one inscrutable glance — Ulys's star seemed on a trajectory of unrestrained ascent. The following morning, after delivering his testimony to the joint committee, he was received with great enthusiasm in the House. Julia watched from the gallery as, shortly after Congressman Daniel Wheelwright Gooch read excerpts regarding prisoner exchanges from Ulys's testimony, Ulys himself was recognized on the floor and the chamber voted to recess so the members could pay their respects. Scores of congressmen crowded around him, eager for introductions, but after several minutes he was escorted to the clerk's desk and formally introduced to the entire body, while the chamber resounded with thunderous applause from officials and spectators alike. A similar scene played out soon thereafter in the Senate, where he was praised and congratulated with such enthusiasm that Julia could scarcely imagine how they would respond when he ultimately won the war.

Later that afternoon, Ulys and Julia attended Mrs. Lincoln's reception at the White House, which Julia overheard several guests remark was in many respects the finest of the season. Mr. Lincoln, gaunt but amiable, assisted his wife in receiving her guests, among whom the most prominent were Admiral Farragut and Ulys himself. Mrs. Lincoln looked elegant and self-assured in a rich lilac gown trimmed with black velvet and narrow ribbon, the neckline cut low to show off her lovely shoulders, the skirt set with diamond-shaped panels of white satin and velvet. Her dark hair was braided and coiled and adorned with a headdress of point lace and feathers, and she completed her costume with a necklace of lustrous pearls, a diamond breast pin, white kid gloves, and a lace fan.

Julia supposed that only one lady could have outshone Mrs. Lincoln that afternoon, but when she looked around for Mrs. Sprague, she did not see the auburn-haired beauty anywhere. A few discreet inquiries among the officers' wives revealed that Mrs. Sprague had spent most of the winter social season at her Washington home, for she was in a delicate condition, not yet in confinement, but far enough along that she declined most invitations.

"Surely she'll attend the inauguration," a colonel's wife told Julia archly. "Chief Justice Chase will be administering the oath of office, and the ball will be the social event of the season. Mrs. Sprague would have to be mere minutes away from her blessed event to be kept away from that." She peered at Julia inquisitively. "Will you and General Grant attend, Mrs. Grant?"

"I don't know." Ulys had said nothing about it, and it had not occurred to Julia to wonder if they might. "I suppose it will depend upon what's happening with the war."

She resolved to ask Ulys the next time she saw him, but when he found her in the crowd soon thereafter, he forestalled her question with a command: "If there's anyone else here to whom you ought to pay your respects, do so now. We'll be leaving soon."

"For the Willard?"

"Yes, and then on to City Point."

"This afternoon? Already?"

With a slight frown Ulys replied, "I would say rather, 'at last.' My place is in the field. I've tarried too long already."

General Sherman had moved on from Savannah into South Carolina, and on February 17, his valiant men captured Columbia. The news filled Julia with wild hope, because if the Union army liberated the prisons, and if the captives had not been marched off elsewhere before the city fell, her brother John might be freed and allowed to go home at last.

The day after General Sherman took Columbia, the Confederates surrendered Fort Sumter and evacuated Charleston. A Union victory seemed more certain than ever before. Julia frequently overheard Ulys tell his most trusted aides that he did not see how the Confederacy could endure much longer. His network of loyal Unionist spies in Richmond had smuggled out reports that clerks serving

Mr. Davis's cabinet secretaries were frantically packing up important documents for transport, and a plan to evacuate the government from the city had been devised and approved. Every day scores of soldiers in butternut and gray deserted the rebel camps and surrendered themselves to Union pickets, while others simply packed up their kits and went home, probably assuming that the war would be over soon anyway and they ought not to get shot in the meantime. Throughout the South, the Confederate military had been conscripting every able-bodied man between eighteen and forty-five, but new laws had been passed allowing for the drafting of boys aged fourteen to eighteen, who formed the junior reserves, and men from forty-five to sixty, the senior reserves. "They're robbing the cradle and the grave," said Ulys regretfully one night as he finished his last cigar. The lives he sought to preserve by bringing a swift end to the war were not all on the Union side.

Even with the enlistment of boys and old men throughout rebeldom, Ulys figured the enemy lost at least a regiment each day, taking into account casualties of battle, deaths from disease, fatalities from natural causes, and desertions. With rebel morale at its lowest ebb, Ulys was impatient for winter to end so he could commence the spring campaign, which he firmly believed would be the last of the war. For weeks heavy rains had drenched the landscape, and the muddy roads had become an impassable morass for artillery and teams. Until the downpours relented and the sun dried the roads, his teamsters could not move the wagon trains and artillery necessary for prolonged fighting in enemy territory. He wanted General Sheridan's cavalry with him too, but they were still maneuvering north of the James, having come from the Shenandoah Valley. Ulys would not set out until Sheridan's forces could join him south of the river.

Ulys's headquarters crackled with activity from before dawn until long after sunset. Unable to move on General Lee's army, they planned and prepared, drilling the troops, studying maps, collecting intelligence, and testing the roads. They were focused, determined, apprehensive, and eager — but often their concentration was broken by visitors from the North, politicians, dignitaries, newspapermen, and often their ladies, eager for a glimpse of the soldiers in their natural setting before the war ended and they would be viewed only in parades. To lift the burden from her husband's shoulders, Julia gladly assumed the role of hostess.

Late one afternoon, upon returning to the cabin after calling on soldiers on the sick list, Julia found Ulys at his desk engaged in earnest conversation with General Ord.

"See here, Mrs. Grant," Ulys greeted her. "General Ord has returned from rebel lines with an intriguing suggestion that terms of peace may be reached through you."

"My good lady," General Ord began, "recently I met under a flag of truce with General Longstreet to resolve some problems with fraternization between the opposing pickets. Our soldiers and the rebels have been trading papers, sharing tobacco, even challenging one another to races and whatnot, and it's high time this was stopped. After settling this little matter, I said to him, 'Longstreet, why do you fellows hold out any longer? You know you cannot succeed. Why prolong this unholy struggle?' "

Julia resisted the urge to ask how Cousin James looked, if he had quite recovered from his dreadful wound, if he seemed to be starving, as so many of the rebel deserters who crossed into their lines did. "What was his reply?"

"He said he would be glad to have peace restored between our two nations."

Ulys sighed and lit a fresh cigar, and Julia thought of Mr. Lincoln's distinction between peace among separate nations and peace within one common country.

With a glance for Ulys, General Ord continued, "It was proposed that a conference between Generals Grant and Lee could be arranged, and that since you are old friends, you and Mrs. Longstreet could cross enemy lines and act as mediators."

"What an intriguing idea," Julia exclaimed.

"It was our belief that you ladies could become the mediums of peace," General Ord explained. "Mrs. Longstreet has already been summoned from Lynchburg to Richmond for this purpose."

Julia would rejoice to see her dear friend again, especially to broker peace. "I'm willing to go the minute you give the word," she told General Ord, and then, remembering herself, she turned to Ulys. "I may go, may I not?"

Ulys smiled but shook his head. "No, I think not."

"Why not?" Julia protested. "I'd be proud to serve my country this way."

"No, that would never do."

Julia approached him and took his hand in both of hers. "Please, Ulys, do consent. Mrs. Longstreet is coming. How will it look if I seem unwilling to meet her?"

"Mrs. Longstreet will understand that it was not your decision." Ulys gave her hands an affectionate squeeze and returned to his desk and the cigar he had left smoldering in the ashtray. "Even if I were willing to put you at such great risk, which I am not, it would be out of the question. The men have fought this war and the men will finish it."

It was not only a man's war, Julia well knew. North and south, women had been engaged in their own battles for more than four years. Though they did not carry rifles and wear Union blue or homespun butternut, many suffered, and many had perished.

CHAPTER TWENTY

February–March 1865

"I'm afraid I might be obliged to leave Washington soon," Jule confessed sadly as she and Emma made their way to church one icy morning in late February, linking arms to steady themselves. Earlier that week, an unexpected taste of spring warmth had melted the ice along the banks of the Potomac and drenched the city in rain, but temperatures had plummeted overnight, freezing puddles and ruts in the muddy streets into a precarious landscape frosted in white. "Maybe for New York or Boston."

"But why?" Emma protested, not daring to lift her gaze from the icy terrain underfoot. "You're comfortably settled. You have almost more work than you can manage. You have dear friends who would miss you terribly." She gave Jule's arm a little squeeze to indicate that she considered herself foremost among them. "Why would you want to start over somewhere else?"

"I don't want to." Jule burrowed her chin into her scarf to ward off the bitter winds gusting down the avenue. "But lately Mrs. Grant's been coming to the capital too often and too unpredictably. Last time I was twenty minutes late for an appointment at the Willard because she was holding court in the ladies' parlor and I couldn't sneak past the doorway."

Emma risked a skeptical glance. "She probably would've been too preoccupied with her callers to notice if you'd hurried by with your bonnet up."

"Maybe, but I couldn't risk it."

Emma halted, bringing Jule to a stop beside her. "Why are you still so afraid to meet her? Surely you don't fear you'll be thrown back into slavery."

"No, not anymore." Jule resumed walking, bringing Emma along with her. Ratified or not, the Thirteenth Amendment had put those fears to rest. "I can't rightly explain it. When I think of her, I feel so much — so much anger and resentment, I'm afraid what I might do or say. We were close once, or at least, as close as slave and mistress can be. For most of my life, I trusted her to look out for me, and to set me free if she could." Jule inhaled deeply, outrage and disappointment simmering. "She married an abolitionist and still kept me enslaved. President Lincoln signed the Emancipation Proclamation, and still she didn't set me free. I know she thinks I betrayed her by running away, but *she* betrayed *me*."

"All the more reason for you to hold your ground, to stay in Washington, where you've made your new home," Emma declared. "If you do happen to run into her, well, simply tell her what you just told me. You'll probably feel much better afterward."

"She might not be my mistress anymore, but she's still the wife of a very powerful man." Jule shook her head. "No, even now I can't risk offending her."

"Don't let her chase you off," Emma implored. "When the war's over, she'll likely go back to Missouri, too far away to trouble you anymore."

"Maybe. I expect it depends where General Grant's posted. Oh, Emma, I don't want to go. I don't want to start over among strangers again. I don't want to put a single mile more between me and Gabriel."

"Then don't go," Emma urged. "At least not before the inauguration. It's not far off, and you'll profit greatly from it. We both will."

Jule's appointment book was already filled with the names of ladies determined to look their best for Mr. Lincoln's swearing-in ceremony and the grand ball the following evening. Her blemish remedies and hair tonics sold almost as quickly as she could fill the bottles. It would be very foolish indeed to

scurry away before the most important —
and lucrative — events of the social season.

"I'll stay," she told Emma, "at least through
the inauguration."

She would let the course of the war determine what she did after that.

In the days that followed, Jule felt her spirits
rising with the joyful, exuberant mood that
swept through Washington as the capital
prepared for Mr. Lincoln's second inauguration. Thousands of visitors flooded the city,
packing hotels and boardinghouses full to
overflowing and spilling out onto the streets,
where hardier folk set up makeshift camps on
sidewalks and in parks. At the Willard, ladies
and gentlemen alike sat up all night in
crowded parlors because no more beds could
be found for them. Every one of Jule's most
loyal clients demanded a place on her card,
and visitors begged to be squeezed in at the
oddest of hours.

On the night before the inauguration, Jule
was yanked from sleep by the crash of thunder and the scour of hail upon the roof.
Groggy, heart pounding, she sat up in bed
and drew her quilt around her, for a moment
believing herself back at Holly Springs or
Vicksburg, confusing the tempest for the roar
of artillery. When she realized it was a storm
and not an attack, and that she was safe
within four strong walls beneath a solid roof,
she lay back down and waited for the storm

to subside so she might drift back to sleep.

She woke before dawn to a gray and drizzly morning, and a glance out the window revealed that the night's torrential downpour had turned the streets into thick rivers of mud. Hoping that the skies would clear before the grand parade, she rose from bed, quickly washed and dressed, put on her older pair of shoes — such a luxury, to own two pairs of sturdy shoes! — and went downstairs for a quick bite of breakfast before hurrying off to her first appointment of the day. She had numerous clients to make beautiful for the president's inauguration and the White House reception that would follow, the wives of senators and generals and visiting dignitaries. Emma, too, would be very busy, Jule knew, finishing up elegant gowns for Mrs. Keckley's wealthy clientele, but they planned to meet later to watch the parade and to hear Mr. Lincoln deliver his inaugural address from the Capitol.

Jule made her way carefully through the mud from her boardinghouse to the Willard, where she dressed the hair of a governor's wife and their two graceful daughters. All three were so pleased with their tresses that the mother indulged the young ladies' desire for not one but three bottles of Jule's hair tonics, one concoction for the eldest's curly hair, another for her younger sister's fine, straight locks, and a third to brighten the fading gold of their mother's.

"How will we tell which is which?" asked the youngest girl, examining the bottles curiously as Jule set them on the table.

"You're holding yours," said Jule, smiling. "The darkest one is your sister's, and the lightest is your mother's."

The elder sister held her mother's bottle and her own up to the light. "They're so close in hue, I'm afraid I'll mistake mother's for mine."

"It won't harm your hair if you do," Jule assured her.

"Perhaps not," the governor's wife said, "but you really ought to label your products."

"Yes, you should," exclaimed the youngest girl. "And use pretty labels, with flowers and a picture of a lady with gloriously beautiful hair."

"You must have an impressive name for each of your concoctions as well," her elder sister chimed in. "Like Doctor Mountebank's Arsenical Lotion or Duchess Mary's Jasmine Cold Cream."

Jule smiled and shook her head. "I'm not a doctor or a duchess," she said, packing her brushes and ribbons in her bag.

"You don't have to be," said the governor's wife, waving a hand dismissively. "I've heard that Duchess Mary is really a perfumer's daughter from Edinburgh. You must use an interesting name, even if it's simply 'Jule of

Washington, Hairdresser.' A clever name would help people remember your tonics — and you."

"Maybe so," said Jule as she accepted her fee, discreetly tucked within a sheet of paper, folded and sealed. "I thank you for the suggestion."

After attending to a few more clients, Jule hurried through the crowded streets to meet Emma at her boardinghouse on Twelfth Street. From there, accompanied by several other young ladies who sewed in Mrs. Keckley's workshop, they joined the tens of thousands of other eager spectators lining the parade route along Pennsylvania Avenue from the White House to the Capitol. Thankfully, the rain had let up, and the procession was as glorious a spectacle as Jule had ever seen, despite the mud underfoot and the cloudy skies above. Graceful horses pranced, soldiers marched proudly, and bands played merry tunes for the ladies, gentlemen, and children who packed the sidewalks, peered out from upper windows, or looked down from rooftops, cheering and waving hats and flags and handkerchiefs.

A team of sturdy horses pulled a model of an ironclad gunboat, complete with a revolving turret that startled and delighted onlookers by firing blanks as it made its way down Pennsylvania Avenue. Uniformed officers of fire departments from Washington and Philadelphia and fraternal lodges from across the North marched proudly, carrying banners and flags. A local printers' society had mounted a handpress on a wagon, printing broadsides and distributing them to spectators they passed along the way. Jule was gratified to see people of color marching in the parade too, a battalion of colored soldiers as well as distinguished leaders of several Negro civic associations.

"This is the first time people of our race have been included in an inauguration," Emma told her. "I mean truly included, part of the celebration and ceremony, not just onlookers or the folks who cook the food and clean up afterward."

For the first time too, people of color would be permitted on the Capitol grounds while the president delivered his address. As soon as the parade passed by, Jule, Emma, and their companions quickly hurried down side streets, avoiding the worst of the congestion as they made their way to Capitol Hill. A massive crowd thousands strong already filled the muddy grounds when they arrived, but they managed to find a place to stand within the fences.

When the president emerged onto the East Portico surrounded by dignitaries, a sheet of paper in his hand, the newly completed Capitol dome rising in magnificent splendor high above, the vast crowd surrounding Jule let out a great roar of welcome and gladness. As Mr. Lincoln came forward to the edge of the platform, the clouds suddenly parted and the sun broke through, and a bright shaft of sunlight shone down upon him like a benediction from heaven.

Jule stood listening, spellbound, as President Lincoln offered his brief, simple, and profoundly beautiful address, clear and poignant and warm, full of forgiveness and reconciliation. He spoke of the war, and how slavery was the undeniable cause of it, and how four years earlier everyone, North and South alike, had wanted to avoid war, but one side would make war rather than let the nation survive, and the other would accept war rather than let it perish. He spoke of their shared belief in one Almighty God, and how peculiar it was that each side prayed to him and invoked his aid against the other. "It may seem strange that any men should dare to ask a just God's assistance in wringing their bread from the sweat of other men's faces," he noted, his high, thin voice carrying to the far edges of the crowd, "but let us judge not that we be not judged. The prayers of both could not be answered; that of neither has been answered fully. The Almighty has His own purposes."

Jule felt Emma's gloved hand close around hers, and she knew the same fervent inspiration filled both their hearts.

It was possible that God had sent them the terrible war as punishment for the offense of slavery, President Lincoln continued, and that the war could be a mighty scourge to rid them of it. People north and south alike hoped, and fervently prayed, that the war would swiftly pass away, but if God willed that it should continue "until all the wealth piled by the bond-man's two hundred and fifty years of unrequited toil shall be sunk, and until every drop of blood drawn with the lash, shall be paid by another drawn with the sword," they must accept that the Lord's judgment was true and righteous.

"With malice toward none," Mr. Lincoln urged his listeners, "with charity for all, with firmness in the right, as God gives us to see the right, let us strive on to finish the work we are in; to bind up the nation's wounds; to care for him who shall have borne the battle, and for his widow, and his orphan, to do all which may achieve and cherish a just, and a lasting peace, among ourselves, and with all nations."

Breathless, her heart pounding with fervent admiration, Jule watched as Mr. Lincoln turned to a tall, imposing, black-robed gentleman, who stepped forward holding an open Bible. The gentleman — the chief justice of the Supreme Court, Jule heard someone murmur — set the holy book on a stand, and after Mr. Lincoln placed his right

443

hand upon it, the chief justice solemnly administered the oath of office. Then the president bent and kissed the Bible, and as the multitudes roared their approval, an artillery salute boomed and the Marine Band played a stirring tune — but Jule stood motionless and silent, President Lincoln's powerful oration reverberating in her ears and heart and thoughts.

"This is history, Jule," Emma said close to her ear, applauding furiously, her eyes shining with unshed tears of joy. "We were here. We saw it happen. How could you wish to live anywhere else?"

She couldn't, Jule realized as she joined in the thunderous applause and ardent cheers of the thousands of citizens, white and colored alike, all around her. Washington City was her home, and she would not let fear and worry drive her from it.

When Julia read of Mr. Lincoln's stirring inaugural address, she wished anew that Ulys had accepted his invitation to attend the ceremony and the lavish ball that had followed, but soon sad news from Covington drove all regrets for celebrations missed from her thoughts. Only a few days after the president's second term began, Jesse Root Grant sent Ulys a black-edged letter bearing the stunning news that on March 6, Ulys's eldest sister, Clara, had died of consumption.

444

"I've known she was on the decline," Ulys admitted to Julia, his voice rough, his head bowed over the pages. "But I still hoped she'd rally. I wasn't expecting to hear of her death so soon."

So intense was his sorrow that he could not bring himself to respond to his father's letter for more than a week, and after that, he buried his grief beneath his stoic exterior. It pained Julia that with so many lives depending upon him, Ulys could not take time to mourn his own loss.

Sharing his heartache, longing to ease his sorrow, Julia arranged for Jesse to withdraw from school and join them at City Point. Ulys was very glad to have his little rascal with him again, and Jesse's merry antics around headquarters amused Ulys's staff officers too. Soon Julia was relieved to see the lines of grief and worry fade from her husband's brow, although his cares were too great for them to disappear entirely.

By the middle of March, spring had come to City Point, and preparations for the great offensive against General Lee's army picked up speed and intensity until the encampment seemed to tremble and hum with eager anticipation. Ulys's chief of intelligence had received a letter from "a lady in Richmond" — the leader of his intelligence network in the rebel capital — disclosing that Confederate troops had been ordered from the city down the Danville road. Warehouses of tobacco, cotton, and other goods had been turned over to the provost marshal, and citizens had been ordered to "be organized," which Julia interpreted as a veiled warning to the people of Richmond not to plunder the city if it were evacuated. She overheard Ulys tell Rawlins and Ingalls that his informant's observations strongly indicated that the enemy intended to retreat southwest to Lynchburg, and soon.

Julia was equally concerned with news from the Union capital. Nearly every day, the newspapers from Washington and New York commented on the exhausted, careworn appearance of the president. Julia's heart went out to him, and she worried that the enormous burden he carried would kill him if he could not set it down, if only for a brief respite.

"Ulys," Julia mused one evening after they had put Jesse to bed, "why don't you invite Mr. and Mrs. Lincoln to visit headquarters and review the troops?"

"If President Lincoln wants to come, he will," Ulys replied. "He won't wait to be asked."

"I'm not so sure." Julia drew her chair closer to his and rested her head on his shoulder. "Ever since the war began he's been unfairly maligned by the press for meddling in army affairs. I don't think he'll ever visit unless you invite him, rather than stir up that talk again."

"I suppose so," said Ulys, but he looked dubious, and when one day and then another passed and no invitation was sent, Julia decided to pursue another tack.

Young Jesse was not the only son of a great man in the encampment, for soon after Union troops had occupied Charleston, a new officer had joined Ulys's staff at City Point — Captain Robert Lincoln, the president's eldest son.

In mid-January, Mr. Lincoln had sent Ulys a humble and sincere letter, which opened with the entreaty, "Please read and answer this letter as though I was not President, but only a friend." His son Robert, he had explained, twenty-two years of age and recently graduated from Harvard, wished to see something of the war before it ended. "Could he," Mr. Lincoln had asked, "without embarrassment to you, or detriment to the service, go into your Military family with some nominal rank, I, and not the public, furnishing his necessary means?" He had hoped that Ulys could find a post for Robert that would neither place him on the front lines nor bestow upon him a coveted position that ought to go to a more deserving veteran soldier, but if Ulys could not, "say so without the least hesitation, because I am as anxious, and as deeply interested, that you shall not

447

be encumbered as you can be yourself."

What the president had not said, but what Julia had heard from others, was that Robert had long sought his parents' blessing to enlist in the army, but Mrs. Lincoln, already bereft of two sons, had adamantly refused. Julia had wondered if Mrs. Lincoln had changed her mind with the end of the war seeming so near, or if Mr. Lincoln had not consulted her.

"I will be most happy to have him in my Military family in the manner you propose," Ulys had replied a few days later, writing on the torn-off, blank half of Mr. Lincoln's letter for want of other paper. He had recommended the rank of captain and the role of assistant adjutant general, which Mr. Lincoln and his son had immediately and gratefully accepted.

In the days that followed, as the president's eldest son had settled into camp and into his new position on Ulys's staff, Julia concluded that he was a noble, handsome young man who had inherited many of his father's genial traits. Robert Lincoln enjoyed telling stories and jokes around the campfire and cheerfully joined in all the social pastimes at headquarters. Ulys observed approvingly that despite his father's exalted position he expected to be treated no differently than any other officer. He never shirked his duties and he was always ready to take on his share of hard work. Julia was impressed that Captain Lincoln was determined to earn his own accolades like any other officer, but she could never entirely forget that he was the president's son.

One bright spring day in the third week of March, when Captain Lincoln came to the cabin to see Ulys on some official matter, Julia took the opportunity to inquire after his father's health. "Why do your father and mother never come down to visit?" she asked. "I'm sure a pleasant sail down the river in such fine weather would be restful and beneficial to them both, and know it would please the troops very much to see them."

"I suppose they would visit," said Captain Lincoln thoughtfully, "if they were sure they weren't intruding."

After the captain finished his business and departed, Julia turned to Ulys and gave him a pointed look. With a wry laugh, Ulys rose from his desk. "You were right, my dear little wife. I'll telegraph to invite the president without delay."

"Perhaps you should appoint me to your staff as an advisor," she teased.

"I might," he said affectionately as he bent to kiss her cheek, "if I weren't afraid of making my officers jealous. Julia, you must know that you're as essential to me as any of them. You've been my sunshine throughout these long, dark days."

"I know," she said, smiling fondly up at

him. He was all that and more to her, and ever had been.

CHAPTER TWENTY-ONE

March 1865

It was no simple matter for the president to leave the capital for the field of war, but after Secretary Stanton was satisfied with the measures taken to ensure Mr. Lincoln's safety, the presidential party set out from Washington aboard the *River Queen.* At nearly nine o'clock the following evening, the steamer arrived at City Point, and Captain Lincoln immediately ran to the Grants' cabin to announce the news.

"Shall we call on them?" asked Julia. "The hour is quite late."

"They'd be happy to see you at any time," Captain Lincoln assured them. "I'd be honored to escort you."

The president met them at the gangplank, greeted Ulys cordially, and, offering Julia his arm, conducted them to his wife, who awaited them in a comfortable stateroom arranged as a cozy parlor. Mrs. Lincoln rose from the sofa and received them most graciously, but Julia thought she looked rather tired and drawn, with shadows beneath her eyes and a despondent air that her polite smile could not entirely conceal.

"If you two ladies will excuse us," Mr. Lincoln said, "the general and I will withdraw so we can talk awhile without interruption. If you'll oblige me, General?"

"Of course, Mr. President," Ulys replied, and after offering the ladies courteous bows, the two gentlemen departed.

With a soft sigh, Mrs. Lincoln spread her skirts and seated herself on the sofa.

"Was your journey pleasant?" Julia inquired politely, sitting beside her.

"How dare you?" Mrs. Lincoln said icily, glaring first at Julia's face, and then at the sofa, where only a narrow gap separated them.

"Oh, I crowd you, I fear," Julia murmured, hiding her surprise as she quickly rose and settled into a nearby chair. She moved on to a topic she was certain the proud mother would relish — Captain Robert Lincoln, how excellently he performed his duties as assistant adjutant general, and how well liked he was by the rest of the staff. Julia might have overstated the case slightly when she described him as indispensable to General Grant, but Mrs. Lincoln responded warmly to the praise of her eldest son. Julia then inquired about young Tad and suggested that he and Jesse meet the next day to explore the camp and ride Jesse's ponies. Mrs. Lincoln accepted so graciously that Julia could almost convince herself that she had misunderstood the First Lady's exclamation and had imagined the icy glare. Since Mrs. Lincoln had always been courteous and kind whenever Julia met her in Washington, she was perfectly willing to forget her brief lapse in civility, especially since it had come after a difficult day and night of exhausting travel.

The following morning, long before dawn, Julia woke to the sound of urgent knocking upon the cabin door. Ulys rose to answer, and when he returned to the bedroom, he swiftly began to dress.

"What is it?" Julia asked.

"The rebels attacked Fort Stedman at about a quarter past four. Bands of sharpshooters and engineers disguised themselves as deserters, overwhelmed our pickets, and cleared obstructions we had set to delay an advance by their infantry."

"Oh, Ulys, no."

"Three companies followed after and stormed the works," Ulys said grimly. "They relied on stealth and speed, and they caught our men entirely by surprise. One saving grace — General McLaughlen managed to alert some of the batteries before he was surrounded and captured."

"Captured! How dreadful!"

Ulys patted her leg through the quilts. "Never mind, my dear little wife. Our artillery is returning fire, and we might have the enemy in full retreat by the time you get up for breakfast."

He went out to the front room, and soon a faint light beneath the closed door and the scrape of a chair told her he had lit a lamp and was working at his desk. Unsettled, she lay awake hoping another messenger would bring more reassuring news, but eventually she drifted off to sleep.

She woke well after daybreak to find Ulys gone. She spent the morning minding Jesse and awaiting news, and she was much relieved when Badeau sent word that General John F. Hartranft's troops had mounted a fierce counterattack and the Union once again held Fort Stedman. They had suffered about one thousand casualties — men killed, injured, missing, or captured — a sorrowing number to be sure, but only one to every four of the enemy.

Mr. Lincoln was keenly interested in visiting the scene of the battle, and when Julia learned that Ulys and his staff were making the necessary arrangements, she entrusted Jesse to an aide and hurried to Ulys's office. If a party was being made up to tour Fort Stedman, she wanted to be included. If it was safe enough for the president and First Lady, it was safe enough for the general's wife.

At noon Mrs. Lincoln and Julia joined a rather sizable group aboard a military train bound for General Meade's headquarters with the Army of the Potomac, about ten miles away. The roadbed was dreadfully rough and jarring, but as she studied the passing scenery, Mrs. Lincoln gave no sign of dissatisfaction but a slight grimace. Suddenly she gasped aloud and pressed her handkerchief to her lips. In the mud beside the tracks lay mangled bodies in tatters of blue and butternut and gray, enemies intermingled in death, faces buried in the muck or staring up unblinking at the brilliant sky.

Julia could not tear her gaze away from the window. Countless bodies passed before her line of sight — arms torn from sockets, chests sunken into wet blackness, skulls fractured with gray matter spilling out upon the grassy slope — and she jumped and clutched her hand to her throat as an arm reached past her and, with a slow, soft scraping of cloth against wood, drew the shade. Startled from her waking nightmare, Julia turned to find Badeau, who regarded her with sorrowful sympathy before moving on to draw Mrs. Lincoln's shade as well.

The railroad did not extend all the way to their destination, so at the terminus, the men continued on horseback, while the ladies, with Badeau detailed to escort them, followed in an ambulance. Their conveyance was a half-open carriage with two seats for passengers and one for the driver, and after Badeau assisted Mrs. Lincoln aboard and offered a hand to Julia, she was careful to ask, "May I sit beside you, Mrs. Lincoln?"

"Of course," the First Lady replied, surprised. Julia thanked her and sat, making room for Badeau to climb aboard and take his place on the front seat facing the ladies, with his back to the driver and the horses.

"Do you think the danger of this morning's attack has quite passed, Colonel?" Mrs. Lincoln asked anxiously as the carriage set out.

"Oh, certainly, madam," Badeau replied. "However —" He hesitated, smiling, as if he were not sure whether he should divulge what he knew. "All wives of officers at the army front have been ordered to the rear, which is a sure sign that active operations are contemplated."

"Indeed?" replied Mrs. Lincoln. Julia, who knew very well that Ulys planned a significant offensive strike as soon as the muddy roads permitted, said nothing.

"Oh, yes," said Badeau. "Not a single lady has been allowed to remain — except the wife of General Charles Griffin, and only because she obtained a special permit from the president."

Mrs. Griffin, Julia knew, was regarded as one of the great beauties of Washington City, and she was about to suggest that they invite her to join their excursion when Mrs. Lincoln drew herself up and fixed Badeau with a piercing stare. "Do you mean to say that she saw the president alone, sir?" she demanded. "Do you know that I never allow the president to see any woman alone?"

"Pray forgive me, Mrs. Lincoln," said Badeau, startled. "I meant no offense."

"That's a very equivocal smile, sir," she snapped. "I will ask the president if he saw that woman alone."

"Dear Mrs. Lincoln," said Julia in an undertone, placing her hand on the First Lady's. "Colonel Badeau made an unfortunate remark. He doesn't mean anything by it. Pray don't let it annoy you."

Mrs. Lincoln shook off her hand. "Stop the carriage," she ordered Badeau, but when he merely stammered protests, she rose from her seat, reached past him, and pinned the driver's arms to his sides. "Stop at once, I say!"

"Mrs. Lincoln, please," Julia exclaimed as Badeau went to the driver's rescue. "Do calm yourself. You'll startle the horses."

None too soon, Julia persuaded her to sit down, and the driver, looking much vexed, was able to proceed. When they arrived at General Meade's headquarters, the general himself promptly approached the ambulance to pay his respects to the president's wife.

With one last glare for Badeau, Mrs. Lincoln descended and took General Meade's arm, and they walked off together.

Julia inhaled deeply and fell back against her seat.

"I had intended to offer Mrs. Lincoln my arm," Badeau said, quietly frantic, "but General Meade is my superior, and he has the right to escort her. I had no chance to warn him. What if she makes a scene in the presence of the foreign minister and the other dignitaries with the president?"

"You've done nothing wrong, Colonel," Julia assured him. "General Meade's father was a diplomat. Let's hope he's inherited some of his father's skill."

"You're a fine diplomat yourself," Badeau said, "and I'm glad you were here to help manage Mrs. President."

Julia inclined her head to him, flattered and yet unsettled. She hoped she never became someone her husband's aides felt they had to manage.

They joined the rest of the party as General Meade showed them around his headquarters. When President Lincoln inquired if he might ride out to view the battlefields, General Meade readily offered to guide him and the other gentlemen in the party. He courteously showed the ladies to a small parlor where they could await the men's return, again with the unfortunate Badeau as their escort.

As soon as the general left, Mrs. Lincoln fixed Badeau with a sharp look. "General Meade is a gentleman, sir," she said crisply. "He says it was not the president who gave Mrs. Griffin the permit, but the secretary of war."

"My apologies, madam," he replied, bowing. Mrs. Lincoln seemed satisfied with that, and she promptly engaged Julia in a lively conversation about the illustrious gentlemen who had accompanied them from Washington. Dazed from Mrs. Lincoln's sudden and dramatic shifts in temper, Julia did her best to keep up, nodding and murmuring perfunctory replies at appropriate intervals.

When the president, Ulys, and their companions returned, they were somber and quiet. The president had ridden over part of the battlefield where the fallen soldiers were being buried, and the experience had depressed him greatly. Melancholy seemed carved into the very lines and hollows of his face, and Julia suspected that not even peace and a reunited nation would ever erase them entirely.

Their train traveled slowly back to City Point, hauling cars full of wounded soldiers. When they arrived, Mr. Lincoln, weary and worn, declined an invitation to dine with Ulys and his staff at headquarters. Instead, he and

Mrs. Lincoln and most of their party retired to the *River Queen* for the night.

As much as Julia liked the president, she was not sorry to see them go.

Later that evening, Julia sought out Badeau to assure him that he had handled Mrs. Lincoln's outburst like a true gentleman. "The whole affair is so distressing and mortifying that neither of us must mention it again," Julia said firmly. "I'll tell the general what happened, but no one else."

"I heartily agree, Mrs. Grant," said Badeau, much relieved.

She waited until later that night, when she and Ulys were alone in the cabin. Ulys listened soberly as she described the strange and disturbing incident. "Mrs. Lincoln's jealousy of Mrs. Griffin was truly extraordinary and extreme," she finished, shaking her head. "If she should complain about Colonel Badeau to you or to her husband, you should know that he did nothing wrong."

"I'm sure he didn't." Ulys sat down on the edge of the bed, reached for her hand, and pulled her down to sit beside him. "Try to be sympathetic with Mrs. Lincoln if you can. The president has confided in me, now and then, about her poor health. She still grieves terribly from the loss of young Willie, and she suffers as I do from sick headaches."

"Was she suffering one yesterday?" asked Julia, dubious.

"She could have been. Why don't we give her the benefit of the doubt, just as we wish people would give me the benefit of the doubt when I'm stricken instead of calling me a drunk?"

Julia agreed, and she resolved to carry on as if the unpleasant incident had never occurred, for she would want the same regard shown to herself. She hoped that as Ulys's star continued to rise, she would bear the inescapable burdens of public life more easily than poor Mrs. Lincoln did.

The following day, a gloriously bright Sunday, a grand review of General Ord's Army of the James was planned for the president, but first his party traveled by steamer to watch General Sheridan's troops cross the river at Harrison's Landing. Julia felt a thrill of excitement and worry as she watched Sheridan's cavalry crowding the heights all along the north bank of the James while others crossed the river on a pontoon bridge. She knew Ulys had been waiting for Sheridan to arrive before he launched his spring campaign, which now loomed imminent on the horizon, dark and rumbling with the promise of victory and destruction.

The party — which included President and Mrs. Lincoln and their two sons; General and Mrs. Ord; Badeau, Porter, and a few other members of Ulys's staff; as well as Ulys, Julia, and Jesse — had lunch on the admiral's flagship, the *Malvern,* followed by a grand review of the naval flotilla. Once ashore at Aiken's Landing, the gentlemen and Mrs. Ord mounted horses, while Mrs. Lincoln and Julia squeezed their hoop skirts into an ambulance. Badeau was again assigned to escort them, but he quickly persuaded Porter to share the duty.

"We're fortunate Mrs. Ord has such an excellent bay to ride, and wasn't it charming that General Ord had ponies for the boys?" said Julia brightly as they set out. The ride was no smoother than the one the day before, and her voice trembled with every bump and jolt over the rough road.

"Charming indeed," said Mrs. Lincoln through clenched teeth. The ambulance jolted along so violently that the ladies' heads were bounced against the ceiling again and again, flattening the crowns of their bonnets. "Why could he not have had mounts for all of us?"

"Oh, do you ride, Mrs. Lincoln?" Julia asked, glad to have found a common interest.

Rather than answer, Mrs. Lincoln frowned imperiously and called out, "Driver, do hurry along. We're falling behind the others."

Julia observed that Mrs. Lincoln kept her gaze fixed on her husband, clearly recognizable even to Julia's poor sight by his height and his tall stovepipe hat, and upon the beautiful Mrs. Ord, whose fashionable hat boasted a long, white plume that bounced merrily in time with her mare's graceful gait.

"What does the woman mean," Mrs. Lincoln suddenly exclaimed, her voice shaking with each jolt of the wheels on the washboard road, "by riding by the side of the president, and ahead of me? Does she suppose that *he* wants *her* by his side instead of me?"

Major Seward, a nephew of the secretary of state, overheard some of Mrs. Lincoln's words but none of their implication. "The president's horse is very gallant, Mrs. Lincoln," he called, dropping back alongside the ambulance. "He insists on riding with Mrs. Ord."

"What do you mean by that, sir?" Mrs. Lincoln asked sharply.

"Only that Mrs. Ord's horse is the mate of the president's horse," said Major Seward, taken aback.

"And a chivalrous creature he is indeed," said Julia, "to want to look after his mate. You're quite right, Major."

His smile long since vanished, Major Seward inclined his head to them in parting, urged his horse to quicken its pace, and soon caught up with the other riders.

"Why do they ride so far ahead?" said Mrs. Lincoln, her voice shaking as much from anger as from the violent rattling of the ambulance. "What is it they don't wish me to see?"

Before Julia could reply, the ambulance struck an exposed tree root in the muddy road, tossing the passengers from their seats into the air.

"Stop this carriage at once," Mrs. Lincoln shrieked. "I must get out, and I will get out!"

The driver — a different fellow than the day before — pulled hard on the reins until the carriage halted. Julia felt her seat shift as two of the wheels mired deep in the mud.

"Let me out at once," said Mrs. Lincoln, climbing stiffly to her feet and reaching for the door. "Call to the riders to come back."

"Please, my good madam, do stay seated," Badeau implored.

"I'll continue on foot," she declared. "Mrs. Ord should have offered me her horse and taken my place in this dreadful conveyance."

"You oughtn't walk about here," the driver remarked. "You might get shot."

Mrs. Lincoln yanked open the door and began to descend. Badeau and Porter bolted to their feet and took hold of her arms.

"Unhand me at once, sirs!" Mrs. Lincoln exclaimed, but out of concern for her safety, they could not obey.

As Badeau and Porter fell back into their seats, Julia reached for Mrs. Lincoln's arm and held it firmly as the mired wheels pulled free and the ambulance rattled down the road. "That was quite startling," she said, with a wide-eyed breathlessness that was not entirely feigned. "I'm quite upset. Please forgive me if I cling to you for a moment."

Mrs. Lincoln glared imperiously and yanked her arm free of Julia's grasp, her lips pressed together in a thin, hard line, her smooth cheeks flushed darkly with rage.

At long last they arrived at the parade grounds, only to discover that the review had begun without them. The band played a lively martial tune; the colors flew; the troops presented arms. Julia spotted the president's cavalcade halfway down the line, and Mrs. Lincoln's sharp intake of breath told her that she, too, had seen Mrs. Ord's white plume unfurling grandly in the breeze not far from Mr. Lincoln's tall black stovepipe hat.

Mrs. Ord spurred her horse toward the ambulance. "Welcome, Mrs. Lincoln, Mrs. Grant," she greeted them, smiling, as she brought her lively bay close. "Have you ever seen such a magnificent spectacle?"

"I see a spectacle, to be sure, but I would never call it magnificent," snapped Mrs. Lincoln. "How dare you parade yourself before my husband in this brazen manner, you shameless Jezebel?"

The blood drained from Mrs. Ord's face. "Mrs. Lincoln," Julia protested. "Mrs. Ord has done nothing of the sort."

Mrs. Lincoln kept her blistering gaze fixed on Mrs. Ord. "Vile strumpet! How dare you take my place at the president's side?"

"What have I done?" Mrs. Ord protested, looking from Mrs. Lincoln to Julia and back beseechingly. "What have I done to deserve such censure?" Shock had rooted the general's wife in place, tears springing into her eyes, the long, white plume dancing gaily in the breeze.

"Nothing," Julia said quickly, laying a hand on Mrs. Lincoln's in a futile attempt to calm her. "Nothing at all. Mrs. Lincoln, please, do quiet yourself."

"Who are you to command me to be silent?" Mrs. Lincoln demanded. "I suppose you think you'll get to the White House yourself, don't you?"

"I am quite satisfied with my present position," Julia replied with all the dignity she could muster. "It is far greater than I had ever hoped to attain."

"Oh! I have no doubt that it is!"

Mrs. Lincoln turned her back upon Julia and Mrs. Ord, red-faced and fuming. Only then did Julia notice that the presidential party had been listening in silence — Ulys, grim and proud, and Mr. Lincoln, as pained and unhappy as she had ever seen him. The review continued, but the soldiers' brilliant, flawless performance was wasted on the distraught visitors.

On the steamer to City Point, Mrs. Lincoln immediately retired to a private parlor, offering her companions a much-needed respite from her temper. "Are you well?" Ulys asked Julia quietly the moment he could take her aside.

"I'm fine," Julia assured him in an undertone, but when her hands began to ache she realized that she clung to the steamer's railing with unnecessary vigilance, and she deliberately relaxed her grip. "I worry far more about Mrs. Ord."

"And Mr. Lincoln," Ulys added. Suddenly he took one of Julia's hands and kissed it. "Sometimes I neglect to tell you how grateful I am to have you as my wife. I am, you know — always, deeply."

"Oh, my." Julia managed a smile. "I suppose I have Mrs. Lincoln to thank for that inspired poetical declaration."

Mrs. Lincoln did not emerge from her parlor until the steamer reached City Point, and as the party disembarked, she was subdued and quiet, her anger burned down to embers. But Julia's relief was short-lived. By the time she and Ulys and his staff joined the Lincolns for supper aboard the *River Queen* later that evening, the fire of Mrs. Lincoln's temper had been stoked and burned as hotly as before. She berated General Ord over the first course, criticized her husband throughout the second, and before the coffee and sweets were passed, she loudly and repeatedly demanded that the president dismiss General Ord immediately. "He is unfit for his place," she declared, "to say nothing of his wife."

None too soon, the meal ended, and while Mrs. Lincoln retired, Mr. Lincoln escorted their guests to the gangplank, where he bade them good night, his expression a study in sadness and solemn dignity.

Ulys walked ahead with Rawlins and another officer, discussing a recent telegram from Sherman, who was expected at headquarters the next day to plan the spring offensive. Colonel Badeau fell in step beside Julia and offered her his arm. "Colonel, I hereby release you from your promise never to speak of Mrs. Lincoln's outburst yesterday," said Julia. "Today's incidents so far surpassed them, and there were so many witnesses, that our silence won't make any difference."

"You don't need to endure her tempers," the colonel replied. "Mrs. Stanton refuses to see her at all."

"Surely not."

"Indeed. Mrs. Stanton told me herself, when she and her husband last visited City Point. I chanced to ask her some innocent question about the president's wife, and Mrs. Stanton replied rather shortly, 'I do not visit Mrs. Lincoln.' I thought I must have misunderstood her, because the wife of the secretary of war surely must call on the wife of the president."

"I would certainly think so."

"Ah, but when I renewed my inquiry, she said, with firm civility, 'Understand me, sir. I do not go to the White House. I do not visit Mrs. Lincoln.' "

"I can't blame Mrs. Stanton," Julia acknowledged, "but I can't emulate her either. Tomorrow, after Mrs. Lincoln has had a chance to rest, I'll call on her aboard the *River Queen*, and perhaps we can yet be friends."

When Julia called on Mrs. Lincoln in the morning, she was informed that the president's wife was indisposed, but when she and Jesse met Ulys for lunch, he told her that Mr. Lincoln had invited them to accompany his family and a few others on an excursion aboard the *River Queen* to the Point of Rocks on the Appomattox River, where legend told that Pocahontas had saved the life of Captain John Smith. Ulys's frown, though slight, told her he disliked the idea of yet another sightseeing excursion that would oblige him to leave headquarters.

"I'll make it my mission to see to Mrs. Lincoln's every comfort," Julia promised, determined to relieve him of at least one concern.

The wind was brisk and cold on the river, and the steamer rocked slightly in the choppy waters, so Julia invited Mrs. Lincoln to join her in the forward cabin. Mrs. Lincoln curtly declined, wrapped her shawl more tightly about herself, and went out upon the uncovered deck near the pilothouse.

Watching the First Lady through the window, considering what to do next, Julia was startled from her reverie by the polite clearing of a throat behind her. "Good afternoon, Mrs. Grant."

Glancing over her shoulder, Julia discovered Captain John S. Barnes, the commander of the armed sidewheel steamer the *Bat,* a blockade-runner that had been assigned to accompany the *River Queen* on the James. Secretary of War Stanton had personally charged Captain Barnes with the president's safe conduct from Washington to City Point and back, which was no small responsibility considering that the *River Queen* was unarmed and unarmored.

"Good afternoon, Captain," Julia replied.

"I'm sorry to intrude upon your solitude, but I thought Mrs. Lincoln would be with you."

"She's on the deck," Julia said, nodding to the window. "I wasn't aware you were aboard. Who's minding the *Bat*?"

"She's in good hands, never fear." Captain Barnes hesitated. "I confess I've joined this trip with some misgivings, and only because the president himself invited me. I regret to say that I'm responsible for yesterday's debacle."

"I think it unfair that anyone other than

Mrs. Lincoln should accept responsibility for her behavior."

"But it was I who told Mrs. Ord that she should ride along with the president," said Captain Barnes. "Afterward I explained to Mr. Lincoln how Mrs. Ord and I had found ourselves in the reviewing column, and that we immediately withdrew from it upon the arrival of your ambulance, but Mrs. Lincoln insists that the troops were led to think that Mrs. Ord was the wife of the president."

"But surely the soldiers know Mrs. Ord," said Julia. "She's been staying at her husband's headquarters for months. They wouldn't have mistaken her for anyone else."

"I like to think any rational observer would reach the same conclusion," the captain said gloomily. "For the president's sake, I'd give anything to placate Mrs. Lincoln, but I'm at a loss for what to do."

"Why don't you begin with a simple act of kindness?" Julia gestured to one of several upholstered armchairs arranged in the cabin. "Mrs. Lincoln prefers to be outside, but she's obliged to stand. I'm sure she would thank you for taking her a comfortable seat."

Julia watched through the window as Captain Barnes wrestled a chair through the doorway, carried it to an ideal spot on the deck, and offered it to Mrs. Lincoln, who promptly declined it. "I failed in my mission," he reported upon returning to the cabin, looking thoroughly miserable.

At that moment Mrs. Lincoln turned, regarded Julia unsmilingly through the window, and beckoned her outside.

Steeling herself, Julia joined Mrs. Lincoln on the deck. "Did you want some company?" Julia asked pleasantly. "I see that Captain Barnes has brought you a chair. How very kind of him."

"Too little, too late," said Mrs. Lincoln shortly. "I am not comfortable with that man aboard this boat. He never should have intruded upon our party."

Julia hardly knew what to say. "I believe Mr. Lincoln invited him."

"Well, I object to his presence." Mrs. Lincoln fixed her with an imperious look. "He is no longer invited, and I want you to inform him."

"We're in the middle of the river," Julia replied carefully. "Invited or not, the captain must remain with us for the present, unless you intend for him to swim back to City Point."

"That is for him to sort out." Mrs. Lincoln waved a hand. "You may go."

"Indeed?" Julia's voice was brittle with astonishment. "*May* I?"

"Yes, you may."

Julia was tempted to remain right where she stood to prove that she was not Mrs. Lincoln's to command, but the idea of quitting her company appealed too much to be denied. Not trusting herself to speak, she inclined her head in farewell and turned to go.

"Mrs. Grant."

Hoping Mrs. Lincoln had thought better of her request, Julia turned around. "Yes, Mrs. Lincoln?"

"Do not ever turn your back to me when you leave."

Julia stared at her, dumbfounded. "Do you mean to say," she asked distinctly, "that you wish me to back out of a room when I leave your presence?"

"I only remind you to show the proper respect, as I'm sure you would not wish to cause offense."

Julia regarded her levelly. "I will not risk injuring myself or tumbling overboard simply to avoid offending you. I'm quite sure *you* would not wish *that*. Good afternoon, Mrs. Lincoln."

Quite deliberately, she turned and walked away, vowing never to conduct herself as Mrs. Lincoln did, regardless of whatever migraines, tragedies, or troubles befell her.

Before long she found Captain Barnes in the pilothouse. "My good captain," she began, fighting to modulate her indignation, lowering her voice so that the officers present would not overhear, "Mrs. Lincoln has sent me on a most distasteful errand."

The captain drew himself up, apprehensive. "Pray continue, madam. I've braced myself."

Quickly, Julia told him what Mrs. Lincoln had said. "I am but the unhappy messenger," she emphasized. "However . . . I encourage you to avoid Mrs. Lincoln for the rest of the excursion."

"I can do better than that," he said, resigned. "When we land at Point of Rocks, I'll have the captain put me ashore on the other side of the Appomattox. I'll get a horse from the quartermaster and ride back to City Point."

Julia thought it a great injustice that a gallant naval officer should be treated so, but Captain Barnes insisted, explaining that he had the greatest sympathy for Mrs. Lincoln. He understood that she was unwell and that the mental strain upon her was so great that it caused her extreme sensitivity to perceived slights. He would not give her another moment's distress, even if it meant great inconvenience to himself.

Captain Barnes's kindness and generosity impressed Julia greatly, and when the presidential party disembarked at Point of Rocks, she remained aboard to see him off on the other shore.

The next morning offered the promise of a fresh start, so after breakfast Julia and Jesse called at the *River Queen* to invite Mrs. Lincoln and Tad to go riding. Tad joyfully

474

bounded down the gangplank to join them, but he said his mother was not well and could not come. Nor did she appear the next time Julia attempted to see her, and as rumors sped through headquarters, she soon learned why.

Although the president had treated his wife with the most affectionate solicitude throughout their visit, her behavior had embarrassed him so much that a breach had come between them. Distressed and ashamed, Mrs. Lincoln had fled back to Washington, leaving Mr. Lincoln and Tad behind.

CHAPTER TWENTY-TWO

March–April 1865

As the last days of March passed, the sun warmed the earth, the roads dried, and City Point crackled with a fierce new energy, filling Julia with excitement and apprehension. She knew they were only days away from the launch of the last great offensive — for Ulys seemed certain that it would be the last, deciding the course of the fractured nation once and for all.

Soon after General Sheridan's cavalry arrived at headquarters, Julia chanced upon him aboard the *River Queen,* his eyes shining with eagerness as he read from a long scroll of office paper. "Ah, General, I see I've caught you reading a most interesting document," she teased. "What is it? It cannot be a love letter. No lady would use that sort of paper to express her affections to a beau."

He smiled, rolled up the scroll, and tucked it away in his breast pocket. "It is much better than a love letter, madam," he replied in a conspiratorial whisper. "It is the order of battle your husband wrote for me."

"It seems to give you great pleasure."

"It does, madam," he said firmly. "It is magnificent."

On the evening of March 27, General Sherman arrived at City Point aboard the *Russia,* a captured Confederate steamer drafted into service for the United States Navy. Julia joined the officers as they gathered around the campfire, where Sherman described in terrible, exhilarating detail the stirring events of his march through Georgia. "I met some people I knew as friends in better days, and they were not ashamed to call upon the 'Vandal Chief' that had invaded their lands," he said. "Otherwise the Southern people regarded my armies as the Romans did the Goths, and the parallel is not unjust."

It was a grand, glorious epic, but after Sherman had enthralled his audience for nearly an hour, Ulys said, "I'm sorry to break this up, Sherman, but the president is aboard the *River Queen,* and I know he'll be anxious to see you. Suppose we go and pay him a visit before dinner."

Sherman immediately rose and the two generals set out for the wharf. Julia knew that there they would be joined by Generals Sheridan and Meade, Admiral Porter, and other officers — a notable gathering to discuss war maneuvers past and present.

It was only after she put Jesse to bed and sat alone with Ulys in the cabin, she at the fireside and he at his desk, that she grew wistful. "Ulys," she said, "why do you never tell me of your plans? You know you needn't fear I'd divulge your secrets."

Ulys looked up from his dispatches and regarded her thoughtfully as he puffed on his cigar. "Would you like to know?"

"Of course I would."

He pushed back his chair and held out his hand to her. "Then come here."

She crossed the room, and when she took his hand, he pulled her onto his lap, wrapped his left arm around her, and with his right indicated the map spread upon his desk. "There is the entire field," he said, sweeping his hand over the Southern states. "Here stands the Army of the Potomac and the Army of the James." He pointed to West Virginia and Tennessee. "There I've placed General George Stoneman with a large body of cavalry to guard the mountain passes." He rested his palm on the Gulf states. "General Edward Canby is here, and Sherman —" His fingers moved across the map and came to rest upon the eastern coast of Georgia. "Sherman's forces are here. Now you have the position of all the armies, and you can see that they form a perfect cordon from sea to sea again."

"Yes," said Julia, studying the map. "I do

see that. What happens next?"

"Well —" Ulys paused for a moment. "I'm going to tighten that cordon until the rebellion is crushed or strangled."

Julia absorbed this in silence, cold grief welling up within her as from an underground spring.

"Julia?"

She took a deep, shaky breath. "I'm sorry, Ulys, but knowing this, I feel only a terrible, deep, abiding sorrow."

"Yes, war is always sorrowful." He kissed her softly on the cheek. "But, Julia, think how dreadful it would be if a cordon like the one I've drawn about the South encircled the Union instead."

She shuddered, imagining it all too well, knowing General Lee would have encircled the North if he had been able.

She knew Ulys had no choice but to draw the cordon tight.

The next morning Captain Barnes took General Sherman aboard the *Bat* and returned him to South Carolina, and General Ord crossed to the southern shore of the James River with three divisions to take his position for the assault. As Generals Meade and Sheridan, too, moved into place, Ulys told Julia something she had long suspected: He had decided to accompany his armies into the field and direct the operations himself.

On the afternoon before Ulys's departure, when most of the officers had already left headquarters for the field, Julia returned to the cabin after an outing with Jesse to discover Ulys packing up his office. He placed his hands on Julia's shoulders and fixed her with a look that allowed for no dissent. "I've decided that you and Mrs. Rawlins and the children should move aboard the dispatch boat for your safety. If my plans unfold as I hope and expect they will, I'll return to City Point soon, and we'll travel together to Washington."

Julia managed a smile, but her voice trembled. "How very proud I shall be."

"But if Lee should escape to the mountains — and I'm concerned that he might, if he moves before I'm ready — there's no telling when this war will end. In that case, you and Jesse must return without me."

Julia threw back her shoulders and lifted her chin. "I'm certain that the next time I return to Washington, it will be at my victor's side."

On the evening of March 29, Mr. Lincoln called on her aboard the *Mary Martin.* The lines of his face seemed deeper, the rings beneath his eyes of a darker hue. She had never seen him look more grave, and she knew the weight of his responsibilities oppressed him.

"When I parted with General Grant at the

station, he was looking well and full of hope," Mr. Lincoln told her kindly, his ineffable compassion bringing light to his careworn face. "I'm confident that his last campaign has begun, and that it will end in victory."

Julia thanked him and assured him that she shared his confidence — for somehow, despite her grave worries, she knew, in that uncanny way she always did, that Ulys would return to her whole and unharmed.

All those left behind at City Point braced themselves for word from the Petersburg front, for jarring reports of bloody battles, for ambulances full of wounded. Julia; Mary Emma Rawlins, Rawlins's second wife; and Antoinette Morgan, the wife of Colonel Michael R. Morgan, spent the long, anxious hours waiting for news, minding their children, strolling along the James, speculating in hushed and anxious voices about what their husbands might be doing at that very moment — and praying, silently and fervently, for victory and peace and the deliverance of the men they loved most dearly.

The day after Ulys departed, he telegraphed Julia from Gravelly Run to report that they were well but enduring heavy rains. "The weather is bad for us," he noted, "but it is reassuring to know that it rains on the enemy as well."

In the days that followed, he wrote to her

frequently, brief notes that were important not so much for what they told her of his military maneuvers — which was very little indeed — but for the assurances they offered that he was alive and well. He sent lengthier reports to the president, who had decided to remain at City Point until the outcome of the offensive could be known, and Mr. Lincoln kindly shared the news with Julia and the other wives.

It was from Mr. Lincoln — radiant, relieved, and beaming — that Julia learned of the fall of Petersburg. After Sheridan's marvelous victory at Five Forks, Ulys had ordered an assault all along the lines, shattering the rebel defenses and taking the city. By early afternoon, Union scouts reported that the Confederate government was evacuating Richmond. Ulys, telegraphing from his headquarters at the Banks House near the Boydton Plank Road, invited Mr. Lincoln to visit the captured works.

On the morning of April 3, Mr. Lincoln rode out with Tad to meet Ulys at Petersburg and to tour the defeated city. But before Mr. Lincoln and Tad could return with news from Petersburg, other reports came by telegraph from Richmond — word of an event that the people of the North had anxiously awaited for years.

At a quarter past eight o'clock that morning, Union forces under the command of

Major General Godfrey Weitzel had entered Richmond.

The Confederate capital had fallen.

Shortly after noon on that bright, sunny Monday, Jule walked to the workshop of Mr. Peter Bryant, a glassblower, to negotiate new terms. For months he had supplied Jule with bottles and jars for her various concoctions in exchange for an ample supply of her burn salve, but her need for more bottles had grown dramatically, in keeping with demand for her products. Although Mr. Bryant had not complained, she knew no one needed that much burn salve, and only kindness restrained him from asking for cash instead.

An assistant sent word of her arrival, and soon he emerged, wiping his brow and smiling. "Good day, Miss Jule," he greeted her warmly, as he always did. A few months before, Emma, who seemed to know at least one person in every profession, had introduced her to the freeborn craftsman, a widower in his early forties, the father of two children. In that time Jule had come to know that he was quiet and industrious, but kindly and generous too. His eldest son, fifteen and broad shouldered like his father, worked alongside him in the workshop, and his daughter, almost twelve, attended school and wanted to be a teacher.

"Good day, Mr. Bryant," Jule replied, smiling back.

The workshop was stiflingly warm, so he offered her a chair outside in front of the shop window. He stood nearby, arms folded in front of his chest, gaze keenly interested, as she opened negotiations.

"I'm glad your business is faring so well that you need so much glassware," he remarked. "I think I can manage a fair price considering the quantity you want."

The price he named was so low that Jule had to laugh. "Mr. Bryant, I think you'll lose money on this deal. This is business, not a favor."

"I know that," he said, looking a trifle embarrassed. "If you're worried about me, you can ask around. You might even find a better rate."

"I doubt that very much."

He extended a hand. "Then let's shake on it."

Her glance took in the old burn scars on his forearm. "Only if you let me include a regular supply of salve in the deal."

"Agreed."

They shook hands, and he held hers longer than necessary, perhaps distracted by a sudden, none too distant burst of artillery fire, followed immediately by whistles and cheers and shouts and a cheerful blast on a trumpet.

Jule gently eased her hand free of Mr.

Bryant's. "I wonder what they're celebrating."

He glanced up and down the street, frowning curiously as merry crowds began to gather, shouting and laughing for joy. "Another victory for General Grant, I hope."

Jule rose from her chair and watched, astonished, as people poured from homes and businesses, tossing their hats into the air, embracing and kissing and weeping for joy. Another artillery salute boomed, and as the blacksmith next door burst from his shop, Mr. Bryant called, "What's happened? What's the news?"

"What's the news, you ask?" The blacksmith beamed, tore off his leather apron, and tossed it over his shoulder through the doorway. "Richmond's fallen — that's the news!"

As Jule gasped and pressed her hands to her mouth, Mr. Bryant cheered, punched a fist into the air, and then seized her hands and danced her about in a circle. Joy bubbling up within her, she laughed and danced along — and then froze as he seized her by the shoulders and planted a kiss on her lips.

She stared at him numbly.

"Miss — Miss Jule," he stammered, releasing her. "Please forgive me."

"It's all right," she said shakily. "It's the excitement. I understand." She took a step back. "We have a deal, about the bottles, isn't that so?"

He nodded, shamefaced and utterly miserable. "I didn't mean to offend —"

"It's all right," she repeated, managing a smile. "I take no offense. I'll see you soon." She nodded and turned, hurrying away home.

Tears filled her eyes as she made her way through the joyful, raucous, exuberant crowds toward home. It seemed that all of Washington City had joined the celebration spilling into the streets, hearts overflowing with joy, happiness shining in the faces of clerks and drovers and housemaids and waiters, white and colored alike. Already citizens were draping patriotic banners and bunting from their windows, and bands quickly formed on street corners and parks to play spirited marches and merry jigs.

"Jule," she heard a voice cry out happily, and when she turned, she glimpsed Emma waving frantically from the other side of the street, rising high on tiptoe to be seen over the crowd. A surge of relief swept the troubling kiss to the back of her thoughts, and she quickly wove her way to her friend's side.

"Oh, Jule, isn't it glorious?" Emma cried, embracing her.

"Yes," she replied, truly understanding for the first time. "Oh, Emma, it's wonderful!"

With Emma and her companions, seamstresses from Mrs. Keckley's workshop and the renowned dressmaker herself, she joined the celebration, linking arms and singing and laughing and marching through the streets. Crowds gathered outside the homes and offices of various dignitaries and called for them to come out and address them, but of the many who complied, only the few loudest could be heard over the din. An eight-hundred-gun salute shook the city: three hundred booms for the fall of Petersburg, five hundred for Richmond. Many revelers indulged in too much liquor, and Jule was at first amused and then alarmed to observe neighbors she knew to be sober, responsible folk tottering down the streets, singing and proclaiming the glory of President Lincoln, General Grant, and the Union army in loud, slurring voices.

Tomorrow they would nurse headaches and sour stomachs, but for the moment, nothing could diminish their rejoicing. Jule could not say the same for herself, for regret tempered her happiness — regret for the unexpected kiss, for Gabriel's absence, for the profound loneliness that only a reunion with her beloved husband could assuage.

That day was coming, she told herself. Every victory General Grant won brought Gabriel that much closer.

As Ulys and the Army of the Potomac relentlessly pursued General Lee's forces, the thrilling promise of victory brought a torrent of visitors from the North down upon City

Point. The president and his wife had apparently reconciled via the post and the telegraph, for on April 5, two days after the fall of Richmond, Mrs. Lincoln and a small party of companions joined the president aboard the *River Queen,* docked not one hundred yards from the *Mary Martin.* Before calling at the presidential ship, Julia enlisted as her escort Congressman Elihu Washburne, a friend of Ulys's from their Galena days. Aboard the River Queen, they were kindly received and introduced to one and all — Senator Charles Sumner; Secretary of the Interior James Harlan and his wife; their daughter Miss Mary Harlan, whom Robert Lincoln was courting; the Marquis de Chambrun, visiting from France; and an elegant, fashionably attired colored woman whom Mrs. Lincoln introduced as her friend Mrs. Elizabeth Keckley, a dressmaker.

After Julia paid her respects, Mrs. Lincoln said, as if continuing an interrupted conversation, "Suppose we ask Mrs. Grant. Let her answer this important question."

Offering a serene smile to mask her sudden wariness, Julia inquired, "What question is that?"

"What should be done with the Confederate president Jefferson Davis," Senator Sumner asked, "in the event of his capture?"

"What should be done?" Julia echoed thoughtfully, stalling for time. Just then her eyes met those of Mr. Lincoln, who regarded her with a friendly smile. Inspired, Julia said, "I would trust him to the mercy of our always just and most gracious president."

"Well said, madame," declared the Marquis de Chambrun.

"A most diplomatic answer," praised Secretary Harlan.

Even Mrs. Lincoln beamed approval, to Julia's relief.

The next morning the sun rose golden and warm in a sky of perfect blue, so Julia decided to invite Mrs. Lincoln and Tad on a picnic. She put on her prettiest bonnet, took Jesse by the hand, and went ashore — only to discover that the *River Queen* was gone.

Puzzled, she inquired among the men working the docks and discovered that Mrs. Lincoln had organized an excursion to Richmond for her companions. "She got upset when she learned that Mr. Lincoln visited the city without her the day after it fell," an ensign confided. "So Mr. Lincoln obliged her with a second trip."

Julia was hurt that she had not been invited along, and her sense that Mrs. Lincoln had intentionally excluded her heightened the next morning, when she called at the *River Queen* after breakfast only to learn that the presidential party had taken a special train to Petersburg to tour the fallen city. "I know Mrs. Lincoln is easily offended," Julia confided to Mary Emma and Antoinette, "but I don't understand how she could have forgotten me."

"Oh, she hasn't forgotten you," said Antoinette archly. "She simply likes you less, as the people like your husband more. Their cries of 'Grant for president!' are like the crash of cymbals in her ear."

"He doesn't want to be president," Julia protested. "He made that perfectly clear before the last election."

"With the war almost won, perhaps Mrs. Lincoln fears he'll be searching for another occupation."

"If so, her fears are entirely unjustified," said Julia, hurt, "as was her ungenerous decision to leave us behind."

"Why don't we make up our own party and take our own boat to Richmond?" said Mary Emma.

Antoinette clapped her hands, delighted. "A splendid idea! We don't need Mrs. Lincoln to enjoy ourselves."

Congressman Washburne, as curious to see the vanquished Confederate capital as they, agreed to escort them, and two other officers were easily persuaded to join the group. Soon the *Mary Martin* set out upon the James, and in the company of her cheerful, loyal friends, Julia enjoyed the warm sunshine on the forward deck, savoring the breeze and the pure, balmy air. The river flowed along majestically, its banks lovely and fragrant with the first sweet blossoms of spring. Beyond them stretched fair fields, the very image of peacetime bounty — but all too often, the illusion of prosperity was broken by glimpses of deserted army camps and ruined forts, the ugly scars of war.

Before long the steamer landed at Richmond, and after disembarking, Julia's small party arranged for carriages to take them through the city. Their pleasant conversation soon fell silent as they rode through the ruins of the former capital, still smoldering after the fires the Confederates had set as they evacuated, destroying valuable supplies rather than leave them for the Yankees. The streets were unnaturally subdued except for occasional patrols of Union soldiers, a few thin citizens in worn clothing who averted their eyes as they hurried past on business of their own, and an occasional colored servant who glared at them as intruders, which Julia felt they were indeed. The streets surrounding the public buildings were covered in papers — letters and government documents, Julia surmised — and the Virginia statehouse where the Confederate Congress had met was in a state of disarray that spoke of fear and haste — desk drawers yanked open, papers scattered, chairs overturned as if their last occupants had fled in alarm.

The scenes of sorrow and suffering grieved

Julia so much that after circling the capitol square she asked to be taken back to the boat. While the others continued touring the city, she gazed out upon the river, listening to the familiar peeping of frogs, so reminiscent of her Missouri home that tears sprang to her eyes. On what was surely the eve of her husband's greatest triumph, she was haunted by the tragedies of the long years of war — the homes made desolate, the hearts broken, the treasure lost, the young lives sacrificed.

Eventually her friends and their escorts returned to the boat, which soon thereafter carried them back to City Point. When they landed, they were informed that the presidential party had returned from Petersburg and intended to depart for Washington that evening.

Later, alone in her stateroom, Julia was mulling over the day when Captain Barnes called. "Would you please escort me to the president's boat?" she asked after they had chatted awhile. "I haven't seen much of their party of late, and I understand that they're leaving tonight. I'd like to pay my respects and say farewell."

"Certainly, Mrs. Grant," the captain replied, surprised, "but aren't you going to the reception tonight?"

"Reception?"

"Why, yes, madam. Have you received no notice of it?"

"No," said Julia, doing her best to sound unconcerned. "But I presume I will in good time."

"I'd be happy to escort you now," Captain Barnes said, discomfited, "if you wish to call on them sooner."

"No, that's quite all right." Julia managed a smile, embarrassed for them both. "I'll wait for the reception."

But after the captain left, she waited in vain for a messenger to bring her an invitation. The stars came out, and scarcely a hundred yards away, the crew of the *River Queen* illuminated the ship with lanterns from bow to stern until it shone like an enchanted palace. She watched from the forward cabin as a military band went aboard, but when the sound of tuning instruments and laughter and conversation drifted to her across the water, she drew on her shawl and turned away, disconsolate.

Sunday dawned warm and clear, with bright sunshine that soon lifted the dew from the grassy riverbanks and softened the mists rising from the river. Julia spent the morning in prayer and contemplation of scripture, and later that afternoon, she and Mary Emma Rawlins received callers in the forward cabin. They were engaged in earnest conversation with several officers from the army and navy, weighing the probability of imminent peace, when a telegraph officer from headquarters appeared, cheeks flushed, eyes wide and beaming, a piece of paper clutched in a grip so tight his hand trembled. "Mrs. Grant," he exclaimed. "May I have a word?"

"Certainly." Rising, Julia followed the young officer into the corridor, where she instinctively lowered her voice. "What's the news?"

"Glad news — but it would cost me my head if old Stanton knew I had told you first."

"I won't tell him. You have my word."

He took a deep breath and blurted, "General Lee surrendered this day to General Grant at Appomattox Court House."

Julia gasped and pressed her hand to her heart, reaching out with the other to steady herself on the wall. "Can this be true? Are you certain?"

The telegrapher nodded and read the terms of surrender. The officers and men of the Army of Northern Virginia would be paroled on the condition that they would not take up arms against the government of the United States. Their arms, artillery, and public property — excluding officers' sidearms, private horses, and baggage — would be turned over to the Union. That done, all officers and soldiers would be permitted to return to their homes and would not be disturbed by the government of the United States as long as they observed their parole and the laws of the places where they resided.

Overwhelming force followed by mercy — she would have expected nothing less from her Ulys.

"I hope I haven't spoken out of turn, madam," the telegrapher said, "but I felt that you should know as soon as anyone else, even the president." He bowed and hurried out, leaving her to stare after him, speechless from disbelief and dizzy with joy. She had not thanked him. She had not even learned his name.

When she returned to the forward cabin, Mary Emma and the officers urged her to tell them what she knew, but she demurred. It was a relief when, twenty minutes later, great shouts of joy rang out along the bluff, loud cries of "The Union forever!" and "Hurrah!" and "Hallelujah!" Julia's companions guessed her secret before it burst from her, but then they laughed and cheered in celebration, embracing and shaking hands and praising God and wiping tears from their eyes. Hundreds of boats crowded the river, carrying sightseers from Washington and New York and Boston and parts beyond, and as word of the surrender spread across the waters, one boat after another pulled alongside the *Mary Martin* to shout congratulations to Julia, beaming and waving hats and handkerchiefs. Other eager well-wishers came aboard, eager to voice the prediction, "General Grant will certainly be the next president."

The next day, dispatches from the front arrived announcing that Julia and her companions could expect their husbands for a late dinner that evening. After making arrangements with the captain for dinner to be served to as many officers as the steamer could accommodate, Julia, Mary Emma, and Antoinette donned their best dresses, arranged their hair becomingly, and gathered with their children in the saloon to await the arrival of their gallant heroes.

The hours passed. The anxious wives watched the clock and peered off the bow to the shore, eager for the first glimpse of the men they loved. The children grew hungry, so their mothers fed them, but although their own stomachs rumbled they denied themselves, determined to wait until their heroes could join them at the table.

Finally the hour grew so late that the children fell asleep curled up in armchairs and had to be carried off to their staterooms and to bed. Soon thereafter, a telegraph arrived for Julia. "Tell Mrs. Grant and party we will not be in as soon as we elected and cannot say at what time now."

They sighed worriedly and resolved to stay up, but finally, at four o'clock, exhausted by their long vigil, they retired to their staterooms — not to sleep, they agreed, but only to rest for a while. After checking on Jesse,

Julia fell upon her bed, still dressed, and sank instantly into sleep.

"Julia." A hand brushed her cheek. "Wake up, my dear little wife."

Julia quickly sat up, blinking sleep from her eyes, and she flung her arms around her husband. "Oh, Ulys, at last!"

"We wanted to return sooner," he said, holding her close, "but the railroad was damaged and our train ran off the rails three times. I'm sorry we kept you waiting."

"It doesn't matter. You're here now." And he was, safe and sound and triumphant. "You're here, and you were never more my victor than you are at this moment."

He held her tightly, without speaking, his arms strong though trembling with fatigue, and when she closed her eyes and inhaled deeply of his scent — cigar smoke and pine and horses and warmth — she could not speak for the love and relief and gratitude that filled her, permeating every thought, every heartbeat, every fiber, every bone.

CHAPTER TWENTY-THREE

April 1865

Soon thereafter aboard the *Mary Martin,* the previous night's dinner was served as breakfast to nearly fifty famished officers, three proud ladies, and several excited children. Ulys ate quietly while his officers reverently described every detail of the surrender ceremony — General Lee's dignified approach on his large, handsome, gray horse called Traveller; his cordial reception at the residence of Wilmer McLean; Lee's striking appearance in a new uniform of Confederate gray, coat buttoned to the throat, fine boots ornamented with stitching in red silk, and long, gray buckskin gauntlets; his handsome sword, of exceedingly fine workmanship, the hilt studded with glittering jewels; the courteous discussion and slight modification of the terms; the formal signing of the documents.

"A little before four o'clock, General Lee shook hands with General Grant, bowed to the other officers, and left the room," Colonel

Porter told Julia. "We officers followed him out to the porch, solemn and quiet. General Lee signaled to his orderly to bring up his horse, and while it was being bridled, he stood on the lowest step and gazed sadly in the direction of the valley where his army lay — now an army of prisoners."

"How bravely he endured it," said Julia, finding herself unexpectedly sympathetic.

Porter nodded. "Everyone who beheld him at this, his moment of supreme trial, understood the sadness that overwhelmed him. He thrice smote the palm of his left hand slowly with his right fist in an absent sort of way, seeming unaware of the Union officers in the yard who rose respectfully at his approach. The arrival of his horse interrupted his reverie, and as General Lee mounted, General Grant stepped down from the porch and saluted him by raising his hat."

"Every officer present imitated him in this act of courtesy," Badeau broke in. "Lee raised his hat respectfully to us all, and rode off at a slow trot to break the sad news to the brave fellows whom he had so long commanded."

Julia could imagine it all, every somber glance shared, every respectful phrase spoken. She was a bit taken aback, then, to discover that not long after the ceremony ended, Ulys's officers, understanding well the historical significance of the day, had quickly returned to the sitting room and bargained with Mr. McLean for various relics and mementos until the room was nearly stripped bare of its furnishings. Ulys had claimed nothing, but General Sheridan paid twenty dollars in gold for the table at which Ulys had written the terms of surrender, General George H. Sharpe ten dollars for the pair of brass candlesticks that had flickered atop it. General Ord had purchased the table at which General Lee had sat, and calling for it to be brought into the room, he proudly presented it to Julia.

"Oh, my goodness," said Julia, quite confounded. "Thank you, but I couldn't possibly accept such a treasure. Do promise me you'll give it to Mrs. Ord instead." The relic would be a small recompense for all his lovely wife had suffered during Mrs. Lincoln's first visit to City Point.

General Ord protested chivalrously, but Julia insisted until he acquiesced.

From a table in the corner, a younger officer called, "General Grant, you'll go up to Richmond now, won't you?"

"No," he replied. "I'll go at once to Washington."

When the officers expressed surprise, Colonel Morgan asked, "Couldn't you run up on the steamer and tour the captured city before starting for Washington?"

"The rebels kept us out so long, it seems a shame to go home without at least taking a look around," another officer chimed in, prompting laughter from the others.

Ulys smiled briefly and shook his head. "No, I think it would be better if I didn't. I could do no good there, and I want to report to Secretary Stanton as soon as possible, to urge him to stop recruiting men and purchasing supplies." When a murmur of disappointment rose, he added, "But if any of you are curious to see the city, I'll wait for you to make the trip. I don't think we'll be ready to leave for Washington until tomorrow anyway."

The men seemed satisfied with that, and as conversations resumed around the room, Julia turned to her husband. "Surely you have time to go to Richmond first," she protested in an undertone.

"Hush, Julia," he said quietly, solemn and earnest. "Don't say another word on this subject. I wouldn't distress the people of Richmond. They're feeling their defeat bitterly, and you wouldn't add to it by having me parade about like some vain conquerer, would you?"

Remembering the forlorn, ruined capital and the haunted look of its inhabitants, Julia was moved by his compassion and understanding in victory. Whenever she thought she could not possibly be any prouder of him, Ulys did something unexpected, something noble, to prove that she could.

On Wednesday afternoon, the Grants departed City Point for Washington aboard Ulys's dispatch boat, accompanied by General and Mrs. Rawlins, Colonel and Mrs. Morgan, and a large number of officers. They arrived at the capital early the following morning — and such a glorious welcome awaited the victorious general that it surpassed Julia's most elaborate expectations. As they approached the wharf, every gun and cannon burst forth with a thunderous salvo, and the bells on every ship and in every steeple rang out. A large Stars and Stripes flew proudly from a tall flagpole on the dock, unfurled to its full length and breadth above the sparkling river.

"Look, Pa! Look, Ma!" cried Jesse, pointing to the flag. "Not one single star is missing. Not one!"

"That's right, darling," said Julia, hugging him. "Not one single star was lost from that blue field, thanks to your pa."

She beamed at Ulys, warm and admiring, until a flush rose in his cheeks, reminding her of the young lieutenant who had called on her at White Haven so many years before.

Ulys accompanied Julia and Jesse to the Willard Hotel, but as soon as they were comfortably settled, he hurried off to the

Executive Mansion to report to the president and the secretary of war. In his absence, Julia was inundated with callers, whom she received in the ladies' parlor until Mrs. Stanton came to her rescue by insisting that Julia accompany her to the War Department. Julia had never seen Mr. Stanton so ebullient as when he showed her the many stands of captured arms and flags displayed in his office. He also possessed a stump of a large tree taken from the field of Shiloh, perforated all around by bullets.

"Shiloh," Julia murmured, tracing the concentric rings with a fingertip, turning her gaze away from the pockmarked bark. The dreadful battle seemed so long ago.

Secretary Stanton also eagerly told them of the arrangements that were being made for a grand illumination of the city that evening. "It will be a glorious spectacle," he promised. "You won't want to miss it."

Soon thereafter the ladies bade the gentlemen good-bye and strolled back to the Willard. "Neither of our gentlemen mentioned it," Mrs. Stanton remarked, "but the president and his wife have invited the four of us to attend the theater with them tomorrow evening."

"Is it an opera?" asked Julia. "The general loathes opera almost as much as I love it. Perhaps that's why he said nothing."

"No, it's a comedy, *My American Cousin.*"

Mrs. Stanton threw Julia a quick, sidelong glance. "I don't wish to gossip or speak ill of any lady, but unless you accept the invitation, I shall refuse. I will not sit without you in the box with Mrs. Lincoln."

Recalling Badeau's allusion to ill feeling between the two ladies, Julia did not need to ask why. "I'll have to speak to the general, but —" Suddenly she felt a sick stirring of dread, inexplicable and staggering. "I'm inclined not to go. I'll send word to you for certain tomorrow."

"Mrs. Grant," said Mrs. Stanton, studying her. "Are you quite well?"

"Yes — yes, I'm fine." Julia managed a smile, though she felt a prickling of terror as if a cruel, piercing gaze was fixed upon her back. She resisted the impulse to glance wildly about for the unseen watcher, fearful of what she might discover. "I'm merely fatigued from excitement and travel. I'll be fine."

"Do get some rest before the illumination this evening."

Julia assured her that she would, and they parted with a friendly embrace and promises to visit again soon.

"Mr. Bryant is handsome and kind," Emma declared as she and Jule strolled to the printer's shop. "He's hardworking and prosperous, and his children obviously adore him."

Jule had to smile. "Yes, Emma, I agree. He'll make some lucky woman a wonderful husband someday. But I'm not that woman."

Emma halted and placed a hand on Jule's arm to stop her. "Why not? What is it you dislike about him?"

"Nothing at all," Jule exclaimed, laughing, though she felt a pang of regret. "I like him very much, but I'm already married." She had not seen Gabriel since October of 1862, and it had been more than two years since he had been sold, but until she knew for certain that he had passed away, she would not consider herself a widow.

"Well, he likes you very much," said Emma.

A forlorn note in her friend's voice confirmed Jule's suspicions. "He understands that I'm not free to marry."

Emma shrugged, dismissing that as of little consequence. She resumed walking and Jule fell into step beside her.

"I spoke to him earlier this morning," said Jule. Mr. Bryant's apologies for the errant kiss had been interrupted by a salvo of artillery fire from the wharf and the pealing of bells throughout the city. Her heart had quaked when Mr. Bryant noted that the clamor was in honor of General Grant, welcoming the victorious hero and his wife to the capital. "He isn't in love with me. That kiss was just — the excitement of the moment. He would have kissed you instead, if you had been standing there instead of me."

"I wish I had been," Emma admitted.

"Then you'll be very glad to hear that he's hired a carriage, and he's invited us to ride with him and his children tonight to see the illuminations."

With a gasp, Emma whirled to face her. "Did he?" Then her eyes narrowed. "Or did he invite you and you asked to bring me along?"

"Does it matter?"

Emma considered. "No," she said, a slow smile brightening her pretty features. "I suppose it doesn't have to."

They soon came to the printer's shop, which was full of customers placing orders and collecting handbills, leaflets, and printed papers of every kind and description. Jule's excitement grew as she waited her turn, and by the time she was called to the counter, she felt breathless with elation — and worry. What if the labels looked nothing like what she had envisioned? What if they inspired mockery rather than respect?

The printer greeted her, disappeared into a back room, and returned with two large boxes, which he set on the counter. Jule held her breath as he lifted the lids, and as she glanced inside, she exhaled in a soft sigh of relief.

"Oh, they're lovely," exclaimed Emma, peering into the first box. " 'Madame Jule's Almond Cream.' 'Madame Jule's Oil of Lavender.' Such elegant script, and that delicate scroll frames the words so beautifully!"

"I like the illustrations myself," the printer remarked, admiring his work. "I think it's a fine idea to put a sketch of the most important ingredient in the lower corner there, for them folks as don't read. It's pretty, too, for the ladies, or so my wife says."

"They're perfect," Jule managed to say, her throat constricting with emotion. "I wouldn't change a single stroke."

She paid for her purchases, and when the printer bade her farewell with a polite, "Good afternoon, Madame Jule," she thought her heart would overflow with happiness and pride.

She spent the afternoon pasting labels to bottles she had already filled and tucking them carefully into a basket for delivery to various shops and pharmacies throughout the city. She would need to sell only a fraction of them to earn enough money to purchase more bottles and new labels. As she worked, she envisioned a design for her burn salve and another for her most popular hair tonic. If they sold well, she would begin advertising in newspapers — and if her business expanded as she hoped it would, she might hire an assistant.

As twilight descended, she changed from her work dress into the prettier frock Emma had made for her, bartered for a generous supply of almond cream and hair tonic. When Mr. Bryant pulled up in front of her boardinghouse in his carriage, Jule was pleased to see that he had collected Emma first and that they sat together on one seat facing Mr. Bryant's son and daughter. Jule greeted them all merrily and settled upon the seat beside the children, and off they rode to admire the illuminated capital.

Emma's cheerful humor soon had Mr. Bryant and his children in excellent spirits. They marveled aloud as they gazed through the windows at a city transformed by light and bunting and banners. Every public building, hotel, restaurant, shop, and residence dazzled with the light of thousands of candles, gas jets, and oil lamps. The Capitol blazed from portico to towering dome and the White House shone like marble. The Willard was lavishly adorned in red, white, and blue Chinese lanterns, while gas jets on the roof spelled out the word "Union" in a brilliant, blazing arc. The Treasury boasted an enormous fifty-dollar bond composed of innumerable pinpricks of candlelight, and across the street a banking house had raised an enormous banner declaring, "Glory to God, Who Hath to US Grant'd the Victory." Rockets exploded and fireworks soared above the Potomac, declaring victory with color and light and noise. Jubilant citizens filled the streets, bands played familiar tunes from nearly every street corner, and every heart seemed overflowing with hope and with a deep, profound longing for peace that seemed soon to be fulfilled.

And yet the illuminated city was not so marvelous that Mr. Bryant was blinded to the charms of the young beauty seated beside him, and of all the wonders Jule observed that night, no sight pleased her more than the glances of fond admiration that passed between the glassblower and the seamstress.

To Julia the illumination had been a marvelous, breathtaking, awe-inspiring spectacle, all the more so because the great general in chief had been by her side, holding her hand.

Mrs. Lincoln had wanted it quite otherwise. Shortly after Julia had parted from Mrs. Stanton at the Willard, the Stantons' eldest son had called with an invitation for Ulys and Julia to accompany them in their carriage to view the illumination, and afterward, to be honored guests at a reception at their home. When Julia told Ulys of the arrangements, he had explained that Mrs. Lincoln had invited Ulys — but not Julia — to ride out with her and the president, and he had accepted.

"Oh, Ulys," Julia had said, crushed. "I

wanted so badly to see the illumination with my victor by my side. Why didn't Mrs. Lincoln invite me too?"

"I'll ride out with you and the Stantons first," Ulys had replied. "Afterward, I'll leave you at their house so you can enjoy the reception. Then I'll accompany Mr. and Mrs. Lincoln, because I know it would please the president."

At nightfall, the Stantons had called for them, and after an enchanting hour's ride, the carriage had brought them to the Stanton residence. Julia and the Stantons descended, and after a quick farewell, Ulys continued on to the Executive Mansion for a second tour of the illuminated city.

Although Julia would have preferred to enter the reception on Ulys's arm, she enjoyed the evening tremendously, the music and dancing, the delicious food and drink. Nearly every guest had wanted to meet her, and she had graciously accepted their congratulations on her husband's behalf. When Ulys had returned from his outing with the Lincolns, thunderous applause had welcomed him, and the band had played a particularly invigorating rendition of "Hail to the Chief."

It had been a glorious, exhilarating day, and Julia had expected to sleep well that night, curled up beside her victor, the quilts drawn softly over them both, a smile on her lips, her arm resting on his chest, his breath warm and steady upon her brow.

But she woke before dawn, breathless and trembling, shaken from sleep by harrowing dreams that faded the moment she tried to remember them. A terrible, dark sense of foreboding oppressed her, and although she lay down close to Ulys and prayed and tried to drift off to sleep again, a nameless, terrible dread kept her anxiously awake.

Her fear diminished with the sunrise, but she knew she could not spend another night in Washington. As soon as Ulys woke, even before he rose from bed and lit his first cigar of the morning, Julia asked if they could leave for Burlington on the early train. "I wish we could," said Ulys, tucking a long strand of her chestnut hair behind her ear, "but I promised Mr. Lincoln that I'd call on him this morning and see what we can do about reducing the army. He also wants me to report to the cabinet about the surrender."

"After that, might we go?" Julia implored. "Please, Ulys. I'm absolutely desperate to see the children."

"I'm sure Helen would have telegraphed us if they were ill. Is something else troubling you?"

"I don't know," said Julia helplessly, wringing her hands. "It's just a feeling."

Ulys studied her. He always took her feelings seriously, no matter how irrational they seemed. "I'll do my best to finish my work in

511

time for us to take the evening train to Burlington."

Julia thanked him profusely, tears of relief springing into her eyes. Jesse came bounding into the room then, hungry and cheerful, so Ulys sent down for breakfast. It arrived shortly after they finished dressing for the day, but on the tray was a letter a messenger had brought over from the White House. Uneasy, Julia watched as Ulys unfolded the page. "It's from the president. 'Dear General: Suppose you come at eleven o'clock, instead of nine. Robert has just returned and I want to see something of him before I go to work.' " Ulys shook his head regretfully as he set the letter aside. "I'm sorry, Julia, but I think this will prevent me from being able to leave this evening after all."

"We must go," Julia insisted. "Ulys, please. We must."

"We will, my dear, if it's at all possible."

Julia knew he could promise no more than that, so she resigned herself to an anxious wait.

As soon as he departed for the White House, she wrote to Mrs. Stanton to say that they would not attend the theater that evening. Even if she and Ulys could not leave Washington, Julia felt too disconcerted to sit in the state box with Mrs. Lincoln, who had snubbed her several times too often.

At about midday, a knock sounded on the

door. "Come in," Julia called, expecting the bellboy with the day's calling cards. Instead, in walked a man dressed in a worn tan corduroy coat and trousers and a rather shabby hat. "Who are you?" asked Julia, startled. "What do you want?"

"You are Mrs. Grant?" the stranger asked gruffly.

"Of course I am."

He bowed. "Mrs. Lincoln sends me with her compliments to say that she will call for you at exactly eight o'clock to go to the theater."

Julia frowned, disliking both the unkempt appearance of the messenger and his message, for the first smacked of discourtesy and the second of command. "You may return with my compliments to Mrs. Lincoln," she said sharply, "and say I regret that as General Grant and I intend to leave the city this afternoon, we will not be able to accompany the president and Mrs. Lincoln."

He hesitated. "But, madam, the papers announce that General Grant will be with President Lincoln tonight at the theater."

"The papers are wrong. Deliver my message to Mrs. Lincoln as I have given it to you. You may go now."

He bowed again, and as he turned to leave, he smiled impertinently. Unsettled, Julia shut the door behind him firmly and leaned back against it, heart pounding, her sense of foreboding surging more intensely than ever. Swiftly she began packing, determined to set out for Burlington the moment Ulys returned to the Willard.

By the time the clock chimed noon, Ulys still had not come back, so Julia took Jesse and met Mary Emma Rawlins and her little stepdaughter Emily downstairs in the dining room for luncheon. No sooner had they placed their orders when four men seated themselves at a nearby table and proceeded to watch them closely. Julia's poor eyes might have deceived her, but she was certain one of the men was the strange messenger who had come to her suite earlier that day.

"Be discreet," Julia urged Mary Emma in an undertone, "but observe the men opposite us and tell me what you think."

Mary Emma calmly studied the men from the corner of her eye and murmured that they did seem quite peculiar, but when Ulys arrived in midafternoon from the White House and Julia told him of their insolent stares, he said absently, "Oh, I suppose they were merely curious."

Julia disagreed, but when he told her they could leave Washington on the evening train, she kept her peace.

About half past three o'clock, the wife of General Daniel Henry Rucker kindly called at the Willard in her two-seated top-carriage to take the Grants, Colonel Porter, and

Captain Samuel Beckwith, a telegrapher, to the Baltimore and Ohio Railroad station.

"How is the president?" Julia inquired as they rode along Pennsylvania Avenue toward the depot. She still regretted not paying her respects to him before he departed City Point aboard the *River Queen.*

"He seemed healthier and more cheerful than I've ever seen him," Ulys replied. "He told us — his cabinet and me — about a curious dream he'd had last night, and I was reminded of you, Julia, and your prophetic gifts."

"Indeed? How so?"

"We'd all hoped for word from the field that Johnston's army had surrendered to Sherman, but no news had come. Mr. Lincoln told me not to worry, for he was certain that good tidings would soon arrive, because the night before, he'd had a particular dream that came to him without fail on the eve of every great and important event of the war."

"What sort of dream?" asked Mrs. Rucker, intrigued.

"When Secretary Welles asked him to describe it, Mr. Lincoln told of standing aboard a ship — a singular, indescribable vessel — moving swiftly toward a dark and indefinite shore. He'd had this dream before Sumter, Bull Run, Antietam, Gettysburg, Stones River, Vicksburg, and Wilmington. When I remarked that not all of those great events had been victories, he smiled and said that he remained hopeful that whatever event his dream heralded would be favorable."

"I hope his presentiment is correct," said Julia, turning her gaze to the window. At that moment, a dark-haired, pale man on a bay horse with a black mane and a long black tail galloped by them, peering into the carriage as he sped past. He rode twenty yards ahead, wheeled his horse about, and returned at the same swift pace, passing closely on Ulys's side and glaring so disagreeably that Ulys instinctively drew back.

"Everyone wants to see you, General," their driver said cheerfully.

"Yes," said Ulys, "but I don't care for such glances as that."

"I'm sure that was one of the men who stared at me at luncheon," exclaimed Julia.

"How dreadfully ill-mannered," said Mrs. Rucker, indignant.

Ulys peered over his shoulder in the direction the rider had taken. "It's just as well we're leaving."

The president of the Baltimore and Ohio Railroad had arranged for a special car to carry them home, and as the Grants and their party climbed aboard, Julia paused to speak to the conductor. "The general urgently needs his rest. Would you be sure to lock the doors to our car so he won't be disturbed?" The conductor assured her he would, but she kept careful watch until he turned the bolt and the train pulled away from the station.

Julia had expected her dull sense of dread to dissipate with every passing mile, but if anything it steadily increased, as if they were speeding toward disaster rather than away from it. Night had fallen by the time they reached Baltimore, and Julia, dozing with her head on Ulys's shoulder and Jesse sleeping half on the seat and half in her lap, woke with a start at the sound of a loud, insistent rattle. Blinking, she discerned a man on the platform, his face hidden in the shadows, trying to open the locked door.

"He must not realize this is a private car," said Ulys as the man wrestled with the latch determinedly. When the whistle blew, he threw his hands into the air in frustration and stalked away.

As the train chugged from the station, Julia glimpsed the man pacing irritably on the platform. "Why, he missed the train altogether."

"Stubbornness cost him a ride to Philadelphia," Ulys remarked, raising his cigar to his lips.

Upon their arrival in the city, they decided to dine at Bloodgood's Hotel near the Walnut Street wharf while awaiting the ferry that would carry them across the river to meet their connecting train. They had scarcely begun when a messenger brought Ulys a telegram. Before he could unfold it, two more arrived in rapid succession.

As Ulys silently read the first, his face went starkly pale. "What's the matter?" asked Julia as he closed his eyes and bowed his head.

"General?" prompted Colonel Porter as Ulys studied the second telegram, and the third.

"I'll read them to you." Ulys's voice shook with emotion. "But first prepare yourself for the most painful and startling news that could be received."

Julia's heart cinched. "The children —"

"No, Julia," he replied quietly, but even as she breathed a sigh of relief, he glanced around the table and warned, "Control your feelings. Betray nothing to the people around us."

Julia steeled herself, envisioning Sherman defeated by Johnston, the war perpetuated indefinitely, but what Ulys told them — reading aloud in a calm, quiet voice while his listeners held perfectly still and silent, their faces careful, expressionless masks drained of all color — was worse, far worse, than anything she could have imagined.

" 'The President was assassinated at Ford's Theater at ten thirty tonight and cannot live,' " Ulys read, scarcely above a whisper. " 'The wound is a pistol shot through the head. Secretary Seward and his son Frederick were also assassinated at their residence and are in a dangerous condition. The Secretary of War desires that you return to Washington immediately.' " Clearing his throat, Ulys passed the telegram to Julia on his right, who read it silently, numb with horror, before handing it to Beckwith. Ulys read the second telegram silently and summarized it for them, saying, "The assistant secretary of war warns me to take precautions." That telegram, too, he passed to Julia, but her gaze rested unseeing, uncomprehending on the paper, her ears ringing so loudly that she scarcely heard the last telegram, something about Vice President Andrew Johnson being in danger.

It could not be true. Mr. Lincoln, that good, kind, compassionate man — he could not be lost to the world when they still needed him so desperately. How could he be snatched from them with the end of the war within their grasp, without enjoying a single day of the peace and unity he had fought for over the past four long, difficult years?

Ulys's hand on her shoulder jolted her from her reverie. "Come, Julia," he said, helping her to her feet. She realized then that the others had risen from the table, even little Jesse, who struggled fiercely to hold back sobs. With a soft moan, she folded her son in her arms and held him, murmuring soothingly until Ulys touched her arm in a wordless signal that it was time to go.

In grief-stricken silence, they returned to

the ferry dock, where Ulys quickly determined that as Burlington was only an hour away, he would return to Washington no later if he first escorted Julia and Jesse home and ordered a special train to carry him swiftly back to the capital.

It was long past midnight when they crossed the river and boarded the train for Burlington, all of them silent and grieving, but sharply aware of their surroundings, vigilant lest a madman attack the general in chief.

"Ulys," Julia asked softly as the train raced northward, "who could have done such a terrible thing, and why? Why?"

"I don't know."

"Confederate partisans seeking revenge?"

"The South had nothing to gain from President Lincoln's death. He was inclined to be kind and magnanimous, and his death at this time —" Ulys shook his head. "It's an irreparable loss to the South. They badly need his tenderness and generosity."

"Andrew Johnson will be the president now, will he not?"

"Yes," said Ulys flatly, "and I confess this fills me with the gloomiest apprehension."

In Burlington, Ulys scarcely had time to look in on his eldest children, still slumbering peacefully in their beds, and to read the telegrams sent after they had departed Philadelphia. The special train was soon made ready to return Ulys to Washington. He and his aides left while it was yet starlight, but Julia could not calm her turbulent thoughts enough for sleep.

It was not yet dawn when callers began knocking hesitantly upon the cottage door, a scant handful that swelled into a crowd with the sunrise, some weeping, some pallid with shock, all wanting to know if the horrifying rumors were true. By midmorning, after her three eldest children had leapt from their beds and had raced downstairs to welcome her home — rosy cheeked and laughing and demanding kisses, oblivious to their youngest brother's tear-streaked face and downcast eyes — their worst fears were confirmed.

"I am requested by the Lieutenant General to inform you of his safe arrival," Captain Beckwith had telegraphed Julia. "The President died this morning. There are still hopes of Secretary Seward's recovery."

Julia carried the telegram with her all day, and when words failed her, when she could not bring herself to tell her distraught visitors the grim news, when she could not believe it herself, the small slip of paper spoke for her.

President Abraham Lincoln was dead.

Never had a nation plummeted so suddenly from joyful hope to utter despair. Grief-stricken mourners sought comfort in churches and in the company of friends. Others took refuge in righteous anger, demanding justice and retribution. Flags that had waved proudly in victory were slowly lowered to half-staff. Even war-weary people of the South expressed grief and dismay. They seemed to realize that they had lost a merciful, compassionate friend who had wanted not to punish them in defeat, but rather to help them recover and rebuild after the long, devastating war.

Julia remained in Burlington with the children throughout the days of lamentation and woe that followed. She did not attend Mr. Lincoln's solemn funeral, where Ulys stood in a place of honor at the head of the martyred president's black-swathed catafalque in the White House. Thousands of mourners paid their respects as he lay in state in the East Room, and tens of thousands more the next day in the Capitol rotunda. On Friday, April 21, nearly a week after the president's death, a nine-car funeral train bedecked with bunting, crepe, and a portrait of Mr. Lincoln carried the remains of the president and his young son Willie, who had died of typhoid fever at the White House more than three years before, on a seventeen-hundred-mile journey to Springfield, Illinois. Thousands of mourners gathered along the rail lines to bid farewell to their fallen leader, lighting the way with bonfires as the funeral train made its slow, circuitous journey west. Julia's heart went out to Mrs. Lincoln when she learned that the bereaved widow was frantic with grief, prostrate with anguish, refusing to see anyone but Secretary Welles's wife and her faithful friend, the dressmaker Mrs. Keckley.

Throughout those dark days, Ulys tirelessly performed the duties of his office, securing the capital, supporting Sherman as he negotiated Johnston's surrender. He collaborated with Secretary Stanton in the relentless pursuit of the assassin and his cronies, and when sketches of the murderer appeared in all the papers, Julia immediately recognized John Wilkes Booth as the strange, pale, dark-haired man who had stared at her so insolently while she dined at the Willard, the same aggressive rider who had glared at Ulys as they rode to the depot mere hours before the assassination.

"There is little doubt that the plot contemplated the destruction of more than the President and Sec. of State," Ulys had written home soon after his return to the capital. "I think now however it has expended itself and there is but little to fear."

Julia was less certain. As federal troops pursued the wretched fiend Booth through Maryland and into Virginia, a letter arrived at the cottage, addressed to Ulys in an unfamiliar hand. He had asked Julia to open all telegrams and letters that arrived for him, and what she read chilled her to the marrow.

"General Grant," the anonymous author began, "thank God, as I do, that you still live. It was your life that fell to my lot, and I followed you to your train. Your car door was locked, and thus you escaped me, thank God!"

Was the letter an expression of remorse, or a warning?

■ ■ ■ ■

PART THREE: CHERISH

■ ■ ■ ■

CHAPTER TWENTY-FOUR

May 1865–November 1868

In the weeks that followed, Secretary Seward and his son recovered from their grievous wounds, but John Wilkes Booth and the four other conspirators would pay for their crimes with their lives. Julia would never know if the anonymous letter writer had been among those hanged on the grounds of the United States Arsenal in Washington on that stiflingly hot day.

In late April, General Johnston surrendered to General Sherman in North Carolina, and in the first week of May, federal troops captured the fugitive Jefferson Davis; his wife, Varina; and a few loyal companions near Irwinville, Georgia. By the end of the month, the remaining bands of rebel forces recognized the futility of their ongoing resistance and surrendered.

Soon thereafter, Washington was the scene of a grand review of the armies, two days of parades and celebration honoring the courageous, triumphant soldiers who had brought victory and peace to the nation. Julia returned to the capital for the glorious event and sat beside Ellen Sherman in a place of honor with their husbands, ranking generals, and the cabinet on the reviewing stand across from the White House. Each glance that took in the Executive Mansion reminded Julia sharply, painfully, of the great and good man who had once inhabited it, and of the distraught, grief-stricken widow who had only recently departed for Chicago, accompanied by her two sons, her doctor, and her faithful friend, the celebrated dressmaker Elizabeth Keckley. Inexplicably, Julia thought of Jule and fervently wished that they could have been friends instead of mistress and servant. Mrs. Keckley, too, had once been a slave in St. Louis, and she had become an intimate of the White House. What great heights could Jule have attained if Julia had granted her her freedom instead of compelling her to run away?

Julia could only imagine, and she knew she would never be able to remember Jule without regret and remorse.

It was comforting to distract herself with the magnificent pageant that flowed past the reviewing stand, the Army of the Potomac on the first day of the review and the Army of the Tennessee on the second. A great banner strung across the Capitol declared, "The

Only National Debt We Can Never Repay Is the Debt We Owe to the Victorious Soldiers." Nearly two thousand schoolgirls in white dresses lined Pennsylvania Avenue, singing "The Battle Cry of Freedom" in their sweet, piping voices. As the troops marched past, their tattered, shot-ridden battle flags told their story of sacrifice and triumph. Onlookers cheered and threw flowers in the path of General George Meade's horse as he rode at the head of his army. General George Armstrong Custer, with his scarlet necktie and flowing golden locks, lost his broad-brimmed hat as his steed dashed ahead alongside the column of cavalry. For six hours each day, as the infantry, cavalry, artillery, and every other branch of the service marched proudly past, ladies on the sidewalks threw flowers in their path and soldiers draped floral wreaths around the barrels of their rifles.

At long last, the war was over.

In a springtime full of warmth and hope, the Grants moved from Burlington into the beautiful residence bestowed upon them by the good citizens of Philadelphia. Julia was utterly delighted with their new home, which she considered perfect in every way, beautifully furnished from attic to basement, the closets full of snowy white linen, the tables and cabinets set with fine glass and silver, the larders and coal bins almost bursting with abundance.

Before long Fred and Buck returned to school in Burlington, while Julia enrolled Nellie and Jesse in local day schools. Ulys remained with them in Philadelphia for a few days, but all too soon he was summoned back to Washington, a pattern that repeated itself with dismaying regularity as spring blossomed into summer. Although Julia made new friends and their neighbors were unfailingly generous and kind, she was lonely at home with only her two youngest children for company — and little wonder, she thought, after four years in the field, surrounded by the bustle and excitement of the military, the marshaling of troops, the grand reviews, the distinguished visitors, and, yes, even the danger.

"I see less of you in peacetime than at war," she complained mildly to Ulys during one of his brief, unsatisfactory visits home.

"It does seem that life is too short to spend it apart," Ulys said, "but when we accepted this house, we promised the Union Club that we'd live here."

"Well, we can't," said Julia firmly. "These past few weeks have proven that you can't make your home so far from your headquarters. I hate to part with this lovely house, but you must give it back."

Ulys tried, but the people of Philadelphia refused to accept it, insisting that it would remain the Grant home even if the Grants were obliged to reside elsewhere. In mid-summer, the family moved to a rented house in Georgetown Heights in Washington, which Julia found large and conveniently placed but uncomfortable and terribly overpriced, and she resolved to find better, more permanent lodgings as soon as she was able. Once more the people of Philadelphia impressed Julia with their inexhaustible generosity. So great was their admiration and gratitude for General Grant that they urged him to rent out the house they had given him, accept the income as yet another gift, and move all the lovely furnishings to their Washington residence.

The house in Georgetown Heights had a fine library, and there Ulys wrote a lengthy, detailed report for Secretary Stanton about the armies of the United States, from the time he had taken command as general in chief in March 1864 until the end of the war. As soon as he finished, Julia put her foot down. "Ulys, you need and deserve rest," she declared, "even more than the children and I need and deserve your company." Ulys loved to travel, and so Julia proposed that they spend the late summer months touring the country, or at least the Northern states, which would surely receive them kindly.

The Grants were gratified to discover that their reception exceeded even Julia's optimistic expectations. Wherever Ulys appeared, thousands of people, many of them his veteran soldiers, met him with fanfare and celebration and an abundance of heartfelt gratitude. Across the North, Ulys was feted with parades, banquets, and receptions and presented with more horses, medals, jeweled swords, and honorary degrees than any single man could ever use. It was not quite the restful vacation Julia had intended, especially since Secretary Stanton had required Ulys to take along a military staff and he was obliged to spend many hours sending and receiving dispatches. Nevertheless, Ulys and the children thrived, happy to be all together at last.

In mid-August, the people of Galena welcomed their local hero home with a glorious procession, stirring speeches, and brilliant fireworks. As the family was driven through the city in an open barouche, they passed beneath a banner that proclaimed, "Hail to the Chief Who in Triumph Advances." Another on Main Street announced that the new sidewalk Ulys had long requested had been built exactly as he had desired. "It looks like you needn't run for mayor after all," Julia teased him over the merry music of a brass band.

The procession halted at the DeSoto House, where their friend Congressman Elihu Washburne embarrassed Ulys and moved Julia to tears with a fond, reverent speech before ten thousand ardent citizens. Afterward the Grant family was escorted up Bouthiller Street to the top of the hill, where the mayor presented them with a lovely residence — an Italianate villa with balustraded balconies and covered porches, exquisitely furnished with everything good taste could desire.

"I almost feel we shouldn't accept this gift," Ulys quietly told his overwhelmed wife as their proud hosts led them on a tour through the beautiful home. "I don't expect to be in Galena very often. I'd hate for this nice home to go to waste."

"We've always loved Galena, and we may very well retire here someday," Julia pointed out. "These good people are our friends and neighbors. If they want to give us a home, let them. Would you embarrass them by refusing?"

To her relief, Ulys needed little convincing, and so they departed Galena with the deed tucked safely in Julia's trunk.

They journeyed on to Dubuque, St. Paul, Milwaukee, Chicago, and Springfield, and there, too, Ulys received thunderous applause and rapturous ovations from everyone he met. The shouts of "Grant for president!" rang out everywhere, but loudest of all in St. Louis. The family managed to escape the crowds at White Haven, where early autumn had blushed the thickets and forests with scarlet and gold. Julia was overjoyed to be reunited with Papa and her sisters and brothers — especially John. At long last he had been liberated from the Confederate prison in Columbia, had come North in the general release of prisoners, and had made his way home, exhausted, ill, and contrite.

Julia had not seen her father in months, and she found him much transformed. He had acquired new respect for the son-in-law he had once dismissed, but the years without his beloved wife had aged him greatly, and Julia and her siblings privately discussed his failing health and wondered aloud how much longer he should live alone with only the servants for company. "When the time comes, he'll have to be convinced to leave White Haven," Julia warned her brothers and sisters, and even as they agreed, they exchanged unhappy, commiserating glances. Although any of them would have been happy to take him in, none wished to depose their father from his cherished pastoral realm.

From Missouri the Grants next traveled through Ohio, visiting friends and family along the way and ending their tour in Covington, where Jesse greeted them exuberantly, his old disappointments utterly forgotten. Ulys's sisters' cries of welcome beckoned Hannah from her chores, and when the victorious general in chief of the Armies of the United States crossed the threshold, she said calmly, "Well, Ulys, you've become a great man, haven't you?" Then she kissed him on the cheek and returned to her work.

In late November, President Johnson and Secretary Stanton sent Ulys on an inspection tour of the South. Ulys wrote to Julia often as he traveled from one city to another, and it was with great pleasure that Julia learned he had finally met Miss Elizabeth Van Lew, his daring spymistress. "She appeared in good spirits," he wrote, "but her loyalty to the Union has earned her the hatred of most of Richmond, and nearly all of her fortune went to fund her intelligence operations. If I ever have the opportunity to help her, I am determined to do so."

Ulys returned to Washington in time to celebrate Christmas, and when he escorted Julia to President Johnson's New Year's Day reception at the White House, the band struck up "Hail to the Chief" and the other guests showered him in thunderous applause. Soon thereafter, in the middle of January — and thanks to generous donors from New York — Ulys purchased a lovely home at 205 I Street, a spacious, four-story residence surrounded by beautiful grounds in a neighborhood known as Minnesota Row.

Not long after the Grants settled into their new home, Papa, in failing health, came to live with them. "You know, Julia," he told her unexpectedly one morning as they sat alone in the parlor reading the papers, "your mother was right about your young man."

Tears sprang into Julia's eyes at the memory of her beloved mother's unshakable faith in Ulys, her certainty that he would do great things. "You know, Papa," she said, "I quite agree."

"Oh, Madame Jule," exclaimed Mrs. Gilbert when Jule arrived to dress her hair for a state dinner at the White House. Mrs. Johnson — or rather, her two daughters, who shared the role of official hostess for their retiring mother — did not entertain as lavishly as Mrs. Lincoln had, but their guests, especially the ladies, remained as eager as ever to look their very best. "You'll never guess who moved in across the street a fortnight ago."

Jule smiled at the eager young woman in the mirror as she unpacked her satchel. Mrs. Gilbert was the judge's second wife, three months married and twenty years his junior, recently arrived from Kansas, and thoroughly delighted with everything about life in Washington. "One of Mr. Johnson's new appointees, I suppose?"

"In a manner of speaking," said Mrs. Gilbert coyly, but then she could withhold the secret no longer. "General Grant and his family!"

Jule felt a peculiar wrenching of the heart. "Is that so?" she said evenly, taking up her comb. "I heard they'd been living in Georgetown Heights, but they plan to move back to Illinois."

"The citizens of Galena did give them a lovely home, but the general's work keeps him in the capital, so here they shall stay." The young bride clasped her hands together in her lap, her eyes shining. "Isn't it marvelous that they chose our neighborhood?"

"Why, yes." Jule gently ran the comb through Mrs. Gilbert's golden locks. "How exciting to have such a celebrated neighbor. Have you made Mrs. Grant's acquaintance?"

"Not yet, but the judge has invited the Grants for supper Friday evening, so I will soon." Mrs. Gilbert gave a little start. "Madame Jule, would you like me to recommend you to her? I'd be happy to do so."

Years of practice enabled Jule to conceal her distress. "That's kind of you, Mrs. Gilbert, but I'm sure Mrs. Grant already has a maid to do her hair. She's newly arrived to the neighborhood, but not to Washington."

"Oh, of course. I'm sure you're right."

"If you'd like my services on Friday evening, though, I'd be glad to add you to my schedule."

Mrs. Gilbert promptly agreed, and Jule distracted her with suggestions for a new arrangement of curls, a Grecian twist, a becoming ribbon, until Mrs. Grant was forgotten.

When Jule left the Gilbert residence, she

buried her chin in her muffler and glanced warily across the street, but she saw no sign of Julia, the general, or any of the children, nothing to set the house apart from any other on the block. Then, just as she turned away, she glimpsed a thin, white-haired figure at a second-story window — and with a frisson of shock, she recognized the old master, much aged, but unmistakably the patriarch she had feared as a child.

Heart pounding, Jule forced herself to keep to a walk until she reached the corner. As soon as she was out of sight of the Grant residence, she quickened her pace until she was almost running.

"I can't stay," Jule told Emma, despondent, the next time they met.

"Nonsense," Emma protested. "What's the worst that could happen, even if you rounded a corner and bumped into Mrs. Grant on Pennsylvania Avenue? Slavery is finished. You have nothing to fear and no reason to hide."

"I know that," said Jule shakily. "I can't explain myself. I know it's unreasonable. I'm sorry."

"Oh, Jule." Emma embraced her. "You don't need to apologize, or to explain. But do promise me you won't leave Washington before my wedding. Peter and the children and I would be so disappointed."

"I wouldn't miss it for the world," Jule assured her.

The wedding, on a lovely afternoon in mid-May, was beautiful — the bride radiant, the groom happy, the guests joyful and thankful and merry. Soon thereafter, Jule considered moving to Texas to search for Gabriel, but President Johnson had recently issued a proclamation declaring an end to the insurrection everywhere but in Texas, and her friends convinced her it would not be safe for a colored woman to travel there alone. As spring turned into summer, Jule contemplated moving to New York, but again Emma persuaded her to delay, this time because of a terrible cholera epidemic sweeping through the city.

But every time Jule found a good reason to stay in Washington, an unsettling encounter renewed her urgency to flee. One afternoon, she went to the Willard to meet a client, only to glimpse the Grant family seating themselves in the dining room. After a moment of panic, she concealed herself behind a folding screen and watched them, frightened and fascinated, long enough to learn that they were celebrating in honor of Fred's imminent departure for West Point, where he had been accepted as a cadet. Jule's eyes filled with tears as she took in the dear faces of the children who had once loved her so wholeheartedly, with such sweet innocence. She had likely become no more than a dim, fond memory to them, the capable nurse who had run away in wartime, abandoning them in — what was it Julia had said? — in her hour of greatest need.

Then, one afternoon in early autumn, a few weeks after General Grant had been named the first four-star general in the nation's history, Julia was dressing Mrs. Gilbert's hair for a ball when the young matron indicated the bottle of Jule's hair tonic on her bureau. "Mrs. Grant came for tea a few days ago," she remarked. "She was kind and very polite but seemed unsettled, and when I asked her if something was the matter, she told me that she had been struck by a familiar fragrance in my home that she could not quite place. Soon we discovered that it was my hair tonic, and she was so keenly interested that I showed her this bottle."

"Is that so?" Jule managed to say.

"Indeed. She went quite pale and still when she examined the label. 'I knew a Jule once,' she said, 'but that was very long ago and far away, and my Jule had no such lofty title.' Isn't that curious?"

"Yes, it is," Jule said, her throat tightening.

Her Jule, indeed.

She resolved to leave Washington before winter, but where would she go? Texas was impossible, St. Louis familiar but perhaps equally unsafe. Jule was torn between New York City and Boston, and Emma was equally opposed to both.

Then one night, Jule was visited by a strange and vivid dream.

She was seated in a church, her head bowed in prayer, listening as a choir sang the old familiar spirituals she had learned in childhood. She heard the crackling of a campfire, smelled the woodsmoke, and even as she took comfort in the familiarity of it, she realized that a Missouri campfire did not belong within the stone walls of a church in the middle of New York City — which, in the manner of a dream, she knew it was. At that moment the preacher began to speak, words of praise and thankfulness for divine blessings, and it was a voice she knew as well as her own and loved more than any other.

She woke, and even as the dream faded, the voice lingered in her thoughts. Jule knew then that of all the prophetic dreams the Lord in his mysterious ways had bestowed upon the already richly blessed Julia, he had spared one for her.

She would go to New York City, and she would find happiness there.

In the first months of his presidency, Mr. Johnson had seemed to appreciate having a man of Ulys's experience and stature at his service as general in chief. He had sent Ulys almost daily notes, had consulted with him regularly, and had sought out every opportunity to be seen in public with the

541

victorious general, basking in the glow of Ulys's popularity as his own precipitously declined. But over time, Julia observed that their relationship became more contentious. While Ulys never failed to do his duty by his country and his commander in chief, he could not ignore the president's innumerable defects of character — just as Mr. Johnson could not mistake the loud cries of "Grant! Grant!" that often drowned out his own speeches when the two men appeared on the same stage.

By spring of 1867, President Johnson was determined to remove Secretary Stanton, whom he despised, from the War Department, and when Congress passed the Tenure of Office Act to restrict the president from dismissing any cabinet member without the consent of the Senate, he simply waited until Congress recessed in August. Then he suspended Stanton — and asked Ulys to accept the position of secretary of war ad interim.

"What did Mr. Johnson say when you refused the appointment?" Julia asked.

"I didn't refuse."

"You didn't?" Julia stared at him. "But Ulys —"

"I consented only with great reluctance, and I told the president so," said Ulys. "It's essential to have someone who can't be used or intimidated in that post."

Julia nodded assent, although her heart

sank with dismay.

In early December, President Johnson had asked the Senate to approve Secretary Stanton's suspension, but on January 13, 1868, the Senate voted thirty-five to six to reinstate him. The following morning, Ulys resigned as ad interim secretary, incurring the president's wrath.

Ulys's consternation and outrage did not go unnoticed by his friends. "I've been with Grant in the midst of death and slaughter," Sherman told Julia on the last day of January, shaking his head and frowning, "but I've never seen him more troubled than since he's been in Washington."

Julia agreed, but she felt helpless to do anything more than to offer Ulys her steadfast support and love.

Three weeks after Ulys left the War Department, President Johnson again suspended Mr. Stanton. Three days after that, the House of Representatives voted by an overwhelming majority in favor of a resolution to begin impeachment proceedings against the president, charging him with high crimes and misdemeanors.

Chief Justice Salmon P. Chase presided over the impeachment trial, which after several grueling, contentious weeks ended in acquittal. Thirty-six votes were required to remove the president from office, and three times the balloting resulted in thirty-five votes for impeachment, nineteen against.

Less than a week after the trial concluded, Mr. Stanton resigned as Secretary of War. Ostensibly Mr. Johnson had triumphed, but everyone, except perhaps the president himself, knew that his political career was essentially finished. He had already lost the upcoming presidential election — indeed, he would almost certainly fail even to win the Democratic nomination — before a single vote was cast.

Ulys remained the most admired man in the nation, and the capital hummed and sparked with energetic speculation that he was certain to be chosen as the Republican Party's nominee. Julia remained, as ever, proud that her husband evoked such tremendous admiration from the people, but she adored being a military wife and doubted Ulys would enjoy the presidency more than his position as general in chief. Once, when she and Ulys were alone, she ventured, "Ulys, do you even want to be president?"

"No," he told her, without needing even a moment's reflection. "But I don't see that I have anything to say about it. The Republican Convention's about to open in Chicago, and from what I hear, they intend to nominate me — and I suppose if I'm nominated, I'll be elected."

"But if you're elected, how can you hope to

serve the country as well as you do now?" she asked. "To satisfy one faction or region you must hurt another. Think about this, my dear, dear Ulys. Think of President Johnson. What a time he's had!"

"Oh, Johnson," scoffed Ulys, dismissing him with a wave of his cigar. "If I'm nominated I must accept the candidacy as my duty, and if I'm elected, I must serve. I wouldn't seek the office, but if it falls to me, I believe I can satisfy those widely separated factions and regions."

"How so?"

"The people of the North support me already, and the people of the South will accept my decisions on matters affecting their interests more amiably than those of anyone else who might be elected. They know I'd be just and that I'd administer the law without prejudice."

Julia knew that too. Of course Ulys would be a good, wise, and just leader, but that didn't mean she wanted him to be president.

The convention met, and mere days after President Johnson was acquitted, the Republican delegates nominated Ulys as their candidate, unanimously and on the first ballot. Mr. Stanton brought Ulys the news at army headquarters, and he brought it home to Julia. That evening she invited a few intimate friends over to celebrate, but Ulys expressed no pride or exultation, merely a quiet acceptance. Papa, much recovered from a dreadful stroke suffered the year before, stood proudly by Julia as Ulys received the compliments and assurances of support from their guests. At that moment, Julia felt her mother's presence more strongly than she had ever felt it anywhere but White Haven.

Ulys resolved not to campaign, but rather to spend the summer quietly with his family in Galena and St. Louis. On the eve of their departure for the West, General Sherman called to bid them farewell.

"Now, Mrs. Grant," he told her with an ironic smile, "you must prepare yourself to observe your husband's character thoroughly sifted."

"What could I possibly have to fear?" protested Julia. "You of all people know he's a man of great integrity."

"My dear lady, it isn't what he *has* done, but what they will *say* he has done. Mark my words, you'll be astonished to discover what a thoroughly bad man you have for a husband, and have had all these years without realizing it."

Soon thereafter, Julia settled happily into their beautiful home on Bouthiller Street in Galena, well content with Ulys's decision not to campaign. They both soon discovered that there had never been any need, for his faithful, loyal soldiers took up his cause with great exuberance, filling all corners of the reunited nation with flags, banners, speeches, and all the old merry martial tunes from the war. His gallantry at Appomattox was praised north and south, and longtime friends and fellow officers eulogized him in every city and hamlet.

But the papers brought distasteful news along with the good, and Julia was distressed and angered when General Sherman's predictions came to pass.

"Listen to this," she declared one morning as she and Ulys read the papers after breakfast, too full of righteous indignation to rest her strained eyes from making out the tiny, infuriating type. " 'General Grant is now lying confined to his residence at Galena in a state of frenzy and is tearing up his mattress, swearing it is made of snakes.' "

Ulys, reading in his favorite armchair, dressed in his white linen suit, smiled benignly at her wrath. "I don't mind what they say, and neither should you. We both know it isn't true." He puffed his cigar and turned a page.

On election night, Julia remained at home while Ulys awaited the returns at Mr. Washburne's residence, smoking and playing cards with the congressman, Badeau, and a few other close friends. He was expected to beat his Democratic rival, former New York governor Horatio Seymour, but nothing was certain until the final votes were tallied.

The hours passed in anxious waiting and quiet excitement. Shortly before midnight, a jubilant crowd began to assemble in front of the Grant residence, and at about half past one, Julia glanced out the window to discover Ulys walking up the hill, surrounded by his proud, beaming companions.

"Well, my darling Julia," he addressed her from the foot of the front stairs, rather sadly, "I'm afraid I am elected."

He joined her on the porch, took her hand, and held it tightly as he addressed the crowd, which burst into cheers and shouts of joy until all of Galena resounded with his name, from the hilltops where they stood to the rushing Mississippi in the valley far below.

CHAPTER TWENTY-FIVE

March 1869–March 1877

Friends and relations filled Julia's beloved home on I Street, Dents and Grants and others who had come to Washington to celebrate Ulys's inauguration. Although the morning broke to a cold drizzle and heavy mist, and the stiff, cold winds heralded an approaching snowstorm, the capital was packed with raucous and rejoicing visitors, many of them proud veterans wearing the insignia of their regiments and companies. Visitors and long-time residents alike seemed to have embraced with hope and thankfulness the brief, memorable words Ulys had uttered when he had formally accepted his nomination: "Let us have peace."

Enmity between the president-elect and his former commander in chief remained so intense that Ulys refused to ride with Mr. Johnson to the Capitol. Instead, Rawlins and a few other close friends accompanied him in his carriage while his predecessor remained at the White House signing bills. Julia left for the Capitol ahead of time in a separate carriage, with the children, Papa, and the elder Jesse riding with her and the rest of the family following. Only Hannah had not come to witness her son's momentous day, her boundless modesty keeping her quietly at home. Julia imagined her sewing by the hearth or planting her kitchen garden, marking the occasion with as much pride as her inherent humility would allow.

Julia and her companions squeezed into the overcrowded gallery of the Senate chamber, enjoying the convivial mood and watching the rear corridor for a first glimpse of her victor. At precisely noon he entered, escorted by two senators and followed by Vice President–Elect Schuyler Colfax. Handsomely attired in a plain black suit and straw-colored calfskin gloves, Ulys seated himself in front of the presiding officer, his expression calm and imperturbable despite the countless pairs of opera glasses fixed upon him. With a sharp bang of his gavel, Senator Benjamin Wade promptly brought the Senate to order and called Mr. Colfax forward to take his oath of office, after which Mr. Colfax offered a few brief and appropriate remarks. Next the newly elected senators were called forward to be sworn in, a lengthy proceeding that provoked impatience from the onlookers in the galleries, who restlessly shifted toward the exits, eager to claim good seats on the platform outdoors, where Ulys would soon take his oath.

It was not quite half past noon when the sergeant at arms directed the audience to proceed from the Senate chamber to the East Portico, with Ulys at the head of the column surrounded by dignitaries. "Thank goodness the rain stopped," her sister Nell murmured as Julia and her companions were escorted to their seats. Julia glanced up at the sky to see that patches of blue and shafts of golden sunlight had broken through the gray clouds, but a cold wind blew, steady and strong, and the air smelled of snow.

Thousands of proud, eager onlookers packed the muddy, waterlogged Capitol grounds. Thousands of faces turned expectantly to the platform decorated with statuary, evergreens, and flags and bunting in the national colors. Cheers rang out from the crowd as the doors swung open, increasing to a deafening roar as Ulys appeared at the head of the procession.

Julia's heart pounded and her cheeks ached from smiling as Ulys came to the front of the platform to take his oath of office. Chief Justice Salmon P. Chase met him there carrying a Bible, somber, tall, and imposing in his black robes.

It was no secret that Chase had coveted Ulys's nomination, but he had fallen out of favor with the Republicans during Johnson's impeachment by presiding over the hearings with impartial integrity rather than promoting the party agenda. Julia doubted he would have claimed the nomination in any case, for Ulys's tremendous popularity would have been impossible for him — for anyone — to overcome.

Thus it was Ulys who spoke the words of the solemn oath that blustery day, who kissed the open Bible and became the eighteenth president of the United States. A salute of twenty-one guns thundered the news to the city. Bugles blared triumphant anthems, and the vast crowd roared its approval so powerfully that Julia felt it as an almost physical force.

When the cacophony diminished, Ulys took from his pocket several pieces of foolscap. Slowly and deliberately he read his inaugural address, concisely enunciating the policies of his forthcoming administration. He would endeavor to promote the greatest good for the greatest number, he said, to execute all laws in good faith, and to the best of his ability appoint to office only those who would do the same. His words were firm, his delivery clear, although Julia doubted his voice would carry beyond the first few rows. "In conclusion," he said before long, and Julia suspected he had never spoken the phrase with greater relief, "I ask patient forbearance one toward another throughout the land, and a determined effort on the part of every citizen to do his share toward cementing a happy union; and I ask the prayers of the nation to Almighty God in behalf of this consummation."

He bowed, and as bells pealed throughout the city and the people again erupted in resounding cheers and applause, he folded the pages of his speech, shook the hands of the distinguished gentlemen nearest to him, and hastened to Julia's side. "And now, my dear," he said, kissing her cheek and placing the pages in her gloved hands, "I hope you were satisfied."

"Well satisfied and never prouder," she declared, smiling.

The ceremonies concluded, the dignitaries and special guests left their seats and mingled on the East Portico, the mood convivial even between rivals. Julia accepted warm congratulations from so many ladies and gentlemen that she knew she would have great difficulty remembering who had spoken which graceful phrases. The children, thankfully, kept close to their parents in the crush, but she soon realized that her father was nowhere to be seen.

Ulys urged them to return home to see if Papa was there, and in the meantime he gave orders for the Capitol guards to keep searching in case Papa had not left the grounds. While Julia and the rest of the family hastened to their carriages, Ulys drove off with a few companions to the White House, intending to remain only long enough to meet the household staff and tour the family's private chambers.

The milling crowds slowed traffic to a crawl, allowing Julia sufficient time to imagine a dreadful variety of disasters that could have befallen her father. At last they reached home, only to discover an unfamiliar carriage parked on the street before the house and the front door slightly ajar. They hurried inside, where they discovered Papa reclining on the sofa in the parlor, three solicitous gentlemen attending him.

"What happened?" Nell exclaimed as the family crowded around their beloved patriarch.

A gentleman who introduced himself as Mr. John F. Driggs, a former congressman from Michigan, explained that as Papa was leaving the Capitol, he had lost his footing on the stone staircase and had tumbled backward to the ground, striking his head, badly injuring his hip, and acquiring a number of scrapes and cuts, but thankfully, no broken bones. With assistance, Mr. Driggs had brought him to a private room and procured a stimulant, and when it appeared that his injuries were not serious, he had summoned a carriage and had brought Papa home.

Papa was well recovered by evening, but he was easily persuaded to remain home and rest rather than attending the inaugural ball. "I could stay to watch over him," Ulys offered, all innocence, but his grin betrayed him.

"It would be just like you to avoid your own inauguration ball," Julia scolded, giving him a playful swat on the arm. "You are the president, and you must go, and finely dressed too."

After much conflict and controversy over where the ball should be held and whether it should be held at all, the inaugural committee, which had been refused permission to host the grand affair in the Capitol rotunda, had settled upon the unfinished wing of the Treasury Building, though evidence of ongoing work remained. There were several rooms for dancing, each furnished with an accomplished band, flooded with warm gaslight, draped in a profusion of bunting, and beautifully adorned with garlands and wreaths of flowers and evergreen. The allegorical painting *Peace* had been brought over from the Capitol and was on display in the Cash Room, another note of grace in a spacious chamber that boasted gleaming polished marble, a beautifully painted ceiling, and an airy balcony encircling all.

Despite her concerns about Papa's health, Julia had a marvelous time. She felt almost regal in her new gown of heavy white satin trimmed in point lace, her neck, ears, and hair adorned with pearls and diamonds. After receiving their six thousand guests, the Grant and the Colfax families withdrew to a private room and dined with their most intimate friends and family. Only afterward did Julia learn that some other guests did not get a mouthful of supper, or lost coats, hats, and wraps in the mad chaos of the cloakroom, or could not find their carriages afterward in the bedlam among the hacks on Fifteenth Street. Many a distinguished gentleman and distressed lady made their way home on foot through slushy streets, shivering without their wraps. "Everything today has been a great success," a correspondent for *The New York Times* later remarked, "but the inauguration ball tonight was too much of a success to be really a good thing."

The Grants and their entourage had no difficulty securing their own carriages, and in the very early hours of the morning they rode home to the Grant residence on I Street, weary but glowing with pride and happiness.

The entire household slept long past dawn, but by midmorning Ulys had reported to his offices at the White House, where Julia knew he was deliberating with his most trusted advisors about the remaining vacancies in his cabinet and elsewhere in the government. Julia spent the day enjoying the company of her family, receiving callers, and tending to Papa. When Ulys returned home for supper that evening, he remarked, "It'll be a great convenience to me, and to my staff, when we reside in the Executive Mansion. You should make ready to move."

Julia adored their home and was in no hurry to relocate, and she had made no secret of it. "It's impossible for me to make any arrangements with the house full of guests," she explained, gesturing vaguely over her shoulder as if all the Dents and Grants stood behind her, affirming her words.

The next day, Ulys returned from his new offices carrying a small parcel wrapped in brown paper. "A gift from the chief justice of the Supreme Court," he said, placing it in Julia's hands. "Mr. Chase had it delivered to you at the Executive Mansion, where he reasonably assumed you would be."

Blushing at his gentle rebuke, Julia untied the string and removed the paper. "Why, it's a Bible," she said, admiring the fine leather cover. A letter from the chief justice informed her that it was the very Bible upon which Ulys had taken his oath of office. " 'His lips pressed the 121st Psalm,' " Julia read aloud. " 'The Book will, I am sure, be to you a precious memorial of an auspicious day; destined, I trust, to be ever associated in American remembrance with the perfected restoration of peace, and with the renewal and increase of prosperity throughout our land.' What a lovely sentiment."

"How fine that Bible will look on display in our private family drawing room at the White House," Ulys said pointedly. Julia responded with a nod and a noncommittal smile.

For a week their guests lingered, but all too soon, they prepared to return to their own homes, and Julia reluctantly accepted that she, too, must make arrangements to depart. The president and his wife must live at the Executive Mansion — it was customary, pragmatic, and far safer for them all. Ulys wanted to sell the I Street residence, and when Julia learned that generous donors from New York wanted to purchase it as a gift for General Sherman, she consented to the sale without further complaint out of friendship to him and Mrs. Sherman.

When the Grants finally moved into the White House in late March, they found the residence in a state of utter confusion and disarray. Upon inspecting the family's private quarters, Julia was so appalled by their dilapidated, threadbare condition that she immediately ordered the installation of new wallpaper, carpets, and furniture. The public rooms also required significant refurbishing, and so Julia set herself to the formidable task of organizing the household, arranging for repairs, and hiring servants.

While Julia was settling into her role as official White House hostess, Ulys was assembling his cabinet and filling other important government posts. One of his first official acts as president was to appoint General Sherman as general in chief of all the armies. This he did over the objections of numerous senators, congressmen, and other advisors who urged Ulys to keep the position vacant so that he could return to it when his term as president expired. That sounded like an excellent idea to Julia, but when she tried to persuade Ulys, he adamantly refused. "I resigned my commission to become president," he said firmly. "If I don't fill the position of general in chief, neither Sherman nor any other general will be promoted. Sherman has always succeeded me as I climbed through the ranks, and I won't deny him this promotion to save a place for myself four years from now. He deserves that office, and he'll serve me and the country loyally in it."

"When you explain it that way," Julia remarked, "I'm not only thoroughly convinced; I'm embarrassed that I ever objected."

Ulys gave her a wry smile. "I hope all of my opponents will be as amenable as you when the facts are placed before them."

"Oh, my dear Ulys," she said, shaking her head, profoundly sympathetic. "No president in the history of the country has ever been that fortunate, though I would rejoice if you were the first."

Ulys's cabinet was complete long before Julia's renovations, and privately she suspected she relished her tasks far more. After so many years of pecuniary uncertainty, it was intoxicating to be able — not only able, but encouraged — to spend lavishly on furnishings and decor. The family quarters and the executive offices at the east end of the second floor received most of her attention, but she took special delight in choosing a new china service for state dinners and official events. She commissioned the artist William E. Seaton to create exquisite floral illustrations to grace the center of each piece, which were transferred to fine porcelain by the celebrated Haviland and Company of France. An elegant yellow-gold border bearing the Grant coat of arms provided what Julia considered the perfect final touch.

Within a few weeks the White House began to assume some semblance of order, and by autumn the house was in excellent shape, the private family chambers comfortable and cozy, the public rooms elegant and magnificent enough to impress foreign dignitaries and heads of state. It was by any measure an Executive Mansion worthy of the president of a powerful, bountiful, and rising nation.

As the years passed, Jule followed her former mistress's rise to the pinnacle of Washington society via the press, marveling at her transformation from a bashful belle of St. Louis to a confident, celebrated society hostess to the nation's elite. Time and distance had softened Jule's anger and whetted her curiosity, so she read with interest — and perhaps even a measure of fondness — of Julia's obvious delight in her role as First Lady. The White House had become a magnificent stage for glorious balls and receptions, levees and state dinners, where Julia entertained foreign ministers, princes, emperors, heads of state, and the most distinguished gentlemen and ladies of her own country.

In January of 1870, President and Mrs. Grant received their first royal guest, Prince Arthur of England, Queen Victoria's third-eldest son. A twenty-seven-course dinner was served in the state dining room, which was elaborately decorated with evergreen wreaths and boughs, a portrait of Queen Victoria, and the American and British flags. The center of the table was adorned with a magnificent floral arrangement surmounted by the royal crown of England and surrounded by nine bouquets representing the queen's most precious jewels, her nine children. "The toilets of the ladies were extremely rich," *The New York Herald* reported. "Mrs. Grant wore a dress of white satin, trimmed with Valenciennes lace and pearly and diamond ornaments. Miss Nellie Grant wore a blue satin, trimmed with puffed lace, and a broad sash of deep blue." Jule could not help wondering who had arranged their hair, and how — thinking, somewhat jealously, that she would have done better.

Whenever she read of such grand occasions, Jule would imagine Julia dressed in fine silk gowns amid distinguished company in gilded and marbled halls, and then she would remember Julia in a faded calico dress pulling weeds from the kitchen garden at Hardscrabble. "What a strange world it is," she would murmur, shaking her head in wonder.

Jule's indignation rose whenever she read the occasional catty mockery of Julia's crosseye and dumpy figure, but she felt an unexpected surge of pride if a reporter praised the First Lady's kindness, modesty, and friendly charm. "Mrs. Grant possesses a wonderful power of conciliating all distracting elements which helps to unite social and political society," one lady reporter wrote warmly. It was little wonder, Jule thought, considering how throughout most of her life Julia had been obliged to reconcile intense contradictions within herself. She was the daughter of a slave owner wed to the son of abolitionists. She was generous and empathetic, and yet she had never felt a twinge of conscience as she enjoyed the comforts that had come from exploiting other human beings — Jule, Gabriel, Annie, Dinah, and too many more.

Jule was satisfied for the nation's sake and

happy for Julia's when President Grant was elected to a second term in November 1872, for she approved of several measures he had enforced to secure rights for people of color. He certainly could do more, Jule and her friends and neighbors agreed, but life was much better for their race under Grant than it had ever been under Johnson. Even so, Jule was less than confident in his position on woman's suffrage, which had become one of her most ardent causes. The General Grant she remembered had been courteous to ladies, but he had never treated them as his intellectual equals. He had listened when his wife expressed her opinion on political and military matters, but to Jule he had always seemed to do so with an air of amused indulgence, as if entertained by the prattle of a precocious child. Jule could not imagine that he would trust Julia, and by extension, other women, with the vote.

Rights for people of color, the vote for women, the care of colored orphans — those were to Jule the most pressing matters of her day. Her business had thrived in postwar New York, and with her success had come prosperity, respect, and a certain amount of fame. She had bought a comfortable home in Brooklyn, and with no children of her own to cherish, she had found fulfillment in supporting asylums for colored orphans. She had made many friends through her congregation, the Bridge Street African Wesleyan Methodist Episcopal Church, and when she realized her home was too large and quiet and empty for one lone woman, she adopted two children, a brother and sister. Charles and Dorothy were sweet and smart and curious and funny, and when Jule fed them breakfast and walked them to school and heard their prayers as she tucked them into bed at night, her heart swelled with happiness and gratitude. She had never expected to be a mother, to have any family but Gabriel, who had been gone so long.

But as thankful as she was for her little family, it felt incomplete.

Over time she had learned the merits of advertising. Her lotions, balms, and tonics had become popular throughout the cities of the East, not only because of recommendations from satisfied customers, but also due to the notices she regularly placed in newspapers. And so she began running "Information Wanted" advertisements in the press — first in New York, then in St. Louis, and after Texas was readmitted to the Union and communication became easier, in Dallas and Houston — seeking information about a man in his late forties called Gabriel, russet skinned and golden voiced, born in Missouri, last known whereabouts in Texas, possibly working as a groom or a minister.

Each notice ended with the same quiet,

urgent plea: "Any information concerning this gentleman will be gratefully received by Madame Jule of Brooklyn, New York."

Julia's darling Nellie was but eighteen in 1873 when she met the handsome, Oxford-educated Algernon Charles Frederick Sartoris at sea while returning from a European tour, and her heart was swiftly captivated. Soon thereafter, Algernon, a twenty-two-year-old English officer assigned to the British legation in Washington, strode into Ulys's study in the White House and declared, "Mr. President, I want to marry your daughter." Ulys demurred, arguing that Nellie was much too young and the two had not known each other long. Unsettling rumors suggested that the young Mr. Sartoris would not be a suitable match for the president's daughter — and more troubling yet, his own parents had written to warn Ulys that Algernon had given them much trouble and they were not optimistic about the marriage. But Nellie was thoroughly in love and swore she would never have another happy day without her Algy, and Ulys and Julia, mindful of their own parents' objections to their betrothal, eventually gave their blessing.

Nellie and Algernon wed in the East Room of the White House on a gloriously beautiful May morning the following year. Flowering trees filled Washington with shade and perfume, and seventy carriages brought two hundred guests to the Executive Mansion — generals, statesmen, diplomats, wealthy businessmen, and their elegant, beautifully attired ladies. Nellie was breathtakingly lovely in a heavy white satin gown trimmed with point lace, the Marine Band played soft, romantic music, and the banquet was a culinary triumph. Their distinguished guests enjoyed themselves tremendously — although many observed that President Grant was silent and tense throughout the ceremony and reception. Later, after Nellie departed on the arm of her bridegroom, Ulys was nowhere to be found. After most of the guests had gone home, Julia went in search of her husband and found him in Nellie's room, sitting on the bed and weeping without restraint.

Five months later, Fred, a lieutenant colonel on General Sheridan's staff, married the lovely, enchanting Ida M. Honoré — not at the White House, but at the Honoré country home near Chicago. Julia and Ulys agreed that Ida was as amiable as she was beautiful, and they delighted in Fred's wedding day as they had been unable to enjoy his sister's. Not quite two years later, Ida gave birth to a beautiful daughter at the White House, and Julia was moved to tears when the happy couple announced that the child's name would be Julia Dent Grant.

But the family witnessed tragedy as well as happiness during their time in the White House. Nellie's first child, a son named Grant Grenville Edward Sartoris, died before his first birthday. Consumption eventually claimed the life of the long-suffering Rawlins, who had served in the Grant cabinet as secretary of war, and two years later, his lovely wife, Mary Emma, perished of the same dread affliction. Jesse Root Grant died in Covington scarcely four months after Ulys's second inauguration, and in December of that same year, Papa passed away at the White House, opinionated and curmudgeonly until the very end.

Nor were all of their tragedies personal, for Ulys's administration was plagued by scandal — the gold conspiracy crisis that culminated in Black Friday, the Delano affair, the Whiskey Ring, the Belknap scandal — and too many others, each with its own odious moniker for the press to bandy about in blistering editorials. Charges of nepotism were so copious that Julia did not even try to keep track of them, but waved them off like so many swarms of irritating, biting flies. Julia staunchly believed that Ulys ran his administration as he had run his armies, with tremendous force of will, great honor, utmost integrity, and steadfast faith in the men he appointed to serve him. But far too often, his trust was betrayed. Time and again Ulys was exonerated of the crimes committed by his subordinates, but that did not quell the grousing of his critics in Congress and the press.

But whatever obstacles appeared before him, Ulys regrouped and moved ever forward, refusing to retreat or retrace his steps. The people had made him president, but nothing could transform him into a politician. He was, and would ever be, a general.

In early spring of 1875, more than a year before the Republican delegates would meet to choose their nominee for the next presidential election, fervent speculation that Ulys would seek an unprecedented third term filled newspapers and drawing rooms and front porches across the country. Julia reveled in her role as First Lady and eagerly looked forward to another four years, but whenever she asked Ulys about his intentions, he evaded her queries with jokes or noncommittal replies.

"I suppose when you finally make up your mind," Julia lamented, "the press will know before I do."

"They'll probably know before either of us," Ulys remarked, ever calm and reticent.

Finally, one Sunday afternoon at the end of May, Ulys informed her that he had written to the chairman of the Republican State Convention at Philadelphia to announce that he had no intention of running for a third term. Profoundly disappointed, Julia sank down heavily in a chair. "Was that kind, to send the letter before telling me? Was it just?"

"You would have tried to talk me out of it, and I've made up my mind."

He was right, of course, but Julia still wished he had given her the chance to persuade him.

Ulys came to her and rested his hands on her shoulders. "I don't want to be here another four years," he said simply. "I don't think I could stand it. Don't lament over this, I beg you."

She placed her hand over his and sighed, too unhappy to speak. She did not like his decision, but she understood it.

If Ulys had pursued a third term, he almost certainly would have spared the nation a great deal of controversy and turmoil. After election returns in southern states were contested and returning boards held recounts, Republican Rutherford B. Hayes was declared the victor over Democrat Samuel J. Tilden, but only after the Supreme Court intervened.

In the last week of February, with the nation still hotly divided over the outcome of the election, Julia passed through the home that had become so familiar to her during her years as First Lady, rooms that had witnessed births, deaths, and a bittersweet wedding, glorious public occasions and private family moments she would cherish forever in her memory.

Soon it would be their home no longer.

On Saturday, March 3, Ulys and Julia hosted a state dinner for the president-elect and thirty guests at the White House, and it was on that day in the privacy of the Red Room that Mr. Hayes took his oath of office, amid threats upon his life and concerns that various angry factions would prevent the peaceful transition of power. Mrs. Hayes kindly invited Julia to accompany her to the public inauguration two days later, but Julia could not bear the thought of attending and politely declined. Instead, as her last act as official White House hostess, Julia arranged a sumptuous luncheon for the Hayes family and their companions, and she was waiting in the foyer to welcome them after the inauguration.

All too soon it was time to depart. Mrs. Hayes, sturdily competent and self-assured, graciously escorted Julia to the door and told her she was welcome to visit anytime.

"Mrs. Hayes," Julia said, fighting back tears, "I hope you will be as happy here as I have been for the past eight years."

Mrs. Hayes inclined her head, and with nothing more to say, Julia took Ulys's arm and allowed him to lead her on to their waiting carriage, and a new home, and whatever else might come after.

CHAPTER TWENTY-SIX

January–October 1884

Jule had intended to let the anniversary pass unacknowledged, but as she and Dorothy sat down to supper together one January evening, she heard herself say, "Today I am twenty years a free woman."

Dorothy's eyes widened. "Oh, Mamma." She reached across the table and clasped her hand. "I wish you had never been a slave. I can't bear to think of you subjected to such cruelty."

"But I was," replied Jule, without bitterness. "I and countless millions of others through the generations. I survived. Maybe enduring slavery made me stronger."

Dorothy pressed her lips together, waiting for her to say more, but Jule merely smiled fondly and took up her fork, and after a moment, Dorothy did too. Jule disliked talking about slavery times, and in this she was not unusual among folks her age. Dorothy and her brother had learned to listen carefully and quietly whenever she allowed them rare glimpses into her past before her flight to Washington City, before her transformation into Madame Jule, before she became their mother.

Charles — twenty years old, tall, sober, sharply insightful — would have insisted they mark the occasion with a cake or small glasses of sherry, but he was off at his second year at Howard University, studying to become a lawyer and perhaps someday a judge. Dorothy, recently turned eighteen, eagerly anticipated finishing school come spring. "You could go to the university too," Jule had told her, or rather implored. She could not bear for her children to squander any opportunity for self-improvement, for advancement in a world that remained adamantly opposed to colored folk rising too high.

"I want to work with you," Dorothy would remind her pointedly. "I enjoy it — and be honest, you need me."

It was true. Jule had worked hard all her life and was ready to slow down, and Dorothy — a confident, clever, briskly efficient young woman with an excellent head for business — was the person she trusted most to succeed her. For the past two years Dorothy had gradually taken over many of the sales and accounting tasks in the Madame Jule Company, freeing Jule to concoct new products and promote them to the great many clients who regarded Jule as a genius of beauty and grooming.

Jule still earned a significant portion of her income from wealthy white ladies, but in recent years, her interests had turned to creating balms and tonics suited for the unique needs of women of color. Skin of all tones could be soft, smooth, and luminous, she had told a much younger Dorothy whenever she had tearfully lamented that her lighter-skinned classmates mocked her deep sepia hue. African hair could be glossy and radiant with good health, and needn't be blond or straight or fine to be beautiful. "We should strive to be well-groomed, dignified, and comely, not lighter," Jule asserted, unable to refrain from bitterly twisting the last word.

Once, in a rare moment of self-doubt, Jule had asked her pastor if her profession was inherently sinful, if it encouraged vanity and pride. The reverend had sat silently for a moment before responding. "Taking pride in one's appearance is not the same as being prideful," he said. "For too long our brothers and sisters have been taught to despise their dark skin. You teach them instead that it deserves admiration and care. I cannot believe this is sinful."

Jule's own skin had taken on a few lines that deepened when she smiled, and her tight curls had become a glossy, silvery white. She doubted anyone who knew her from her slavery days twenty years before would recognize her if they passed on the street, not even Julia.

Winter softened into a balmy spring. Dorothy finished school and gladly came to work full-time for the Madame Jule Company. Jule found herself with more time to read, to attend lectures, to serve on the board of the orphan asylum where she had discovered her children, and to be active in her church. The Bridge Street Church advocated for many causes dear to Jule's heart, and often they invited eminent speakers from across the country to address the congregation.

One Sunday as services were ending, the pastor mentioned that the following week, he would be joined in the pulpit by a renowned minister, former slave, and advocate for civil rights for people of color, the Reverend Gabriel Brown. A frisson of shock and hope ran through Jule, pinning her to her seat long after the rest of the congregation began to file from the church.

"Mamma?" asked Dorothy worriedly, standing in the aisle, studying her from above. "Is something wrong?"

"I need to speak to the pastor," she said, rising, trembling, steadying herself on the back of the pew.

Dorothy accompanied her outside, where the pastor stood on the front stoop bidding his flock good-bye. "Do you know this Reverend Gabriel Brown?" Jule inquired, breathless from excitement and renewed hope. She had ceased placing advertisements years before when nothing had come of them, and part of her had accepted that she was in all likelihood a widow. And yet his name, his profession, his history — this minister could be her Gabriel.

"I've never met him," the pastor replied, "but I'm familiar with his writings, and we have mutual acquaintances."

"Has he come from Texas?" asked Jule urgently. "Do you know if he sings? Do folks remark about his wonderful voice?"

"He's been called a powerful orator, but no one has mentioned his singing to me. And he comes from Virginia, not Texas." The minister's brow furrowed. "My dear sister Jule, is something the matter?"

Virginia, not Texas. "No, Reverend." Jule wrenched her frown of bitter disappointment into a semblance of a smile. "I thought I might know him is all, but I was wrong."

She turned quickly to hide the tears gathering in her eyes — and yet hope did not leave her entirely.

Never did a week pass more slowly. "Mamma," Dorothy told her gently one evening as she stared unseeing out the window, lost in thought, "this minister is probably not your long-lost husband."

"I know that," Jule replied. "But the sooner Sunday comes, the sooner I'll know. The sooner I can stop hoping."

Through the years, waiting and not knowing and always wondering had tarnished all the bright silver of her happiness. If this Gabriel Brown was not her Gabriel, Jule resolved to accept that he was lost to her forever. Acceptance would change nothing about how she spent her days, but perhaps she could finally bring herself to mourn him properly and leave the past in the past.

She had intended to arrive a half hour early on the chance that she might be able to meet the illustrious guest before services, but her anxious nerves got the better of her and she arrived ten minutes late. Murmuring apologies to those seated around them, she and Dorothy slipped into their usual pew just as Reverend Brown was introduced. Jule stared at him as he came forward and shook hands with the pastor, desperately searching his face for features reminiscent of the young man she had loved — and finding them. And when he spoke, his voice resonated as her husband's had, less pure in tone but richer with dignity and gravitas.

She became aware of Dorothy beside her, glancing from her to the minister and back, her eyes widening as she sensed the intensity of her mother's response. "Is it he?" she whispered.

Jule felt as if she were illuminated from within as she nodded, as the tears began to stream down her face. It was Gabriel, her Gabriel.

He knew her too.

Their eyes met as he preached, and for one long, radiant moment, he fell abruptly silent, staring at her, shocked and disbelieving, but then he caught himself and resumed his sermon, faster than before, as if he could not wait to reach the end. When the choir sang, he bent his head close to the pastor's and they conferred briefly, urgently. By the last chorus they were both looking straight at Jule, the pastor utterly astonished, Gabriel as if he dared not look away for fear she would vanish.

The service ended, and although church deacons and respected dowagers gathered around to meet their renowned guest, Gabriel nearly leapt down from the pulpit to come to her, to take her hands, to pull her to her feet.

"It's you," he said, his voice full of wonder. "It's you. My Jule. My love. My wife."

"Gabriel," she choked out, smiling through her tears. "Oh, praise be to God, at last."

Swiftly the story spread through the congregation, and all around them the people erupted in joyful cheers and songs of thanksgiving. Surely the grace of God had descended upon their church that day.

"I tried to find you," Jule told him later, at home, when they were alone, Dorothy having kindly gone out to visit a friend to give them time alone, together. "For so many years, I tried."

He clasped her hands so tightly that she imagined they might fuse to his, ensuring that they would never be parted again. "And I tried to find you."

He had stayed in Texas less than a fortnight before running away, he told her. He assumed Jule would be with Miss Julia, so he tried to reach military headquarters, only to be caught up in the waves of contraband following General Grant's army. Months later, when he heard that Julia had joined her husband at City Point, he had made his way there, only to discover that Mrs. Grant's favorite maid had fled long ago. With no other home to return to, he had settled at Freedman's Village, a contraband camp established on part of General Lee's captured estate in Arlington, Virginia. There he had tended horses for the Union army and had preached the Holy Gospel until the end of the war, when a benevolent society had sponsored him for the seminary, allowing him to formally continue the studies he had begun in secret as an enslaved child at White Haven.

"You were so close," Jule said. "All the while I was in Washington City, you were so close, and I never knew."

"I'm closer now," he said, pulling her into his embrace, kissing her cheeks, her forehead, her lips. "And if you still want me after all these years, I'll stay."

"Of course," said Jule, laughing at the very idea that she would ever let him go. "Let us never be parted again."

"I swear we never will be, while we both live."

She kissed him, and as they laughed and cried and held each other, she felt as if she had been a long time traveling and had finally reached the end of the road, only to discover that a new one lay before her, a smooth path, bright with promise and newly beginning, one she never need travel alone.

When Ulys bit into a peach one lovely day in early June of 1884 and complained of excruciating pain, Julia felt no shadow of foreboding that it marked the beginning of the end.

There was no reason she should have, not when she and Ulys were distracted by what seemed to be more serious concerns. A month before, the brokerage firm managing their finances had gone bankrupt, and they had lost every cent of their investment. Their entire fortune, scrupulously earned and saved over many years, was gone.

The calamity struck with a force as utterly unexpected as it was swift and devastating. Buck — Ulysses S. Grant, Jr., as he was known to all but family and friends — had attended Exeter and Harvard and had earned his law degree from Columbia. He had married Fannie Josephine Chaffee, the daughter of Colorado senator Jerome B. Chaffee, who had earned a multimillion-dollar fortune from his investments in silver mines. When the financial tycoon Ferdinand Ward proposed that he and Buck establish a Wall Street investment firm, between Ward's experience, connections, and capital and Buck's revered Grant name, their success seemed preordained. At Ward's suggestion, they took on another partner, James D. Fish, a respected New York financier and president of the prestigious Marine Bank. When Grant & Ward quickly found its footing and began to reap astonishing profits, Buck invited Ulys to join as a partner, and after he agreed, many other members of the Grant family entrusted their savings to the firm.

For three years, Grant & Ward prospered. Every morning, Ulys reported promptly for work at his offices on the second floor of No. 2 Wall Street, cordially greeting the potential investors Ward courted, lending the weight of his august presence to meetings and transactions. To Julia's delight, Ulys's initial investment of ten thousand dollars grew to three-quarters of a million, and they were at last free of the lurking fear of debt and poverty. They kept a lavish home on East Sixty-sixth

Street in Manhattan, and Ulys gave Julia a generous monthly allowance of one thousand dollars to spend however she pleased, while he indulged his love of good cigars and fine horses.

"You needn't trouble yourself to save for the children," Ulys told her one Thanksgiving as they prepared for a family visit. "Ward is making us not only secure, but wealthy."

But in the early months of 1884, Ulys frequently came home from his office with a furrowed brow, troubled by rumors circulating on Wall Street that Ward was mishandling his investors' funds and that Grant & Ward was on the verge of crumbling.

Then, on the morning of May 4, a quiet, peaceful Sunday, Ward unexpectedly called at the Grant residence. "The Marine Bank needs a twenty-four-hour loan of one hundred fifty thousand dollars," Ward told Ulys, his voice trembling with dread. "Our investments are imperiled."

Listening just outside the doorway, Julia heard Ulys sigh heavily. "I'll do what I can," he said, as Julia had known he would. The firm was in jeopardy, and therefore, so was his good name.

After seeing Ward to the door, Ulys went out and returned a few hours later, unsmiling, cheeks flushed with embarrassment as if he were a young lieutenant again. In his pocket he carried a check from his old friend and political supporter William Henry Vanderbilt, the enormously wealthy railroad magnate. "He told me he cared nothing for the Marine Bank and very little about Grant & Ward," he told Julia, "but he cares a great deal about me, and so he offers this as a personal loan."

Ulys delivered the check to Ward, but in the days that followed, the Marine Bank closed, creditors would not honor Buck's checks, angry crowds gathered outside the firm demanding payment — and Ward disappeared with Ulys's money.

Grant & Ward went bankrupt. Ulys and every member of the Grant family that had invested in the firm had lost everything.

Ulys came home despondent from an emergency meeting at No. 2 Wall Street. "I've made it a rule of my life to trust a man long after other people have given up on him," he said dully as he sat in the library, with its shelves full of treasures from their world travels and expensive volumes donated by admirers from Boston. "I don't see how I can trust any human being again."

As the collapse of Grant & Ward and the failure of the Marine Bank shook Wall Street, the press began to speculate about Ulys's culpability in the financial disaster. "Is Grant Guilty?" *The New York Sun* queried in a bold, front-page headline. The *New York Post* savagely editorialized that "General Grant's influence was used in some highly improper way to the detriment of the government and the benefit of Grant & Ward." It was not true, of course, but to Ulys, who prized his honor above all else, the criticism was a heavy blow. He took Julia's hands and solemnly vowed that he would repay every penny of the debt, and he would not rest until he found a new way to provide for her and the children.

"I know you will, darling," Julia said soothingly, alarmed by his vehemence. "I'm not afraid."

Ulys made no reply except to squeeze her hands once, quickly, and to retire to his study at the top of the stairs. There, with the same determination and resolve he had applied to planning military campaigns from his headquarters at City Point, he tallied his assets — their homes in Philadelphia and Galena, two parcels of undeveloped land in Chicago, and White Haven, which he had purchased several years before. He gathered his mementoes and prizes from the war — the jeweled sword he had won by popular vote at the great Sanitary Fair at Palace Garden, others equally ornate that had been bestowed upon him by the grateful citizens of towns throughout the North, the gold medals, gilded humidors, campaign maps, uniforms, and papers that might be of historic interest. He calculated their worth, and when he found the total insufficient, he and Julia gathered the treasures they had collected on their two-year world tour following his second term as president — teakwood cabinets, jade and porcelain given to them by Chinese statesman Li Hung-chang, an eleven-hundred-year-old gold-lacquer cabinet given to Ulys by the mikado, cloisonné from Japan, enamels and malachite from Russia, jeweled and gilded caskets containing scrolls representing the freedom of cities they had visited, Persian and Turkish rugs, a Bengal tiger skin, two elephant tusks given to them by the king of Siam, a Coptic Bible taken by Lord Robert Napier from King Theodore of Abyssinia, and every other precious memento.

For her part, Julia unclasped the chased gold locket with the daguerreotype of her beloved young lieutenant, which she had worn by its narrow velvet strap about her wrist every day since she and Ulys wed. "Every little bit will help," Julia said. "A jeweler wouldn't appraise it as highly as these other treasures, but it would surely fetch a fine price from one of your admirers for its historic and sentimental value."

"But to us it's priceless. Julia, I forbid you to give away my wedding gift to you."

Quickly blinking away tears, Julia nodded and fastened the strap about her wrist again.

Though Mr. Vanderbilt thwarted Ulys's every attempt to repay the debt, Ulys's honor would not bear such generosity. When Mr.

Vanderbilt departed for an extended European tour, Ulys and Julia turned over mortgages to their real estate and securities for the treasures to his lawyers, who agreed to present them to Mr. Vanderbilt upon his return.

Within a fortnight, police detectives traced Ferdinand Ward to his brother-in-law's home in Brooklyn, and on May 26, he was arrested and indicted for fraud. Their silent partner, Marine Bank president James D. Fish, was arrested soon thereafter. Julia hoped that Ulys's one hundred fifty thousand dollars could be recovered, but it was long gone.

"Never mind," Ulys consoled her. "Our debt to Mr. Vanderbilt is satisfied, and the criminals responsible for our unhappiness will be brought to justice. All will be well."

Upon becoming president, Ulys had retired his military commission to allow General Sherman and his other subordinates to be promoted, so he would not receive a pension from the army despite his many decades of distinguished service. Unable to pay the household bills, Julia had become quietly, frantically desperate when their good friend Matias Romero, the ambassador from Mexico, called to express his sympathies and secretly left behind a check for one thousand dollars. A day later, a gentleman they had never met from upstate New York mailed them a check for the same amount, folded within a letter that described the payment as "a loan on account of my share for services ending in April 1865." Julia was grateful, but she knew they could not depend upon spontaneous acts of generosity over the long term.

At the end of May, the Grants closed up their New York mansion and retired to their summer cottage in Long Branch, New Jersey. The four-story, twenty-eight-room residence could not be lost to the bankruptcy because it was not truly theirs; George Childs, publisher of the *Philadelphia Public Ledger,* had purchased it during Ulys's first term as president, with the understanding that Ulys should consider the idyllic retreat his own. Before long, their eldest son, Fred, who had lost nearly everything in the collapse of Grant & Ward, rented out his home in Morristown and moved his family in with them.

Ulys spent many hours gazing out at the sea, smoking and contemplating his options. At sixty-two, an age when he ought to retire and enjoy the rewards of a life well lived, he had been forced to start over.

A few days later, as the family lingered at the table after luncheon, Ulys took a peach from a bowl, bit into it, and started as if in great pain. "Oh, my," he exclaimed, bolting to his feet. "I think something on that peach stung me."

"Are you all right?" asked Ida. She remained as lovely, bright, and amiable as she had been on her wedding day, and she was devoted to Fred and their two darling children, little Julia, age eight, and Ulysses, three.

His hand to his throat, lips pressed together, Ulys frowned and shook his head. He paced the length of the room and out to the piazza, returning to the kitchen to rinse his throat again and again. "Water hurts me like liquid fire," he said hoarsely when he returned to the table.

The sharpness of the strange, sudden pain diminished, but Ulys's discomfort persisted, intensifying whenever he ate anything acidic. He accepted the soothing remedies Julia and Ida offered him but refused medical treatment. "I don't need a doctor," Ulys said, more curtly each time Julia suggested that he see a physician. "It'll be all right directly."

A week later, Ulys decided to break his self-imposed exile by speaking at a convention of army chaplains in nearby Ocean Grove. Fred, who had achieved the rank of lieutenant colonel before resigning to accompany his parents on their world tour, escorted his father to the gathering, where the audience greeted Ulys with a standing ovation. Dr. A. J. Palmer, an old friend of Ulys's, had introduced him, declaring, "No combination of Wall Street sharpers shall tarnish the lustre of my old commander's fame for me."

A few days later Ulys traveled to Brooklyn, where the Society of the Army of the Potomac elected him their president. The veteran soldiers' faithful kindness worked wonders on Ulys; the strain left his visage, the tension in his jaw and shoulders eased. Once again Julia was moved to thank God for the valiant United States Army.

At the reunion, Ulys had enjoyed a cordial conversation with Richard Watson Gilder, senior editor of *The Century*, so it did not come as a complete surprise when his colleague, associate editor Robert Underwood Johnson, called on Ulys at Long Branch to invite him to write a few articles for their magazine.

As the two men spoke on the piazza, Julia concealed her surprise as Ulys frankly acknowledged his financial troubles. "Despite my well-publicized need, I'm reluctant to accept your proposal," he said, offering Mr. Johnson a cigar, which he declined. "I'm not a writer, and others have already written a great many articles and books about my campaigns. I don't know what I could add to what's already in print."

"An article from the former general in chief of the Union army and United States president would inherently be more informative than anything previously written," Mr. Johnson replied.

Julia felt as if she were holding her breath while Mr. Johnson suggested that Ulys write four stories, one each about the Battle of

Shiloh, the Vicksburg campaign, the Battle of the Wilderness, and General Lee's surrender at Appomattox. Each article would earn Ulys five hundred dollars, an extraordinary sum. When Ulys agreed, Julia clasped her hands to her heart and said a silent prayer of thanksgiving.

Ulys immediately commenced work on an article about Shiloh. To refresh his memory, he studied official reports, dispatches, and articles by witnesses, but sometimes he merely sat in quiet reflection, gazing out at the ocean and puffing on a cigar. He wrote every word himself, toiling about four hours every day throughout the month of June. On July 1, his handwritten manuscript arrived at the *Century* offices in New York.

Mr. Gilder promptly replied to thank him, and a few days later, he returned to Long Branch with the annotated manuscript in hand. Noting well Mr. Johnson's careful praise and tactful suggestions, upon his departure, Julia detained him on the piazza. "I gather that the general's article is not quite right for *The Century,*" she said in an undertone.

Mr. Johnson hesitated. "It's factual and clear," he said, glancing past Julia to the doorway, as if wary that Ulys might suddenly appear. "But there's no life in it, no sense of General Grant — what he felt, what he was doing or thinking. One might almost think he wasn't there."

"He's written you a battle report, you mean."

"Yes," said Mr. Johnson, looking relieved. "That's exactly it."

Julia placed her hand on his forearm. "You should tell him what you want, as straightforwardly as you can. He's a soldier. He can bear it."

Mr. Johnson looked dubious, but he thanked her, and the next time he visited, she overheard him encouraging Ulys to add more personal anecdotes to his story — for that was what it was supposed to be, a story, complete with plot and characters. "What we need is for you to approximate such talk as you would make to friends after dinner," he said, "some of whom would know a great deal about the battle and others who would know nothing at all. The people will be especially interested in your point of view — everything that concerned you, in what you planned, saw, said, and did."

On subsequent visits, Julia observed Mr. Johnson asking Ulys about particular incidents from the war, and in his replies, Ulys chronicled events in rich detail and offered frank descriptions of his fellow officers and his feelings. "You should put that in the article," Mr. Johnson would say after Ulys finished a tale, and Julia hid a smile when she discovered the editor's trick to drawing out the recalcitrant general.

"If I had known what he wanted from the beginning," Ulys remarked to Julia one day after Mr. Johnson departed for New York, "I would have given him that."

"Think of these early drafts as your apprenticeship. Now you're ready to begin your masterpiece."

He gave her a wry look as if to say his intentions were not that grand, but he resumed his work with a new determination. She enjoyed sitting with him while he wrote, but she worried that he often grimaced and absently touched his throat, and that he ate and drank very little.

"Is your throat bothering you again?" she asked one afternoon when he refused the sweet, cool tea she had left on his desk hours before.

"It never stopped hurting entirely," he replied, without looking up from the page. "It comes and goes."

"I do wish you'd see a doctor."

"I don't have time. Johnson and Gilder want this article by the end of August."

Julia knew that nagging him would accomplish nothing, but one day, when Ida summoned a doctor to the house to examine her feverish, coughing daughter, she persuaded Ulys to consent to a quick examination. Julia watched the doctor's expression closely as he peered into her husband's throat. "The back of your throat is quite inflamed," he said, frowning. "You should consult your family doctor immediately."

He wrote a prescription for a mild pain-killer, and the moment he left, Julia declared, "You heard him. You must see Dr. Barker right away."

"Dr. Barker is in Europe," Ulys said. "I'll schedule an appointment the day he returns."

"Do you promise?"

"Yes, my dear little wife," he replied. "I promise, if you promise not to badger me anymore."

Julia nodded her assent, knowing she had negotiated the best terms Unconditional Surrender Grant was likely to concede.

By the middle of August, Ulys had produced an entirely new version of his account of the Battle of Shiloh — and it was riveting. "You have a gift for clarity and simplicity of expression," said Julia, "and a wonderful eye for detail. I felt as if I were there, riding along with you and your officers. If your letters home had been so terrifying, I might have begged you to resign your commission."

As Mr. Johnson and Mr. Gilder eagerly prepared to publish the article, Ulys turned his attention to the Vicksburg campaign. But he had always resisted retracing his steps, and it proved to be a difficult task even with pen and paper. Fred — an accomplished author in his own right, having authored a book about his service on the Yellowstone Expedition with the Fourth Infantry — continued to be of great help, and Ulys soon recruited Badeau, author of a successful three-volume history of Ulys's military career. They checked facts, verified dates, reviewed drafts, and often sat in on Ulys's conferences with Mr. Johnson.

By early September, Ulys finished the first draft of his article on Vicksburg and commenced the first draft of a piece on the Chattanooga campaign. Soon after he began, Mr. Johnson arrived at Long Branch accompanied by Roswell Smith, president of the Century Company. Although the summer season had passed, the resort town was full of tourists enjoying the sunshine and balmy air, and Ulys often liked to write on the piazza, nodding cordially to passersby who waved as they strolled along the sidewalk between the cottage and the sea. Ulys's voice was raspy as he welcomed the gentlemen, whose curious gazes lingered on the scarf Ulys wore around his neck despite the summer heat.

Julia served them lemonade, and as she quietly seated herself in a wicker chair at a discreet distance, where she could observe but would not intrude, Mr. Smith broached the subject of Ulys writing his memoirs. His articles were brilliant, Mr. Johnson chimed in, and his swift progress proved that he was more than capable of producing a book. Ulys listened intently, nodding from time to time as the editor and publisher described the project they envisioned, how they would work to create and promote it — and, of keen interest to Julia, how Ulys would profit from the sales.

"Do you really think anyone would be interested in a book I could write?" Ulys asked.

"General," said Mr. Smith, astonished, "would not the public avidly read Napoleon's accounts of his battles, if they existed?"

Ulys remained silent, but Julia could tell that the high praise of the comparison impressed him.

"What do you think, Julia?" Ulys asked later, when they were alone.

She thought the gentlemen's proposal was a godsend, but she said, "When Mark Twain urged you to write your memoirs, you told him you were no writer, that you were sure no one would want your memoirs, and that you would be embarrassed to see a book published under your name."

"That was three years ago," said Ulys. "That was before — all this."

Julia nodded, acknowledging that indeed everything had changed in a matter of months, and that old, trusted decisions must be reconsidered. She could only imagine what other changes yet awaited them, but if

Ulys's memoirs could save their family, he would find the way.

CHAPTER TWENTY-SEVEN

October 1884–February 1885

At the end of October, the Grants left Long Branch and returned to their home in New York. Ulys was eager to continue work on his articles for *The Century,* but Julia insisted that he first put down his pen, set aside his papers, and keep his promise to call on Dr. Fordyce Barker.

"Well?" Julia asked the moment Ulys returned home from the appointment, only to discover that Dr. Barker had not offered a diagnosis. Instead, upon examining Ulys, he had referred him to Dr. John Hancock Douglas, the preeminent throat specialist in the East. Ulys and Dr. Douglas had met professionally early in the war, while Ulys led the assault on Fort Donelson and Dr. Douglas served on the United States Sanitary Commission.

"I have an ulceration at the base of my tongue," Ulys informed Julia, Fred, and Ida, after consulting with Dr. Douglas. "The doctor applied a muriate of cocaine to the swollen area, and it gave me immediate relief. He also treated me with Iodoform to reduce the pain and disinfect the sore so I can eat and sleep. I'm to visit him twice a day so he can reapply the medicines."

"Twice a day for how long?" asked Fred, brow furrowing.

"He didn't say. Until it's run its course, I suppose." Ulys smiled briefly and began climbing the stairs to his study, but then he paused, his hand on the banister. "On my way home, I stopped at the *Century* offices and told Smith that I want to write my memoirs."

The four articles he had already planned would form the foundation for his book, Ulys told them that evening at supper. He expected that it would be a relatively simple matter to bind them together with accounts of his other battles and campaigns and stories from his youth. He worked throughout October, his newfound enjoyment of researching and writing a delight for Julia to see, but his appetite was little improved from before he began Dr. Douglas's treatments, and Julia and Ida agreed that he had lost weight.

"You know what a stoic your father can be," Julia said to Fred and Ida in a hushed conversation while Ulys toiled over his manuscript in his second-floor study at the top of stairs, alone except for his longtime valet, Harrison

Tyrell. The faithful Harrison, as the family referred to him affectionately, watched over Ulys almost possessively, bringing him fresh paper when he filled a page, adjusting the scarf about his neck when it came loose, plumping a pillow for his back. "Perhaps Pa hasn't been entirely forthcoming with the doctor. If Dr. Douglas truly understood how much he suffers, he might offer a more aggressive treatment."

They agreed that Julia and Fred should call on Dr. Douglas and share their concerns.

Dr. Douglas was a handsome man perhaps two years younger than Ulys, with flowing gray hair and an abundant beard. His expression grew progressively more serious as Julia and Fred took turns describing Ulys's symptoms and suffering at home, but not for the reason they imagined.

"Mrs. Grant, Colonel Grant, I'm going to be as frank with you as I was with the general," he said. "General Grant has cancer. A carcinoma at the base of his tongue has spread to several other small lesions in his throat. Over time the cancer will grow into his neck, making it nearly impossible for him to eat, and eventually, to breathe. The progress of the disease will be lengthy, excruciatingly painful, and ultimately fatal. All we can do is to make General Grant as comfortable as possible in the time remaining to him."

Julia sat utterly still, ears ringing. Fred queried the doctor further, but the back-and-forth of questions and replies scarcely registered in Julia's mind until Dr. Douglas addressed her directly. "Mrs. Grant," he said distinctly, as if aware he was speaking to her through a thick fog of shock, "I could instruct you how to apply the topical pain relievers to your husband's throat. It isn't a difficult procedure, and it would spare him the inconvenience of coming to me for treatment twice a day."

Wordlessly, Julia nodded, and she forced herself to concentrate as the doctor described what she must do to ease Ulys's pain. When he finished, Dr. Douglas regarded them gravely and asked if they understood all that he had told them.

Fred assured him that they did, but Julia asked, "Is it curable?"

Dr. Douglas hesitated. "There have been rare cases when it has been cured."

"How rare?"

"Extremely so, madam."

Julia took her son's arm as they left the building, and although they had planned to take the streetcar, Fred took one look at her face and quickly summoned a carriage. "Pa concealed his condition out of a desire to protect us," he told her as they rode home.

"He shouldn't have." Julia inhaled deeply and shook her head. "Except for the growths in his throat, your father is healthy, temperate, and strong. Why should he not be again?"

"Mother —" Fred studied her for a moment before closing both of his hands around one of hers. "Dr. Douglas is the foremost throat specialist on the East Coast. He knows this disease, and he said nothing to encourage us to hope for a cure."

"He might know cancer, but he doesn't know your Pa," Julia countered, a fierce new strength filling her. "I cannot believe that God in his wisdom and mercy would take this great, wise, good man from us, to whom he is so necessary and so beloved. It simply cannot be."

Julia persisted in her belief that her victor would triumph over his illness, even after she applied the painkilling opiates for the first time and her heart quaked to behold the three scaly, inflamed lesions far back on the roof of his mouth, the swollen gland on the right side, and the membraneous tissue at the base of his tongue that formed the surface of the carcinoma.

"I had hoped to spare you all this," Ulys said ruefully when she had finished.

"Oh, nonsense," scoffed Julia, corking the bottles and setting them aside. "We've been married thirty-six years. Why should you start sparing me now?"

Her confidence wavered only slightly when Dr. Douglas froze part of Ulys's ulcerated throat, excised some of the tissue, and sent it to the renowned physician and microbiologist Dr. George Frederick Shrady, who with absolute certainty confirmed a diagnosis of lingual epithelioma, or cancer of the tongue. After examining Ulys, the stern, forthright physician urged Ulys to give up his cigars, but if he could not, he must limit himself to three a day. Dr. Shrady also advised against surgery, noting that the cancer had already ruptured and spread its poison throughout the surrounding tissue, and nothing would slow the carcinoma's relentless growth. An operation would only increase Ulys's discomfort while accomplishing nothing.

"What he means is that it's too late," Ulys told Julia, holding her gaze steadily. "You do understand, don't you?"

"Of course," Julia said. Surgery would not work, so Dr. Shrady would simply have to find another course of treatment.

As the autumn passed, Ulys worked on his articles for *The Century* and commenced his memoirs, but all the while the pain in his throat worsened, despite Julia's faithful applications of the medicines and frequent visits to his doctors. Julia and Ida plied him with wholesome soups and custards, easy to swallow and full of flavor and nourishment, but Ulys could scarcely eat enough to maintain his strength. "If you can imagine what molten lead would feel like going down your throat, that is what I feel when swallowing," he told Julia as she begged him to take just one more spoonful of beef broth.

Writing provided Ulys with a distraction from his pain and an ambitious goal to focus his thoughts. From early morning until well into the evening, Ulys toiled away in his second-floor study at the top of the stairs, a knit cap upon his head to ward off the chill of early winter, a shawl wrapped around his throat. Two windows looking out upon Sixty-sixth Street illuminated his desk, tidily arranged with his manuscript pages in the center and neat stacks of notes all around. Upon a nearby folding table, Fred and Badeau had arranged several useful maps for Ulys to consult as he retraced the progress of his armies' movements.

Fred worked with his father's tireless diligence, but Badeau had come to the project somewhat reluctantly. When Ulys first requested his help, Badeau had refused, explaining that he was working on a novel that demanded his full attention, but eventually Ulys persuaded him, even offering a comfortable bedroom in the Grant residence as part of his compensation.

Every day Ulys followed a diligent routine of researching, outlining, writing, editing, and revising. Working from a nearby room, Fred and Badeau compiled research, read sections as Ulys completed them, verified facts with their records, jotted notes in the margins, and returned pages to Ulys for revision. Julia often observed the men as they worked, watching quietly as Ulys sat at his desk bent over his manuscript, the nib of his pen scratching on the paper, Harrison keeping vigil in the corner he had claimed as his own.

Julia knew that the faithful Harrison was much more than a valet to Ulys. A man of color not yet forty, in the years he had been in Ulys's employ, Harrison had been his messenger, confidante, devoted friend, and increasingly, his nurse. He applied the soothing opiates to Ulys's throat more often than Julia did, and twice a day, he brought a glass of milk on a tray to the study and insisted Ulys drink it. Harrison was protective of Ulys's time, and Julia was grateful for the solicitous yet firm way he managed to keep interruptions at bay and tried to ensure that Ulys received adequate rest.

But as the cancer grew, Ulys's throat gradually constricted and his breathing became more labored. He developed a chronic cough, his throat burned with pain, and his voice began to fail. Julia felt as if a knife turned in her heart to watch him suffer so, and from day to day her moods shifted dramatically between sunny optimism and the bleakest despair. She threw herself into a vigorous regimen of prayer, convinced that only that could save her beloved husband, and that it surely would, if her faith did not waver.

With the onset of winter, Ulys rarely went out, but occasionally friends would call, and he would interrupt his work long enough to cordially shake hands and converse as much as he was able. Good friends quickly discerned that he was unwell, kept their visits short, and required him to say almost nothing, but invariably a well-meaning admirer would linger until Ulys was hoarse and weary.

One caller who could never overstay a visit was the writer and humorist Mark Twain, who like Julia had been born and raised in Missouri. Ulys and Twain — whose real name was Samuel Clemens, although his many admirers, including the Grants, addressed him by his pseudonym — had shaken hands but had exchanged hardly a word the first two times they had met, once at a reception in Washington in the winter of 1866, and later at a White House levee during Ulys's first term. They did not become friends until ten years later, when Twain was asked to deliver a toast at the Army of the Tennessee's banquet in Ulys's honor at the Palmer House in Chicago. As he confided to Julia several years after the fact, Twain had watched as Ulys listened impassively to one laudatory toast after another, and he resolved to make the famously stoic general laugh. He succeeded, too, and in quintessential Mark Twain fashion, by following up another speaker's toast "to the Ladies" with his own "to the Babies," whom he pointed out had never been mentioned at a banquet and had been denied that honor too long.

"In still one more cradle, somewhere under the flag," Twain declared as his toast reached its conclusion, "the future illustrious commander in chief of the American armies is so little burdened with his approaching grandeurs and responsibilities as to be giving his whole strategic mind, at this moment, to trying to find some way to get his big toe into his mouth, an achievement which, meaning no disrespect, the illustrious guest of this evening turned his attention to some fifty-six years ago."

The crowd, which had been guffawing only seconds before, fell into a stunned, embarrassed silence.

But Twain was not finished. "If the child is but a prophecy of the man," he said, his voice ringing with good cheer, "there are mighty few who will doubt that he succeeded."

Ulys was the first to laugh, loudly and heartily, slapping his knee. The rest of the gentlemen in the smoke-filled banquet hall soon joined in, and all raised their glasses to toast "the Babies" — and the stoic former president had proven that he could laugh at himself.

After the Grants moved to New York, Twain

called on Ulys often to reminisce about the war, chat about mutual friends, and discuss Twain's writing career. In October of 1881, over a lunch of bacon, baked beans, and coffee, Twain urged Ulys to write his memoirs, to preserve for future generations the story of his life, his battles, and his presidency. Ulys refused, despite assurances that the book would have enormous sales and that Twain would employ his hard-won experience to protect Ulys from signing a contract with an unscrupulous publisher. Ulys insisted that he would never write his memoirs, and when he changed the subject, Twain did not persist.

Early one morning three years and a month later, Twain called at the Grant residence, his manner to Julia as courtly as ever, although he seemed a trifle harried. "Is the general in?" he inquired as Julia showed him inside.

"He's in the library with Fred going over some documents," Julia told him. Ulys rarely left the house anymore, knowing that his appearance would incite speculation. His doctors came to him, and he declined invitations with the excuse that his writing demanded all his attention. "I'm sure they'd welcome your company."

"My dear lady," he asked urgently, seizing her hands. "Are those documents by any chance from the Century Company?"

"Why, yes," she replied, surprised. "It's a publishing contract."

"For his memoirs, I presume. Has he signed it yet?"

"Probably not. He and Fred wanted to give it one last careful examination."

"Thank you, madam." Twain planted a swift kiss on the back of her hands and strode off toward the library.

Bemused, Julia watched him disappear around the corner, wondering what possessed him.

The gentlemen remained sequestered in the library for quite some time, long enough for Julia's curiosity to prompt her to bring them some tea and cake, which she knew Ulys would refuse. She found the men in the midst of an earnest discussion about the publication of Ulys's memoirs, and she quickly deduced that Twain had urged Ulys not to sign the contract, which he decried as insultingly stingy. He instead wanted Ulys to enter into an agreement with the American Publishing Company of Hartford. They had published several of Twain's novels quite successfully and, Twain insisted, they would certainly offer Ulys a far more generous, more lucrative arrangement than the Century Company had.

"Smith and Gilder were my benefactors in my time of great need, and it seems disloyal to desert them." Ulys coughed hoarsely, and concern flashed across Twain's features. Ulys had been careful to conceal the nature of his affliction, giving neither the public nor his friends any indication that he suffered from more than a bad cold.

"If they can offer terms as good as the American Publishing Company, you won't have to," said Fred. "This isn't a matter of sentiment, but of pure business, and should be examined from that point of view alone."

Julia was inclined to agree, but before she could venture an opinion, Ulys said, "Yes, but I feel a certain loyalty to the Century Company because they came to me first."

"In that case," declared Twain, smiling beneath his thick brown mustache, "I'm to be the publisher because *I* came to you first. It was little more than three years ago in this very room that I urged you to write your memoirs and offered to help you do it."

Ulys looked thunderstruck. "Well, that's true," he acknowledged.

Julia lingered as long as she reasonably could, pouring tea and offering cake, and she left the room just as Twain turned the conversation to the benefits of subscription rather than trade publication. Later, after the men emerged from the library and saw Twain to the door, Fred told her that Ulys had agreed to set aside the Century Company's contract for a day and seriously consider his friend's proposal.

Ulys slept unusually well that night, and so when Twain returned the next morning, he found him in good spirits. This time, Julia accompanied the gentlemen when they retired to the library, and she listened intently as Twain made his case for Ulys's memoirs.

"My good friend General Sherman published his memoirs several years ago," Ulys said, "a two-volume set, very well made. He told me that his profits were twenty-five thousand dollars. Do you believe I could get as much out of my book?"

"I'm sure you'll make an even greater profit."

Julia drew in a slow, quiet breath — but she let it out, deflated, when Ulys gingerly shook his head. "I don't think you can be right about that."

"I'm certain that I am." Twain slapped his palms flat on his knees. "I'll tell you what, General Grant. Forget about my publisher. Sell your memoirs to *me.* I'll pay you twice what General Sherman got for his book. Take my check for fifty thousand dollars and let's draw up the contract right now."

Julia gasped. Ulys stared at Twain, stunned, but eventually he shook his head, wincing from the pain. "I can't do that. We're friends, and I would hate it if you failed to make a profit. I could never allow a friend to run such a risk."

"I'm taking a very small risk, I assure you," Twain replied. "I expect to make one hundred thousand dollars from your book within six months."

"Ulys," Julia murmured, wanting desperately for him to shake Twain's hand and accept his check.

Ulys sat for a long while in silence, thinking. "Put your terms in writing. I'll refer the matter to my friend Mr. George Childs." Twain inclined his head; the newspaper publisher and philanthropist was known to all as a man of impeccable integrity. "I'll have him compare the Century Company's offer to yours and make his recommendation. That's all I can promise at this time."

The two men shook hands on it, and Julia clasped hers together tightly in her lap. With two publishers contending for Ulys's memoirs, surely the family would be saved from financial ruin.

Ulys promptly wrote to Mr. Childs in Philadelphia to request that he come to New York to review the two proposals and negotiate the final contract. While Ulys labored over his chapters on the Mexican War, Mr. Childs and his lawyer carefully reviewed the competing proposals. In early December, Mr. Childs was convinced that Twain's offer was the superior one, but more negotiations followed before the terms were settled and his verdict made official.

Mark Twain would publish Ulys's book. Now everything depended upon Ulys completing it.

Writing increasingly exhausted Ulys, and by mid-December, his throat throbbed with pain so intense that relentless nightmares jolted him awake, shouting and disoriented. One harrowing night, Ulys told Julia of a dream in which he was traveling alone in a foreign country. "I carried a single satchel and I was only partially clad," he said hoarsely, sitting up in bed. "I found to my surprise that I was alone, without money or friends. I came to a fence, but after climbing the stepping stile up one side, I discovered there were no stairs on the other. I went over the fence anyway, only to discover that I had left my satchel on the other side. Then I thought I would return home and borrow the money from you, but when I asked, you replied you had only seventeen dollars, which was not nearly enough. And upon realizing that, I woke."

Though Julia assured him that she found no prophetic warnings in his visions, the nightmare visited him again several times thereafter. To anyone else it would sound like a strange, perhaps even silly dream, but Julia easily recognized all the elements of her husband's worst fears — of being forced to retrace his steps, of poverty, of being unable to provide for her.

The dreams and the pain became so severe

that Julia and Harrison had to coax Ulys to bed every night. Two great dreads had seized him — that he would choke to death while he slept, and that he would be unable to complete his book, rendering his family penniless and unprotected. By Christmas he had plunged into the deepest melancholy, exhausted, unhappy, and unable to work.

One night, gasping in pain, exhausted but unable to rest, Ulys was in such deep distress that he asked Julia to summon Dr. Shrady. The physician came at once, applied his medicines, and calmly assured Ulys that the pain would pass and that he should lie down with his head on a cool pillow.

Julia stood in the doorway and watched silently while the doctor helped her husband into bed. "Pretend you are a boy again," Dr. Shrady told him. "Curl up your legs, lie on your side, and bend your neck while I tuck the covers around your shoulders." Obediently, Ulys did as he was instructed. "Now go to sleep like a good boy."

Ulys quieted, and Dr. Shrady stood observing him until he fell asleep at last.

When Dr. Shrady turned to go, he seemed abashed to discover that Julia had witnessed the scene. He stole from the room and joined her in the corridor. "My apologies," he murmured while Julia softly closed the door, leaving it slightly ajar. "I do hope the general won't think my methods demeaning. My only intention was to ease his pain."

"There isn't the slightest danger of that," Julia assured him. "The general is the most simple mannered and reasonable person in the world. He doesn't like to be treated with unnecessary ceremony."

Dr. Shrady regarded her with a potent mixture of sympathy and sternness. "Mrs. Grant, I should warn you that there shall be many more nights like this to come."

"I know it." A slight tremble in her voice betrayed her apprehension. "I also know that he's lost interest in his book, the one endeavor that gave his days purpose."

"This is natural. Sometimes the general will feel like giving up. Sometimes he'll refuse to eat and be unable to sleep. He'll reject his work and become fatalistic. This is the normal and necessary preparation of the mind for a person who is terminally ill." The doctor rested his hand on her shoulder and held her gaze. "The general is stronger and more disciplined than an ordinary man, and I believe eventually he'll come to accept his illness and resolve to work through his pain."

Julia's eyes filled with tears, and she thanked him, though she wanted to cry out that she did not accept that Ulys's illness was fatal and would never encourage him to do so.

Ulys's melancholy persisted as the year came

to a close, but when he heard that his old friend William Sherman was in New York, he relaxed his ban on visitors and invited him to call. Julia knew what an effort it was for Ulys to conceal his suffering for the two hours he and Sherman sat in the library and talked. Ulys told him he was writing his memoirs and that he was ill but was recovering under his doctors' care. Afterward, as Julia escorted him to the door, Sherman paused in the foyer. "Mrs. Grant," he asked suddenly, "we are friends, are we not?"

"I should certainly hope so, after all these years."

"Then may I beg the liberty of a friend and ask you a direct question?"

Julia felt a stir of trepidation. They should have known Sherman would recognize Ulys's pain and thinness for what they were. What would she say if he asked her for the truth? "Of course you may," she replied, steeling herself.

"Forgive me, but when I look around your beautiful home, I can't mistake the signs of your material distress."

"Oh, that? Well, yes." Julia uttered a tiny, helpless laugh. "It's true that we aren't as comfortable as we were before the failure of Grant & Ward, but Ulys's writing will provide for us."

Sherman frowned slightly as he bowed and bade her farewell, and a few days later, the

Grants learned that he had raised a subscription for Ulys's benefit. "I appreciate both the motive and the friendship which have dictated this course on your part," Ulys immediately wrote in response, "but, on mature reflection, I regard it as due myself and my family to decline this preferred generosity."

To Ulys's chagrin, his letter found its way into the hands of the press, and it was published in the *New-York Tribune* on January 8. Then, mere days after he hinted at his illness in a letter to another friend, mentioning that he was weak and could not sleep, a Philadelphia newspaper reported that Ulys was ill, and attributed his condition to his financial difficulties. When the New York press besieged Ulys's doctors, Ulys scripted their answer: He was ill, but cheerful and comfortable, and they expected a quick recovery.

Nothing could have been further from the truth. Not even Julia could pretend otherwise any longer. "My tears blind me," she wrote to Mrs. Hillyer, her dear friend from their St. Louis and Holly Springs days. "General Grant is ill. I cannot write how ill."

And yet, in the bleakest midwinter, Ulys seemed to steady himself, and his spirits noticeably improved. Every morning he rose early, allowed Harrison to wrap him in a warm shawl, and went to his study to resume writing.

"Whether those persistent rumors in the press about his poor health have spurred him on, or he has remembered his commitment to Twain," Julia confided to Dr. Douglas, "he seems to have discovered a new wellspring of strength."

"I'm not surprised," Dr. Douglas replied. "I believe the general now understands the adversary he faces, and he has proposed to fight it out on this line if it takes all winter."

Julia glowed with recognition of the doctor's paraphrase of her brave victor's famous words from the Battle of Spotsylvania Court House — so unexpected, so perfectly suited to his ordeal.

Twain had traveled most of the winter on a speaking tour, and when he returned to New York in the last week of February, he promptly called at the Grant residence. Ulys was upstairs in his study, his writing momentarily interrupted by Dr. Douglas's regular examination. Although Ulys could barely speak above a hoarse whisper, while Dr. Douglas finished his tasks, Ulys and Twain chatted about his new novel, *The Adventures of Huckleberry Finn,* which had taken him nine years to write. It had been out only a few days and he and his publisher were still awaiting the first reviews.

"For a while the book seemed plagued by bad luck," Twain confided, settling himself into a chair. "Some unscrupulous scoundrels were trying to sell their own versions of my novel, and a lascivious engraver nearly sabotaged our first printing with a deliberate error to one of the illustrations that showed one of my characters, Silas Phelps, with his —" He caught himself and glanced at Julia. "Well, let's just say the picture left no question that he's a male of the species."

Julia smiled in spite of herself, and the men laughed — all save Ulys, who struggled not to, for the great pain laughing caused him. Twain regarded him curiously for a long moment. "*The New York World* reported yesterday that you're suffering not from cancer," he said, "but from a case of chronic inflammation of the tongue brought on by excessive smoking. I was very glad to see the news."

"Ah, yes," said Ulys, smiling faintly. "I read that too. If only it had been true."

"The general's condition is serious," added Dr. Douglas, "and it will worsen."

Julia could bear no more. She hurried downstairs to the parlor, where she sank into a chair and fought back sobs. Soon she heard Fred escorting Twain to the door, discussing the manuscript and a few details in the publishing contract that had yet to be settled.

Their footsteps paused in the foyer. "I tell you in strictest confidence that my father is very ill, and he isn't expected to recover," Julia heard Fred say. "His doctors believe he may have only a few weeks to live."

"I had no idea it was so serious," said Twain. "How could a man so robust decline so quickly?"

"Don't be concerned —"

"How could I be otherwise? Your father is a very dear friend of mine."

"What I mean is that you shouldn't worry that his work will be affected," said Fred. "My father writes diligently each day, and everything is proceeding on schedule. The first volume of his memoirs is finished, and work on the second is progressing very well."

"My dear fellow," replied Twain, his voice gruff with grief and kindness, "I'm far less concerned about the book than the man."

CHAPTER TWENTY-EIGHT

March–July 1885

Like every other resident of the city, Jule had known of General Grant's poor health for months. Nevertheless, on the first day of March she was shocked to read on the front page of *The New York Times* a bold headline surrounded by a black border: "GRANT IS DYING."

Other New York papers quickly took up the story. "Sinking into the Grave!" one announced. "Dying Slowly from Cancer," lamented another, and a third, "Gen. Grant's Friends Give Up Hope."

"Mrs. Grant would never give up hope," said Jule, disbelieving. "She would pray for her husband until she had no voice left before she would give up hope."

Gabriel put an arm around her shoulders and gently turned her away from the lurid proclamations of despair and imminent death. "Do you want to call on Mrs. Grant to offer your sympathies?"

In an instant, alternate scenes played out in her imagination: a tearful reunion on Julia's doorstep, a hasty retreat as the mistress hurled recriminations at her faithless servant, bewildered questions evoked by an utter lack of recognition.

"I don't think she would thank me to intrude upon her now," Jule replied.

But she could not resist strolling past the Grant residence late the following afternoon, drawn by sympathy and sorrow. Reporters from all the New York newspapers had assumed posts on Sixty-sixth Street, and Jule was appalled to observe several try to peer into the second-floor window — General Grant's study, someone in the crowd said. By the time she returned later that week, reporters from Baltimore, Boston, Philadelphia, and Washington had joined them, and after a fortnight, well-traveled newspapermen from Chicago, St. Louis, Los Angeles, and San Francisco swelled the crowd. It was called "the death watch," Jule learned to her horror, and at any given hour, throngs of curious citizens threatened to outnumber the press.

Day after day, she found herself almost unwillingly joining them.

She did not recognize the dignified Negro servant who braved the gauntlet of reporters nearly every day as he came to and from the house, apparently to run errands for the family. Harrison — or so the newspapermen addressed him, shouting questions whenever he left or returned — must have joined the household after she had run away.

Harrison impressed Jule with his calm response to the barrage of queries. "The general is fine, thank you," he might say, or "I'll tell him you wish him well, sir," or his apparent favorite, "General Grant grows better every day, thank you."

"He doesn't mean it," Jule told Gabriel one day when he accompanied her on what had become an almost daily vigil. "I can tell from his face, from the look in his eye. The headlines are true. The general is dying."

Gabriel pressed her hand where it rested in the crook of his elbow. "General Grant saved the Union, he and Mr. Lincoln both."

"He wasn't a perfect man or a perfect president, but he was a loving father and a devoted husband." Jule took a deep, shaky breath. "Listen to me, talking like he's already gone." She fixed her gaze on a window that seemed to look into a parlor, willing Julia to come to it, to glance outside, to spot her in the crowd. "He was always kind to me, though, me and all the Dent slaves."

"We're all sinners in need of the Lord's redemptive grace and forgiveness." Gabriel's voice was as quiet as if he stood at the ailing man's deathbed, yet it rang with love and certainty. "General Grant and his wife too."

"I do forgive her," said Jule, understanding

what he did not say. "She couldn't help herself. She did the best she could with what she thought to be right."

She watched each window in turn, but the curtains were drawn as if the household was already in mourning.

"Let's go home," she said, gazing up at her beloved husband, heartened by the sight of him, by the miraculous fact of his presence by her side. "I'll come back at Easter and place flowers on their doorstep, but for now, we've paid our respects, and I think it kinder to leave the family in peace."

After all, at long last, her own heart was at peace.

With Ulys's consent, his physicians decided to release twice-daily bulletins, carefully phrased to divulge little about the inexorable progress of his disease. Julia knew that their purpose was not to keep the public informed, but to preserve Ulys's privacy.

"Everything must be done to ensure that the general gets sufficient rest and keeps to a regular schedule so he can finish his book," said Dr. Shrady in the corridor outside Ulys's bedchamber while he dozed fitfully within.

His emphatic remark met with nods of agreement from Dr. Douglas, Badeau, Fred, and even Harrison, but Julia felt her heart cinch. "No," she said emphatically. "The harder he works, the weaker he becomes. He must abandon his writing — or at least cut back on it drastically — and conserve his strength."

The men regarded her with astonishment. "Forgive me, madam," said Dr. Douglas, "but the general's interest in completing his memoir is all that prolongs his life."

"I'll read to him instead," Julia countered. "Reverend Newman will divert him with scripture and prayer."

"I've noticed a direct correlation between the general's ability to work and his desire to live," said Dr. Shrady, shaking his head. "If you remove one, you will almost certainly remove the other."

"My husband's condition worsens every day. He requires rest, not more toil."

"But, madam —"

"I will finish my book."

The thin, hoarse whisper drifting from the bedchamber silenced them.

"I will finish it." Ulys coughed, inhaled deeply, and let out a long, shuddering breath. "Julia, this book will provide an income for you and the children when I am gone. I must finish it."

Heartsick, Julia abandoned her protests.

A few days later, while reporters circled like vultures and Ulys worked and wrote through the pain, Grover Cleveland was inaugurated as the twenty-second president of the United

States. On the last day of President Chester A. Arthur's administration, Twain joined Ulys, Julia, Fred, and Badeau at the Grant residence. For months, General Sherman had acted the gadfly in Washington, lobbying Congress to reinstate Ulys to the rank of lieutenant general, thus restoring the military pension he had relinquished to become president — and to allow Sherman to assume the role of general in chief. A combat veteran himself, President Arthur had made Ulys's reinstatement one of the primary concerns of his administration, but if the Senate did not approve the bill before his term expired, it would not pass.

The hands of the mantel clock turned slowly, and in the early afternoon, a telegram from the president pro tem of the Senate finally arrived. As Fred read it, a look of deep satisfaction filled his visage. "It's done," he said, handing the telegram to his father. "You're reinstated. Another victory for General Sherman."

Ulys read the telegram, a faint smile on his lips.

"Hurrah! Our old commander is back," Julia exclaimed, embracing Ulys tenderly.

As a retired lieutenant general Ulys would earn an annual salary of thirteen thousand five hundred dollars, and when the time came, as his widow Julia would receive a stipend of five thousand dollars a year for the rest of her life.

That would suffice, Julia thought. Ulys could set his book aside and rest, and perhaps his strength would return and he would astonish doctors and reporters and naysayers alike by vanquishing the sinister disease once and for all.

But even as hope rose in her, giddy and effervescent, it burst against the surface of rough, unrelenting truth, and her sudden rush of ebullience went flat and still.

She knew Ulys would not stop writing — just as she knew that even if he did, it would not add a single day to his life.

A week after *The New York Times* ran its devastating headline, Chief of Police Adam Gunner informed Julia that he had assigned officers to patrol Sixty-sixth Street in order to control the reporters and keep the ever-increasing crowds at bay. Devout citizens prayed loudly on the sidewalk in front of their home. Every day the mails brought home remedies shipped from all corners of the nation, potions and teas and plasters that were guaranteed to cure the suffering general. Veterans' groups and women's auxiliary clubs sent gifts, and admirers from all over the world sent letters and telegrams. On one occasion Julia glanced out the window to discover a one-armed veteran marching back and forth in front of their home as if passing in review before his general — or, as she was suddenly, dizzyingly reminded, as if he were an honor guard at the catafalque of a slain leader.

In mid-March, Ulys was heartened to be reunited with his precious daughter. Nellie's husband had finally granted her permission to return to New York from England, but he had refused to allow her to bring their three children — Algernon, who had just celebrated his eighth birthday; Vivien, almost seven years of age; and little Rosemary, four and one-half. Nellie had become a lovely matron of not quite thirty years, her skin as luminous as it was the day she wed, her brown eyes as soft and guileless, her thick, dark hair shining like rich satin in a Grecian twist with a long cascade down the back. And yet there was a sadness in her expression that pained Julia to see, for she knew it sprang from a broken heart.

Ulys brightened beneath his daughter's affectionate gaze and smiled when she spoke to him in their familiar, companionable way. Only when alone with Julia did Nellie's composure falter. "I didn't expect to find him so transformed," she confided, choking back sobs. Julia folded Nellie in her embrace and murmured words that had no power to comfort.

The invigorating effects of Nellie's arrival proved sadly ephemeral. To help Ulys conserve his waning strength, Twain arranged for a stenographer to assist him in preparing the manuscript. In the third week of March, Twain arrived at the Grant residence and triumphantly presented Ulys with the proofs for the first volume of his memoirs, which Ulys accepted with a silent nod and a look that spoke of pride and triumph.

On the evening of March 25, Ulys suffered a violent choking fit, so severe that he was promptly sedated with a mixture of cocaine and morphine. He woke the next morning ready to resume his work, but another dreadful choking fit struck that evening and every evening that followed, until on March 30, his condition had become so precarious that his doctors warned that he would not survive the night. Ulys's good friend Matias Romero made a statement to the swarms of reporters, and Julia sat vigil at her beloved husband's bedside, listening for his last labored breath and weeping.

Yet Ulys did not die. He struggled between life and death, but by the evening of April 1, his breathing grew steady and he slept peacefully. The next day he was out of bed, walking gingerly around the room on Fred's strong arm. He slept soundly that night too, and the next morning he rose, asked Harrison to wrap him in a shawl, and went to his study to write. A few days later, on April 9, Ulys asked Dr. Shrady if he might celebrate the anniversary of General Lee's surrender at Appomattox with one or two puffs on a cigar. Dr. Shrady consented, and so Ulys indulged in his old vice one last time.

Ulys determinedly pushed on at the same relentless pace as before, drafting page after page, often dictating for three or four hours at a stretch. Anxious, Julia urged him to rest, to conserve his strength, but Ulys firmly rejected her appeals. "As time goes on, I'll have fewer days without pain," he said. "I must work when I can."

By early April, Twain was closely examining the proofs and making notes for possible revisions, but his suggestions were so minor and so few in number that Ulys became concerned. "Maybe Twain is silent about my work because he believes my writing isn't that good," he fretted hoarsely one afternoon as Julia, Ida, and Nellie tidied his study.

"You're a wonderful writer, Pa," Nellie declared. "I've saved and cherished every letter you've ever sent me."

Ulys looked gratified, but he rasped, "You, my dear, are a fond daughter and a forgiving audience. The vast majority of my readers will not be."

Troubled, Julia discussed his remarks with Fred, and when Twain called the next day, Fred detained him before he could disappear into Ulys's study. "I thought you should be aware," he said, "that the general is concerned about your opinion of his work."

"He shouldn't be," replied Twain, bemused, his hand already on the banister, his foot on the bottom step.

"Perhaps not," Julia said, "but you've never offered any remarks about his work, whether to praise or to censure."

Twain's brow furrowed beneath his shaggy mane. "I thought the excellent quality of his writing was self-evident," he said, looking from Fred to Julia for confirmation. "It never occurred to me that a man who had defeated General Lee and had governed a great nation could worry about so small a thing as a book."

A few days later, Julia was sitting with Ulys and Twain in the library while Ulys read letters and Twain reviewed new pages for the second volume. "I've recently reread Caesar's *Commentaries,* and I can't help comparing it with your memoirs," Twain suddenly remarked. "In my judgment — which I'm sure we all agree is authoritative — the same merits distinguish both books: clarity of statement, directness, simplicity, unpretentiousness, manifest truthfulness, fairness and justice toward friend and foe alike, soldierly candor and frankness, and soldierly avoidance of flowery speech. It is my opinion that both books share equally in greatness."

He promptly returned his attention to the manuscript.

After a long moment of silence, Ulys whispered, "I'm glad my book meets with your approval."

Twain raised a finger in warning. "Of course, I have not yet read the whole thing. I may be obliged to revise my opinion later."

"Mr. Twain," Julia admonished, but Ulys smiled.

On Easter Sunday, Ulys waved from the window of his study to the kindhearted admirers who left abundant, fragrant bouquets on their doorstep in honor of the holiday. Later, leaning on Fred's strong arm, he came out to the front stoop to listen to a serenade of hymns sung by the Excelsior chapter of the Masonic Council — the man who had always barely tolerated music rousing himself to acknowledge the singers' respect and affection. That afternoon, when his doctors issued their usual medical statement, Ulys included a note thanking friends and strangers alike for their prayerful sympathy and interest. Julia had suggested the addition of the word "prayerful," and Ulys had obligingly allowed it.

Less than two weeks later, Dr. Shrady discovered that the cancer had spread to the right side of Ulys's jaw and that his mouth and gums were covered in malignant growths.

April 27 was Ulys's sixty-third birthday, and Julia was determined to celebrate as usual.

"A carriage ride through the city would be a fine birthday present to myself," he said hoarsely and settled in to tour the city with Julia, Nellie, and Harrison. He enjoyed the ride so much that when they returned home, he suggested they set out again. His grandchildren, innocently unaware of the shadow lying over their beloved grandpapa, drew pictures for him and recited poems, and Julia almost wept to see how tenderly he thanked them and kissed their sweet faces. A few close friends called to give him their regards, and Andrew Carnegie had sixty-three beautiful roses delivered. In the late afternoon, the New York Seventh National Guard Regiment passed in review before the house, where Ulys stood at attention at his study window.

That evening at supper, Julia decorated the table with sixty-three candles, bathing the faces of their loved ones in gentle, benevolent light. Julia and Ulys exchanged looks across the table that revealed the same unspoken thought — they had been truly blessed. They had known great love and great joy amid the pain and suffering of life, and in spite of the great grief they all knew awaited them, their hearts were full, their joys abundant.

By that time, Ulys had finished his four articles for *The Century* and had plunged into the most difficult part of his memoirs, the months from the end of the Wilderness campaign until General Lee's surrender at Appomattox. He had selected the maps he wanted to include, outlined the remaining chapters, and made copious notes on the material yet to be covered. The force that compelled him had not diminished, and yet Julia could not mistake the subtle changes to his writing routine. His penmanship, once strong and bold, had become spindly, the letters weakly formed, the strokes wavering. Fred had taken to drawing lines on the blank pages with a straightedge to ease the strain on Ulys's failing eyes.

But the biggest change came with the abrupt departure of Adam Badeau.

As Ulys's writing had hit its stride, and as Twain had become more involved in reviewing and editing the manuscript, Badeau had been relegated to the position of clerk, fetching maps and reports, sorting notes, and providing encouragement. Eventually the disgruntled Badeau moved out of his room in the Grant residence, and soon thereafter, reports appeared in *The New York World* that Ulys was not the author of his memoirs but had delegated the task to a ghostwriter.

"The work upon his new book about which so much has been said is the work of General Adam Badeau," the reporter claimed. "General Grant, I have no doubt, has furnished all of the material and all of the ideas in the memoirs as far as they have been prepared;

but Badeau has done the work of composition. The most that General Grant has done upon this book has been to prepare the rough notes and memoranda for its various chapters."

Julia, who had witnessed every day of the book's composition and had measured the enormous physical toll the effort had exacted upon her husband, recalled the lessons of their years in the White House, when she had learned not to trust the press. But whereas she was indignant, Twain was enraged, and he vowed to sue the newspaper for libel. "The general's work this morning is rather damaging evidence against *The World*'s intrepid lie," he stormed to Fred and Julia, pacing in their library while upstairs in his study Ulys dictated new material to the stenographer. "A libel suit ought to be instituted at once. No compromise or apology will do. Press for punitive damages. Damages that will cripple — yes, disable — that paper financially."

"Let's try a more circumspect approach first," said Fred, raising his hands, but the calming gesture had no effect upon the furious author. "This story is nonsense and can easily be struck aside, and I'd rather not subject my father to the rigors of a lawsuit."

When Julia chimed in her agreement, Twain reluctantly agreed, and so Fred issued a simple statement explaining that General Grant was dictating his account of the Appomattox campaign to a stenographer, but every word was his own, a perfectly straightforward and lucid account drawn from his dispatches and other records. Ulys followed that with a letter to the editor, refuting the accusations point by point.

"It's far better to embarrass *The World* than to sue it," Twain later acknowledged, but he was not yet satisfied, and with Ulys's blessing, he tapped his network of friends within the press to track down the source of the false claim. Soon he was able to confirm what Julia already suspected — Badeau had sparked the rumors himself. Then the once trusted aide committed what Julia considered an unforgivable offense: He wrote to Ulys demanding additional compensation for his past contributions to the memoirs — and in exchange he agreed not to claim authorship of the work.

"But he is *not* the author," Julia protested. "He demands that we pay him not to lie?"

Summoning up his boundless resolve, Ulys adamantly refused to capitulate, responding in a strongly worded letter that the two men "must give up all association so far as the preparation of any literary work goes which bears my signature." Ulys had written so prolifically — plans of battle, instructions, reports, official documents bearing the presidential seal — that the public had become too accustomed to his style of writing to believe that the words had come from anyone else's pen.

In late May, Ulys began the final sections of his memoir, spending up to five hours a day writing and dictating his account of the end of the siege of Petersburg and General Lee's retreat to Appomattox. By then his neck was so swollen from the unrelenting spread of the cancer that he could barely speak. His pain kept him awake, so while the rest of the household slept, he stayed up alone working on his book, late into the night and into the early hours before dawn. Sometimes Julia woke to discover him dozing fitfully upon his two favorite leather chairs set facing one another, manuscript pages scattered on his lap and on the floor all around.

On June 8, Ulys informed Twain that he had finished the first draft of the entire second volume. There was still much to do, he warned in a shakily scrawled note, for he intended to review every page.

To give their patient respite from the oppressive summer heat of the city, Dr. Douglas and Dr. Shrady decided he should relocate to Mount McGregor in upstate New York. Mr. Joseph Drexel, a Philadelphia financier and philanthropist, had offered his summer home adjacent to the luxurious Balmoral Hotel. "There among the pines," Dr. Douglas told the Grants, "the pure air is especially beneficial to patients suffering as General Grant does."

As for his precious manuscript, "I'm not yet finished," Ulys told Twain, "but I'll be done in time, certainly by September fifteenth, when the family plans to return to New York."

No one — not Julia, not even Ulys himself — expected him to see another autumn.

Mr. Vanderbilt provided the train that carried Ulys, Julia, Nellie, and Fred, Ida, and their two children north to Mount McGregor. It boasted a locomotive, a luxurious dining car, and Mr. Vanderbilt's private coach, where porters carefully placed Ulys's two comfortable leather chairs. Dr. Douglas, Harrison Tyrell, nurse Henry McQueeney, and Ulys's stenographer, Noble E. Dawson, completed the party that left New York on the hot, sultry morning of June 16. Word had spread that Ulys was leaving, and a crowd of onlookers saw them off from home, and another bade them good-bye as they boarded the train at Grand Central Station.

The train chugged through the Hudson Valley, lush and green with the foliage of early summer. Ulys dozed in his chairs dressed in a long coat and skullcap, his neck wrapped in a scarf despite the heat, his chairs turned away from the smoke of the locomotive. Silent crowds gathered at the depots to pay their respects, and now and then, Julia spotted a gray-haired veteran standing at attention among them. Ulys slept through most of the salutes, but Julia woke him when they passed West Point so he could see the academy where he had set his life's course.

An honor guard met them at Saratoga, where they were obliged to change trains, but although the soldiers had hoped for the general's inspection, Ulys was too weak to do more than nod and raise his cane to them as he hobbled on Harrison's arm from Mr. Vanderbilt's coach to the smaller-gauge train that would carry him the last twelve miles of his journey.

When they arrived at Mount McGregor, the cool, fresh air seemed to revive him, and Julia was well pleased with Mr. Drexel's cottage, a spacious, airy, two-story home with a broad, wraparound porch, furnished simply but elegantly with everything they needed. Ulys would have the front bedchamber, where large windows offered abundant morning sunshine and views of the surrounding forested hills of northern pine. Dr. Douglas had arranged for their meals to be brought to the cottage from the nearby Balmoral Hotel to spare Ulys the walk.

As Julia and Ida saw to the unpacking, a crowd of curious onlookers wandered over from the hotel to observe them from a discreet distance. Ulys merely nodded to them politely from a comfortable chair on the porch and fixed his gaze upon the scenery. The people dispersed before Julia joined him there, pulling a chair close enough to touch his. "What do you think of our pretty cottage?" she asked, taking his hand and drawing it onto her lap.

"Very pleasant," he whispered. "A good place to finish my work."

The air was cool and crisp that night, and Ulys enjoyed his first restful sleep in many weeks. In the morning he woke refreshed and curious, and to Julia's surprise, he announced his intention to go exploring. Harrison accompanied him as he slowly but steadily climbed a nearby knoll. At the top was a wooden bench that afforded a magnificent view across the valley toward Saratoga, but Ulys paid for the prize with exhaustion.

Later that afternoon, Harrison arranged Ulys's two favorite leather chairs in his bedchamber, and on a nearby table, Fred set out his research materials in the same order Ulys had kept them in New York. His voice had become too weak to allow for dictation, so he wrote in his own shaky hand and gave the pages to Dawson to copy. Sometimes Dawson would read aloud sections of the manuscript, and Ulys would nod in approval or shake his head and scrawl notes for revisions.

As June passed in soft breezes scented with

pine, Ulys worked on his book, often in his bedchamber, sometimes on the broad, shaded porch, while their grandchildren played among the trees, their footfalls cushioned by a carpet of fallen pine needles. On June 27, sure that he was within pages of completing the second volume, Ulys wrote to Twain at his summer home at Quarry Farm asking his help in revising his *Century* articles and making corresponding changes to the memoir. When Twain arrived the next morning, he said nothing about Ulys's dramatically altered appearance — his once thick brown hair and beard had gone entirely white, and his famously rugged frame had become skeletal — but the author's stricken expression told Julia that Ulys's deterioration had not gone unnoticed.

Twain had intended to stay with them at the cottage only until the revisions were complete, but even after he and Ulys were satisfied, he stayed on when he heard that Jesse would soon join them. Twain and Jesse — twenty-seven, four years married, and living in California — were partners in a prospective business plan to build a railroad from Constantinople to the Persian Gulf, one of many such unusual projects in which Twain habitually invested.

"We're all coming together again," Ulys remarked happily later that evening as Julia helped him back into his two leather chairs, which he preferred to the bed, and kissed him good night.

"Not all of us," she said wistfully. Ulys nodded, probably thinking she referred to Buck and his family, who in April had been blessed with their third child, a baby girl. Julia was thinking of them, of course, but also of all the loved ones they had lost through the years. Mamma and Papa. Ulys's parents, his brothers Simpson and Orvil, and his sister Clara. Nellie's first precious baby, who had died within a year of his birth — too many losses. A family circle was never truly complete except in memories and in hopes for the future.

Even after Jesse settled in, Twain lingered — hoping, Julia suspected, that Ulys would finish his manuscript and allow Twain to take it home for editing. When it became apparent that Ulys was not quite ready, Twain made arrangements to return to Quarry Farm without it. On the day of his departure, he received a telegram from the publishers, which he immediately read to Ulys and Julia. Although the subscription campaign was only half over, sixty thousand editions of Ulys's memoirs had already been ordered. "This will guarantee you royalties of at least three hundred thousand dollars," Twain announced, jubilant.

Julia's head spun so dizzyingly that she was obliged to sit on the arm of Ulys's porch chair. "I never dreamed it would be so much."

"I am astounded," Ulys said in a thin whisper. "I cannot say how relieved I am that my family will have this provision, and I have you to thank for it."

"Not so," said Twain gruffly, clearing his throat and tucking the telegram into his pocket. "The credit is all yours, General. You're writing the thing."

Later that evening, Ulys struggled so desperately to breathe that Dr. Shrady dosed him with morphine, which Ulys hated because it clouded his mind and rendered him unable to write. But he had little choice. Every day violent fits of coughing shook him fiercely, ceasing only after Ulys choked on his own blood, vomited, and thereby cleared his airways. Julia found it terrible to witness, but she steeled herself and held Ulys's hand as he suffered, soothing him as best she could, driving her own anguish inward so he would feel only her strength.

Ulys wrote on, slowly and deliberately, his work frequently interrupted by old friends who traveled from near and far to pay their regards to the ailing leader — in truth, Julia knew, to say good-bye.

In early July, Fred arranged for the use of a bath chair, a wheeled conveyance that reminded Julia of the rickshaws she and Ulys had seen in Japan. Harrison would assist Ulys into the chair and wheel it wherever Ulys directed him to go — to the shade of a stand of pines, to a sunny bank above a trickling creek, along the forest path where birds trilled in the boughs overhead and squirrels and rabbits rustled the underbrush below.

Julia often accompanied them on their excursions, and as they walked along she reminisced aloud about other scenic places they had explored in days long past — the beautiful, leafy wood at White Haven, the snowy woodlands of Michigan, the marvelous landscapes they had traversed on their world tour, the White House lawn, the pretty gardens Julia had cultivated wherever they had made their homes.

On the fourth of July, they celebrated Independence Day quietly, reminiscing about Vicksburg and marking the birthdays of Nellie and their grandson Ulysses S. Grant III. Ulys was surprised and pleased to receive a telegram from the emperor of Japan, and he dispatched Fred to send a reply before he settled down to his writing again. It pained Julia to see how thin he had become, his bony, almost translucent hand gripping the pen, the dark hollows of his cheeks. He was starving to death, and it wrenched her heart to watch him waste away.

"I fear the worst the day the general completes his book," she overheard Dr. Douglas tell Dr. Shrady one afternoon as Ulys and

Fred and Dawson toiled over the manuscript, and she was obliged to go off by herself into the pine forest, sink onto a soft mat of brown pine needles, and weep as if her heart were breaking, for surely it was.

The next day, the air smelled heavy with rain. After breakfast, where Ulys sat lost in thought at the table while his family quietly ate, he asked Harrison to wheel him out to a clearing with a broad view of the sky so he could watch the thunderclouds roll in. He asked Julia to accompany them, so although the iron-gray skies and the distant rumble of thunder provoked her anxiety, she agreed.

They went along in silence until Ulys gestured for Harrison to stop. As soon as he saw that Ulys was as comfortable as his affliction would allow, Harrison strolled a discreet distance away to give the couple privacy, ready to return swiftly if Julia called for him.

"Married almost thirty-seven years," Ulys rasped, "and still we require a chaperone."

Julia laughed, but it came out as a sob, full of grief and fear and longing. "I don't know what sort of trouble they fear we'd get into," she said, as breezily as she could manage. "I've grown too stout to squeeze into that bath chair with you."

"If we put our minds to it," Ulys whispered hoarsely, "I'm sure we could think of something."

This time Julia's laugh was genuine, and it rang out pure and true. Hearing it, Ulys smiled and asked her to sing for him, and so she did, all the sweet, plaintive, romantic tunes from their courtship long ago.

When her last melody faded away, Ulys said, "Do you remember how your father and my parents objected to our marriage?"

"I do." Julia reached for his hand. "I suppose we proved them wrong."

A faint smile lifted the corners of his mouth. "Your father offered me Nell instead."

"Yes, and you've teased her about it ever since."

"Your father insisted that you wouldn't care for the military life," Ulys reminisced in a voice scarcely louder than a breath. "He said you wouldn't like all the traveling, and yet you followed me throughout the war, and to the White House, and all around the world."

"I would follow you now if I could," she said with sudden vehemence, her tears spilling over.

"Julia, you don't mean that."

"I do. I've always hated being left behind. You know that." Kneeling beside his chair, she pressed the back of his hand to her lips, her forehead, her heart. "Who am I without you, Ulys?"

He regarded her silently for a long moment, marshaling his strength, his eyes tender, sad, and full of enduring love. "You are Mrs.

Grant," he told her. "You'll always be my dear little wife. Don't I always go ahead and find a place for us, and call you to me when the time is right?"

"Yes." Julia fought back her despair for his sake. "You always have."

"Julia —" He coughed then and his voice failed him, but she already knew all he wanted to say.

A few days later, Julia was sitting quietly on the front porch, resting her eyes, an unfinished letter to her sister Emma on the table beside her, when she heard Ulys shift in his chair. She glanced up as he handed a sheet of paper to Dawson, then settled back, smiling almost sadly, though his eyes shone with contentment. "It's finished," he whispered. "There is nothing more I could do to it now."

Julia's heart was heavy as she congratulated him.

After examining Ulys the next morning, Dr. Douglas took Julia aside and warned her that Ulys had expressed his readiness to die, since he could not be cured, and she must prepare herself. She almost laughed. What else had she been doing all those many months if not that?

On the morning of July 20, Ulys asked Harrison to take him in the bath chair to the top of the knoll he had climbed the day after they arrived at Mount McGregor. Fred, Jesse, and

Dawson accompanied them, while Julia, Ida, and Nellie quickly tidied and aired his bedchamber. Julia waited anxiously all the while he was away, wishing she had gone with them and had not been dissuaded by her sons' warnings that she would find the climb too difficult.

When the men returned, Ulys looked pale and weak, although Fred told her he had enjoyed the view and had breathed deeply of the cool, clear air. But the heat and humidity rose with the day, and by evening Ulys was uncomfortable and struggling to breathe, so Harrison settled him on the porch and Dr. Douglas administered morphine. As the family gathered around him, seating themselves in wicker chairs and chatting companionably, Julia took Fred aside and asked him to telegraph Buck to tell him to come in all haste.

Buck arrived the next morning. Throughout the day and into the evening, Ulys remained awake, smiling at his children and grandchildren, gently pressing Julia's hand whenever she took his in her own. Once he asked for water, and when the hour grew late, he rose shakily from his chair and whispered that he wanted to lie down. Julia's heart thumped as she and Fred and Harrison leapt to make everything ready and settle him upon his bed. Ulys had slept in his two leather chairs every night for months, not only for comfort but also out of fear that he would choke to death in the night if he reclined. The danger remained, but apparently Ulys no longer feared it.

Julia sat vigil at Ulys's bedside into the early morning hours of July 22. The grandchildren were kept away under the watchful care of their nurse, but the children sat with them from time to time throughout the long day. As night descended, Dr. Douglas ordered the exhausted family to get some sleep, promising to watch over Ulys until they woke in the morning.

Julia obeyed, and she soon sank wearily into her bed, only to be gently wakened at dawn by the touch of Jesse's hand upon her shoulder. "Ma," he said urgently, his voice shaking, "Dr. Douglas says we should come at once."

Quickly Julia scrambled out of bed and flew to her husband's side. Dr. Shrady was there, and Harrison, and as Dr. Douglas explained that Ulys's breathing had become shallow and faint, Fred, Buck, Jesse, and Nellie gathered around his bed wrapped in shawls and dressing gowns, silent, anguished, their faces wet with tears.

There was no expiring sigh, no last, raspy breath Julia could later reflect upon as the moment her beloved Ulys passed from life into death. He slipped away so quietly, so peacefully, that they waited a full minute before they accepted that he had truly left them.

As wrenching sobs broke the solemn hush, Fred crossed slowly to the fireplace and stopped the hands on the mantel clock.

It was eight minutes past eight o'clock, and Ulys was gone.

Julia was inconsolable.

She withdrew to her bedchamber and sobbed until she was too exhausted and wracked with despair to release another tear. There were decisions to be made, children and grandchildren to comfort, but she had no strength for that. She was utterly bereft and could not imagine ever being whole again.

Later that day, cajoled from her room by Nellie and Ida, she sat on the front porch beside Ulys's bath chair, one hand nestled in the folds of the blanket he had left behind. She imagined that she could still feel his warmth in the soft wool.

"Mrs. Grant."

Jolted from her reverie, she looked up to find Dr. Douglas standing beside her, a folded paper in his hand.

"Forgive me for disturbing you, madam," he said, his voice low and kind. "We found this in the pocket of the general's dressing gown."

Julia blinked at him uncomprehendingly for

a moment, and then, with great effort, she reached out to take the paper from him. At the sight of her name in Ulys's familiar, even script, every loop and whorl and line as well-known to her as his face or his voice or the feel of his beard against her cheek, she knew immediately that he had written the letter knowing that he would be gone when she read it, that she would remain behind, desolate, longing for one last word from him.

Mt McGregor, Saratoga Co. N.Y.
June 29th 1885.

My Dear Wife,

There are some matters about which I would like to talk but about which I cannot. The subject would be painful to you and the children, and, by reflex, painful to me also. When I see you and them depressed I join in the feeling.

I have known for a long time that my end was approaching with certainty. How far away I could not venture to guess. I had an idea however that I would live until fall or the early part of winter. I see now, however, that the time is approaching much more rapidly. I am constantly losing flesh and strength. The difficulty of swallowing is increasing daily. The tendency to spasms is constant. From three or four in the afternoon until relieved by morphine I find it difficult to get breath enough to sustain me. Under these circumstances the end is not far off.

We are comparative strangers in New York City; that is, we made it our home late in life. We have rarely if ever had serious sickness in the family, therefore have made no preparation for a place of burial. This matter will necessarily come up at my death, and may cause you some embarrassment to decide. I should myself select West Point above all other places but for the fact that you would, when the time comes, I hope far in the future, be excluded from the same grounds. I therefore leave you free to select what you think the most appropriate place for depositing my earthly remains.

My will disposes of my property. I have left with Fred a memorandum giving some details of how the proceeds from my book are to be drawn from the publisher, and how disposed of.

Look after our dear children and direct them in the paths of rectitude. It would distress me far more to think that one of them could depart from an honorable, upright and virtuous life than it would to know that they were prostrated on a bed of sickness from which they were never to arise. They have never given us any cause for alarm on this account, and I trust they never will.

With these few injunctions, and the knowledge I have of your love and affection, and of the dutiful affection of all our children, I bid you a final farewell, until we meet in another, and I trust better, world.

Your loving husband,
U. S. Grant

P. S. This will be found in my coat after my demise.

EPILOGUE

1901

As the wedding day of her granddaughter Vivien approached, Julia accompanied Nellie from their home in Washington to New York to shop for the bride's trousseau. It should have been a merry occasion, but Nellie's misgivings about the match had cast a shadow of gloom over her ever since Vivien had accepted Archibald Balfour's proposal.

"Tell Vivien how you feel," Julia urged as their train chugged northward. "If your father and I had been more forthright with you, we could have spared you a world of grief."

Nellie gave her a wan smile. "Don't blame yourself. I wouldn't have listened. I was too much in love."

Julia smiled sympathetically in return, for she doubted that anything more than infatuation had ever existed between Nellie and Algernon, and even that had been fleeting. Five years after Ulys's death, unable to bear her husband's cruelty, debauchery, and neglect any longer, Nellie had separated from him — though in truth he had left her long before, living in a separate home on his parents' estate when he was in England, boldly going about in the company of foreign women when he was traveling abroad, overindulging in drink everywhere. Julia was not ashamed to admit that his death from pneumonia in 1893 had come as relief, for only then had Nellie been free to bring the children to America, where they had lived with Julia quite contentedly ever since. Nellie worried that her own unhappy marriage had made her unreasonably wary and suspicious of her daughter's suitors, especially Englishmen, but Julia believed that a mother should heed her instincts.

"Tell her," Julia repeated emphatically. "I'm not suggesting that you forbid her to marry, only that you express your concerns and let her decide for herself."

With a wistful sigh, Nellie promised that she would.

They checked into a comfortable suite at the Fifth Avenue Hotel and ventured out to the fine shops up the avenue, and at Madison Square and Gramercy Park. The elms and sycamores lining the sidewalks provided pleasant shade, and the sounds of children playing and gleaming carriages passing offered a charming backdrop for their excursion. When they returned to the hotel with their purchases, they agreed that shopping for a lovely bride-to-be could be a pleasant experience even if one was not fond of the groom.

"Since we've finished our errands," Nellie said as they rested in their rooms before dressing for dinner, "tomorrow I'd like to spend the day visiting friends, if you'll forgive me for abandoning you."

"There's nothing to forgive," Julia assured her, smiling. "Enjoy yourself. I'm sure I'll find some way to occupy myself."

In fact, she would be glad for some time on her own, for she, too, had a friend she was eager to visit — Mrs. Varina Davis, the widow of the Confederate president.

The boutique on Fifth Avenue was one of Jule's favorites. Not only did it prominently display the full line of Madame Jule beauty products in a prominent location — and consequently sell more of them than any of her other purveyors — but also the shopgirls never flinched when Jule and her companions swept in through the front entrance rather than humbly knocking on the back door, and the clerks addressed all customers, white and colored alike, with the same solicitous courtesy.

"It's because they're French," Emma had replied when Jule had written to her longtime friend about the unexpected and much

654

welcome show of respect. Jule had laughed to read it, even though it was unclear from the words on the page whether Emma was joking.

Though Emma had never visited the boutique, whenever Jule crossed the threshold she was reminded of her dear, absent friend, now a successful dressmaker, contented wife, and devoted mother in Washington City.

From behind the counter, the proprietress offered a gracious nod when Jule entered with Dorothy, and she raised her elegantly arched eyebrows to indicate that she would join them as soon as she finished assisting a pair of customers. Jule nodded back, and as she turned to inspect the Madame Jule display, her gaze passed over the two ladies making purchases. They were chatting with the proprietress in low, decorous voices, but then the elder of the two, stout and gray haired, let out a light trill of a laugh.

Jule forgot to breathe.

Slowly she turned her head just enough to observe the two women from the corner of her eye as they collected their packages, exchanged farewells with the proprietress, and exited the boutique.

"Mamma?"

Jule inhaled sharply. "That was her." Her voice was strangely rough. She cleared her throat and tried again. "That was Mrs. Grant."

Dorothy's eyes widened. "No."

"Ah, your mother is quite correct," said the proprietress as she approached, her sonorous voice graced with the accent of her native country. "It was she. Mrs. General Grant, the late president's wife. She calls here whenever she visits New York."

"And the woman with her," said Jule, feeling strangely light-headed and unexpectedly sad. "Was that her daughter, Nellie?"

"*Oui.* Mrs. Sartoris. Her daughter is getting married soon, and they bought many lovely things for her trousseau." The proprietress smiled. "I am pleased to say both ladies carried away several bottles of Madame Jule beauty potions even as you watched. Mrs. Grant values her privacy or I would have introduced you. I'm sure you understand."

"Of course," said Dorothy, before Jule could reply. "We wouldn't dream of inconveniencing Mrs. Grant."

If the proprietress detected the sharp, bitter undercurrent in Dorothy's voice, she gave no sign of it.

When their business was concluded — orders made, payments accepted, products delivered — Dorothy scarcely waited until the shop door had closed behind them before she whirled upon her mother. "Should I have called after her?" she asked, her shoulders squared, her face ablaze with righteous anger. "Are you sorry you didn't speak with her?"

"No, to both questions," Jules replied shakily. "The very thought of confronting Mrs. Grant in the finest boutique on Fifth Avenue — oh, dear me, no."

"If I hurry I might be able to —"

"Dorothy, dearest, she's long gone. Even if she weren't, I wouldn't have you chase the poor woman through the city."

"But she walked right past you. She didn't even know you."

"I wouldn't expect her to recognize me. Too many years have passed."

"You knew *her* on sight."

"Yes, but I've seen her pictures in the papers more times than I could possibly count." Jule smiled, reflecting. "She probably imagines me still as the stubborn little ginger maid who left her at the train station in Louisville, if she thinks of me at all."

Sometimes she still imagined them that way — ginger and cream, two little girls with hands clasped, long ago and far away.

"Come, Dorothy." Jule linked her arm through her daughter's and led her off down the street to catch the omnibus that would take them back to Brooklyn. "We don't want to be late."

Dorothy began to protest, but something in Jule's expression abruptly silenced her. Though her misgivings were obvious, she nodded and said no more about Mrs. General Grant.

The family was expecting them, and Jule would not keep them waiting so that she might pursue Julia and — do what? Demand recognition? An apology for half a lifetime of forced servitude? Gabriel had taught her to forgive, and even the most humble and sincere apology from her former mistress would give Jule nothing she wanted that she did not already possess.

Gabriel was waiting at the church where their grandchildren would likely finish choir rehearsal any minute now. Charles and his family were visiting from Boston, and Jule had a lavish supper planned with all of their favorite delicacies. Jule needed nothing from Julia Grant. Her life and her heart were full.

"I still say she should have known you," Dorothy said. "The years have not changed you as much as all that."

Oh, but they had, in ways Dorothy in her freeborn innocence could not possibly understand — and for that Jule was thankful.

"It's all right," Jule said, patting her daughter's arm affectionately. "I always did see Julia Grant more clearly than she saw me."

It was, perhaps, an unlikely friendship, the fondness that had developed between Mrs. General Grant, former First Lady of the United States, and the wife of the president of the Confederacy, but the two widows had discovered much in common when they met in the summer of 1893. Julia had left the oppressive heat of Washington behind for the cooler climate of Cranston's Hotel on the Hudson, and when she learned that Mrs. Varina Davis had checked in too, she reflected for an hour or so before resolving to make her acquaintance.

The bellman kindly told her the number of Mrs. Davis's suite, and soon thereafter, Julia rapped upon the door. After a moment it opened, and a stout woman of seventy-five years — like herself — with large dark eyes, an olive complexion, and fine threads of gray in her dark hair, stood before her.

"Good afternoon," the woman said, a question in her voice, although she could not have failed to recognize her visitor.

"I am Mrs. Grant," Julia said simply.

Mrs. Davis extended her hand. "I am very glad to meet you."

She invited Julia in, where they enjoyed a cordial chat, expressing great pleasure in finally making each other's acquaintance and parting with hopes that they would meet again. Their words were no mere pleasantries, for as the days passed they were frequent companions, strolling on the verandah together, talking over tea, going for carriage drives along the river. They were well aware that the sight of the two famous Civil War widows together delighted the other guests, who saw in their blossoming friendship the perfect symbol for the reconciliation of North and South, once so bitterly divided.

Julia was amused by the fuss made over their simple, quiet meetings. While they were still enjoying their visits at Cranston's, a front-page article in *The New York Times* announced, "Celebrated Women Meet," and the next day reported that their acquaintance promised "to ripen into warm friendship." The prediction proved true, for after they returned to their homes in the city, where they resided about twenty blocks apart in Manhattan, they exchanged calls and went for carriage rides together, occasions that rarely escaped the notice of the press.

Julia found nothing so extraordinary about her friendship with Mrs. Davis that it merited mention on the front page of *The New York Times*. They were both Southern women raised in slaveholding families. They had both been public figures by virtue of marriages to prominent gentlemen, although Julia tactfully refrained from noting that she did not consider Mrs. Davis a former First Lady, because like Ulys, Julia did not accept that the Confederacy had ever been a sovereign nation. They both enjoyed writing; Mrs. Davis was certainly the more successful of the two, with a biography of her husband and numerous magazine and newspaper articles to her credit, compared to Julia's mere handful of pieces. They had both been criticized for allegedly wielding too much influence over their husbands, and they had both experienced the terrible war from a close, intense, and unique perspective. Privately they agreed that northerners and southerners were more alike than they were different, more alike than they realized. They could also discuss frankly, as they could not with their northern friends, the South's "peculiar institution," which they had once accepted as the natural order of the world, and which they had eventually learned had never been a benevolent system established by divine law as they had been taught.

"I think, deep down, we always knew it was wrong," Julia had once confessed to Mrs. Davis. She had never admitted as much to anyone, not even Ulys. "We reassured ourselves with the opinions of our forebears and justified our actions with carefully selected verses from scripture, but we must have known."

"A dear friend of mine, a South Carolinian whose husband served in Mr. Davis's administration, told me that she often wondered if slavery was not a curse to any land," Mrs. Davis had replied, sighing. " 'God forgive us, but ours is a monstrous system and wrong and full of iniquity,' she said. I still remember the ferocity and shame in her expression as she spoke."

"But that's over now."

"Yes, and now we are all equal, white and

colored, just as we are all one united nation, North and South."

Mrs. Davis spoke ironically, as was her habit — but something in the lilt of her voice reminded Julia of Jule. Months would pass in which Julia would not think of her erstwhile maid, and then something — the glimpse of a dove-gray shawl, the fragrance of almond oil or lavender, an advertisement for ladies' hair pomade — would call her to mind with such vivid intensity that they might have parted at the train station in Louisville only yesterday. Once, in New York, when Ulys was yet living, still toiling over his memoirs, Julia had glanced out his study window and imagined she spotted Jule among the people holding vigil on Sixty-sixth Street. For a moment Julia had been tempted to hurry outside to speak to the strangely familiar woman, but a reluctance to expose herself to the stares and whispers of the curious throng restrained her. She knew, at heart, that the woman could not possibly have been Jule, who — by all rights and in all likelihood — had never forgiven Julia for keeping her enslaved. Jule, if she yet lived, had surely forgotten their ginger-and-cream days, though to Julia they often seemed more real, more present, than the long, lonely years she had lived without Ulys.

Julia's friendship with Mrs. Davis endured even after Julia sold her New York residence and moved away, first to spend several months in California with Buck and Jesse and their families, and then back to Washington, where she resided contentedly with Nellie and her children. She and Mrs. Davis kept in touch through frequent letters, for although their friendship was new, they understood each other as not even the most sympathetic longtime friends could. Their shared experience of being famous widows of men whose deeds had not yet faded from public memory, men who remained after death both exalted and condemned, united them in a way that could not be measured in years.

Only a few months before, when Owen Wister published his dreadful, caustic biography of Ulys, Julia's loyal friends and devoted children had staunchly supported her, but it was Mrs. Davis's letter that had provided her the most consolation. "If I had not learned to steel myself against such attacks I never would have known an hour of peace or comfort," she had written. "Genl. Grant's and Mr. Davis's records are complete, and posterity will judge for itself, even if every idle critic in the land or envious defamer should write scurrilous opinions from now until the end. In another half century when you and I are where we shall 'see clearly' and shall have our merited rest, the world will judge fairly, and commend justly."

Even so, Mrs. Davis was not content to wait

until the afterlife for justice. In response to a request from *The New York World,* Mrs. Davis wrote an extraordinary article about Ulys titled "The Humanity of Grant." Julia had known the essay was forthcoming, for Mrs. Davis, who had never met him, had asked Julia for anecdotes from their family life to include in the piece, but she had not expected such a striking, powerful refutation of Mr. Wister's worst accusations. Mrs. Davis's thesis — which she argued convincingly — was that Ulys was a decent person as well as a great man who had refused to humiliate General Lee and the people of the South in victory, and who had regarded human life as precious. In war he had used overwhelming force not because he was a butcher, but because he believed it would bring about a quicker end to the battle, thus ultimately saving lives.

Julia had been greatly moved by Mrs. Davis's bold, public refutation of Mr. Wister's book. Although she had written to express her gratitude the same day the article appeared in *The World,* she was determined to thank her friend in person at the earliest opportunity, which the shopping trip for Vivien fortuitously provided.

Mrs. Davis received her warmly at her gracious home on West Forty-fourth Street. Julia knew that many people of the South considered it an outrage and a betrayal of the highest order that the widow of President Davis had made her home among the Yankees, but the northern climate was better for her health, and, as she confided to Julia, even if it had not been, she adored New York and could not imagine living anywhere else.

As they sat in her sunny parlor sipping tea, Julia thanked Mrs. Davis for praising Ulys in the papers. "Every word I wrote was true," Mrs. Davis demurred, as if that made her gesture any less kind and noble.

"Speaking of writing . . ." Julia set down her teacup. "I have a confession to make. I've decided to try again to publish my memoirs."

"Oh, Mrs. Grant, how delightful," Mrs. Davis exclaimed, smiling. "I'm sure they'll be a great success."

"Nothing to rival General Grant's, of course," said Julia modestly. Ulys's memoirs had been published in December of 1885 to great acclaim and had enjoyed sales that defied all expectations. Over three hundred thousand copies had sold, earning Julia more than half a million dollars and becoming the best-selling American book in the nation's history.

Julia and the children had been well provided for, just as Ulys had promised. Julia had written her own life story not from pecuniary need, but for posterity.

"That's not a fair comparison," Mrs. Davis

protested. "No one should expect their book to match the success of General Grant's. Nevertheless, I look forward to reading yours."

"I may be no more successful in finding a publisher this time than I was before."

"Nonsense. I'm confident that your book will be published, and then, at last, you can set the record straight."

Julia sipped her tea, thought for a moment, and returned the cup to its saucer. "I wouldn't put it quite like that. Ulys wrote nothing that wasn't true, but he left out a great deal. I don't mean to set the record straight, but rather to fill it out."

Mrs. Davis nodded sagely. Julia had told her how disappointed she had been to read Ulys's wonderful book only to discover that she had played but a very small role in it. They had been married almost thirty-seven years, and she had spent almost all of them at his side. Even when he had gone to war, she had been with him more often than not. And yet anyone reading Ulys's memoir would be forgiven for believing that Julia had been hundreds of miles away all the while. Anyone reading Ulys's memoir would know that he was a great man, but they would never guess that he had enjoyed a great love.

The conversation turned to other things — their children, women's suffrage, the astonishing changes time had wrought upon Washington and New York. Ideas and institutions that had once seemed everlasting, inviolable, had crumbled to dust, while new marvels they never could have imagined as young belles were appearing every day. The world was changing so swiftly, they agreed, that they often did not recognize the country their grandchildren would inherit.

But some things were eternal and unchanging — love, family, faith. The blessing of friendships, old and new.

"When the great story of our age is finally told," Mrs. Davis said afterward as she escorted Julia outside to her carriage, "I wonder if posterity will write it as a tragedy."

"Not a comedy?" asked Julia, amused. "Not a grand and glorious adventure?"

"A tall tale or a satire, perhaps, if your friend Mr. Twain writes it."

"He probably will," Julia remarked. "He already has."

They shared a laugh, exchanged farewells, and promised to continue their correspondence. With one last wave, Julia settled into the carriage and rode back to the hotel, lost in thought.

A tragedy, a comedy — none of those forms suited her life with Ulys, her life as Mrs. Grant.

Theirs was a love story. It could only and always be a love story.

ACKNOWLEDGMENTS

Mrs. Grant and Madame Jule is a work of fiction inspired by history. Many events and people appearing in the historical record have been omitted from this book for the sake of the narrative. Although the lives of Ulysses and Julia Grant are well documented, almost nothing exists about Jule beyond a few brief mentions in Julia Grant's memoirs. Thus her life as depicted in this story is almost entirely imagined.

I offer my sincere thanks to Denise Roy, Maria Massie, Liza Cassity, Christine Ball, Brian Tart, and the outstanding sales teams at Dutton and Plume for their ongoing support of my work and their contributions to *Mrs. Grant and Madame Jule.* I appreciate the generous assistance of my first readers, Marty Chiaverini, Geraldine Neidenbach, and Heather Neidenbach, whose comments and questions proved invaluable. I also thank Nic Neidenbach, Marlene and Len Chiaverini, and friends near and far for their support and encouragement.

I am indebted to the Wisconsin Historical Society and their librarians and staff for maintaining the excellent archives I have come to rely upon in my work. The resources I consulted most often were: George Rollie Adams, *General William S. Harney: Prince of Dragoons* (Lincoln: University of Nebraska Press, 2001); Adam Badeau, *Grant in Peace: From Appomattox to Mount McGregor. A Personal Memoir* (Hartford, CT: S. S. Scranton & Co., 1887); Julia Cantacuzene, *My Life Here and There* (New York: Charles Scribner's Sons, 1922); Emma Dent Casey, *When Grant Went a-Courtin': The Personal Recollections of His Courtship and Private Life* (New York: Circle Publishing Company, 1909); Joan E. Cashin, *First Lady of the Confederacy: Varina Davis's Civil War* (Cambridge, MA: Belknap Press of Harvard University Press, 2006); Charles Adolphe de Pineton, Marquis de Chambrun, *Impressions of Lincoln and the Civil War: A Foreigner's Account,* trans. General Aldolphe de Chambrun (New York: Random House, 1952); Catherine Clinton, *Mrs. Lincoln: A Life* (New York: HarperCollins, 2009); Julia Dent Grant, *The Personal Memoirs of Julia Dent Grant,* ed. John Y. Simon (New York: G. P. Putnam, 1975); Ulysses S. Grant, *Personal Memoirs of Ulysses S. Grant* (New York: Charles L. Webster, 1885); Ulysses S. Grant and Jesse Grant Cramer, *Letters of Ulysses S. Grant to His Father and His Youngest Sister, 1857–78* (New York: G. P. Putnam's Sons, 1912); Ulysses S. Grant and John Y. Simon, *The Papers of Ulysses S. Grant* (Carbondale: Southern Illinois University Press, 1967); Ulysses S. Grant, E. B. Washburne, and James Grant Wilson, *General Grant's Letters to a Friend, 1861–1880* (New York: T. Y. Crowell & Co., 1897); Elizabeth Keckley, *Behind the Scenes* (New York: G. W. Carleton & Company, 1868); H. A. M., "The United States Through English Eyes," *Fraser's Magazine for Town and Country,* vol. 61 (February 1860); Mark Perry, *Grant and Twain: The Story of a Friendship That Changed America* (New York: Random House, 2004); Horace Porter, *Campaigning with Grant* (New York: Century Company, 1897); Ishbel Ross, *The General's Wife: The Life of Mrs. Ulysses S. Grant* (New York: Dodd, Mead & Company, 1959); and Jonathan D. Sarna, *When General Grant Expelled the Jews* (New York: Nextbook, 2012).

As always and most of all, I thank my husband, Marty, and my sons, Nicholas and Michael, for their enduring love and tireless support. I could not have written this book without you.

ABOUT THE AUTHOR

Jennifer Chiaverini is the *New York Times* bestselling author of *Mrs. Lincoln's Dressmaker, The Spymistress, Mrs. Lincoln's Rival,* and the Elm Creek Quilts series. She lives with her family in Madison, Wisconsin.